CW01509418

FAINT CHANCE

Brent Ayscough

MINERVA PRESS

LONDON

MIAMI   RIO DE JANEIRO   DELHI

FAINT CHANCE
Copyright © Brent Ayscough 2001

All Rights Reserved

No part of this book may be reproduced in any form
by photocopying or by any electronic or mechanical means,
including information storage or retrieval systems,
without permission in writing from both the copyright
owner and the publisher of this book.

ISBN 0 75411 584 4

First Published 2001 by
MINERVA PRESS
315–317 Regent Street
London W1B 2HS

Printed in Great Britain for Minerva Press

FAINT CHANCE

To Indira and Usha

Chapter One

The beige Land Rover bounced up and down and tossed from side to side on the narrow, sandy, windy Laotian mountain path hardly wider than the vehicle itself. It was not one taken by other vehicles. The top down, the riders were bouncing about as the vehicle went over the huge bumps and dips in the road so large that their speed was often slowed to that of a brisk walk. As nothing as wide as the Land Rover came through to clear the vegetation, huge tropical foliage smacked the sides of the vehicle, and occasionally the leaves struck the persons in it as they bent around the windscreen posts.

The driver, a square-faced, healthy-looking German man of thirty-five years of age, maneuvered the vehicle over the bumpy path. In the back was the equipment and gear that he used to look for gemstones of Laos. The gear was tied down, but it still bounced around much to the concern of the German. Falk was in Laos working for a German company seeking out new areas to mine for the native gemstone treasures of Laos, and was prospecting in the northern mountains where hardly anyone from the West ever went. The area was only recently open, as it had only been a few years since America had dropped thousands of tonnes of bombs nearby on the Ho Chi Minh trail, and there were continuous reports of people being blown to bits from stumbling inadvertently onto unexploded American bombs from the huge number dropped.

Sitting beside Falk was his Laotian wife, a lovely woman of twenty-four with coal-black hair. On her lap was their stunning four-year-old daughter, Sangmouane – named after her mother. Apart from the coal-black hair of her mother, the young girl did not particularly resemble either of her parents with her mixed blood. Sitting on the lap of her mother, the Land Rover gave her a ride like an amusement park as it bounced up and down on the bumpy path.

Appearing in front of them suddenly was a working elephant traveling the same direction with a young Laotian man sitting atop his neck, guiding him with the assistance of a stick. There was no way to go around the elephant, and the foliage at that part of the path was much too dense for the elephant to move to one side to allow the Land Rover to pass. Falk let it be known that he wanted to pass by driving up close to the elephant as though to intimidate it, but the elephant hardly noticed.

"BEEP BEEP!" Falk tooted his horn at the young man and his elephant frustratingly blocking their progress. The young man looked around slowly at the Land Rover, and then turned his head back towards his direction of travel, as there was nothing he could do to allow the vehicle to pass at that spot of the path.

Rain began to fall, but it was a light rain. It was hot enough that the couple did not mind the cooling effect of rain on them, and so they did not stop to erect the canvas top yet – they would wait to see if the rain would remain light. The wetting of clothes provided some refreshing coolness to the hot, Laotian day.

Finally the path widened, or at least the foliage on the sides did, such that Falk could pass the elephant. Falk hit the horn again, and the young man steered his elephant to one side of the path without slowing his pace.

Falk seized the opportunity, and gunned the motor and zipped around the big creature, brushing its swinging tail as he did. He had felt restrained and frustrated by the slow pace of the elephant, and began driving faster than he had been, and faster than he should, given the fact that he was completely unfamiliar with the area.

Rain made the sandy path slicker than it was, and the front wheels of the Land Rover slid around the tight curves as Falk maneuvered it for another half hour. Falk was not sure exactly where he was, and only had an idea of where he was going from an earlier look at a map.

Rounding a tight turn, the direction ahead obscured by green foliage, Falk realized he had made a mistake. Suddenly there was nothing in front of him but air! They had come upon a gorge with vertical cliffs eight hundred feet straight down to a river below. He was going too fast, and could not make the tight turn to follow the path to the left. He stomped on the brakes, and turned the wheel smartly to the left.

The Land Rover's wheels locked in the left turning position, and even though it was only going fifteen miles per hour, the speed was still too much to make the turn and the front end slid over the edge of the sharp cliff – the vehicle was now airborne. The rear end of the vehicle went over the front, upside down on its long fall to the bottom of the gorge. The adult passengers were helpless on the way to their demise.

But the force of the Land Rover tumbling over the cliff threw young Sangmouane out of the arms of her mother. As it went straight on down towards the bottom, Sangmouane landed miraculously in the brush that grew out of the side of the cliff twenty-five feet down from its edge. She was surrounded by unusual purple flowers with bright orange centers.

The brush was comprised of roots sufficiently large to grab and hold the light Sangmouane, and her clothes caught up in it, stopping her fall. She could go nowhere, helplessly lying there, as her parents continued their fall. The last sound she would hear of her parents was the noise of the Land Rover hitting the bottom of the gorge, crushing everything in it.

Chapter Two

Two days later, a native tribal man, dressed in a local traditional village outfit, out on a hunt from his village with his teenaged son, came to the cliff and stopped to look down at the frightening sight of the gorge below.

Standing at the edge of the eight hundred foot gorge, he said, "This is where a special plant, the *ton mai piiset* grows, son." He pointed down to the colorful plant twenty-five feet below growing out of the cliff side.

As they looked on, a huge, black bird with red tips on its wings flew menacingly out in front of them a hundred yards away in the middle of the gorge, watching the two men looking over the cliff. The bird's nest was apparently not far off and although threatened by the humans' presence, it showed no fear.

"I see it, Father!" the young man said, looking at the purple and orange plant growing out of the side of the cliff below them.

"This is the only place left where it grows, in the soils from ages past," the man said to his son. "You must come for the *ton mai piiset* for your wedding."

"What is that in the brush?" the son asked his father, pointing over to one side of where they were standing and looking. In a spot of thick brush growing out of the side of the cliff was something in light-colored fabric.

"It moves!" the young man said excitedly.

"I think it is a child!" the father said.

"I will go down the path to see," the father said, and went over to one side some distance away where a very narrow, perilous, pathway came up to the cliff's edge. From there it was possible to sidestep down to the area where the child was stuck in the brush, next to the colorful plant.

Chapter Three

Three years later, sitting across from the Chief of a remote northern Laotian village was a couple that arrived in the village.

"We are Mr. and Mrs. Oosterlink. We are missionaries from Holland, but we have been living at a Christian mission in Vientiane. We are very pleased to meet you, and may God bless you," Mr. Oosterlink said to the Chief. The couple were in their fifties, attempting to spread Christianity.

The couple had been taken to the Chief's house when they came upon the village. The Chief would interview any such stranger that came to the village, which was a rare event as the village was so remote. The Chief's house was, like the other houses in the village, a primitive structure with wooden sides that let in some light between the joints of wood. The roof was thatched material from trees. There was a doorway and two small windows through which the majority of light came into the primitive dwelling. Some additional light came in through some knot holes and the cracks between the horizontal wood planks. There was no glass to be found anywhere.

"You have come a long way," the Chief told them. "Did you come to see my tribe?"

Mr. Oosterlink said, "No, not specifically. We actually did not know of your tribe. It does not appear on our map. We knew only that there were remote tribes in these northern Laotian mountains, and came to bring the word of God as His missionaries to whoever we can find that has not yet been enlightened by Him."

"I will not have you spreading your religion here. There were other missionaries here before, years ago, also from Europe. My tribe will do quite well as is," said the Chief.

"Please allow us to bring His words to those who wish to hear," Mrs. Oosterlink pleaded.

"No, you may not do that," the Chief told them. "You must

leave. My tribe is quite happy without the religions of other places. I will provide you with food and water for your return journey. But you must leave without attempting to spread your religion."

The missionaries' attention turned to a beautiful girl of seven years of age as she wandered into the Chief's house. She made a big smile and came next to the Chief.

"Who is this charming girl?" Mrs. Oosterlink asked the Chief. "She does not look like the other children."

"This is my adopted daughter," the Chief said. "She was left orphaned when I found her. I was on a hunt with my son some distance from here, and we found her. I believe she was in a vehicle with her parents that went over a cliff – they were killed. She was caught in some brush growing on the side of the cliff which kept her from falling to her death. She was near death when we found her, and we brought her here to the village. That was three years ago."

"What is her name?" Mrs. Oosterlink asked.

"Sangmouane Sayasithsena," the Chief answered.

"What a beautiful child!" Mrs. Oosterlink exclaimed as she looked at the young girl. "Were her parents foreign?"

"The father was a white man. Sangmouane remembers that he looked for precious stones to mine. The mother was Laotian. She speaks Laotian, and some European words. I have given her mother's last name to her rather than the father's so that she would have a Laotian name and not seem strange to the other children. She has learned the village dialect."

"Do you plan to keep her here in the village?" Mrs. Oosterlink asked.

"I have thought about this often as I have watched her grow. She had much of the western ways in her by the time she came here," the Chief said. "I think she hungers for a western education, and the things that you have in the cities where she came from. I think it would be better for her to go to the city and get a city education."

"Do you plan to take her to a place where she can get such an education?" Mr. Oosterlink asked.

"There is nowhere to take her near here. There may be some

place in the capital city of Vientiane, but I have not been there myself. It would be a long journey. I have no way to take her there, and I have no one there to take her to."

"We came from a Christian mission in Vientiane," Mrs. Oosterlink said. "We have been doing our work there for several years now, and felt that to do His work, we needed to go out and reach the needy that have not been touched by Him. We learned our Laotian at the mission in dealing with the local people. We will go back there when we do our best to bring Christianity to those who have not been touched by His miracles." She whispered, "Amen."

She continued. "We have a Land Rover on the road several days' journey from here. We would be pleased to take this young child to the mission when we leave if you will allow. The mission sometimes takes in orphans and finds homes for them. Would you let us take her to the mission? I can assure you that she will be cared for, and we can do our best to find her a nice home in the city with a good family."

Mrs. Oosterlink turned to her husband and said in Dutch, "Oh dear, do you think that God led us here to find this young lost soul?"

"It may very well be His will," Mr. Oosterlink said to her. "It could be that God sent us here for just this purpose, to save this young soul."

Mrs. Oosterlink raised her hands in prayer and closed her eyes to pray. Mr. Oosterlink joined her.

"We will do this, as we believe that we have been instructed to do this as His will," Mr. Oosterlink told the Chief. "But we would be obliged to attempt to teach her of God and His miracles, as it is our mission in life to do so. Do you object to that?"

The Chief said, "She has some knowledge of your God from her European father, so it will not be new to her. I suppose she could do worse. She really does not belong here, and you may be the only chance that she has to leave."

Making the decision, he said, "You may take her with you to Vientiane to the mission there. I will spend this last day with her, and then you may go with her tomorrow. There are some things that she and I must say to each other before she goes. I have loved her as though she was my own child."

"Of course," Mrs. Oosterlink said. "She is such a lovely child, and so in need of His words. I know now why God led us to this village. It was to save the soul of this poor child that lost her parents and to return her to Christianity. Praise the Lord. He works in mysterious ways."

In the late afternoon, atop a hillside overlooking a field of village crops below, the Chief and Sangmouane sat alone. The Chief said, "I believe it best for you to return to the outside, and so you will leave with the missionaries tomorrow. They will take you back to your own people."

Sangmouane had suspected something was wrong when her father brought her there with the strangers still in the village. Tears at once formed in her eyes.

"It is best. You can return one day, when you are older. You will go to city schools, and learn the western ways and things you cannot learn here. It is what is best for you."

With her little arms, she reached out to hold on to her father, as the tears flowed from her cheeks. She clung to him as he sat her in his lap.

"Now stop crying, and let me give you something very special."

The Chief took out a small silk bag from a satchel, and opened it. Out came crushed purple leaves, resembling tea except for the unusual color, as he poured the contents onto a piece of cloth.

"Do you see these leaves? They come from the *ton mai piiset*."

Sangmouane tried her best to listen over the sadness of the moment. "Yes, father."

"Unlike many people in the place that you will be going, we believe that spirits live in plants and certain things. This *ton mai piiset* has very special spirits that live in it, that have great powers. In our tribe only I as the Chief, and my bride, have summoned the spirits of this *ton mai piiset*. When taken at the wedding time with the proper prayers, the spirits can be asked to give your child special abilities that one day your child will lead others.

"It is a very rare plant, and only grows in a very special place in soils of ancient times. I found you at the place where it grows, and

I believe that your karma is tied to it, although I am not exactly sure how. My parents took the plant, and that is why I was able to be the one who speaks to the spirits, the *Maw Pii*. I took it with my wife when we were married, and our son was born with those special abilities that will make him a good Chief one day.

"I love you as my own daughter. I do not want to let you go, but I believe it to be best for you. You are not well suited for the simple life here in the village. In the city you will get a formal education and also get things that I do not have to give to you. So, it is best."

Tears streamed down Sangmouane's cheeks. "I do not want to go!" She clung on to him as though it would keep her there.

"You must do as I say, my Sangmouane. I want to keep you, but you are not best suited to be a village girl. And, you can come back one day to visit when you have grown. It is best."

The thought of losing Sangmouane brought a tear to his own eye. "Now that you are leaving, I will not be able to teach you further."

He held her for a time, and then said: "This *ton mai piiset* is something that I can give you that you cannot get elsewhere, and I want you to have it as my special present. This is the most valuable thing that I can give you." He put the strangely-colored leaves back into the cloth bag and gave it to his daughter.

"Now you must listen carefully and remember what I am going to tell you. You will marry one day. Beginning on your wedding night, you and your husband are to take some of these leaves each night for several days until they are gone. And, you must also take some of the dark mushroom that grows here. The mushroom will not last like the leaves, and so you must obtain one for the ceremony. If you cannot get one of the dark mushrooms where you are when you marry, you can take northern-made 'Lao Lao', a local whisky, in place of it, as the dark mushroom is used in the making of Lao Lao here in the north of Lao. It must be Lao Lao from the north, not from the south, as the mushroom is not used in the south of Lao in making it since it does not grow there. You must also learn two special prayers that I am now going to teach you. One summons the spirits, and the other asks for the powers to be given your child. When you do this, the spirits that live in the *ton mai piiset* will be summoned and give your child the special powers. Do you understand?"

"Yes, Father."

"Now I will teach you the prayers." He took out some strings from his satchel. "You must first put on baci strings on your wrists and on your husband's, like this," he said showing her, tying white strings spun by hand on her wrists. "And you pray like this," he said, holding his hands together in a prayer position. He then chanted the first prayer for her.

"That is the prayer to summon the spirits," he told her. "Now you do it."

She performed the chanting prayer for him.

"That is correct. You must repeat it for both you and your husband a number of times. Then you must pray this prayer," he said, and he chanted a different prayer for her. "Now, you do the second prayer for me."

Sangmouane chanted the second prayer.

"That is right. You must also repeat this prayer in the ceremony a number of times. Now do both," he told her.

Sangmouane performed them again, chanting the prayer as he had taught her.

"Once more."

She performed it correctly again, and he smiled at her in satisfaction. She looked to him through her tear-soaked eyes, knowing that she had done it well and that the occasion was a parting event between them.

He interrupted her thoughts. "You may only take the baci strings off three days after the wedding, or longer, and then you must not cut them – you must only untie them."

"I love you, Father."

"I shall always remember my daughter Sangmouane." As the sun set over the field of crops, the two embraced the moment and each other.

Chapter Four

Fifteen years later in America

"Cameron, why don't you find yourself a nice woman and settle down with a nice family?" Sharon, the busybody secretary of the architectural firm they worked for, asked him.

Cameron sat at his drafting bench, working on plans for a small shopping center, trying to ignore the question as though he had not heard, hoping he would not get snagged up in her busybody topic.

She refused to accept non-compliance with her offer to set him up with what she assumed was a perfect catch, that being her girlfriend, and continued, "I have been married now for six wonderful years and have two wonderful children. You are the only bachelor in the office. I know you would be a lot happier once you do start a family. Why don't you let me fix you up with my friend?"

Cameron could not successfully ignore her further, and answered, "The idea of getting married doesn't scare me, but the thought of children does. These days the women want to work and have their own career, and so both the father and the mother are always running around to day-care centers, and making arrangements for the kids to be here or there, at the doctor, at a friend's house, the movies, doing this or that – your whole life becomes one for the children. And that lasts until they go to college twenty years later. And nowadays they want to move back in after they move out rather than continue to pay rent. You can't get rid of them! No thanks!"

Cameron continued, "Look at what you have to do. If you don't pick your kids up from the day-care center by five thirty, on the second occasion you are ten minutes late they are expelled from the center. How could I stay late and do my architectural work under threats like that? Last night I was here until nine.

How could I ever be a success with an overriding commitment like that?"

Sharon said, "Oh, you don't really mean that. I know you. You love kids just as much as anyone. You just say that."

"Dream on. I am not going to spend my life chasing around for kids."

The owner of the architectural firm walked into the area and said, "Cameron, can you come in my office for a minute on some changes to the center that the owners want?"

"Sure," Cameron said, welcoming the interruption. He looked at Sharon and said, "Well, back to work."

Chapter Five

"Candice and I will be taking a year-long sabbatical, and leaving in two months," Spencer, his brother-in-law, said to Cameron at the dinner table. "We are making preparations now, and have cleared everything with our employers at the institution. We still have a great deal to do, from handling mail to paying utilities here. We are going off to India first, and elsewhere in Asia, and do not anticipate returning for an entire year. We have told the attorney to make up wills for us in case anything happens, and we have made you executor."

"An entire year!" Cameron said. "Good Lord! How does one do that? I couldn't even consider that!"

Of the two siblings in the Harrington family, Spencer was the oldest and a research doctor, and Cameron, the younger, an architect. Spencer had married, but had no children yet. Cameron had not married. Candice, Spencer's wife, was also a research doctor. They both worked at the same research hospital, but in different wings. There were no children yet to carry on the name of Harrington.

"I am tired," Spencer said. "I need a sabbatical."

"Me, too," Candice joined in.

Cameron directed his words to his brother initially. "But you have become such a name in the field of research medicine for lowering cholesterol. You are invited to go all over the world to give lectures to doctors who need continuing education credits to keep up their licenses. And you, Candice," he then looked at his sister-in-law, "your research in genetics. How can either of you possibly go away for a year? And, you have traveled so much already!"

Spencer spoke. "When I go to a lecture, I spend a day going, a day coming back and usually two days there at most. On occasion I only spend one day. I only get to see the inside of the hotel, and the meeting hall of where I give the lecture. I am always taken to a dandy dinner somewhere, but as the captive of a few of the local doctors. I rarely get to do anything else.

"When I am in the city of the lecture, usually several of the doctors and their wives have a dinner planned for me, or for both of us if Candice goes. Their conversations are all the same. Hospital cutbacks, government cutbacks, cutting back on their ability to earn as much as they used to, ungrateful patients, avoiding malpractice claims, the horrors of continually increasing socialization of medicine, being on call and having to stay nearby the hospital on weekends, how the government makes them be on call for indigents who are many more times likely to sue for malpractice, problems with the raising of their children, how expensive it is to provide higher education for their kids, and so on. Boring."

Candice said, "I am almost always invited with him with a free ticket. But I don't get the invitations for lectures like Spencer, as genetics is not the rage like cholesterol. But, I must say, we do get first-class tickets when we are invited. When doctors request another doctor to come and lecture, they never question expenses. For a doctor to question the travel expenses of another would be sacrilegious," she said with a smile.

Cameron said, "Aren't you going to miss all that?"

Spencer said, "Well, it was fun for a while. We got to visit a good number of places. But now it seems more like work. I am bored with it all. I want to go off and meet people who are not doctors. And Candice loves her photography. We want to go into India first, and wander off into places that are not just first-class hotels and tourist spots. We want some adventure, and to experience something new and different. In Asia, we were only invited for lectures to Sydney, Singapore, and Tokyo. We did go once on a tour organized by a medical organization that we paid for to China, which took us to Hong Kong, Beijing, Macao and Shanghai. That is the extent of our Asia experience so far.

"Also," he continued, "I want to go to Bangalore, India, where there is supposed to be spiritual enlightenment at an ashram."

"Don't tell me you are going to go off and see some weirdo preacher," Cameron said.

Spencer answered, "Well, that is just a highlight. I hear this one fellow, Saaid Baba, makes quite an impression on his audience there in Bangalore, and people from all over the world go there to see him."

"Let me show you how exciting India looks," Candice said as she went to the bookcase for a large book. "I bought a picture book of travel in India. Here it is." She opened it up to show the pictures. She turned to a picture of an extremely foreign-looking Indian man in a white outfit, a big yellow turban, huge mustache, riding a camel.

Cameron took the book, and flipped through some of the color pictures. The architecture caught him up. He looked at a picture of the interior of a building that was hand-carved marble. Below the picture it said: "Porticoed hall of a Dilwara temple, on the plateau of Mt. Abu, in the Aravali mountains of Rajasthan".

"This is amazing architecture!" Cameron said. "I would love to go there for some architectural inspiration myself, if there is much of this sort of thing," he said as he looked through the book intently. "I might benefit from a trip to a place like this."

Candice said, "You ought to consider it, too. Before long, we will be old. These containers, our bodies, are frail containers once you are in your forties. Just as a person gets to the age of some value in his calling, he finds out how vulnerable his body is. Cancer, heart attacks, and a long list of other maladies can afflict us."

"God," Cameron said. "You make me feel like I have only moments left. But isn't going away for a year going to put a pretty big financial dent in things?"

"What better way to invest than in experiencing the wonders of the world?" Spencer said. "We would much rather do this than to just go buy some eighty thousand dollar status symbol car to run around in to impress other doctors."

"Well, you make a good point. And you, Candice, made a good meal!" Cameron said, as he ate the Epicurean delight Candice prepared. "You really are fantastic!"

"Thank you, my sweet brother-in-law. But, getting back to the trip – in addition to my photography, I hope to learn about the recipes of Asia," Candice said. "There are so many spices and wonders I will never possibly learn unless I go there – I really have to go."

Spencer looked to his brother Cameron and said, "Now that Dad has died, and we have some extra money from the inheritance, the finances will be okay. And, we still have no children, so this is the absolute best time for us. We will never get to do it once we have a child."

Candice added, "We want to go while we are still young. Once we have a child, travel will only be to places like Disney World."

Cameron asked, "What will happen to your research when you are gone for a whole year? Aren't you the guru of lowering cholesterol?"

"There are plenty of things set in motion to more than occupy a year without me," Spencer said. "Right now I have set up methods of increasing, not decreasing, one of the types of cholesterol, called HDL. This is like a 'good' kind of cholesterol. Finding methods of that without increasing others will more than occupy the year for the staff."

"Well, the trip sounds like high adventure. I will help hold down the fort here while you two are gone by looking after the house."

"My genetics research can wait. Humans are millions of years old. Our travels away from the lab won't make a big dent in mankind," Candice said. She would later learn that would not be the case.

Chapter Six

"There it is!" Spencer showed his excitement to Candice as they walked through the entry courtyard to the arched opening where tourists get their first glimpse. It stood one hundred yards away from where it was first viewable. The afternoon sun made a yellow glow on the magnificent structure in front of them. The white marble structure with its inlaid semi-precious stones glowed in the radiance of the sun's rays. A reflection of the structure gave a second image in the water pond in front of one of the world's most famous examples of architecture.

"The Taj Mahal! It is even more beautiful than I imagined!" Spencer said, but Candice was already getting her camera warmed up with settings and walking forward through the arched opening that separates the entry courtyard from the magnificent structure. She was overwhelmed, and began furiously taking pictures from different angles. She moved from spot to spot, snapping away, stopping occasionally to change filters to enhance the preservation of the moment on film.

Spencer followed her reading aloud from a small book he bought at the airport in New Delhi on the Taj Mahal. "It was built as a mausoleum by Shah Jahan in memory of his favorite wife, Mumtaz Mahal. It is entirely inlaid with semi-precious stones. It took seventeen years to build."

"Mumtaz must have been some kinda honey!" he added. "I wonder what she did so well?"

"I am so glad we came!" his wife, Candice, said, ignoring her husband's comment in the presence of the structure before her. "This is truly the most magnificent structure in the world. I wish Cameron, as an architect, were here to see this. Can we spend an extra day here in Agra so I can photograph it in the morning light?"

"Why not?" Spencer said. "Maybe we can find out more about this superwoman."

"You are hopeless," she mused with him, shaking her head at him with a smile, and resumed moving in closer using different angles for more photographs.

Chapter Seven

Three months later at a café in Kerala, south India, Spencer and Candice sat outside at a table sipping Indian beer, the only alcoholic beverage the Indians made that was drinkable, watching the people going by. The day had been hot, and they were recovering from another sightseeing excursion earlier in the day.

Sitting nearby at another table, also sipping beer, was a light-haired, tall, slender young man appearing to be in his early twenties. In front of him was the large-sized Kingfisher beer, the Indian brand. He had the backpacking, rustic look of a traveling college student.

Catching them looking at him, he said, "Hi. Where are you from?"

"The US. You?"

"Germany." But that was obvious from his accent, as their accent must have been obvious to him. "Have you been in many places in India?" the man asked.

Candice answered, "Yes. We have covered a great deal of India. We stayed on a houseboat in Srinagar, Kashmir for five days and went around the area. From there we went by car up to Gulmarg, and skied the Himalayas. We traveled by steam engine through Rajasthan out to Jaisalmer to see the old trade routes. There we rode on camels, and saw the architecture of the past. The same train took us to Agra, where we saw the Taj Mahal. We have also been to the erotic temples of Khajuraho. Oh yes, not to forget the castles in Aurangabad. We then moved off the main routes and went into the countryside and traveled through many small villages. We went mostly by car, with a driver and guide. We have seen many things, and it has all been fantastic."

"Das ist gut. How long are you traveling?" the young man asked.

"We are taking a year-long sabbatical. We are both research doctors. How about you?"

"I am still in school. I am alzo taking off a year to do the travel, with my girlfriend," he said. "Are you going elsewhere besides India?" he asked them.

Spencer said, "We are open to go anywhere. We have been here nearly six months now. We have just come back from some travel into some of the small villages in the central region and here in the southern parts. The poverty gives you a different perspective on life. But the Indian people are wonderful."

"Yes, ze people are wonderful. Where are you going next, after India?"

"We haven't decided. What do you recommend?"

"You should go into Lao," he told them.

"Is that the same as Laos?" Spencer asked.

"Ja."

"Tell us about it," Spencer said.

"My girlfriend, who is at the hotel taking a nap just now, und I too are backpacking, und zleeping out often. Lao is more like a frontier than India. Traveling in Lao gives you the feeling that you are going back in time."

"How long were you there?" Candice asked.

"Two months. We only took a hotel once in a while. The hotels are very cheap, but we are traveling on a student budget." He tilted up the glass, and his beer was emptied.

"Let us buy you a beer while you tell us about it," Spencer offered.

"Ja, sure."

Spencer hailed the waiter and ordered a large beer for the traveling student, and one for him and Candice to share. The cold Kingfisher beer arrived. The heavy beer looked very refreshing as it was poured into their glasses in the hot, southern Indian sun.

"Very cooling," Candice mused as she drank down the nice, heavy Indian beer, utilizing the Indian expressions of 'cooling' and 'heaty'. She continued, "The Indian-made liquor is undrinkable, but this beer is good."

"What is so interesting about Lao?" Candice asked the student, as she sipped the cold beer. The effect of the beer made her more talkative.

"Well, there are some very interesting remote villages,

especially in the highlands in the north. They are as though from many centuries past. There is no electricity, no mail, und no contact with the outside. Alzo you can take a boat trip down the Mekong River, from Ban Houei Sai to Pak Ban and then to Luang Prabang. If you go be sure und take that trip."

"How does it compare to India?" Spencer asked.

"India is much larger, and with many more times the population. One billion compared to five million. The population is much more dense in India. Crowded is the word. Alzo, Lao does not have beggars like India. Und, there are not zo many tourists. It is much more remote."

"What about photo opportunities?" Candice asked, always involved with her passion for photography.

"There is zo much in India to photograph as it is zo much larger, but Lao is quite a gut photo opportunity," he told them. "I brought a camera myself. Things are very cheap in Laos, und ze people are very nice. I got gut pictures in both places."

"Maybe we will do Laos," Spencer said, looking at Candice. "We have pretty much done India."

"You will enjoy," the German said. "My girlfriend und I are going next to China, and later home. We are traveling as long as our money holds out. We camp outside most of the time."

Spencer said, "That is too adventurous for us. We stay in hotels."

"But you are working, ja, und we are only students," he said.

Spencer responded to him but looked at Candice, "You are more adventurous than we are. If we were as adventurous as you we would have done what you are now doing when we were younger. We envy your adventurous spirit."

Candice nodded in approval, and they toasted the German. He had no trouble finding an excuse to take a gulp of the good beer.

"Well, it has been nice talking to you, but I must get back. It is only on occasion that we have a hotel room, und I want to make use of it. Thank you for ze beer."

"Thanks for the information," Spencer told him.

"Auf Wiedersehen."

"Goodbye and good luck in your adventure!" Spencer said. The German was off.

"God, can you imagine backpacking in places like this?"

"We are just too old and too used to our luxuries and security, luv," she told him affectionately.

"What do you think, luv?" Spencer said. "Laos next stop?"

"Let's check into it," she said. "The idea of going to a frontier makes it alluring."

"Besides, I have acquired a beef deficiency! There is none here in India anywhere," Spencer said jokingly, but in actuality referring to the fact that he had gone without beef since arriving in India as none of the Indian restaurants serve beef, with the Indians considering the cow as sacred.

Chapter Eight

Spencer and Candice opened the door with their hotel key and walked into the hotel room in New Delhi. Spencer put down his parcels and looked at the visas for Laos that they had just obtained. They had also been given a packet of advisories to review.

Spencer said, "Boy, getting these visas to go to Lao has been a chore. Without help from the US Embassy I don't think we could have gotten them."

Candice said, "At least I collected some cookbooks on curries while we have been waiting this week," as she organized them on the hotel room table. "I will send them home rather than lug them around."

Spencer said, "You should see some of these advisories that they gave us at the US Embassy on travel in Laos. Here, just listen to this:

The Lao People's Democratic Republic (Lao PDR) is a land-locked country between Thailand and Vietnam, whose borders with Lao PDR are 1,730 km and 1,957 km in length respectively. To the south is Cambodia with 492 km of border, to the north-west is a border of some 230 km with Myanmar (formerly Burma), and to the north the border with China is 415 km long.

70 percent of the territory is mountain range, highlands and plateaus. One range, the Annamite Chain, stretches roughly north–south and spans part of the border with Vietnam. It averages 1,200 m in height on the Lao side, forming a geographical barrier between the two countries. A less formidable obstacle – the Mekong River – forms a large part of the border with Thailand.

Population: 4.8 million.

Density: 16 inhabitants/sq. km.

Ethnic groups: Lao 48 percent, tribal Thai 14 percent, Sino-Tibetan including Hmong and Yao 13 percent, Mon-Khmer 23 percent, Vietnamese and Chinese 1 percent, other 1 percent.

Per capita income: US $350 per year.
Number of doctors: 1 for every 11,000 people.

Spencer then turned to Candice and said, "Wow! One doctor for eleven thousand! Maybe we should practice medicine in Lao. They have almost no doctors! We would have a near monopoly!"

Candice smiled in return, and waited to hear more from the materials that Spencer had obtained, wondering if Lao was going to be part of their Asia trip.

"Oh, oh! There are medical advisories provided," Spencer continued, flipping through several pages. He read and condensed parts to her. "Internal parasites, such as worms and unicellular organisms, can enter the body by penetrating unbroken skin but most are ingested when eating fecal-contaminated or under-cooked food. Parasites eaten in egg form hatch out and become viable for years. Since not all of the parasites are detected reliably with single stool tests, it is suggested that you undergo de-worming twice a year."

"De-worming?" Candice repeated. "I wonder how you do that?"

"There is more," Spencer read on. "There is a whole section just on malaria. Of the four species of malaria, a unicellular parasite transmitted by the anopheles mosquito, plasmodium vivax, ovale, malaria and falciparum, the falciparum, or 'brain malaria', can be fatal within a few days. The malaria mosquito bites mainly during night-time, starting in the early evening up to the early morning. One can recognize the anopheles mosquito in its sitting position: its abdomen is tilted upwards and its head is bent downward to the surface it is sitting on. The best way to prevent getting malaria is to avoid being bitten," he read, skipping through the materials.

"Hah! Can you imagine being so close to one that you can see how it tilts its head? And, avoid being bitten!" Candice said. "That is funny!"

Spencer read on, "It actually tells you. Wear long trousers and sleeves if outside at night; apply repellent; avoid wearing dark clothes and perfume because they attract mosquitoes; use a sleeping net; screen the windows and bring your children in before dark."

"Hah!" Candice said. "Bring your children in before dark! That is rich!"

Spencer continued, "Suggested treatment for falciparum malaria is quinine 600 mg every eight hours and doxycycline 250 mg every six hours. For vivax malaria, chloroquine tablets, four every eight hours starting dose."

"Sounds wonderful!" Candice said. "Can there be something else to watch out for?"

"Dengue fever, a viral disease transmitted by an aedes mosquito which bites in the morning. So far there is no treatment for dengue fever because it is a viral disease. Symptomatic treatment is bed rest, two Tylenol every four hours, and three liters of electrolyte fluids daily with bananas, rice, salt or potato for better absorption. Do not take aspirin as it increases the risk of hemorrhaging."

"Charming!" Candice said.

Spencer said, "There is more. Japanese Encephalitis, a mosquito-borne viral disease by a night-biting mosquito culex is found where pigs are bred, peaking between June and August."

"So, it is simple. Don't go out at night to avoid the anopheles mosquito. Don't go out in the day to avoid the aedes mosquito. Just don't go out!" Candice concluded. "What else?"

Spencer read on, "To avoid hookworms, which penetrate the skin, be sure to wear shoes when outdoors. Before eating lettuce or unpeeled, uncooked fruit, clean it with a brush and soak them in a solution of one teaspoon of iodine to one liter of water for twenty minutes. Wash hands before eating to avoid Hepatitis A and B. Every household should have Coca-Cola or Pepsi on hand for bacillary dysentery as they contain more electrolytes."

Candice said, "I think I have got the hang of it. Don't go outside ever. Bring iodine to soak fruit and vegetables. Be especially careful of mosquitoes that sit with their heads tilted down. Keep your entire body covered."

"Wait! It gets better!" Spencer said with a smile as he read on. "Avoid certain routes as there are 'insurgents and bandits' and it identifies the routes. It says to stay clear of areas where a group called the 'Hmongs' are active."

Spencer continued, "There are over two hundred people killed yearly from unexploded bombs that were dropped on the Ho Chi Minh trail in Laos during the Vietnam war. More bombs were dropped in Laos than the entire world dropped during World War II. My God!"

She said, "No wonder no one goes to Lao! Anyone interested gets scared off by our own government," Candice said, looking at the papers on the health risks. "It sounds like the government wants to scare everyone off so that they won't find out about all the bombs dropped on the place!"

Spencer read on, "Here is one for you. Women should not attempt to touch monks. Monks are not allowed to touch women. Hah!" He laughed at the directive as he knew it would get her skin up.

"Now I call that a tiny bit old-fashioned," Candice said. "About two hundred years."

Then she asked in a serious tone, "What do you think the chances are that we would come into contact with something that would affect our lives?"

Spencer thought about it as they had to make a serious decision in the face of all the advisories. He applied his medical research background as a cholesterol research doctor and gave her what he thought was a correct estimation. "There is only a faint chance."

Candice said, agreeing, "The government probably puts up these warnings for most Third World places. Anyway, we wanted adventure, and this has got to be it. What the heck, let's go."

"I have a list of hotels here in the capital city Vientiane," Spencer said. "But the embassy said they do not take reservations. Can you imagine?"

Candice said, "This may be more adventurous than we first imagined."

Chapter Nine

The jet wheels chirped as they hit the Laotian ground at Vientiane, the capital. The pilot was a little rough with the landing, but not so much as to scare most of the passengers.

"Welcome to Laos!" Spencer said to Candice as the small jet went off the runway and on to the taxiway towards the small terminal at Vientiane.

"The Laotians say 'Lao', not 'Laos', and the adding of the 's' is done by the West," Candice reminded him as they taxied up to the small terminal.

A little blue taxi with *tuk-tuk* painted on the back was available outside the small terminal. It appeared to be a combination of a motorcycle and a car. The back was a bed like a pickup, but covered by a metal roof, the sides open. Spencer walked over to it, and showed the driver the name of a hotel on a list he obtained at the embassy in New Delhi. The driver recognized it, or so it seemed.

"Let's go!" Spencer said, and they crawled in the back and off the little popping motorcar went, towards the center of the city. The *tuk-tuk* had a little 100 cc motor that popped like a coffee percolator as they motored towards the heart of the city at 30 mph on the rough road.

The *tuk-tuk* pulled up in front of the hotel. The detail to the grounds was something unusual to the doctors. Flowers were everywhere, and the entrance to the lobby was impressive. "Look at this beautiful teak," Spencer told Candice as they went in the lobby. "The floors, doors, and trim are all in thick teak, and grand. Teak comes from here. And look at these high ceilings! I always have wondered why the US had lost the high ceilings. I only see high ceilings in old movies. Cameron would love all this."

They wandered through the hotel's central courtyard filled with beautiful flowers. Raised rectangular frames of teak wood, three feet wide and six feet high, held up spectacularly-colored bougainvilleas growing inside the frame, the multicolored branches supported by wooden trellises jutting out at upward angles from the handmade frames. The effect was to create cascading bougainvillea branches of different colors, high enough that one could walk underneath them. It was spectacular.

After settling in, and after Candice went through a roll of film, she joined Spencer at the lobby desk behind which a young man was standing, and Spencer asked, "How can I find a good tour agency?"

The young man listened intently, and then just smiled. It was obvious he did not understand a word of what Spencer was asking.

"This could get agonizing," Spencer said, turning to Candice with a twisted expression on his mouth trying to exaggerate his despair.

Aware that the couple at the desk needed something that he was not providing, the young man went to the back. Out came a girl who had a slightly better command of English. After explaining what he wanted several times, the girl pointed to several small stacks of brochures standing up in a holder that were in English. One was obviously from a travel agency.

"May I use the hotel phone?" he asked, looking at a phone on the edge of the desk. She brought it over to him, and smiled. He showed her the number on the brochure which she then dialed for him.

Much to Cameron's relief, an English-speaking man answered. When Spencer hung up, he said, "Cool! I have hired a private coach for tomorrow."

"Well, we still have the afternoon left," Candice said. "Downtown is close, so why don't we walk down there now and look around – some window shopping? This is the capital, and there is supposed to be a concentration of Laotian goods here, according to a handout I have."

"I'm game," Spencer said. "Let's go!"

Chapter Ten

As they walked down the short main street, they observed small appliance stores, a place that sold essentials such as soap and toiletries, but nothing of interest otherwise. They both formed an early impression that shopping opportunities were modest. There were no clothing or handicraft stores in the area. The stores were open to the sidewalk, with a metal pull-down door that would be used at night to close off the shop from the street.

"Perhaps we are not in the tourist area?" Spencer suggested to her in the form of a question. "Do you want to continue in this heat?" Spencer's shirt was getting moist from the heat. There was no breeze in the area, and the heat was taking its toll on him.

"Let's walk on down to the end of the street there," Candice said, looking ahead towards the end of that strip of stores ahead. "Maybe there is something ahead."

After walking three blocks further, they came upon a shop that had glass windows, looking very much more up-scale than the previous shops. It obviously had air conditioning as the front door, in glass, was closed. The air conditioning was a welcome enticement to come in from the heat of the afternoon. As they looked more closely, they saw that it was a jewelry store. Not particularly caring what it sold, as they wanted to cool down, they went in to enjoy the air conditioning.

In the shop was its Indian owner, a dark-skinned Tamil of forty-five years of age. He was dressed in dark trousers, wearing a white shirt without a tie. The whiteness of his shirt made his extremely dark Tamil skin look even darker.

The shop had a square of glass showcases in the center, such that one had to walk around the square to see what was for sale. The walls had glass cases displaying gold necklaces and other jewelry items. The shop seemed to have a good inventory. Spencer and Candice began to look at the jewelry on display so as to justify their using the air conditioning.

As their eyes adapted to the interior of the store, they both noticed another person standing in the back section of the inner square. They both turned their attention from the glitter of the jewelry to the other person working there. Capturing their attention in this manner was the shopkeeper's assistant, a girl in her early twenties. They could not help but stare.

She was tall, olive-colored, with long, rich, coal-black hair. She wore a blue sinn, the Laotian tubular skirt, with gold silk embroidery around the bottom, and a plain, blue, western-styled shirt with short sleeves that was the accepted style with the Laotian women. Her skin was radiant and rich, appearing as though from an ad of a person selling suntan lotion. She wore medium-dark lipstick, and bright blue eyeshadow, nearly iridescent. On just anyone, the eyeshadow might have been too much – but on her, it was exotic.

As they approached her, she smiled politely at them, and gave a *nop*, the slight bowing of the head with the hands in front in the prayer position. The subservient attitude that was displayed by the *nop* melted down any resistance that either of them had to looking at the shopkeeper's wares.

Most of the small shops they had been to in Asia had staff consisting of family. But her skin was so much lighter than the Tamil's that it did not seem as if she was part of his immediate family – an enigma. They walked about the shop looking at the jewelry in the glass cases, the graceful girl standing in the background, in case they had a question, never closing in so as to make them feel uncomfortable.

Two other shoppers came in and spoke to the Tamil in English, but with a German accent – they were most likely from the German Embassy. They did not look like tourists, with dress shirts and ties, but no coats. They engaged the Tamil in conversation about something they wanted.

With the Tamil owner occupied with the Germans, Spencer went to the glass jewelry case nearest the girl, hoping to get her to wait on them rather than the owner taking over for her.

"We would like to look at Laotian stones," Spencer said, looking down at the glass case but not pointing to anything specific.

The Tamil turned away from the Germans, and it looked as if he might take over, which neither Spencer nor Candice wanted. He said to them, "Would you care for tea or soda?" He was trying to lock them in as customers by offering a drink, something Spencer and Candice had experienced in rug shops in Kashmir, India.

"Thank you, but cold water would be better," Cameron responded. "It is hot outside."

The Tamil barked off something towards the back of the shop, where a dark-skinned, young Tamil man suddenly emerged from seemingly nowhere and presented himself to the store owner as though at military attention. The Tamil gave a command to him, which was apparently to fetch water. He scurried out the front door, going the opposite, longer way from where Spencer and Candice were standing so as not to interfere with their presence in the shop.

Spencer and Candice pulled up two high chairs that had been under the glass counter. They looked at the gemstones laid out for sale unmounted in little open white boxes. The two Germans occupied the Tamil owner, asking him to pull out things to look at, and were in the process of buying or ordering something. That left the girl to wait on them, and so the timing was good to ask for help.

The young Tamil assistant quickly returned through the front door with two plastic bottles of cold mineral water for them. It was already hot outside, and the water was a very welcome inducement to stay and look at the stones for sale. The Tamil had hooked them in now with the complimentary mineral water, and they were obliged to look at some of his wares – he was a good salesman. But they wanted to meet the girl.

Looking directly at the girl, Spencer said, "We would like to look at some Laotian rubies and sapphires." He then looked down at red and blue stones appearing to be just that, but in reality he had no idea what he wanted or what sort of stones came from Lao. He pointed to a bracelet to his right, away from the owner in hopes the girl would wait on them and not the owner. "Could we please see this?"

By asking her to take something out of the case, he realized he would probably end up buying something just to be polite. This girl could sell anything, he thought. He pointed to a bracelet and she picked it up inside the case and put it on top of the glass case, on a felt pad. She moved closer in like a dancer, without weight.

"This one is sapphire," she spoke as though her voice was made of sapphire as well. She had a British accent.

Taking it out from the glass case, she handed it to Spencer. "The bracelet is of twenty-two karat gold, and completely set all the way round with these dark blue sapphires," she said, displaying it. The sapphires were a quarter-inch in size. It looked far too expensive to consider. Spencer handed it to Candice, whose eyes opened in amazement at the piece.

"This is beautiful!" Candice said.

Spencer looked down into the glass as Candice examined the bracelet and other objects, considering the sapphire bracelet too expensive.

"Are these in fact real sapphires and rubies, and not man-made?" Spencer asked, referring to the entire lot of stones in front of them.

"Oh yes, sir! These are very real indeed!" she assured them, looking rather puzzled as to why they made a comment that the gems might not be genuine.

Looking towards the sapphire bracelet that mesmerized Candice, the salesgirl said, "These sapphires are from the mines at Bokeo, near the Golden Triangle where Lao, Myanmar and Thailand meet. They are said to be of the finest in the world. See the beautiful color," she said, holding a few she lifted out under the spotlights that all jewelers have over their glass cases.

Spencer looked down at some stones, and the girl took out stones in the white open boxes that Spencer seemed to be focusing on and put them on a mat on the glass.

"May I show you how to look at sapphires?" She picked up a piece of white paper from the desk in the center of the glass cases that surrounded it, and put it on the counter. She put some sapphires on it.

"Look through the stone this way. You can see if the stone has been artificially colored. Notice how these are uniform through-out, and have no striations."

"How do we identify a striation?" Candice asked.

The alluring girl took some of the unmounted stones from under the glass. "Here. These are the less expensive ones. Look at some on the white paper and you can see."

"I can see!" Spencer said. "Look, Candice. She is right! You can see the lines on this artificial one."

"There is a German company in Lao that has a method of impregnating the stones of lesser color with more color. They are still pretty, but not as nice. And, of course, not as expensive."

"Although we cannot afford it," Spencer said, establishing his right not to purchase it just because he looked at it, "I would like to know how much this is." He held up the bracelet that the girl had first pulled out, which was covered in sapphires. It looked like it cost many thousands.

Their beautiful salesgirl turned behind her, and picked up a calculator from a desk in the center area behind the glass cases that encircled it, and tapped in numbers to arrive at the US equivalent of their currency. "Two hundred and seventy US dollars."

As the quote was recited in US dollars, Spencer wondered how she knew they were Americans. Or did she? Were they so obvious? Or was it that, as in India where they had just come from, the US dollar was the standard of currency for foreigners and she would have recited it for other foreigners as well?

Candice, not concerned at all about such issues when looking at such a beautiful piece of jewelry, excitedly burst out, "So cheap! That is the price of costume jewelry back home!" She knew it was imprudent to talk that way in front of a shop clerk, but the price was so little that it never even occurred to her to bargain.

"We will take it!" Spencer said. "Lao is some place to shop!" He laid out the asking price in US dollars, thinking the price was too cheap to haggle over – anyway, there was something about the thought of haggling with this girl, who looked like a world-class model, that seemed to be out of the question.

Candice said, "Thank you, luv!" She gave him a big kiss on the cheek, which he resisted as somewhat out of place in public. Ecstatic, she gleefully put on the bracelet and held up her wrist to capture more of the store spotlights on it and to make it more prominent. She then spun around slowly, all the while looking at her new treasure.

Spencer said to the salesgirl with a big smile, "I guess we have made her happy!"

She replied, "I am sure she will always treasure it."

Spencer said, "Now that we have done our shopping, would you mind if we asked you to recommend to us a good place to go for dinner? Perhaps you would be good enough to write it down in Lao, so we can hand it to a *tuk-tuk* driver. We like to ask locals where to go, as they usually know best."

"Is there any particular food that you prefer?" she asked of Spencer.

When he did not immediately respond, she, trying to find out if they had some religious or other type of limits on certain types of food, changed the question to, "Is there any particular food that you do not take?"

"We have no particular diet," Spencer said. "We would like to sample the local cuisine and like to try most everything. We would like to sample Lao food, something like you yourself eat."

"I do not think you would like the places that I sometimes go to as much as the spots that the tourists and embassy staff frequent," she said.

"We would like to go to some place that has good Lao food," Candice said, thinking the same as Spencer.

The salesgirl responded, "There is a new place that the foreigners go to that I have heard of that is supposed to be very good. I have not had the opportunity to go there, but have heard from some of the embassy staff that come to the store talking about it from time to time. It has been open only for a month or two. I think that would be best for you. I have heard that the place has a variety of Laotian dishes and western ones as well."

Spencer and Candice looked at each other and without any words spoken each nodded affirmatively to the other. They communicated well.

"Would you show us tonight and be our guide? We would be honored and treat you if you would be so kind," Candice asked her. Coming from the wife, the invitation, Candice thought, would be more proper. They were anxious to get someone local to tell them about Lao, and this girl spoke English. She hoped the girl would show them a slice of the local real food. If she would, they would have someone local to talk to, order the food and to tell them about Vientiane and Lao. They had learned that getting in touch with a local was the best way to experience a foreign country. Candice herself was also charmed by the girl.

"Oh, I can get the directions for you. You need not take me."

"Actually, we would much prefer to have someone local to talk to, to help us order the food, to tell us about Lao and what to see in the country," Candice said, hoping she would join them.

She hesitated a moment, and then said, "If you are absolutely certain that it would not be a problem for you, I would be delighted to join you."

"I think we are in for a delightful evening," Spencer said. "Should we come for you in a *tuk-tuk*?"

He realized that was a fairly bold statement after saying it. How was he going to communicate anything to the taxi driver? If her address was not something that, once written down and shown to the taxi driver, was not understandable to the driver he wouldn't be able to find her.

"I don't live too far away, but you may not be able to find it easily," she told them. "The *tuk-tuk* drivers do not speak English. I can come to your hotel. It is easy for me. Let me do that, if you please."

"Will eight be a good time?" the girl asked.

"That will be fine," Candice responded. She gave the name of the hotel.

The girl said, "My name is Sangmouane Sayasithsena."

"I'm afraid that may take some doing for us to pronounce properly," Spencer said. He realized that he could not pronounce it right away, and did not try at this early moment of meeting her so as not to sound like a complete boob to her.

Candice realized that Spencer had not introduced them, and said, "I am Candice Harrington, and this is my husband, Spencer Harrington." She also avoided attempting to pronounce her name at this time. She would give it a go later on, she thought.

Chapter Eleven

"It is half past seven," Spencer said to Candice in the hotel room. "I see you are already having a drink. The sun has gone over the yardarm, so I guess I will join you. Why don't we take our drinks down to the courtyard? There are so many neat flowers there."

Drinks in hand, they walked down the hotel's teak circular staircase to the lobby and out into the floral courtyard to wait for their new contact. The hot Laotian day was now cooling down.

The hotel featured an interior courtyard through which they walked, under trellises of bougainvilleas of many different colors. The sun was no longer shining directly on the bougainvilleas, as it was partially hidden by the hotel structure.

Admiring the flowers, Candice said, "This would be spectacular in the sunlight. I must come down in the sunlight tomorrow and get some shots."

Their new restaurant guide arrived as promised. She looked like a model arriving on a set, as her attractiveness was out of place. She wore a maroon-colored *sinn*, the tubular skirt, with ivory-colored embroidery, and an ivory western top. She greeted them with the *nop*, as she had at the jewelry store, again pressing the palms together, prayer-like, at chest level, and momentarily lowering the head to show respect to her hosts. Spencer and Candice were not used to such treatment, and it presented a very warm greeting.

"*Sa-bai-dee*," she said greeting them in Laotian. Then she gave them a big smile. Her bright teeth glowed against her olive skin and coal-black hair. This girl could melt down anyone, the two of them both realized as they stared at her radiance.

They had already concluded that this gesture was to be returned on occasions, so they both tried returning it to her, clumsily as they were at it. She acted pleasantly surprised, as though they had done it correctly.

"I see you have learned some Lao," she said.

Spencer said, "Hardly. We only know '*Sa-bai-dee*' and '*kop chai lai*', thank you. Not much of an accomplishment in learning a new language. Shall we go to dinner?"

Standing outside, a *tuk-tuk* pulled up, and they climbed in the back. Their guide spoke to the driver, and off they went down the dusty unpaved street. On the way, they observed little open-front shops, staying open late, with the hard-working owners trying to make a go of it.

The restaurant was very newly decorated in western decor. The patrons were all western, and apparently embassy staff, which the doctors guessed by looking at them. They spoke in a number of languages, according to what the couple could hear from their own table.

Sangmouane explained what the dishes were. Spencer and Candice picked one each, and told her to pick three others. They realized that five dishes might be too much, but they wanted to try what they could since they had someone to order for them. And, the prices were cheap. She ordered the local sticky rice, or "*kiiao tiee-ow*", which they were shown is eaten with the fingers.

"We also pick up foods with the sticky rice," she explained.

"You must show us," Candice told her. "We want to eat in the same fashion as you."

The restaurant owner, trying to cater to the various government and embassy staff members from foreign countries, came and proudly told them that they had wine available as though it was something very special to have, and presented a list of imported wines.

"Bring us this one," Spencer said. "I have no idea what I am ordering. However, it is an import."

"That is a good one," the restaurant owner said, and left for the wine. He returned with the bottle and poured it for them.

Spencer looked at their new friend and asked her, "How do you pronounce your name again?"

"Sangmouane Sayasithsena."

"That is impossible to pronounce!" Spencer said, trying to pronounce her name. She smiled at him approvingly, but it was obviously a corruption of the name.

Candice gave it a try.

Sangmouane said it for them again. "Sangmouane Sayasithsena."

Spencer said, "That is a very tough one. I don't think we will ever get it right."

"Is the Indian man in the shop your father?" Spencer asked, wanting to learn about her. He knew that the Tamil proprietor of the jewelry store could hardly be her father with his dark coloring, but the question seemed to be the most diplomatic way of broaching the subject.

"My real parents are no longer living. He is my adoptive father, and the second one at that. I am only half Laotian. My real father was a German who was in Lao prospecting for gems, and met my mother, a Laotian. My name is from her. They were traveling in the north in a remote area looking for new mines, when they were killed when their Land Rover went off a cliff. Only I survived. I was only four."

"Oh my! That is quite a story!" Spencer became very interested.

She continued, "I was caught in brush on the cliff's side. I lay there until I was found by a tribal chief out from his village on a hunt. He was from a local village, a remote one, and saved me and took me to his village, adopting me as his daughter. There are still villages like that in Lao that have almost no visitors, and still live much like there is no rest of the world. The village I lived in was in the mountains that have almost no contact with the outside world. There life is like it has been for centuries. There is no electricity, no phones, nor hardly any contact with the rest of Lao. Nothing from the modern world has come, even today, to such villages. Only rarely are there any visitors. The one that I lived in is even more remote than most others, since it has no road to it."

"Have you returned to visit?" Candice asked.

"No. I have not been able."

"Do you write to the Chief now?" Candice asked.

"No, it is not possible. There is no mail service."

"Now that *is* remote," Spencer said. "Imagine, a place with no mail! Wow, Candice, just think, no ads!"

"How did you come to leave the village?" Candice asked, now mesmerized by the story.

"When I was seven, two Christian missionaries came to the village. When they learned of me, they told the Chief that they would take me to the mission here in Vientiane if the Chief thought it best. The Chief agreed with them that it would be best for me to go back to a city, as that is where my people came from, and that I get a city education. There was no formal education in the village. One can only learn the ways of the villagers. So the missionaries brought me here to Vientiane, to their Christian mission. The nice people there tried to find Christian parents for me, but could not find any Christians to adopt me."

Her audience was listening intently, so she continued her story. "My present parents, who had migrated to Lao from India, heard about me. My new mother was unable to have a child, and when they were looking to adopt a child, they met me and decided to take me. I was so lucky!"

"That is a very interesting story!" Candice said. "You look different from the Laotians we have seen so far."

"That is because my natural mother was Laotian, and my natural father German."

"Oh yes, of course, I forgot. What languages do you speak?" Candice asked. "You have a British accent."

"My parents spoke mostly English at home. They learned their English in India. That is perhaps why the Americans all say I have a British accent, as the English spoken there is from England. And I speak Lao, of course. My father and his wife also speak Tamil, which I can also speak a little of because I hear them speak it. They speak Hindi as well, and I learned a few words of it. There is a fair amount of French spoken in Lao, and I have learned some amount of that. And, there are occasional Germans in the store, and I can speak some German. And I know the village dialect from the village I was in as I told you about, but I have not heard or used it since."

Spencer said, "Communication, or the lack of it, is what either allows or keeps most people from getting ahead in the world. If you did not speak English, we would not have met."

"Yes," she said. "I am so lucky to have had my English-speaking parents."

Candice said, "You are very beautiful with your mixed blood.

It is no wonder why your Tamil parents chose you!"

Sangmouane blushed. "You are too kind." As though to shift the subject from her, she asked them, "What do you do in America?"

"We are research doctors," Spencer said. "I do research in cholesterol, and Candice in genetics."

"That must be very interesting, but I do not know of such things. I feel so honored to meet two medical doctors. Do you have any children?"

"No, we do not," Candice told her.

She looked a little surprised that they did not. It was not routine in Asia not to have children. "Do you plan to have children?"

"Yes. We do," Spencer spoke. "When we get back from our trip."

"I think one child would be enough," Candice added, announcing that she still wanted to pursue her career in research medicine, and not give it up to be a full-time mother with a big family.

"You will enjoy this," the restaurant owner said, interrupting their conversation, as he approached the table. Following him was a waiter and an additional helper behind, each with a large tray with their food.

Sampling the first one, Candice said, "This is very good. Please tell us more about it." They felt so lucky that they had found someone local to guide them.

Sangmouane described each dish and what was in each one.

"I hope to learn to make some of these," Candice said. "Do you know how to cook?"

Sangmouane said, "Yes. I can make Lao food. I can also make Indian food, especially south Indian food. I was taught by my mother."

"We are trying to get to know people on this trip, and hope to be able to do more than just see monuments and that sort of thing." Spencer asked her, "What is of interest here in the capital?"

"Tomorrow a girl I know is to be married. Would you like to come to a traditional Lao wedding? It may be interesting for you to see, and it is not the sort of thing that a tourist would normally get invited to."

"Absolutely! That is just the sort of thing that we have been hoping to get to do on our trip. We would love to be able to get to do such a thing," Spencer said.

"Will it cause any problem, bringing us?" Candice asked.

"Not all at. There will be a lot of people there, and it will be fine that you go."

Candice said, "What sort of present could we bring?"

"Money in an envelope would work very well," Sangmouane said.

"This is really very nice of you to let us see a slice of the local culture. Thank you so much for inviting us," Spencer said. "I can hire a private chauffeured car, so we won't have to take a *tuk-tuk*."

"The wedding is at eleven. I will meet you at the hotel at ten. There will be food served following the wedding."

Candice said, "That sounds perfect! That is the sort of local thing we want to do most, rather than sightseeing. We really appreciate what you are doing for us."

Chapter Twelve

The wedding ceremony was performed with the bride and groom sitting in front of a wreath, four feet in diameter, laced in flowers. Everyone else sat on the floor as well. The wreath was almost in the middle of the room, and the guests, far too many for the room, all sat around. A man who knew the proper chants, but wasn't a minister, sang the chants in a mix between chanting and talking, with repetition. The man chanting was on the other side of the wreath, facing the couple through it. By custom, everyone tied pieces of handmade white string, called baci strings, onto the wrists of someone near, who could be a stranger or someone familiar, and announced a wish, such as good health. Many were tied on Spencer and Candice.

Sangmouane said, "The person whose wrists get the baci strings is not to take them off for three days, and then not to cut them, only to untie them. In this way the wish or prayer will come true."

On three occasions during the ceremony, everyone in the room touched the person in front of them at the same time with the fingertips of one hand, and there was prayer-chanting in unison. Nearly all tied a baci string on the bride and groom. Some of the strings had a bill of money rolled up and tied in the string. During part of the ceremony, a shot glass of Lao whisky was passed to the bride and groom, who then drank it, with the crowd encouraging them with another chant.

"It is over," Sangmouane said. "Let's go outside." Spencer and Candice had a hard time getting off the floor after sitting that way so long. The Lao people, who were used to it, stood quickly without groaning.

Outside in the courtyard an enormous feast had been set up on tables that had been pushed together. Rented plastic tent tops covered the table tops, which were filled with all sorts of delicious Laotian foods. They went around the tables filling their plates and then found three chairs together to sit and watch. A sound system had been set up, and there were some singers. The music was apparently some sort of mixture of modern and Laotian, but the words were in Laotian. A man did much of the singing, and then there were two women who sang alternately. As usual at such events, the volume was too loud. They sat in the partial shade from the hot Laotian sun, and the merrymaking continued.

"When do we give the money present?" Spencer asked. Following the advice of Sangmouane to bring money, Spencer had brought an envelope along from the hotel, and passed it to Sangmouane. "Would you address it please? And, how much money do you think we should give?"

"Your American money goes a long way here," she told him.

"Well, we could use some sort of advice," Spencer said. "Please tell us what you are giving."

"I am giving thirty thousand kip, which is seven American dollars."

Spencer was shocked at the small amount. He realized this was a very poor country, and that the amount spent on wedding gifts here would naturally be much smaller than he was used to giving. Sangmouane had an envelope in her purse, and showed it to them. The envelope was a hand-printed one, very artistic.

Spencer said, "I tell you what. Here." Spencer handed her a fifty dollar bill, and told her, "Give them this for all three of us. You keep your kip, and make this part of your gift as well."

"That is a very large amount of money!" she said. "They will be delighted!" She put the bill into the envelope he brought from the hotel, and wrote on the unpainted side of the envelope in Lao, identifying the additional western guests who were making the large gift. "Do you want to put your addresses on it as well? They will write to you later on with thanks."

"Just put our names, with yours, as your American guests, and let their thanks go to you. You brought us here, and the experience and food are wonderful," Spencer told her. Sangmouane went to a special box for the money gifts on a table and dropped the envelope in it.

Riding back in the chauffeured white minivan they had hired for the day, Candice told Sangmouane, "We really appreciate your taking us to the wedding. It is the sort of genuinely local thing that we wanted to do most on our trip. We would never have had such an opportunity if it were not for you."

"Oh, I am sure that given all the people there that it was no inconvenience. And, your gift was enormous!"

Arriving at the hotel, she said, "I have to go to work now, for several hours." The statement implied she would be free later.

"Can we take you to dinner again?" Candice asked.

"That would be very nice. I will come back at eight again tonight if you wish."

Candice said, "We could try the hotel restaurant. We peeked in last night, and the food looked very good. Have you ever eaten at our hotel?"

"No, I haven't," she answered.

Candice added, "Let's eat there. We can let the car go on back, and pick us up again tomorrow."

"And, the hotel restaurant has a full bar!" Spencer chuckled.

Chapter Thirteen

At half past seven, the phone in the hotel room rang, in bursts of two rings close together.

"Meestah Harreentun, your guest is here," the man from the hotel said on the phone.

"Thank you. Tell her we will meet her in the lounge," Spencer said.

The hotel lounge was very nice for a small hotel. The entire floor was teak, and the ceiling high. The bar area was all done in teak, as were the coffee tables. There were arched openings in the stucco walls without glass, and ceiling fans moved the air in the room in a welcome manner.

As they entered the lounge, Sangmouane was there, standing out – she was too striking to be part of the regular scenery. She wore a sinn skirt and matching western top in bright blue. In the local fashion, there was embroidery at the bottom of the sinn skirt, this one in a silk hand-woven pattern. Her long, rich, thick black hair contrasted against the bright blue outfit. Bright blue eyeshadow complemented the outfit, which, on her, made her look like a model on assignment for a commercial shoot. She could easily be a professional model in the West, both Spencer and Candice agreed. Her skin radiated as though it had a life of its own. Having someone so beautiful to escort them made them feel special.

"So nice to see you," Spencer said.

She greeted them with the *nop*. "*Sa-bai-dee*," she said to them. Then came her irresistible smile.

"*Sa-bai-dee*," said Spencer, and then Candice, trying the *nop* as well, although much more clumsily than Sangmouane.

Spencer looked to the bartender, and said, "Vodka martini, dry, for me. Ladies?"

"The same," Candice said. "How about you?" she asked of Sangmouane.

"I will take the same as you."

"A girl that takes a proper drink!" Spencer joked, admiring her taste as similar to his. "Bring them over to the table," Spencer added, which was completely unnecessary; there were only a few other people in the lounge. The group went over to a corner area with open windows on either side of the corner, and an overhead fan. They sat so they could face one another.

"The wedding was fabulous!" Candice said, looking at their hostess. "I took all sorts of neat pictures. We cannot thank you enough for inviting us. We would have never got to see a Lao wedding otherwise."

The drinks arrived, and Spencer sampled his and proclaimed, "Ah, a civilized drink!"

Candice asked Sangmouane, "Please don't let us impose on you, and do not hesitate to say no. But I am going to ask you if it would be in any way possible for you to take us about as our tour guide tomorrow? We would be glad to pay you to act as a tour guide if you could take time off from the jewelry shop for a day. We would be glad to pay you as much as the agency charges, if you could do that for us."

"I can take off a day," Sangmouane said. "There is no need for you to pay me any money. I do not take a salary, as I just help out my father and he supports me. He will not mind. I would enjoy showing both of you around."

"We are so privileged that you are showing us about," Spencer said. "Are you so nice to everyone?"

Sangmouane was quiet for a few moments. Then she said, "I had a feeling come over me when I met you in the store that there would be something in my future with you. I think it was my karma that I would come to know you."

"Karma," Spencer said. "Well, perhaps it is our 'karma' that we came to know each other. What do you want to do most with yourself, as you are so young and have so much life ahead of you? Do you plan to marry?" Spencer tried again to pronounce her name, again without success, "Sangmouane Sayasithsena," but it did not come out like that.

"Well," she answered, "I will probably marry one day." She said it as if that was something to fall back on, for the lack of some better alternative, as the chances of much else in Lao were limited.

As her answer left hanging some other thought of an alternative, Spencer asked, "What would you do if you could do whatever you wanted?"

Sangmouane answered, "If I had my wish, I would travel to the West. America would be my first choice. I have heard so many wonderful things about it. I love Lao, but there are not many opportunities here."

Spencer, influenced by the drink, finally could not help himself and asked what he had been trying not to ask. "Do you think that you might ever come to America one day?" He meant it as a question of migrating, not as a tourist to see Disneyland, as he, and she, knew that coming as a tourist was ridiculous given the income of Laotians. The embassy material given to him about Lao said the average Laotian annual wage was three hundred and fifty dollars per year. He realized after asking it there was a considerable distance of more than just miles between them.

She gave what Spencer and Candice both found to be a very unusual and provocative answer. Her answer took into consideration the seeming impossibility of going to America due to the expense, the restrictions put up by America to keep out a flood of others wanting everything from wealth to the scourge of welfare, but still not wanting to believe that there was no chance at all to come. In her British accent, especially on the "a" sound, she answered, "I suppose there is a faint chance."

Spencer was so taken by the answer that he thought a while before speaking. "A *faint chance*," he repeated aloud. He looked at Candice, and he could see she was moved by the answer as well. Here was a girl who was very smart, full of youthful ambition and energy, charming, spoke English, and was incredibly beautiful. Her answer represented knowledge of the reality that there was no likelihood of coming to America, but at the same time was an answer that did not absolutely foreclose forever the possibility of coming – leaving it open as something to wish for. It was sort of like a dream – she was young, and still had hopes of something better. Notwithstanding the seeming impossibility of the expensive and visa-requiring travel to the other side of the earth to a place she had only heard of, she refused to completely eliminate the possibility that she might one day get to go to such a place. It seemed the perfect answer, covering all parameters.

"What a lovely answer." Spencer said. "Given the fact that your real name, 'Sangmouane Sayasithsena', is impossible for me to pronounce properly, would you mind if I gave you a nickname? I propose 'Faint Chance!' I love that name!"

Candice said, "I love that name too. Do you mind it?"

"I like it too. It is a very nice name," she politely replied with a warm smile.

"So, we will call you that, if you don't mind then," Spencer said. "Faint Chance," he continued saying it with a British accent, especially on the "a" in "Chance", which he pronounced like "ah".

"Faint Chance," Candice repeated.

Spencer held up his drink and said, "I propose a toast to the new name, Faint Chance!"

Candice held up her glass and clunked it against his, and then Faint Chance, catching on, did the same, joining in the toast. A waiter came around in a white, cotton uniform top with brass buttons. "Another round," Spencer said, without asking the girls if they wanted one. But their glasses were empty too.

At dinner in the hotel restaurant, the three of them ordered a bottle of wine. The seed of her desire to travel to America having been planted, and Spencer, with a substantial dose of alcohol narrowing his focus, pondered how unfair the world was, and how such a charming girl who spoke English could not go where she wanted due to a lack of money and mobility to do so.

"You really should come to America one day," he told Faint Chance. Suddenly he realized that he had already asked her earlier, and that it was not possible for her to consider. Her expression changed to somewhat hurt, as she felt inadequate in that she knew she would never have that much money or opportunity. Spencer realized he was inadvertently rubbing in the fact that he and his wife had so much mobility, whereas Faint Chance had none. An embarrassing feeling of clumsiness and lack of manners overcame him. Wanting to rectify this, and the alcohol making him less subtle, he blurted out, "How would you like your possibility of coming to America to be greater than just a *faint chance*? How would you like to come to America?"

Faint Chance looked puzzled and asked, "How can that be? I would need a sponsor, and a lot of savings."

"What do you think about us sponsoring her?" Spencer asked openly to Candice.

Oh, oh! What are you committing us to, Spencer? Candice wondered silently to herself. I can still say no. Should I? How much do we really know about this girl? What if she gets sick? What if it did not work out for some reason? It was a large commitment to be responsible for someone as a sponsor. They would be totally responsible for her. She wished that he would have discussed it with her before making the invitation. His drinking had made him bold and open. What to do? It would be nice to do something for the underprivileged that they had seen so many of in India in the first six months of the trip, and now in Lao, but there was really nothing that they could do to help. They had discussed in their travels, especially in the first part, in India, how it would have been a great experience to have worked there for a year, but the best time for that would have been when they were just out of medical school – their jobs at the research institute would not allow that now. But, the idea did provide a warm feeling of satisfaction, a good feeling to be able to help someone without the same privileges as they enjoyed. Well, she thought, here we go!

"Yes, we would love to have you come live with us," Candice added to her husband's open offer. I really must chastise him later for handling this the way he did, she promised herself.

"Would you really do that for me?" Faint Chance asked again, as she was in a state of disbelief.

"We insist! We would love to have you come over and stay with us," Spencer said emphatically to make sure it was not taken as an offer that was to be politely rejected.

"Absolutely," Candice added, confirming the offer. Why not? she pondered. Faint Chance was such a delightful breath of fresh air, and would bring a nice change of pace for them from their dreary and boring medical friends. And anyone as beautiful as her would no doubt wind up getting an offer to marry soon and be gone – in fact, probably before they ever tired of having her around.

Faint Chance's eyes opened in surprise at the prospect – it was something that she really never believed could happen to her. Something big was happening!

Candice asked, realizing that maybe this was too hastily conceived, "But can you leave your parents and the store? We don't want to be the cause of breaking up your family."

"My father knows one day I will leave him to be married and to go off to raise a family, so my leaving is expected one day. He will be happy for me. He had very little in India, and will understand the meaning of such an opportunity. I can hardly believe it. I had a special feeling when I met you that there was something in my karma with you." Her eyes watered as emotion overcame her.

Spencer, to try to downplay the event a little so Faint Chance would stop with her watery eyes, said, "It really is not much of a gift. We will have to sign for you, and guarantee your support in the United States as your sponsors. It may take some doing to get you a visa, and will take some time for the government to provide you with papers." He added this so that she would not get the idea that she could just jump on a plane. Spencer did not know what was involved, and worried that he might be raising false hopes of immediate travel to America. He was aware that a single foreign girl could not simply just go get a green card without some considerable obstacles, whatever they might be.

"Oh, I am aware of that," she responded. "But, once in America, how can I live? Is work available?" In her excitement she asked a small battery of questions at once.

Spencer said, "You can live with us for as long as you wish – indefinitely for that matter. After you get settled, and get a good job, you can do what you want. And yes, there are many jobs, but first you will have to get a work permit. In the meantime, you can learn to drive, and you can show Candice how to make Laotian cuisine. How does that sound?"

Faint Chance said, "I have not been so happy since I was adopted by my Indian parents as a little girl. I am truly lucky!"

Candice said, "It is our pleasure, and really is not much for us to do. We enjoy the feeling of helping someone, and you have taken such good care of us here. We will enjoy having you at our house."

Spencer said, "I will go to the US Embassy before we go and get the papers for you to start the process. The American government will be asking your Laotian government if you have any criminal background, for proof of birth and citizenship, and that sort of thing. There are restrictions on people coming into the United States, such that there may be some delay on your coming, depending on how quickly the American government acts on the application. We will not be finished with our trip for another several months, and it will undoubtedly take more time than several months to get your clearance, so, it will work out time wise." He really did not know what was involved, but he had heard of such obstacles when people wanted to migrate to the US.

"It all seems too impossible to be true!" Faint Chance said. "I saw a vision of my future when I met you, and now it is coming true!"

"How come we don't see such things in the future?" Spencer said to Candice.

"Good question," Candice responded. "Perhaps if we stayed slightly more sober!" With that, they all laughed.

Chapter Fourteen

The following morning, the same driver arrived with the tour company's little white van. Faint Chance arrived shortly afterwards in a gold-colored silk sinn with a brown top. The sinn had brown silk embroidery at the bottom in the shape of figurines, and the brown matched the color of the western top, also in silk. Laotian girls do not expose their shoulders as do the westerners, Spencer and Candice later found out. A tank top would be considered obscene. The western shirt on the Laotian girls makes them look modern, but the tubular skirt looks like something from a different place – a curious combination to the western eye.

Her eye make-up was less intense than the blue they had seen her in previously, and gave a more natural effect. The morning sun reflected intensely off her gold silk sinn. She had a natural sway to her hips, as she walked from the *tuk-tuk* to the hotel entrance where Spencer and Candice were all ready to go, watching their exotic guide.

She greeted them with the *nop*, and said, "*Sa-bai-dee.*"

"*Sa-bai-dee,*" said Candice.

"What suggestions do you have on where to go?" Candice asked her.

Faint Chance said, "You must see the silk weaving. You will love that, and I know some very good places where you can see the making of the materials."

"It sounds very exciting," Candice said.

The van pulled up to a building where silk weaving was the business. Faint Chance spoke to the female owner in Lao. The owner let them pass, and became their tour guide as they walked about the open-windowed, silk-weaving business.

Spencer said to Faint Chance, "This is really nice of you to take us about in this manner. We get to see so much more, and from a local perspective. We really appreciate it."

"You are most welcome. All Laotian females wear a silk tubular wraparound dress called a 'sinn'. The full name is 'pan sinn', or cloth sinn. The materials for sinns are made here. Also made here are wall decorations, and other smaller articles. Bedspreads are made at other places, with bigger looms. Let's go to the back, to see how the silk is processed."

Spencer and Candice watched with great interest in the open back as a girl took raw silk thread and wound it into bundles two feet in diameter on home-made wooden boards with pegs. Nearby a dye master was busy making his dyes from berries, tree bark and other things he had learned to use. He had no artificial dyes. The various dyes were made in buckets in which he put the tree bark, berries or whatever material he used with water. Then some of the colored water would be put into a can heated underneath with burning wood. Salt was added, and when it was just right, he put in a bundle of silk, and then took it out and beat it on a wooden rail. The results were stunning, with the colors of the freshly-dyed silk bright and beautiful. Girls put the silk on wooden spools, and then onto large wooden bobbins to end up with the weavers – all a primitive process as though out of the distant past.

Inside the other part of the building, weaving girls sat at wooden looms, five to six feet high. The method of putting the silk together to make the patterns was very elaborate. The patterns were all done by the girl pushing a bobbin of a certain color from the point just before two or more rows of silk thread came together from the loom. She knew just how to change colors and when. So many hours, even days, went into a single piece of cloth.

After an hour, Faint Chance said, "Now I would like to take you to a teak forest, since we have the car. It is out of town in this direction, and you may not have seen a teak forest."

"That is for sure," Spencer said.

Faint Chance directed the van driver out of town an hour away from the silk weavers. As they approached the teak forest, it began to rain. The trees did not provide much shelter, as the odd-looking teak trees did not have spread-out branches. The teak leaves, a foot in diameter, grew close into the trunk of the tall, thin, pole-like trees.

"We don't mind a little rain," Spencer said as they exited the van at the roadway near the forest. Candice got out her camera, and began taking pictures of the odd-looking trees.

After a time, Candice realized that there was a world-class model in the teak forest, and she was missing a great opportunity by shooting only the trees. Suddenly the trees were not so important after all. Candice began to shoot Faint Chance, and focused on her figure, which her wet clothes exaggerated. She provided a model of perfect proportions, and her soaking hair did not seem to ruin anything. Faint Chance did not seem to mind being the subject, and did her best to act natural for Candice. She added life to the pictures of the teak trees, which had become the background. The water built up on the large leaves, and came down occasionally near the base of the teak trees in huge drops. Candice wiped one off her camera, and continued the shoot.

The three of them walked deeper into the forest, and out of sight of the van that was waiting at the road with the driver. After slowing now and then for pictures, they came to a waterfall, coming down a rock formation a hundred feet high, landing in a huge, odd-shaped pool, a hundred feet or so in diameter, and only a foot or two deep. The pool drained out into two other smaller pools below, and the water then went down the hill in smaller streams. Crystal clear, without any mud or debris, the water had a blue cast to it, looking very drinkable. The sound of the waterfall was very loud, adding to the intensity of the scene. It was just too much for Candice to not take advantage of. Red wild flowers surrounded the waterfall, as though the scene had been made for a photographer. It was a photo opportunity extraordinaire.

"Wow, this is too much! I can't believe something like this exists!" Candice said, as she moved from spot to spot with her camera. She began taking pictures. "Imagine this, Spencer, right out here in the middle of nowhere! Perfect!"

The rain let up, and rays of sun began to fill parts of the scene, making it even better. Faint Chance stood by, in her rain-soaked silk sinn and western silk top, watching Candice shoot pictures.

After taking a roll of film, Candice paused to go to her camera bag to put in another, and when doing so looked over and suddenly remembered again who was with them. What a waste! Candice suddenly realized she was completely missing the mark with the "natural" photos.

Candice decided to get bold like a good photographer and said, "Faint Chance, you are already soaking. Would you mind terribly getting in the waterfall? It would look so exotic!"

"Sure! It looks very inviting," Faint Chance said. She took off her shoes, and walked right on into the falling water. Candice was ecstatic. Faint Chance began to dance about in the waterfall, providing a perfect subject for Candice, who was taking pictures at a rapid rate. She did a modified form of a traditional Laotian dance, with movements of the fingers, hands and head, and the knees occasionally raised in the air. The dance looked something akin to Thai dancing to Candice. Spencer stood back, smiling, taking it all in. Then, to the complete surprise of Candice, not to mention Spencer, Faint Chance began to undress!

She first took off her brown silk western top, and tossed it on a rock nearby. She next took off her black bra, and did the same with it. Her mixed blood had bestowed upon her very full breasts, much larger than the smaller Laotian variety, which made her quite the model for Candice. But she did not stop there. She undid her sinn, and put it on the rock as well. She then took off her black panties, and did the same with them. Standing there naked, she washed herself in the falling water, providing contest-material photography for Candice. The shape of her legs was nothing less than perfect, and her olive skin was without lines anywhere. Faint Chance acted without a trace of inhibition, as though dancing naked outside in a waterfall was the natural thing to do. Candice suddenly realized she had become mesmerized by the sight and had stopped taking pictures! She immediately regained her senses and started to snap the moment onto film, a once-in-a-lifetime opportunity – this sort of thing was not normally available to tourists. Shot after shot, there could not be too many pictures of this, Candice realized as she moved about from different vantage points, looking intently at her subject through her single-lens reflex mirror camera.

"These are going to be fantastic shots," Candice said aloud, but the strong sound of the waterfall drowned out any chance of someone hearing her as she snapped away.

Chapter Fifteen

The following morning Spencer and Candice walked to find the US Embassy of Lao. It was situated behind a stucco wall eight feet high. The entrance was not on the high street, but down a narrow side street, with the continuation of the eight-feet-high stucco walls on either side. The area was kept very clean, and two uniformed off-duty policemen stood outside at either side of a very large, strong, iron gate twenty feet wide and eight feet high. Across the gate was the familiar gold Eagle, a warm sight in such a foreign place.

Another man on the inside of the gate approached them through the big iron gate and asked, "What is your business?"

"We are Americans, and are here to see someone about the immigration of a Laotian to America," Spencer told him.

The man behind the gates told the guards outside something in Laotian, and they jumped to the task and pushed the big gate open manually. It was on rollers to move open to the left, and so big that it took both of them to move it.

They walked inside the embassy courtyard, and into the building. Inside the door, there was a wall with a glass top separating the employees from the visitors, with a window opening. A lady came forwards to greet them.

"We need the forms for a Lao citizen to apply for immigration to the United States, and also whatever forms we need as sponsors," Spencer told her.

The lady went over and spoke to a secretary, who got up quickly and went to a filing cabinet. She collected a series of forms and brought them forwards. They were to learn in talking to her that the process was a long one, and involved more than just simply filling out and submitting some forms. They looked over the forms to be sure that they understood them as best they could from a brief reading.

"Is there anything to expedite the process of immigration?" Spencer asked.

"These forms have to be completed and submitted to the Department of Immigration and Naturalization," the lady told them. "Here is a duplicate copy of each form you will need."

"Thank you," Spencer said. "Can I use your phone for a local call?"

She led him to a phone, and he called the jewelry store. Faint Chance answered.

"Hi! This is Spencer. Can you come by the hotel after work? We have forms for you from the embassy."

"Yes, I can be there after work at six thirty."

Leaving the embassy, Candice said, "Spencer, let's go to the shopping area. It is just across the street."

They walked across the street, and entered a Vientiane version of a shopping mall, a large cluster of shops in a building that had no walls, and which had additional stalls added to the perimeter with other vendors. They walked through it once, and found most of the little stalls sold woven silk goods such as sinns and scarves, handicraft and some inexpensive jewelry on a smaller second level.

Candice said, "Spencer, I want to shop for a silk sinn for myself, and maybe a scarf for a gift or two. You will get impatient. Why don't we meet back at the hotel in a couple of hours? I will take a *tuk-tuk*. Okay?"

"Sure. I want to look at some of the handicrafts. See you there."

At the hotel, Candice was inside and waiting for Spencer. There was a knock on the door.

"Yes?" Candice said.

"It's me!" Spencer said.

Candice got up and went to the door, and opened it saying, "Spencer! Wait'll you see my neat new silk sinn!"

Spencer walked in with a sheepish grin, barely fitting through the door, and holding on to an incredibly realistic wooden-carved elephant's head three feet high, with carved ears nearly as wide as its length. He looked as if he had bagged it as a trophy.

"Oh my God!" Candice said.

"Perfect, eh?" Spencer said. "And cheap!"

"We will have to ship that! We are not going to lug that all over Asia!" Candice said. "It'll cost more to ship than it cost!"

"Minor details," Spencer said. "How can you put a price on love?"

Chapter Sixteen

Faint Chance arrived at their room. Spencer read over the papers with her and they filled out each of their sets as best they could. She would have to get some records to attach to her copies later.

"Let's have a drink now and toast your coming to America," Spencer said. He poured drinks for the three of them.

"Here is to our new guest in America!" Spencer said, raising his glass. The three of them clanged their glasses together, and took a sip. Faint Chance looked so pleased.

"I have never been happier!" Faint Chance said.

Later, they sat in a seafood restaurant that Faint Chance took them to. It had a full bar, and they were having another round of drinks.

Faint Chance said, "May I please be so forward as to ask you a personal question? I would not do this, except that you are leaving, and I have good reason to be so intruding on one subject. I hope you will not think it rude, and if so, please do not answer the question and forgive me."

"Of course," Spencer said.

Candice nodded. "Ask away."

"Are you ready to make a child at this time?" Faint Chance asked.

Spencer and Candice looked at each other when confronted with this very curious question, without saying anything to each other. Spencer spoke first. "Well, it has occurred to us that if we are going to have a child, that we had better do so soon."

Candice said, "If I do not do so, I will be too old and problems become higher risk with women who are past my age. I suppose this is as good a time as any. Actually, if we were to start now, the baby would be born well after we got back, and we would have all the benefits of US medicine. It would not ruin our trip, as we would be back before I would get heavy."

"If you are willing to make the baby at this time there is something very special that I will do for the new child to be."

"What on earth can that be?" Candice asked, her medical curiosity aroused.

"Yes, what are you referring to?" Spencer added.

"Remember the Chief of the village that I told you about who took me in and adopted me?"

"Yes," Candice said.

"When I was leaving the village with the missionaries, the Chief gave me a gift that he would have only given his own child. It is for my wedding one day. The gift is the means to summon special spirits that will give a child special powers, so that the child will have special abilities and can be a leader one day. It involves special prayers to summon spirits."

Oh no, Candice thought. Not a bunch of "spiritual stuff". Now we are probably going to have to be subjected to some sort of prayers. But, we must try to be polite, as Faint Chance no doubt takes all this very seriously, and we don't want to offend her. I hope she doesn't want to insist on bringing a bunch of prayers and things like that to our home! Maybe I should let her know I don't go in for that sort of thing.

Faint Chance continued, "As you have given me such a great gift by inviting me into your family in America, I want to give your new child that special gift that the Chief gave to me."

Faint Chance took the little bag out of her purse that the Chief had given her years earlier, and put it on the table. She produced a small bottle of clear fluid and some small white strings each a foot long. She opened the bag to show them its contents – dried, purple-colored, crushed plant leaves.

"It is a tradition of the tribe I lived with that, on the wedding day of a member of their family, the Chief and his bride undertake a special ceremony that will make their future child very special. The ceremony summons spirits that live in these leaves. The ceremony asks them to give the child to be conceived special powers. They will do that, and the child will be born with those gifts and will have the special qualities to be Chief one day."

"Isn't the tribal Chief always a male?" Candice asked, feeling discrimination. The men always get the good spots, she thought.

"As far as I know," Faint Chance said. "But I believe that if the child to be is a female the child would still be special."

"This is fantastic!" Spencer said. "Tell us more." This was exactly the sort of fantastic local experience that he had hoped to find by taking the sabbatical and year off from work.

"I want to give you this very special gift. You must eat it when I say special prayers, and then make your child. Your child will be very special."

Oh God, Candice thought. This local, marginally-educated girl now puts out some local plant and wants us to take it in some ceremony, no doubt. God knows what sort of hygiene or lack of it is involved in eating some crazy weed. How can we back out of this "most generous offer" without offending her? There must be a way.

"But we have already been married for some time now," Candice said, making reference to the fact that the ceremony was said to be for a wedding couple, which they were not. "Won't it only work at a wedding?" She was hoping that would be an easy way out, looking for some excuse to not have to go through with having to ingest some strange leaves from God knows where.

"This will work even if it is not your wedding night, as the prayers summon spirits for the offspring, and are not for the marriage. The Chief taught me."

Spencer's research involved testing uncommon substances and their effect in lowering unwanted cholesterol, and therefore did not dismiss the idea out of hand. "Where are these plant leaves from?" he asked, in a surge of scientific curiosity.

"They only come from a very special place, some distance from the village where I lived. They come from the spot where the Chief found me, and that is the only spot. It is so rare that it has no specific name in Lao or in the dialect of the village other than 'Special Plant', or *ton mai piiset* in Lao. The Chief referred to it as a plant for the *Maw Pii* who is the one that can talk to the spirits. He was the *Great Maw Pii*. So, plant of the special person who can talk to the spirits would be the closest name. It has very strong spiritual powers."

As the doctors looked on with skeptical scientific curiosity, she continued, "The Chief gave me this when I was leaving with the missionaries. He wanted me to have a child with the abilities of one of his own children, since he considered me as his own child. He said that since I was found by him at the place where the plant grows, that it was in my karma to have his gift."

Karma? Candice thought, skeptically. She realized that this girl was no scientist and that the whole thing sounded like some old wives' tale.

"And now, since you are to be my new family across the seas, and are to have a child, I want you to have it."

Trying not to be rude or disrespectful, the two doctors listened on intently. "What is in the bottle?" Spencer asked.

"That is northern Lao Lao, the Laotian whisky. This must be taken at the same time as the *ton mai piiset*, and the spirits can only be contacted if the right prayers are used."

"Was the Chief special?" Candice asked.

"Oh yes, the Chief was the wisest man in the village, not just respected for his bloodline. He was the *Great Maw Pii* to the villagers, the one who could talk to the spirits. He solved the problems of the people in the village. Sometimes even people from other villages would come to him to speak to the spirits and to solve problems."

Spencer said, "This *Great Maw Pii* sounds like the equivalent to the Hindi name given Mohandas Karamchand Gandhi, 'Mahatma'. Mahatma had very special abilities, and some Indians give the term the English translation of 'Great Living Soul', or 'Great Soul'. Go on please. This is really great!" Excitement was building with him as he thought of it, and he propped forwards in his seat, listening intently.

"What is involved in the ceremony?" Spencer asked. "When we go back, do we have to slaughter a goat on top of an Aztec pyramid during the full moon to make it work? Or, sacrifice a sixteen-year-old virgin? But there are no sixteen-year-old virgins left in America."

Candice smiled, but Faint Chance did not laugh at his jokes. Spencer realized that whether she understood his jokes or not, this girl was dead serious and giving up her most precious possession, so he would have to ignore the effects of the drinks he had and would have to try to be more serious. She had just offered the contents of her tiny hope chest to them. She was too poor to have a dowry or anything else to offer to a potential husband, and she was now offering the only thing she had of value. It was indeed a solemn occasion. He must be quiet and go along with it.

"If you take these plant leaves in the ceremonial way, the spirits will bring you a special child," Faint Chance went on. "I was taught the prayers, and can perform them for you when you take the plant. The child will have wisdom, and be respected."

"Those plant leaves were given to you when you were seven and left the village. Can they still be good? How do you know that it is not poison?" Candice asked.

Faint Chance frowned a little and answered, "The Chief said that the leaves are where the special spirits can be contacted, and he was very wise. The spirits are contacted by the plant, regardless of its age," Faint Chance said with the utmost sincerity, a little upset at Candice's skepticism. "The spirits do not die."

Candice noticed from her expression that Faint Chance could sense she was being doubted, and it was rude to treat this royal gift so nonchalantly. This was the most valuable thing this poor girl owned, and she was offering it to her and her husband. She decided to break the ice that was forming, and hopefully back out of having to accept this bizarre gift by saying, "Faint Chance, we are deeply touched by this great gift and privilege you are bestowing on us, but we cannot possibly accept anything so valuable from you. This is for your wedding, and not for you to give. This is your most valuable possession, and you must keep it for yourself – you do not owe us anything. We are happy to sponsor you without remuneration, and we will be quite content with only your company. No gifts are necessary."

Faint Chance answered, "I can get more. You must accept this. Not to do so would be very rude in Lao." She was not being entirely truthful with them, as she had no way for certain to get more of the plant, but she made it clear that she wanted them to accept her gift.

Both Spencer and Candice wondered if it really would be rude to decline the special gift. The idea of consuming some strange plant, especially after having read all the medical warnings about

Laos before they came made the doctors very apprehensive. But she was playing her trump card, accusing them of rudeness if they did not accept.

"And just how does this ceremony work?" Spencer asked, hoping to reduce his apprehension by learning more about it.

"I have to do it. If you wish to accept the gift, and are prepared to create a child, I will summon the spirits with the special prayers the Chief taught me. They will be summoned, and, if they agree, it will happen."

The drinks they had consumed, the lateness of the evening, their intense desire to live and experience local customs and the wonder of it all, made Spencer and Candice look at each other affirmatively, albeit reluctantly. It was all too irresistible. Here they were on the other side of the world, where so few had been, and offered a chance to make a child with a Chief's powers. Who could refuse such an offer?

"How about doing it right now?" Spencer said.

"Why not?" Candice said.

"Well, the prayers take some time, are loud to invoke the spirits. They may not want to be brought here to such a public place. We must go to your room or someplace else to be alone."

"Let's go to the hotel room," Spencer said.

Faint Chance bagged up her present, the baci strings, the plant leaves and the bottle of northern-made Lao Lao, that she had displayed to the recipients of her most precious possession, and off they went.

Chapter Seventeen

In the hotel room, Faint Chance set up her things on the teak wood table in the sitting area, and made ready the baci strings, the northern Lao Lao whisky with glasses and the bag of plant leaves now opened and lying in a small pile. Spencer and Candice did their best to get serious, knowing how much this meant to Faint Chance.

"You sit here, and Candice, you here, please," she said to them pointing where they should sit on either side of her. Faint Chance held the inside of Spencer's wrist, and began a chant. Spencer had not the foggiest idea what she was saying. She rubbed the first baci string on one of his wrists, pushing downwards towards his hand, which Spencer figured must be to cleanse the soul or body of bad spirits. Then she put one of the prayer strings on his wrist, and the prayer chant changed, with loud moments, as though the loudness might drive something into his spirit, or perhaps drive something out. In the latter case it would be like an exorcism, he thought. After completing the first wrist, she then did the same to the other. Faint Chance then held both of his wrists in her hands, and said the chant again.

Faint Chance then turned to Candice, and went through the same ritual with her.

"Now take the leaves. You must also swallow them with some of this northern Lao Lao whisky."

Spencer gulped to build his fortitude, and took a pinch of the plant leaves, swallowing it with the clear Lao Lao whisky. As he took it, Faint Chance began a chant, and as it went down she made a loud sound ending in what seemed like an "uuuurrrrr" sound. It wasn't all that bad, he thought, and he finished his portion of the leaves in three rounds.

"It really has no taste, Candice," he told her to reduce her fear.

It was Candice's turn. She took a pinch of the plant leaves, and downed it with a swig of the Lao Lao. She then followed this with three shots of the Lao Lao. Faint Chance chanted the prayer for her in the same way.

Then she put their hands together in front of her, and put her hands on top of theirs. She began a prayer chanting in her mysterious language of the village.

She then took the wrists of both Spencer and Candice, each in one of her hands, and held them tightly. She chanted the prayer again, and this time she looked up and closed her eyes. She then held her hands together in the prayer position, and repeated the chant.

Spencer felt something first, as he was the first to eat the plant leaves. Something strong was in those leaves! He became a little scared that he might have consumed something like LSD. But the visions ahead were so wonderful that he set his fears aside and watched the spectacle. Bright lights appeared and consumed his vision. Pastel colors appeared and images of winged angels moved about. He found himself weightless and soaring as though flying in clouds, ascending towards the brightest of the lights ahead, as though he were an angel coming home. What is this? he thought. Ahead of the angels was a focal point – was it just distance and lines of great length converging, or was it a narrow point ahead? As he ascended, he could see something ahead – it was a very bright light. Was it the focal point? There was something there. What was it? As he looked, there appeared to be a comforting image of a benevolent figure, but the image was none too clear.

A kaleidoscope of colors covered Candice's field of vision. Her first reaction was also one of fear, as she realized that the plant leaves had some strong hallucinatory powers. How long would this last? But her fears subsided as the most interesting streams of colors and beautiful arrangements of flowers appeared and entertained her as she watched in amazement. Music was present, a strange sort of tune that she did not recognize. The wonderful smell of the fragrance of flowers then satiated her senses, but the scent did not give rise to the memory of any particular flower that she had previously experienced. Taking a deep breadth, she found the intensity of the senses to be increased. She found herself traveling through an endless array of flowers and colorful scenes, water and oceans, sunlit beaches, and faraway places.

Slowly, for both of them, the experience subsided, and the room and the surroundings returned little by little. They realized that they were still holding hands with Faint Chance who was right there, between them, not going anywhere. How long had they been away?

"Wow!" Candice said first. "That is strong stuff!" Looking at Spencer, she asked, "Did you feel it too?"

"I sure did!" he answered. "I think I just had an epiphany, a vision of the Almighty."

"Mine was more like a hallucination." She was not at all religious like Spencer, and was not inclined to attribute the unknown to religious causes.

"It has passed, whatever it was," Spencer said. "That was really something! I still feel a little light-headed."

"That is not just some local weed. It is strong stuff!" Candice added. "I wonder what is in it? Maybe it is like peyote?" She was always the scientist.

"Did you know that it gives hallucinations?" Candice asked of Faint Chance.

"I only knew that the spirits that are summoned are very strong," she answered. "I have not taken it myself but I could feel their presence in you."

"Well, something made me lose complete contact with my surroundings," Candice said.

"Me, too," Spencer added.

The ritual concluded – they released hands and a feeling of relaxation and gratification came over both Spencer and Candice. They were both quiet. Faint Chance appeared as though she were reviving herself from a trance.

Faint Chance spoke. "The spirits have been summoned, and now they will give special powers to your child if you consummate your marriage now as you did on your wedding night."

The strange feeling gone, Spencer decided to break the serious mood that had overcome everyone, and said, "Candice, if we are going to do it the way we did on our honeymoon night, we will have to take a cruise on a ship, and I will have to pass out."

Candice said, "Hah! Some Romeo you were that night!" Then she turned to Faint Chance and asked, "What if we do not conceive the child tonight?"

Faint Chance answered, "Should you not, once the ancestors are summoned, they will stay with you for a time. You should continue to try and conceive the child for some time. And, you must not take off the strings for at least three days, and then do not cut them, only untie them."

Spencer said, "Let's polish off this Lao Lao."

Candice said, "What an adventure to tell about back home!"

Faint Chance frowned at the remark, and said, "It might be best if you do not tell others, but that is up to you, as it is your gift," she said. "I will leave you now to conceive the child."

Spencer said, "Yes, well, that is something I guess we should do alone! So, I guess this is goodbye for now. But you have our phone number and address, and you can call collect any time. If there is a problem with the immigration, call. I am hoping that everything will work out quickly and we will see you in a matter of months. I cannot thank you enough for showing us about, and for everything you have done for us." Spencer then took her and gave her a hug. Teary wetness formed in the eyes of the sensitive Faint Chance, and she kissed Spencer on the cheek.

Candice then said, "Don't worry about a thing. I will have your own room set up for you when you come and everything will be ready. We look forward to having you over." Candice gave her a kiss on the cheek and Faint Chance kissed her back.

"I am so happy!" Faint Chance said. "I look forward to coming to my new family in America. There should be a new child there soon, and the child will be special. I know."

"Ah, yes, to be sure," Candice said, of course not believing anything other than the fact that she had just taken something strong like peyote.

Faint Chance had performed the ritual as her adoptive father had taught her, and she was satisfied that it had been done correctly. She could now leave them to conclude the next step in making the child. One last smile at the door, and she was gone.

Spencer and Candice, in the spirit of trying to experience the local traditions, which was what the trip was all about, had sex later that night without their usual contraception. The only things they wore were the baci prayer strings.

Chapter Eighteen

Cameron, having received only a few postcards from Spencer and Candice thus far, and having not heard from them in over two months, was quite surprised to turn on his computer to see an email from Spencer and Candice.

Dear Uncle Cameron,

We are finally at a hotel that has computers in the rooms! We are in Kuala Lumpur, Malaysia. We were given an access code when we checked in, and can send emails from our very modern hotel room.

Guess what? You are going to be an uncle! Candice is nearly four months along now, and getting bigger. It's a good thing this didn't happen at the beginning of the trip! We are sampling the marvelous Malay cuisine. This country has some really delicious foods. Just check these names out from a cookbook we just got: beef rendang, chicken korma, mee goreng, laksa, pietee, satay, nasi lemak, murtabak, roti canai, meerubus, meesiam, roti jala, ayam percik, ketupat bawang, serunding daging, otak-otak, rojak suun and soto ayam. Does that sound good or what?

Malaysia is our last stop, so we got a ton of spices and seasonings. Candice will be cooking up some spectacular meals at home and you will be invited to try our new recipes.

We will be coming home in three weeks, and are looking forward to it. The trip could not have been much better. We have so much to tell, and Candice has dozens of rolls of pictures to develop. We will notify you of the flight information. We look forward to seeing you, and to coming home.

Spencer and Candice

Cameron read the message again in disbelief! Uncle Cameron? How rude! A child! How morbid! Revolting! Cameron thought of the commitments of having a child, of giving up his pastimes. He thought of his Harley Davidson in the garage, his carefree lifestyle, and things that would have to go if he ever had a child.

Ugh! Oh well, he thought, at least Spencer and Candice were well and were coming back.

Chapter Nineteen

Spencer and Candice looked a little different to Cameron as they walked out of immigration towards him. Spencer was healthy, suntanned and a bit slimmer. Candice looked different too, but she had gained in the stomach with the child on the way.

Perhaps the different look had to do with the experiences that they had gained, and it reflected in their faces as some change in their personalities. After the big hugs, and getting their bags into Cameron's car, they began talking non-stop about some of their experiences.

Cameron interrupted once to ask, "Did you ever get sick from the local water or foods?"

Candice said, "We were both sick twice, at different times, but fortunately not for too long. We both got sick in India for several days, but at different times, even though we only drank bottled water. Oh yes, and Spencer got sick for a day in Thailand from bad shrimp. That lasted a day and a half. But nothing too serious. We recovered."

Cameron said, "Don, Brenda and I watched the house for you. There were no problems."

They pulled up the drive, and Spencer said, "Home sweet home! It is good to be back." They brought in their bags, and began putting things away. At the last stop, in Malaysia, they had bought some things as they were coming straight home from there and did not have to lug extra things all over Asia with them. Candice alone had two full bags of spices.

Candice said, "How about Saturday night for dinner here? Today is Wednesday, and that will give me enough time to get organized. I want to go to the lab tomorrow, if I am not a zombie from the jet lag." She added, "I will put some of these spices I bought to the test."

She opened up one of the bags of spices she had recently bought in Malaysia, showing Cameron the inside of a soft bag. It was full of packets of spices in foil, plastic bags and in bottles.

"That sounds wonderful," Cameron said.

On Saturday night, Candice put on a spectacular dinner. She had in fact learned many new recipes, and brought delicious spices to use not available in America. Don and Brenda were invited since they had helped take care of the house, along with Cameron. Also invited was a colleague of theirs at the medical research lab, Lawrence, who brought his wife Linda. An East Indian nurse friend, named Kala, was also invited. Candice was rather large in the stomach, her pregnancy showing.

Candice said, as she set a huge stack of photo finishing envelopes on the coffee table, "I have not had time to organize these, as I only had time to take them to a one-hour photo shop. Look at them, but please one batch at a time so they do not get mixed up from their negatives. Okay?"

"Sure," Brenda said, and picked up an envelope and began looking at some of the photos. "You really are an excellent photographer, Candice. You could do this professionally!"

"The most interesting shots were from India and from Lao," Candice said.

Don asked, "Which is more interesting, India or Lao?"

Spencer and Candice paused and looked at each other, and finally Spencer answered, "Probably Lao. That place is really more like an undiscovered frontier than any other place we traveled to."

They began focusing on Lao as they told of their adventures. Finally, the topic could come up, and Candice said, "Then, you'll never guess what we did! We completely lost our heads in Lao! We met this absolutely beautiful girl, and were so taken with her that we offered to sponsor her to come to the United States. She should be here in a few months, depending on delays with immigration. I have pictures of her."

"What is her name?" Brenda asked.

"That is a tough one to pronounce. So we call her Faint Chance," Spencer answered.

The name Faint Chance cracked everybody up into a good laugh. Spencer and Candice realized that the name sort of had a sexual overtone attached to it, and it sort of sounded like one's slim chances of having sex with her.

"Is that really what you call her?" Brenda asked.

"It sure is. It refers to her own remark when we met her as to her assessment of what her chances were of migrating to America," Candice added.

Cameron said, "Let me guess. She has a brother named 'Slim' and two sisters, 'Fat' and 'No'."

Hearty laughter followed Cameron's joke.

"You're really so funny, Cameron," Kala told him. Being single herself, and admiring Cameron, she complimented him whenever possible.

Don said, "Tell us more about her," wondering what qualities she possessed that made her so interesting to them as to invite her over to live with them.

Spencer spoke. "She is beautiful, a mix of Laotian and German. She was orphaned at age four, and actually lived with a tribal chief of animists – people who believe that plants and objects have souls and spirits! She was then taken to the city by missionaries at age seven and later adopted by a Tamil Indian couple. We met her in a jewelry store owned by the Tamil Indian."

Brenda asked, "What possessed you to sponsor her to come to America?"

Candice said, "We had seen so much poverty in India, and we wanted to do something to help the underprivileged people we saw. But there was so little we could do. After India, we were in Lao, and met this beautiful girl, who had so little, and who took time off work just to show us around. So, we decided to invite her here."

"Do you think she will like it here?" Brenda asked.

Candice answered, "There is not much opportunity or wealth in Lao, so how could she not? In Lao, the future for a woman is to marry, and spend her entire life caring for her family and home with very primitive means to do so, such that it leaves very little time for anything else. But now, I will leave you for a while, and do the final preparations for dinner. It should be ready in fifteen minutes."

Conversation at the dining table went back and forth from

miscellaneous experiences that Spencer and Candice had on the trip, to various news items that came to mind about people at the research laboratories where they worked, and to some of their mutual friends.

Changing the subject, Brenda asked, "How is it that you decided to have a baby in the midst of all that travel?"

"Well," Candice answered, "we have, of course, been thinking about it for a long time. And, we had a good deal of time to talk to one another on the trip and we had decided that when we got back we would go ahead and have a child. We would not have had a child in Asia, medicine being what it is there. And also, we were traveling, not childrearing. But then we were out for dinner in Lao with Faint Chance, and the most extraordinary thing happened. She gave us the most valuable thing she owned, a present from her tiny hope chest that consisted of only one thing. It was a special plant leaf from a very remote area in the north of Lao that she believes has spirits residing in the plant that can give special abilities to the child being conceived."

"Don't tell me you actually did this?" Brenda asked, raising an eyebrow in suspicious quandary that her friends may have taken some hallucinatory drug in Asia and had their brains fried in the process.

"We sure did!" Candice said. "The whole nine yards! We had the ceremonial ritual, took the plant leaves, and had prayer strings on our wrists for three days afterwards. It was really cool. We were really into it!"

Brenda said, "Don't tell me you ate weird plant leaves when conceiving your child? Ugh! You are probably going to give birth to Medusa!"

"Or an alien!" Don added. "Like in one of those movies."

"*Rosemary's Baby*," Lawrence added, smiling.

Candice continued, "When this girl gave us this most valuable thing that she owned, with us not wanting to hurt her feelings, combined with the fact that we got caught up in this most amazing story of hers about the special plant that was meant for a tribal chief, we took the potion as though we were having a tribal chief's wedding."

"Tell 'em the truth, luv – we were drunk!" Spencer said.

That broke everyone up into laughter. Spencer was known to them for his imbibing.

"Do you suppose there is anything to it in reality?" Don asked.

"I don't," Candice said. "We ran across many rituals. We were in Bombay and learned of an Indian sect that believe that fire is sacred, but when they die, they do not cremate the body, but instead put it on the roof of a special building and vultures come and pick the bones clean, and the bones are later dissolved in an acid. We witnessed the religious significance of the Ganges River to the Indians, and how they, if they can afford it, bring the bodies of their deceased ones there, burn the remains with sandalwood and put the bones in the river. That was very eerie. We saw many such things."

"I feel that there may be something to it," Spencer said. "I had a very strange experience when we did the ceremony, which I believe was an epiphany."

"A vision of Christ?" Lawrence asked.

"I believe it was. It was a very strong experience, whatever it was. Candice also had an experience as well, didn't you, Candice?"

"I did have a strange experience, but I don't attribute anything to religion or the supernatural. I am, after all, a scientist! I think the plant leaves had some chemical that gave a rush, or a hallucination. I definitely had something like that. It was pretty strong."

Kala said, "That must have been quite an experience! Do you think there is anything to it?"

"Probably just superstition," Lawrence said, acting the scientist. "Were most of the superstitions you ran into connected to religion?"

Spencer answered, "Religion and superstition are close bedfellows. When you consider the number of monuments, and major sights of interest, most are connected to religion in one sense or another. We saw so many Buddhas. There is a shrine where Buddha gave his first sermon on the Ganges River in Varanasi, India. That is a very eerie place, with many people burning the remains of their loved ones on the shores of the river, praying. In parts of India, in Thailand and in Lao, a shrine housing a relic is called a 'Stupa'. That usually has a big, gold-painted Buddha inside."

"Stupa? I'll show you Stupa!" Cameron said, as he got up and poured himself another whisky. Everyone broke out laughing.

Chapter Twenty

The baby was born a very healthy boy, and was named Devan. There were no complications. He had no crying spells – an unusual quality according to the doctors and nurses who commented.

A month later, Candice called Cameron. "Cameron, it has been a whole month since Devan was born, and you have yet to so much as come by. We want you to come over this Saturday evening, and I will make dinner. You cannot stay away forever! You have to come and see him some time. He is very well behaved, and you will not dislike him."

"I know, I know," he admitted. He had let it be known to her many times that he had no interest in children, whether family or not. "It's just that I don't go in for cuddling infants. But I guess I had better get it over with. About seven thirty okay?"

"That will be fine," Candice told him.

He hung up the phone in disgust, thinking of a "family affair" with an infant. They will no doubt want me to hold the little rodent, he thought.

Chapter Twenty-One

Come Saturday, Cameron arrived to make what was sure to be a revolting, but obligatory, appearance. He would lie and tell them he had to do some work at home before bed so he could leave early, imagining that the entire conversation would be how cute the little cockroach was, and the disgusting topics of childrearing. He brought some baby clothes as an obligatory gift that he let the busybody secretary at the office pick out, all to her great delight. As he drove up to the house, he thought to himself that he was entirely correct, and genuine, in his dislike of anyone younger than a grown person. To have a child, one should have to go to court and show cause. Otherwise, the parents and the child should all be put to death for having the temerity to have one on their own.

"Hi, Cameron!" Candice said, opening the door. "Come on in."

"You are trim and in good shape already!" Cameron said, exaggerating to the point of complimenting his sister-in-law. She had lost much of the fatty look, and was returning in her shape, but there was more to go. Kids! The ruination of everything! So happy he was not to be burdened with a parasite, sucking off him until he died, like an Amazon leech.

Regaining his composure, and returning to the real world, he said to his sister-in-law, "Here. A small present." He handed her a box with baby clothes. The damn clothes cost as much as his. How the Hell do baby clothes cost so much? It must be that the buyers aren't in the mood to shop, and the merchants take advantage of that.

Candice took his angry thoughts off the idea and opened the box. "Oh, thank you so much, darling Cameron!" And she kissed her brother-in-law on the cheek. He did not like the kiss as he suspected germs were being transmitted to him from Candice since she had no doubt recently kissed the little rodent.

"Cameron!" Spencer said, coming out of his study. "How is the famous architect?"

"Just working long hours, that's about it," Cameron said.

"So, where is the new one?" Cameron asked, as though referring to a specimen of AIDS virus.

Spencer and Candice led him to the crib. He thought to himself that he was supposed to look pleasantly surprised and pass out compliments on the new little rodent. He went up to "its" crib. He refused to give anything so revolting as a child the dignity of a "his" or a "her". "It" would do just fine, for any little crying, diaper-wetting and fouling, obnoxious vegetable like an infant.

Cameron looked in the crib, and bent over a little bit to look directly into the face of Devan.

To his surprise, the infant was not the usual little mass of disgusting flesh, but seemed to have a sort of personality already.

Cameron then further noticed something unusual about the child's face. His eyes followed him from side to side as he moved about, and did not leave his face, concentrating on him as he moved. The little fellow had very good coordination of his hands, and could reach out and grab something in front of him, such as Cameron's finger. As he watched him, he actually turned himself over onto his side in bed, by himself!

Cameron asked, "Have you seen him turn about by himself?"

Candice replied, "I have seen him move about in the crib, but I don't think that is unusual."

Cameron said, "I think it is. I wasn't aware that any infant could do that."

Spencer said, "He does seem to be aware of things. I think he will be extraordinarily smart."

Cameron said, "There is something uncanny about this boy!" Spencer and Candice did not seem to think so, this being their first, apparently thinking it was to be expected that he was very able. *Rosemary's Baby*, Cameron thought to himself, enjoying the idea and his own humor. Still leaning over the crib, Devan rolled back over onto his back, and looked at him. Cameron said, "Hi! I am Cameron, your uncle."

Devan looked him right in the eyes, and said, "Hi, Uncle."

Cameron was completely startled. He stepped away from the

crib and turned to look at Spencer and Candice.

"He said, 'Hi, Uncle', to me! He is only a month old!" Cameron practically shouted.

Spencer and Candice came over and looked at Devan. All three were gathered around him now.

"What?" Candice asked, coming over hurriedly to the crib to look in.

"That is impossible!" Spencer exclaimed. "No one-month-old infant can utilize its vocal cords to make words, as his central nervous system is not sufficiently developed to do that," he added, recalling what he had learned in medical school.

They all gathered around him, and gazed. Devan said it again. "Hi."

They stared at him for a while. Devan looked at them, as though to wonder why they were staring at him. It was obvious that Devan was somewhat aware of what was going on around him.

Candice said, "I cannot believe this!" She and Spencer looked at each other dumbfounded.

"Do you know your name?" Cameron asked him.

"Devan."

They were spellbound, and eventually all moved over to the dinner table, and sat down, speechless.

Spencer said, "What could have possibly happened to Devan to make him so accelerated in his development? Could something on our trip have had something to do with it? I mean, what are the chances of a one-month-old baby talking?"

Spencer and Candice looked at each other for a few moments, then to Devan, then back to each other, and they said simultaneously, "Faint Chance!"

Chapter Twenty-Two

"I am, after all, a genetic research doctor, and who better to analyze any difference in the DNA of Devan that the plant may have caused than me?" Candice asked herself aloud as she utilized the lab equipment to run tests on cells she had taken from the inside of Devan's cheek. She had been conducting tests, using a technique called hybridization of DNA, on samples taken from Devan ever since the discovery that he was not normal.

Candice and Spencer had decided that they dare not let out news about this phenomenon as it would become a media event if the story had credibility. And to the extent that it did not, they would be the subject of much skepticism. Candice confided only in her lab assistant, Tadashi Uto, a Japanese man of twenty-one years of age. He was an employee of the lab, not as a doctor, but as a lab technician assigned to her as her research assistant who had been there two years. As far as letting him in on what was going on, she took a chance and filled him in on the studies, because it would have been impractical to impossible to do any testing at the lab where he assisted her full-time while trying to keep it a secret. And, she needed someone to cover for her when she was working on this project instead of her usual work.

Candice spoke to Tadashi, "Devan definitely has different DNA than an ordinary person. One difference has been the acceleration of the development of his central nervous system. This was brought about by one or more different, substitute amino acids that caused a difference in his DNA chain. Something brought about one or more substituted amino acids."

Tadashi asked, "What is known to cause a change in DNA?"

"The three things we know of are ultraviolet light, radiation and poison."

"Is this one of those?"

"There was no radiation or ultraviolet light involved with Devan. The plant leaf from Lao would be somewhat like a poison, as contrasted to ultraviolet light or radiation. Pretty neat poison! But, what is a poison? Too much of something good can be poison. Then again, maybe a fourth way will be identified, and maybe this is that new category. We really need to get a specimen of the plant and study it, as now all we have is the effect, that is, Devan. Without the plant, we will never be able to do anything other than speculate on what might be in it that can cause such changes." She continued, "These studies take time, and I have only begun. To make matters worse, whenever I run into someone that I have not seen since before I left on the trip, I have to give some condensed version of the trip to them. With all that, and now Devan, I am pressed for time to do the research."

"Do you think that you could synthesize the chemical in the plant if you could identify it?" Tadashi asked.

"Synthesizing it would most likely be easy, if I had a sample. But there is none. We look at what the effect is, and then postulate what might cause that. Imagine if we had a specimen and could synthesize it? It could be made into a pill, like a drug, and everyone would want it. Think of the significance!"

Chapter Twenty-Three

"Hi, Uncle Cameron," Devan said to him as he came in the door.

"Hi, Devan. How are you?" Cameron asked the two-month-old boy.

"Fine, thank you." Devan went back to a building block puzzle he was working on.

Candice said, "Come on and sit, the food is ready." She laid out home-made Indian bread called roti pratha as Cameron took a seat at the table.

"What do you call that outfit?" Cameron asked.

"It is called a 'sinn'. It is the tubular skirt of the Laotians. They wear western tops, but I chose to wear a tank top. Do you like it?"

"Fantastic!" Cameron complimented her, as he sat and went to the basket of bread, sampling a slice.

"This is delicious bread," Cameron said, tasting it. "You really learned a lot of interesting things in your Asia travels." Candice sat down after serving Cameron and Spencer.

"Thank you," Candice blushed.

"What have you learned about Devan?" Cameron asked.

Candice sat and adjusted her chair, and assumed a professorial role. "It is my assumption at this time that Devan's DNA chain was altered by the plant. This is confirmed by some preliminary studies. One, and possibly more, amino acid substitutions may have resulted in a new or stronger enzyme or enzymes that accelerate development of the central nervous system. This includes the brain and the spinal cord. The result is that Devan is developing his central nervous system at a very rapid rate. It must have begun in the womb. My womb. I imagine that he might have heard and remembered noises from before he was born! This rapid development explains how he can walk and talk at two months old."

As she spoke, Devan was walking about the living room, and

was quite able to identify objects by name, know his own name, and the names of others.

She continued. "Devan has a level of speaking already equal to that of someone two or three years of age. He does not make many noises that are not proper words in the way infants do. When he makes a sound, it is generally a proper word, or a small sentence. 'I'm hungry', for example. It is uncanny. To go along with his ability to speak, his muscular coordination is very good, and, as you can see," directing her attention to Devan walking about, "he walks fairly well at two months. His accelerated ability to control his muscles is nothing short of astonishing.

"There was something in those dried up leaves from that special plant that Faint Chance gave us that must have done this to him," Candice continued. "I am quite certain that the fertilization of one of my eggs occurred when Spencer and I took the special plant leaves in Lao. The substance taken by both Spencer and me, at the time of conception, created one or more substitute amino acids, which caused a difference in the DNA chain. The result is that the design for the central nervous system is different such that it develops much more rapidly than in a normal person. Ability to focus the eyes, process sounds, motor skill development, ability to think and reason, bladder control, self-control, ability to learn and intelligence itself are accelerated and possibly enhanced. This explains Devan's ability to be able to think, walk and talk at such a young age.

"But the significance may not just be that the child learns more quickly in life due to a more rapidly developing central nervous system. I have an idea that it may be much more significant than you might imagine! It is my notion that this may make for a whole new dimension of human intelligence. If you think of it, young ones spend years learning to use their muscles and learn coordination, and that of course includes the brain as the main component of the central nervous system. That includes speech. Humans spend, or waste, if you think about it, many years trying clumsily to learn. They are twenty or twenty-five years old, or even older, before they get out of school, and then have only a short number of years, maybe twenty, of useful energy and life before things like cancer, heart attacks, diabetes, hardening of arteries, high blood pressure, strokes, Parkinson's disease, senile dementia, thinning of the bones, cataracts, loss of close-up visual accommodation, fading hearing, kidney failure, arthritis and various other maladies set in and get rid of us like beings that have served their useful purpose and should go. These show up significantly in the forties, and of course very much so soon after the forties. Brain cells actually begin to die."

Cameron said, "That is certainly true."

Candice continued, "The present design of humans is to not allow them to be able to gain much intelligence when growing, and that ability is further impeded by a lack of emotional control over the body by the central nervous system.

"Now," Candice went on, "this plant could be something really significant in more ways than just the fact than it can enhance the ability to learn earlier in his life. It may not be just that he learns at an earlier age, but that he can utilize his formative years to become many times more capable than an ordinary person! As an example, if this accelerated nervous system continues, he could perhaps be in college at age seven or eight, and then go on to some level of achievement far greater than any normal human. He will still be able to continue to learn more and more in his best formative years, and it will be as though he started out higher learning where we left off."

"But how could a youngster have the ability to use, say, lab or other delicate equipment at the bungling age of seven, for example?" Cameron asked.

"When the central nervous system develops, so does the coordination to use the brain. In other words, he should have the muscular coordination of a person of his corresponding development of brain, if my notion is correct," Candice answered. "You have seen how he could follow you with his eyes from the crib, and now he is walking at age two months. He also uses small sentences, and has an extraordinary vocabulary, considering," Candice responded. "So, if I am right, he will not be a 'bungling seven year old' as you refer to. He might be in college!"

She added, "The development of the central nervous system in this fashion will also result in earlier and better control of one's emotions. The onset of puberty, the problems of adolescence, should be much more under control, and cause less problems. This thing may be like coming out of the Stone Age in terms of human development. You have noticed how Devan has never seemed to have fits, crying spells or emotional outbursts like others of his age."

"What does it mean," Cameron asked, "in terms of overall development?"

"We cannot be sure," Candice answered. "These things will not be able to be tested for some time. There is no one to compare him to, unless we compare him to much older people. But his present state of development is easily compared to others. It seems obvious to me that he will far surpass normal intelligence, and who knows, maybe by double or more!"

"Sort of like an Einstein of science or a genius in business, and at an incredibly early age!" Cameron said. "A young person could start out at some early age where everyone else leaves off and achieve new heights! The person would have the intelligence of a fully matured adult at an age maybe one quarter or one third of his peers. From there he could be able to continue to use his youth and best learning years when he would have the ability to acquire information and skills without his body deteriorating, and create achievements yet unknown! A new race of super humans. And, he would be in better control of his emotions, which are the cause of such a waste of human energies, especially in adolescents. Without even trying to be, anyone this way could sort of begin applying themselves where everyone else leaves off, and still be a teenager, or even younger! It is amazing!"

"Just that, if I am right," Candice said. "Anyone born in the future without this influence would be considered from the Stone Age. This is the next step in human evolution. And Cameron, you surprise me! You sound like you actually like Devan! Is this a change in my brother-in-law?"

"I am still quite content to let you be the one with the baby. Just because he is interesting from a scientific point of view does not mean that I am going to go off and have a child," Cameron said. He added, "Are you absolutely sure that the difference in Devan came from your ingesting the plant leaves that Faint Chance gave you?"

"From a scientific point of view, it is the only thing that can explain it. Either that, or Devan just happens to be the most extraordinary child ever."

"He lives!" Cameron joked, making reference to the reincarnation of Hitler as in the *Boys from Brazil* story.

"Hah! That's funny," Spencer said, appreciating his brother's joke.

Candice said, "I cannot confirm scientifically that the plant leaves are in fact the cause since I don't have any to test."

Cameron said, "So, the plant business might be just a bunch of 'mumbo jumbo'?"

Candice said, "I am firmly of the opinion that it was in fact the plant leaves. I remember at the time that I had something like hallucinations, so it was something powerful."

"What is the opinion of the famous cholesterol doctor?" Cameron asked, looking at his brother.

Spencer said, "I, too, had a very interesting experience at the time, but I think it was a vision."

"You have been getting more religious lately, haven't you?" Cameron asked. "Did the trip have anything to do with it?"

"It has clarified my views," Spencer answered. "I simply cannot believe that there is not an order and purpose to the world, and to life."

"More than mathematical order?" Cameron asked.

"Yes. More. As an example, take an apple. It is a bright red fruit, designed to attract by its color. It is wet, sweet, delicious and healthy. It does nothing for the tree on which it grows. It just hangs there until some human, or some other animal, goes and picks it. If no one does, it eventually falls off, where it might be eaten by a hog or possibly some other animal – or it might just rot. But the point that I make is that the apple takes energy and substances from the tree which don't help the tree. So, the apple is clearly 'designed', if you will, for others – in this case humans or animals. Why does the apple tree exist? Is its existence owing to a random chance happening, or is it there because of a design? A purpose. This is my view on God. It is a form of purpose for things."

Cameron spoke. "As you know, my good brother, I cannot

subscribe to the notion of some fellow sitting 'up there' in a chair guiding us through life 'in his image'. It is so much nonsense."

"Well, how do you explain our existence?" Spencer asked.

Cameron answered, "Well, I cannot attribute any purpose to the existence of man whatsoever. Man is just another creature like an insect or anything else. The only difference is that man uses more of his brain than other creatures on this planet. But I don't think that man has much brain to use, or doesn't use much of it. Most of his brain is put to use for pursuits other than the quest for knowledge. I think that Freud was right, in that man's energy is largely fueled by sexual energy. Man dresses himself, or herself, to be attractive. How do you explain a person buying an eighty thousand dollar car just to get around, when that consumes a significant portion of his paycheck? Driving an expensive car is, to me, just like a peacock or some other critter showing off its colors to attract a mate. It is an extended form of a mating ritual, or a pre-mating ritual."

Candice broke in. "I think that Devan represents a step in human evolution. He definitely has an advanced central nervous system, and therefore has more control over his emotions. Sort of like less of the Freudian person you describe, Cameron. And I think it is from the plant."

"But the origin of Devan's difference, if it is the plant," Spencer said, "is still from God, in my opinion. The plant was a naturally occurring substance right here on the earth. It is not something from a computer or a lab."

Cameron said, "But just because it grew from the ground does not necessarily mean it was placed there by a supreme being."

"Well," Spencer said, "I really don't like such explanations as it being put there by a visiting alien or a random chance happening. Have you an explanation?"

"Just leaning on God to answer the unexplained is no answer at all, as far as I am concerned. From a fundamental point of view, the earth is largely divided into things that require some other thing to continue. Trees take in carbon dioxide, and give off oxygen. Men do the opposite. If life stems from simple cells from millions of years ago, it is my view that the division left a link open to later bring them together. In other words, part of the cell would one day become the apple, the other a human to eat it. So, if this special plant caused the change in Devan, it is like the apple and was waiting for man to find it to provide a more advanced step in his development, much in the same way as an apple provides nutrients for his body."

"But aren't you necessarily conceding a purpose to the existence of the plant in your analysis?" Spencer asked.

Candice interrupted, "Hey. I am the one that made dinner. No religion or politics at the table please." She smiled at the two intellectual brothers that she was so fond of.

The brothers smiled at her, and at one another, and realized that she was right. The dinner table really was no place for debate on such basic matters as theology that generally never get resolved, only discussed.

"Right," Cameron agreed. "Let's turn our attention to the meal. This is a very interesting dish you have made here. What do you call it?"

Chapter Twenty-Four

Two Japanese men sat together in the first-class cabin, talking quietly in Japanese at a level that could not be heard about them over the sound of the engines propelling the 747 across the Pacific towards Los Angeles.

One of them said to the other, "Morio, why do you want to buy this expensive marijuana from the US, when we can get it so cheap from Columbia?"

Morio Uto responded, "The fifteen parts per million THC, or tetrahydrocannabinol, of Humboldt County, California brings from several to many times the street price of Colombian. The users know the difference, and cannot be fooled. Actually, the Hawaiian harvests are nearly as good, but dealing with the Hawaiian growers is very frustrating. The Hawaiian growers have an attitude, even a saying, about selling marijuana that if you don't like what I sell you, I'll take it back and I'll smoke it myself! They are not business-like, with a tropical island lack of motivation."

"Then why deal with the Hawaiian growers?"

Morio continued, "It is better to have more than just one source. This gives us a better leverage and knowledge of the going price. I am buying from Hawaii in addition to California."

"Is the Hawaiian crop as good?"

"Most think it can be as good as Humboldt County. Of interest, the crops grown on the mainland of Hawaii are actually largely grown on United States federal government land. There is much government land in Hawaii, and the growers prefer to grow it on there so as to protect their homes and properties from confiscation in the event of a bust, and it makes it more difficult to prosecute if the harvest seized is not on one's own property. There are two to three yearly harvests on mainland Hawaii, the summer crop yielding a much taller and larger plant. The larger plants are as high as six to seven meters in the best season, with a bud as large as one-half to two-thirds meter in diameter. The big ones yield as much as a kilo each of premium marijuana. The winter plants are much smaller, usually four to five feet high, and produce a corresponding lesser amount of product."

"What about in California?" Morio's accomplice asked.

"In Humboldt County, the growers are more scientific about growing, and the crops seem to be more consistent, and give a higher yield. However there are always those who use too much of their own crop and do things like play music to the growing plants."

Morio continued, "The street price of this high THC product in Japan is one thousand dollars per ounce! It is two-thirds the price of cocaine! We are going to set up a big purchase this time. Arrangements to get it into our markets have already been made."

"Is there much to learn about growing it?"

"Sure, but we don't have to deal with that, since we are buying a finished product. With experienced growers, constant care is taken to go in now and then and remove the male plants. Marijuana plants have a sex, and the male plants pollinate the female ones. The expert growers remove the male plants as soon as they are identified, as this makes the female plant continue to produce the sap while waiting for pollination, which does not occur when there are no male plants about to pollinate it. To make matters more difficult, marijuana plants actually can change their sex! So, the growers have to go in and look for the male ones often. The high content THC comes from the sap and gets higher and higher as the female plant continues to produce it without pollination. Humboldt County also has a fair amount of indoor growers, who have taken to that to avoid the federal and state police, and they use artificial lighting."

"How much are we buying?" the partner asked.

"We will be bargaining for six metric tons this trip."

"Wow! That is a bunch of money. I take it this is not your deal alone?"

"No. I am working with the Oyabun."

"What market are you intending to sell to?" his accomplice asked.

"Mostly for the American market, but we will also sell some in

Japan."

"Is it going to be good business selling in America?"

"Yes, very good. The Colombians are raking in a fortune selling it in America."

"What do the Hawaiians do with their product?"

"The Hawaiians mostly grow it for resale to the tourists that come to Hawaii. They send it by boat to Maui and Oahu, but have trouble getting it to the mainland because of the federal police looking for such shipments. We will not have such trouble. We will send it to Japan which they will not be looking for, and then bring it back in cartons of electronic products of which there are so many. I am intending on putting it, as well as the product from California, into sealed, airtight television tubes, inside televisions. The dogs cannot sniff it in the airtight tubes. The main loss will be the cost of the wasted television set, which is relatively minor compared to how much a large tube will hold."

Chapter Twenty-Five

Tadashi always felt inadequate around his brother Morio. Morio always had the most stylish clothes, expensive sunglasses, fancy watches, chauffeured cars, and always had a bundle of spending cash when he came to visit, which was usually once a year. Tadashi thought he was working in a number of business investments, with his primary business being that of an owner of a fancy nightclub in Tokyo. Tadashi did not know his brother was a gangster.

Morio was staying at a hotel nearby, and as usual, looked up his younger brother Tadashi when he came into town. Even the gangster has family ties.

Upon hearing from his brother, Tadashi and Morio arranged a meeting at a Japanese restaurant for lunch. Tadashi got there first and took a table. Morio came in with his stylish clothes, looking very successful. Tadashi envied his brother's success.

As they spoke at the lunch, Tadashi could not help himself. He had only a modest wage as a lab technician, and a nice medical plan as most do who work in medicine, and he wanted to impress his older brother Morio to show that he was also a person of substance. This was hard to do as a lab technician since his brother Morio, when he came over, had spending cash for everything including escort girls of any price. On one occasion, he had brought a good-looking escort girl to Tadashi's house. Morio preferred tall, blonde escort girls.

"You will never guess what I am working on at my job," Tadashi told his brother Morio. "I am working on a project that is potentially worth a fortune. My boss is working on identifying a special substance that, when taken during conception of a baby, will make the baby able to develop his motor skills and intelligence at a supernatural rate, and surpass normal people in intelligence and learning by a great deal. It comes from a special plant from Lao. My boss had taken the plant herself along with her husband, and her own son has these qualities. He could speak words at one month, and is now walking and talking at just a few months old and already learning things that only a child of five or seven years or more of age would learn."

"Why is that so valuable?" Morio asked.

"If the substance can be synthesized, it can then be concentrated, refined and then produced. Then it can be marketed in a pill for every couple that is going to make a baby. Just imagine! Every couple in the world will want to have it! Anyone who does not take it will give birth to only an ordinary child. Ordinary children will be retarded by comparison to anyone born by this substance. Everyone who learns of it will insist on taking it, unless they don't want to have super intelligent kids. Initially it could be sold to the super rich, and eventually marketed to the ordinary person. People would pay anything they could to have extraordinary children. After it is learned of, who would want a child without it? This could be the most valuable thing ever!"

"How could one go about making money off of it?" Morio asked. He was used to dealing in illegal products, not legal ones, and was slow on the take when it came to legal enterprise.

"Once formulated, my boss can patent the process and the formula, and it will only be obtainable from whatever source she chooses to manufacture it. The major countries recognize reciprocal agreements with America regarding patent enforcement, and will honor the patent. So she, as the patent holder, could have an unimaginable monopoly! It would be sort of like selling an expensive drug, much in the way that Prozac or some other drug is sold. But think of how much people would pay for a dose," Tadashi went on. "They would pay any amount they can afford to pay. Initially the rich would pay one hundred thousand dollars for a dose! As soon as it became available, it could be sold for one thousand dollars a dose, or whatever price one wanted to sell it for. This thing I am working on is really incredible!" Tadashi said, boasting, and finally able to stand up tall in stature to his considerably more financially successful brother.

Morio asked, "Is that what your boss has plans for?"

"Not really. Whenever she discusses it with me, she is more

interested in helping the poor, like those she saw in India, by making it available to all, rather than selling it for the maximum profit. She does not want anyone to not have it because of money. She has said that she wants to control it, and she will be quite happy with just the royalties and the success that it will bring her in her research. But just think that even if it only cost a few dollars in poor countries how much could be made. Every time a couple has sex to have a baby, each would be taking a pill."

"Does she have it patented yet?" Morio asked, not being familiar with the patent process, a legal concept.

"No, there is nothing to patent yet. If she can isolate the chemical, or if she could get a plant, then she and I can go to work synthesizing it. Then, she can patent the formula and the process. This I am sure can be done, and I will be working on it with her," he boasted. "I am sure she will give me credit in the journals. I will probably get some of the royalties, too. I would like to get a Mercedes like you!"

Hmmmm, Morio thought to himself quietly. A person could make a bigger fortune with this stuff *legally* than *illegally* – a concept completely new to him. And, help the poor? Screw that, he thought. If I had it I would sell it for whatever I could get for it.

"Have you synthesized this at the lab yet?" He had already been told the answer, but as his interest peaked he wanted to go over it again with his proud younger brother. Whoever got this patent first would be the rich one, and that might be him!

"No, not yet. Our studies of the effects are one thing, but those studies do not leave the formula exposed, only its effects. My boss only had the plant in Lao. We will have to do a great deal more work to find out what the substance is, and that could take a long time – in fact, it might never happen. She has mentioned several times that she would like to go to Lao or send someone there to try to get a specimen of the plant. Maybe she will send me! Right now we are only working on separating substitute amino acids that have altered the DNA chain in her son. But synthesizing it should not be nearly as difficult as working on these DNA chains. You would be surprised to learn just how small, and how complicated, a DNA chain is."

Tadashi proudly went on, able to communicate to his brother for the first time on a different level than before. From that point on, Morio listened politely but did not comprehend nor did he focus his attention on the scientific aspect of how it affected the DNA, which Tadashi so proudly began lecturing on. Morio was wondering how he might become the producer of it.

By the end of the visit, he had impressed his brother, but felt a little worried that he should not have revealed the confidence of his boss who had been so nice to him. He said to Morio just before he left, "By the way, please do not mention this work that I am doing to anyone, as it is done in confidence at this time. My boss is holding off publishing it until she either isolates the substance or gets more of the plant, and we get it synthesized. She will then apply for the patent, and then publish the work. It will make us very famous in the research community. So, you must treat this in the strictest of confidence – I tell you this only because you are my brother and I want you to know what I am doing."

"Don't worry, you can trust your brother," Morio told him. "I am very impressed with what you are doing. I will stop by the lab to see you before I go. You can show me around."

Chapter Twenty-Six

Cameron was called by Candice to come to dinner again. Given the phenomenal growth in intelligence of the baby, and all the happenings, he figured he had better come, but he suspected that there was something wanted from him, which no doubt stemmed from the existence of the child. Only problems could come from having a child, he confirmed to himself as he drove over to the house of his brother and sister-in-law.

Inside, Candice treated him with respect, only confirming his suspicions. She took his jacket, which she did not normally do, and guided him to the kitchen area that was used as a bar and offered him his choice in a subservient manner as there was something to be asked of him later. "What would you like?" she asked.

In order to see if he could come up with a drink that she could not fix, he said, "I will have a Rob Roy, perfect, up, with a twist and a cherry." This was the sort of drink that only a very seasoned experienced bartender might know.

To his surprise, Candice opened the drawer next to the bar and took out a bartender's guide and looked up the drink. After a few moments, she turned to him and said, "Coming up."

Jesus, Cameron thought. They must want something from me. Maybe I am supposed to babysit while they go abroad again? They have another thing coming if that is what they have up their sleeve. I prefer to kill myself than to babysit. True, Devan might be different, but it is not my bailiwick to be a babysitter. I am not rated for children, nor will I ever be.

"Actually, that is too sweet before dinner," Cameron said, surprised she could actually make that drink. "Just make it a vodka martini."

"That is easier," Candice said, and poured vodka into a shaker over ice.

Cameron sat at the bar stool and sampled the drink. "Very good, thanks."

Spencer came out from his room, and so Candice said, "Dinner will be ready in a few minutes, so I will go back to it."

Spencer greeted him. "Hi, Cameron. How have you been?"

"Fine. Very busy at the office. How is young Einstein doing?"

Spencer answered, "He continues to develop his learning abilities at a very accelerated rate. He has no emotional outbursts, and amazes us daily with his knowledge. We are looking into hiring a special tutor for him already."

"He truly is amazing," Cameron acknowledged.

"Dinner is ready," Candice said. "This is a week night, and I know you have to get home early, Cameron, so I made the dinner-time early."

Spencer led Cameron over to the table, where they sat while Candice served. Something was definitely up, Cameron knew.

"Cameron, you are my guinea pig for a new recipe," Candice said as she set down in front of him a large soup bowl filled with a yellowish soup and noodles. The center was topped with crispy fried noodles sticking out of the broth, put on top of the other noodles. "I haven't tried this dish, nor the spices that went into it. This is made with the spices that I brought back. They simply are not available here. I hope you like it." Candice put down two more bowls and joined them.

Taking a spoonful of the broth, Cameron pretended not to know something was up and he sipped the soup slowly. After deciding that the taste was indeed nice, he savored it. It was in fact a delicacy. "This is spectacular. What is it?"

Candice said, "It is called 'Khao Soi', which is curried coconut noodles. It is northern Thai food. It is made best with fresh egg noodles, coriander seeds, turmeric, ginger, shallot, dried red chilies, white soy sauce, black soy sauce, chicken and coconut milk."

Cameron asked, "Where do you get *fresh* egg noodles? I thought noodles were noodles."

"You can buy fresh noodles at the oriental market. They are freshly made, and have to be kept chilled, as opposed to dried noodles. The dish is a soup in the north of Thailand, and has the noodles in the soup. But note some additional noodles that have been deep fried until crisp are on the top as garnish. How do you like it?"

"Fantastic! You continue to put on the best dinners ever. I have never had anything like this. But this must be a lot of work for just the three of us."

Candice spoke. "We have invited you this evening and no others because we need to talk to you about something."

Ah hah! Cameron said to himself. Here we go!

"There is no practical way to ever reproduce whatever it was that changed the DNA in Devan. I have Devan's cells to look at, but to undertake a program to try and see if chemicals could be isolated that cause similar results is impractical. In the first place, it would be such a large undertaking that it would require a staff of people, perhaps years of work, and there is absolutely no guarantee that it could even be done at all. And, of course, experimenting would be limited to mice, not humans. Unless you gave the project to Josef Mengele, the project would probably never get tested on humans for many years, and that assumes it could be duplicated in the first place."

Cameron interjected, "*The* Josef Mengele? From Auschwitz?"

She answered, "I was just joking to make a point."

"Got it! Sorry, I am a little slow," Cameron said. "I am not in medicine, you know. But I have read that some drug companies sometimes spend several hundred million in testing a new drug before it is released. So I see what you mean."

"Frankly, it probably can't be done," Candice admitted. "Something that can make extremely precise changes in human DNA could probably never be made up from scratch, at least not in our lifetime. Something in the plant must create a different amino acid, but it is an impossibly complex thing to try to do without a model to follow. But, on the other hand, if we had a specimen of the plant that Spencer and I took, synthesizing it could very likely be done. We have instruments that can measure exactly what is in something, and what something is made of. Duplicating something is infinitely more easy than trying to backtrack from the effects of it and then trying to recreate what caused it."

She continued, "I have now begun to realize the incredible importance of this discovery. If I could get a specimen of the plant, and replicate the chemical formula in a lab, it could be made available to everyone and become a new dawn in human development. Imagine children that spend only a few years getting the normal high school education. What levels of intellect a human could achieve if he could get a college degree at ten or twelve, and then utilize the remainder of his best formative, educational years to achieve after that? I believe that someone born with the benefit of this plant can possibly achieve twice the IQ as one without it. Easily!"

"Why do you think it will double the IQ, rather than just make whatever quotient of intelligence the kid is going to have come on at an earlier age?" Cameron asked, exploring the subject.

Candice answered, "You know the old adage, 'you can't teach an old dog new tricks'. Take it a step further. The first third of a person's normal lifespan is best suited for education, and there is no reason to assume that you cannot learn at a much higher rate, and much sooner. Much, if not most, of that period is wasted. It is obvious when you think about it. You waste a number of early years from birth just learning to walk, learning coordination and basics. You only begin school at five or so, and then start a long, slow process of education, when the system finally puts you out on the street with a degree at age twenty-two or so if you go to college, or twenty-eight if you go into medicine or some advanced field. Just think if you could do all of that in a fraction of the time. I have good reason to believe that a person could put much more into that early portion of his life if he could just learn more rapidly. It is not a matter of growing a bigger brain, which would work too, but putting efficiency into it by learning more quickly by having a more finely-tuned system that can take in the data and analyze it. Birds can fly in just a very short while. Many animals can fend for themselves fairly well in just days. If you think about it, what a waste of a third of your life just getting a basic education! Humans have the most wasteful design in that regard. You spend a good third of your life getting an education, and then you have about another third to perfect or use that education and then your body starts falling apart. I personally believe that cancer is one of nature's ways, so to speak, of weeding out the pack. It is such an inefficient design that humans have such a short time to be good at something once they finally acquire the ability."

"But how do you know that this plant doesn't just race the person to an earlier death, that is, maybe the person will learn more and quicker, but also die quicker?" Cameron asked.

Candice responded, "We have no reason to believe that is the case. Devan is not aging faster, only accomplishing more. His condition is not one of rapid aging. Millions of cells reproduce, happening all the time. There is something, somewhere, in the DNA chain that directs the body after a time to stop making certain kinds of cells, or changes the way they are made, that makes us grow old and expire. Why couldn't the design just keep making us continue? Perhaps one day that aging can be altered. But to be absolutely certain as to what happens to Devan at a later date, of course, we have to wait."

Candice added, "As an added benefit from this potion, there is something else. From watching Devan, you can see that he is quite in control emotionally. He does not cry, unless he hurts himself, and has much better overall control of himself. There is an incredibly valuable added benefit in this potion. The accelerated and more finely tuned development of the central nervous system has put him in control of himself as well as his emotions. Today lots of mothers work and still want kids. They have all sorts of trouble finding day care, babysitters, and the like. The length of time of care for infants and day care would be shortened by a fraction of what it is presently. A six year old might be able to be alone, and work on his computer, rather than need a babysitter!"

She continued, "The advanced development of his central nervous system has given him more intellect and control over emotion, and he will be able to focus his youthful energies when growing to intellectual matters, rather than let his emotions control and waste them. That alone could be a multiplier of his achievements over the same period of others. You know how many youngsters, especially in adolescence, have so much trouble accepting things. This may put a stop to that, or nearly so."

Cameron said, "I have a question. What happens when Devan

begets a baby. Will he need the potion again? Or, is he transformed forever?"

Candice said, "That is a very astute question. I believe he is transformed, as you put it, forever. Devan's DNA has been altered from that of us, his parents. If he was to be tested for DNA in a lab to establish paternity of us over him, it would be concluded by the ordinary tests that he was not our baby. So, there is no reason to believe that his children will not be the same as him. In other words, he should not need the plant to create an offspring like himself, at least if the partner was born of it, too. As to whether or not his child would be the same if he had an ordinary partner and no plant, who knows? But this is really a step, possibly *the step*, out of the Stone Age of evolution, and it will be done not by a substance from outer space, but from a plant located right here on earth. It was here all the time!"

Cameron asked, "Are you sure that plant did not come from outer space?"

Spencer spoke. "I believe that the plant was put here on purpose for man to find, and to consume as part of his destiny."

Cameron said, "Spencer, that is a religious explanation."

"The changes in Devan's DNA are so acute, and so discrete, that I cannot believe otherwise," Spencer answered. "How else would something exist, in the form of a plant growing out of the earth, that could make such precise changes in someone's DNA and not otherwise adversely affect him?"

Cameron said, "Candice, you say the changes are from chemicals. Spencer, you say the matter has a divine explanation. And I understand Faint Chance believes the explanation is a spiritual one."

Candice spoke. "We suspect that the tribal villagers believe that the wisdom and essence of the forefathers goes into the offspring of the Chief by a spiritual event. As animists, and uneducated, this is what we expect to find."

Cameron said, "So the tribal people think it is spiritual."

Spencer said, "Life in those remote villages remains today an extraordinary window of the past. You would be quite surprised to visit one. We visited several when in Lao. In one we went to they would run and hide from any camera."

"Well, as a matter of fact, the only instance that you know of, your own, where the plant was ingested was with use of the prayers to summon the spirits, right?" Cameron pointed out.

"Very true!" Spencer said. "We have no other examples of it to compare."

"Why do you suppose this plant is not growing everywhere, or that man did not run into it earlier on and obtain its benefits sooner?" Cameron asked.

Candice answered, "I have been wondering if this plant was not growing here for man to find and consume once he gained enough intelligence to realize its importance. It is, however, very remote, to say the least, and probably not plentiful. It could be that it was more plentiful at one time, but got wiped out by something like that which killed the dinosaurs."

"I have a thought," Cameron said. "Perhaps it was put here, from whatever of the three explanations, in such a small quantity that it was not meant to be found until such time as man was capable of reproducing it."

"That is a very interesting thought," Spencer replied, and he went into deep thought pondering it.

"If you could make up the formula for this, you could patent it and make an absolute fortune," Cameron realized and told them. "Now people are paying as much as five dollars for antibiotics per pill. Imagine what they would pay to have a chance at a genius offspring! Even if every person could have a chance of having some little beggar better than normal, wouldn't that be worth a thousand? Ten? Anyone wanting a child would hold off until they had a chance to buy this stuff. You are sitting on the world's largest gold mine."

Candice said, "Yes, I realize that. And, I could produce it if I could get it here and synthesize it successfully. I could patent the formula and the process, and retain control over its marketing. However, I would not be interested in selling it for gluttonous profit. Rather, I would control the price and sell it for a reasonable price in places like the US and wealthy countries. The profits would subsidize the provision of it for those who cannot afford it, like those wonderful people we saw so many of in India, and other places that we did not get to go. Spencer and I were deeply moved by the poverty, and felt so helpless that we could not give. This could be the way. Children born by this would have the intelligence not to breed like flies, and would have the where-withal to come out of poverty. This could be considered as the next step in human evolution. As for Spencer and me, we would be happy with just enough to be wealthy, and retire to whatever limited research that we could choose to do. We are not interested in seeing how much of an empire we can build. And, in our fields of research medicine, it would be the ultimate medical publication. We could literally retire and feel like we had accomplished a sufficient lifetime of work."

Cameron said, "Even if you only charged a royalty in western countries of several dollars per dose, you would still be the richest person in the world. The magnitude of this thing is beyond belief!"

"But such luxuries as being so rich as to be able to help the poor come later," Candice continued. "I need a specimen of the plant, or its leaves."

"Why not ask Faint Chance to go get some more?" Cameron asked.

Spencer spoke. "She really has no way to do that by herself. She has never been back to the village since she was taken away at age seven. She doesn't know exactly where the village is, only approximately. The journey to the village could be a dangerous one, and getting there would be no doubt a jungle expedition. Maybe the village has changed? Gone? Who knows if the plant still exists? Who knows if the Chief would release the prized plant even if there is more of it?"

"What is the situation on Faint Chance's visa application?" Cameron asked.

"We are still waiting for the US Government to act on it. We don't know how long it will take."

"Isn't there some way to expedite it?" Cameron asked.

Spencer said, "Maybe we should amend her visa application: 'Please expedite this visa, as she is bringing back a plant that will alter the course of human evolution and mankind really cannot wait any longer!'"

Everyone at the table laughed heartily.

Cameron asked, "Did you go to any villages similar to the village that Faint Chance lived in?"

Candice answered, "We don't know for sure. The ones we visited were accessible by very windy, bumpy, dirt and sand roads, but at least accessible. The most remote one that we went to in the north was Ban Hmont Houei Sala, a highland village. Although Faint Chance told us of her village, going there would have required some further difficulty, and she was not able to join us after we left the capital of Vientiane. And, of course, we had no idea at the time that the plant would really work!"

Spencer said, "Faint Chance said her village was some distance from the nearest road and to get there requires hiking. There were differences in the villages, but the primitive aspect of them was similar. In one we went to, the women, even the little girls, all wore a certain dark blue home-made one-piece dress, and a bright violet waist string around it, and no other dress is allowed at all. But, after seeing several of them, we had the experience of observing that primitive lifestyle and saw no reason to go and visit more of them."

"And, we could not communicate with them," Candice added. "They either speak Lao or, if remote, one of several local dialects, and the people are very timid. They usually run and hide when the camera comes out. I have pictures here of the villages, but only a very few with the villagers, because if they saw me taking pictures they would go and hide for a while until I put the camera down."

Spencer added, "There was no real reason to go into the jungle so deeply. And, there were some good reasons not to. Wait until you see the warnings from the State Department."

"But once we have fully disclosed the dangers to you, we want to tell you what we would like you to do, and we rather think that you would like it," Candice said to her brother-in-law with a big smile.

Cameron raised an eyebrow.

"Spencer and I just got back from a one-year-long sabbatical, and neither of us can take off again to go on a journey. To compound that, I took off a few weeks to have Devan not too long after we got back. We would definitely be in serious trouble with our positions, and our responsibilities where we work, if we tried for leave again. On the other hand, you have never been to Asia, and you may be able to take off for a while, and have a little adventure as well. We would like you to go to Lao, meet Faint Chance and go get some of the special plant. We think you would enjoy that immensely, and have memorable experiences. And, if you find this plant, and bring it back, we will of course make you a full partner in whatever financial gain there is to make of it."

"That could be more than you might make as an architect in a million years or so," Spencer joked with the exaggeration, but it was designed to pique his brother's interest.

"Is that a third or a half," Cameron said amusingly, not really caring, and pointing out that there were three of them, and two were aligned – Spencer and Candice.

"If you want a full half, you'll have to pay for your own air fare and expenses over there," Spencer chuckled. None of them, including Candice, cared about such matters at the time. But it was a convenient way for Spencer and Candice to avoid paying for Cameron's expenses which was particularly good since the two of them had just spent a year spending money instead of making it. They all were so close that they did not even consider putting anything into writing, a formality, they all assumed, that would be rude to undertake.

Candice said, "We want to make it perfectly clear that we have no assurance that everything will come to fruition, and so if you go and pay for your trip, we guarantee no more than a probable high adventure. Maybe the plant won't be available, maybe the tribal chief will forbid leading you to it, maybe you won't be able to find it, or whatever. We simply have no idea what to expect. It has been years since Faint Chance was there when she got the plant."

"Actually, once you meet Faint Chance, you may decide to run off with her and never come back," Spencer said jokingly, but to make the trip sound better. But in his heart there was a thread of truth to it, as he had been carrying her often in his thoughts since he had been with her.

"I have a few pictures of Faint Chance here," Candice said.

"Wait until you see what she looks like. You will definitely want to go then." Candice found a picture of Faint Chance under the waterfall and handed it to Cameron.

Cameron's eyes opened wide at the beautiful naked Faint Chance in the natural waterfall, dancing in the water. "Wow! That settles it! I am definitely going! How can I resist?"

"A picture is worth a thousand words," Candice said with a big smile.

"Before you say yes so quickly, you had better look at the travel advisories and warnings from the State Department about Lao," Candice warned. "And, if you go off to the remote village to look for the plant, you will be going into a real jungle, far from help and civilization. You should wear long sleeves and pants to avoid the mosquitoes and other insects, and be careful about what you eat. As you will be in remote areas, near the Ho Chi Minh trail, unexploded bombs dropped on Lao during the Vietnam war remain a genuine threat. It is necessary to be very careful."

"And, we still have to contact Faint Chance and see if she will agree. She puts the plant in the context of a serious spiritual ceremony, and we have not yet asked her if she will help us make it known to the world," Spencer added. "But I think she will do it for us. On the other hand, we cannot be too sure if the tribal chief will help, or if there is any plant left. Or who knows what? We cannot just pick up a phone, or have Faint Chance pick one up, and call the Chief. The village has no electricity, no mail service and no regular contact with the outside world at all. There are so many 'ifs'."

Cameron said, "This sounds like a true adventure. Okay, I will do it. If you line it up, I will go."

"I will call Faint Chance at her shop to ask her if she will agree to help. The phone service to Lao is not so great, but I will see what I can do. Without her help, there is no plant, and no hope," Spencer said.

"No 'chance'," Cameron corrected him, smiling.

"If everything gets lined up, Spencer and I will put together some medicine for you in case you get some bad water or bacteria in the food. But there are a number of things that you could get that they will not cure. You must read these advisories," Candice said, as she spread them out on the table having obtained them from a drawer.

"I will write to Faint Chance tomorrow," Spencer said. "I will also attempt to call her at the jewelry store where she works."

"You will have to sneak the plant into America," Candice said. "Had we not gone recently and learned what we did, you could have gone to all the trouble and expense to find and bring the plant over here, and then have it confiscated by customs. One of the problems will be that when you return, the US makes you sign something to declare any plants or foodstuffs you are bringing back to look for medflies and similar pests, and will confiscate any plants you declare, or that they find if they search your bags. So, you will have to figure out a way to conceal the plant, if you succeed in finding some. I recommend a spice packet or jar," she went to the cupboard to show him one of the many she had brought back. "Just put it in a spice jar and call it a spice. Customs will allow that."

"It sounds like committing a 'high crime and misdemeanor'," Cameron said, thinking of the words from American politics used by the press. "But then, what the heck?"

Chapter Twenty-Seven

In making plans, Cameron stopped at Candice's lab to see what she was doing on the project, and to get a better feel for what he might bring back if there were to be any choices to be made. In the lab was Tadashi Uto along with Candice. Cameron had met him before at a Christmas party at Candice's house.

"Tadashi, you remember my brother-in-law, Cameron. He is an architect."

"Yes, of course. We met at the Christmas party. I think that being an architect would be a great profession," Tadashi said to him, admiringly.

Cameron looked around the lab, and said, "This is only the second time I have ever been to the lab."

Candice said, "Tadashi, Cameron is fully informed of the project, and will be the one to go over to Lao to attempt to get us a specimen of the plant."

Tadashi said, "We are very anxious to get a specimen. Candice has expressed positive predictions that we can synthesize it if we have a specimen," he boasted as though he were an integral part of the group. "I wish I could go myself, but I cannot take time off from the lab. How long will you be gone?"

Cameron said, "I have only taken leave for a month. I hope to succeed in bringing a plant back in that time to analyze."

"When are you leaving?" Tadashi asked. "We are very anxious to get a specimen so we can start working on synthesizing it."

Cameron answered his questions for him, as Candice had said he was fully informed about the discovery.

Chapter Twenty-Eight

"We have reached Faint Chance," Candice told Cameron that weekend at his house at another Saturday night dinner. "I got through by phone, believe it or not. Both of us talked to her. The connection was terrible, but we were able to set things in motion. She was a little apprehensive about going to try to find more of the plant."

Cameron said, "That is no surprise. Assuming she can go back and find the place, maybe she would be put to death if she tells the Chief that she gave away the wedding present he gave her to westerners who offered her a ticket out of Lao, and would he mind giving her another so her friends can give it to the world!"

"Hah!" Spencer laughed. "I think her apprehension comes from the possibility of offending the powerful spirits that reside in the plant."

"Did she say she wouldn't do it?" Cameron asked.

"She didn't say no, she just sort of went along with it. I told her you would be coming, and I can't imagine that she would allow all that expense and effort without telling us beforehand that she would not help," Candice said.

Spencer said, "We have made an itinerary for you whereby you will meet her in the north, at a city that has an airport. She has not flown before. She can take the local airline and meet you. We will send her some money by an international wire transfer so she can get about and meet you."

He continued, "Since there is no such thing as a direct flight to Lao, and you have to go to a nearby big airport, we have tried to make the trip as interesting as we can so you can see a little of one other country on the way, and that is Thailand. You will first fly to Bangkok where you will spend two days getting over jet lag and taking in the sights since you have not been there. Then you will fly a short hop to Chiang Rai, Thailand, which is a beautiful resort area in the north of Thailand, for another two nights. You will love that, and you can look around and go to the Golden Triangle. Then you will take a chartered car to the Mekong River, which is the borderline between Thailand and Lao. The meeting we have planned for you is to have her come up from Vientiane, the capital in the south, on Lao Air, which has propeller planes, to Ban Houei Sai, Lao. She will meet you there when you come across from Thailand on a boat across the Mekong River to Lao. This is what we believe is the best and most interesting method for your trip, and puts you into Lao nearest the northern village where Faint Chance lived as a youngster. You will meet at Ban Houei Sai, and from there, you will be as near as we can put you to the approximate area of the highland villages where her adoptive tribe is most likely to be found."

Cameron said, "Most likely to be found? Does that mean maybe we won't find it?"

"It is not on our Laotian map, but Faint Chance says she knows where it is," Spencer admitted. "She has never returned so we cannot be absolutely certain that she can easily find it – but we think that she can."

"Wonderful," Cameron said. "Nothing like certainty in travel. What about reservations in Ban Houei Sai?"

"You must be kidding," Candice said, laughing.

"Right! I understand," Cameron said.

"Okay, assuming I am naive enough to go, what do I need?" Cameron asked.

"The main thing is to check your passport, and then you need to fax the Laotian consulate for a visa. A visa is required to go to Lao," Candice said.

Spencer said, "On the way back, you can go to the south, down the Mekong River, returning with Faint Chance. You will enjoy this route."

Candice asked, "We think you can arrange for you to go in three to four weeks. Will that work for you?"

"I will start preparations," Cameron said. "I must get advice from both of you on what to take. And, Candice, what sort of camera to take? I might get some neat architectural shots for ideas."

"Only take one camera and make it light," Candice said.

"When I think of all the places I hefted my camera bag, I wish in hindsight that I had taken only one light camera. I was on camels and elephants in India, and places where toting the bag was a chore. Make it light. And besides, you are going off into the jungle somewhere. I recommend a 35 mm camera with a single, variable focal length lens, wide angle to short telephoto. This is going to be mostly jungle trekking, so I don't think you will want to lug a long telephoto lens along. One small, light, 24 to 85 mm zoom should be just right, which I will lend you. And, I will lend you a lead foil bag for the film so it doesn't get partially exposed in the X-ray machines at the airports. They all say the X-ray machines are film safe. That is a lie, so use the lead bag. If you have film in the camera, take out the film, or take out the camera and don't put it through the X-ray machine. Trust me!"

"I will just let you handle the camera selection, Candice. That is your specialty."

As they spoke, there was another conversation going on elsewhere about the same topic, Cameron's travel plans to Lao as Candice had told Tadashi at the lab. This was between brothers Tadashi and Morio Uto at Tadashi's apartment. Tadashi was puzzled as to why his brother Morio, back in town, was so interested in the project that he was working on, as he had never shown any interest at all in science. But he was quite gratified that he was doing something of merit that gave him recognition with his brother.

Chapter Twenty-Nine

Morio Uto pushed the button to the side of the heavy, solid rosewood door with polished brass hardware. A Japanese man of thirty-five, without any trace of a neck, standing over six feet tall, with huge shoulders, and weighing nearly three hundred pounds, answered the door, wearing a dark gray two-piece suit, a white shirt, and a black tie that was mysteriously tied somewhere in the crevice that would be a neck on a normal person. He had a very rough face. There was no smile or other greeting as he stood solidly in the doorway. He was obviously a bodyguard. If he put on fat, he could pass for a sumo wrestler.

Uto addressed the neckless man in Japanese. "Morio Uto. I have an appointment with the Oyabun."

The strange-looking man stepped to one side, opening the door for Uto to enter. He closed the door behind Uto, and Uto heard electronic bolts fasten it when it closed. The entry of the home was a spectacular indoor garden, with a koi fish pond, waterfall, colorful plants and various Japanese water features, receiving its light from a glass ceiling above which was a movable panel that was partially open at the time. Considering the average Japanese family of four lives in a five hundred square-foot apartment, the twelve thousand square-foot home in Tokyo was nothing short of a mansion. It had its own helicopter pad on a flat part of the roof. The neckless man led Uto through the indoor garden towards a study. He knocked on the door of the study, and after "enter" was heard, he opened the door and let Uto in, following behind. After closing the door, the neckless man stood there for a time just inside the door.

The Oyabun, the Japanese Godfather, sat in an easy chair behind a coffee table that had some financial records on it that he had been reviewing.

Uto walked in, stopped and then bowed deeply in great respect to the most powerful crime lord in Japan.

"Sit." And then the Oyabun looked to the neckless man, and told him that he could leave them. He then left the room and closed the door behind him.

The Oyabun was in his late fifties, with a medium build, dark complexion and a wide, heavy jowl. The side of his face bore a scar from a long time past. He wore a dark gray suit and white shirt, but had no tie. His shoes were expensive.

Uto gave him the report. "I have purchased six metric tons of marijuana that has over fifteen parts per million of THC from California and from Hawaii. I sampled it myself, and it is of the best and should bring the highest price. The Hawaiian crop will be coming in soon, packed with Hawaiian pineapples. The crop from California is also coming with California fruit. For the American market, I will have it delivered to your electronics division to have it encased in large television tubes, and installed in televisions. The tubes are completely sealed to the atmosphere, and when they are delivered, if the customs people bring their dope-smelling dogs around as they usually do, they will not be able to sniff anything. Our man in America will know which boxes contain the marijuana, as they will be marked with a special sign in Japanese, and he will get them from the warehouse. The cost of the useless televisions is relatively minor compared to the profit on the amount that a large screen television can hold. I have also taken precautions on the import duties. There is import duty on TVs into America, and we must not undervalue the TVs to save money on the duty, as America is keeping track of the cost of TVs so as to keep us from what they call 'dumping' of excess goods on their market. I have brought you the records of the costs of purchase," Uto said, handing a file over the table.

The Oyabun looked down at the table, indicating that he wanted it placed on the table rather than given to him at this time.

"I am pleased with your arrangements. I will look to see how much profit this recent purchase yields," the Oyabun said. "I will review your expenditures later. Now, what is this new matter that you said on the phone earlier that you wanted to talk to me about?"

"I have come across something that could be very big. A plant has been discovered in Lao by a genetics research doctor that my younger brother works for in America. When taken at the time of conceiving a child, it makes the child very smart by more rapid and enhanced development of his central nervous system."

"How can this discovery be of use to us?" the Oyabun asked.

"The research doctor is sending her brother-in-law to Lao soon to go for a specimen of the plant. She intends to have it analyzed and then synthesized so that it can be made into a pill. If it works, everyone in the world will want to take it when having a child. It could be the biggest-selling legal drug of all time. The potential is fantastic."

"How do you know that it works?"

"The genetics research doctor and her husband ate the plant leaves in Lao when they were having sex to have a child, and have already given birth to a gifted child. The child could talk at age one month! It does work!"

"This could be something very big!" the Oyabun said, showing interest in the project. "How can we do anything with it if she is going to do it in America?"

"She will get the plant, and then analyze it in a lab to figure out what special formula it is made of. After figuring out how to synthesize it, she will apply to patent the formula and the process to make it. Most all of the countries recognize international patents, and they will then have a legal monopoly on the pill. But, the plant is natural, and anyone who can get it first, or get a lab to synthesize it first, can patent the synthesized chemical formula and the process to make it first and make a fortune."

"Does your brother know where it grows?"

"Only that it comes from nearby some remote mountain tribe of Lao."

"How do you intend to find it?"

"The doctor that my brother works for knows a Laotian girl who knows where to find it. She is the one who gave it to the doctors when they were in Lao. The doctor's brother-in-law is going to Lao soon to meet with her, and she will lead him to the village to get the plant specimen. I propose to follow him in, wait until he gets the plant, and then take it from him."

"Where will you take it from him?"

"I think the best place would be in Lao. Then I would get it back here, and you could have a lab set up to synthesize it right away and hurry to get it patented. As the plant is a naturally-occurring substance, there should be no way that anyone can challenge the person or company that is first to apply for a patent. The patent process would be perfectly legal, and belong to who applies first."

"Do you know for sure that it can be synthesized?" the Oyabun asked.

"No, I don't. That part is the gamble. But there is so much at stake, that it seems like a very good risk. I do not have the resources to do the lab synthesis myself, and so I bring it to you. I want only a share in it if it works, as there will be considerable investment needed to synthesize it and produce it."

"You have done well by bringing me this," the Oyabun said to him. "I will undertake to do this. What will you need?"

"I will need one man, some capital for expenses and weapons in Lao."

"Do you want to use one of my men, or your own?"

"I will use my own. Can you arrange weapons for me in Lao?" Uto asked.

"I do business in Bangkok with a man who can sell you weapons there. I have no one in Lao. But you can cross the river into Lao with weapons and not be caught with them." The Oyabun got up. Uto stood up when the Oyabun did. The Oyabun walked over to a lacquered ornate box on a table and opened it. "Yen or American dollars?"

"I think some of each," Uto said.

The Oyabun took out some stacks of money from each side of the box, as one side had Yen and the other American dollars. "Here," he said, handing Uto two stacks of money. "You will account for everything spent, as usual."

One did not cheat the Oyabun, and Uto said, "Of course, sir."

"This sounds like a very profitable venture. I want you to keep me informed as it progresses," the Oyabun said.

"It may not be easy to contact you often from Lao, as the communications there cannot be expected to be very good."

"Report in when you can. If you need help I will try to arrange it. I must look around for a suitable lab to be prepared to synthesize the plant when you get it. I do not expect you to fail."

Uto found that remark very discomforting.

As Uto left, the Oyabun sat back and thought about the project. He then realized that he, himself, who had no children, might consider having a son with the special plant.

Chapter Thirty

Chiang Rai makes Bangkok look like a big, dirty city, Cameron thought as the hotel van drove him from the small airport to the hotel. The hotel was beautifully decorated outside with flowers everywhere. The driver got a cart for his bag, and Cameron walked into the marbled entry. The ceiling was an incredible thirty-five feet high, and the sounds of waterfalls and fountains inside were amplified by the marble floors. A swimming pool the size of a small lake came right up to the back of the lobby, surrounded by colorful flowers and plants. It was the most beautiful hotel he had ever been in. He realized he should travel more often, to enrich his architectural background.

Cameron checked in, and his room key was presented to him in a cone made of a green leaf, with an orchid in it, which fascinated him as he held it and looked at it. He told the desk clerk to phone a tour agency his brother had arranged, for him to inform them of his arrival. It was only ten in the morning, as he had taken an early flight from Bangkok, a short hop in a small jet. After he settled in, he went to the lobby to wait for his tour guide.

Within minutes a bubbly Thai girl of twenty-one years, only five feet tall, came in the marble entry. There was youthful excessive energy in her gait. She had white jeans, a white shirt, with a pink tie and a white vest. She had to be the one from the agency. The outfit style reminded him of a sailor's costume.

"Are you from the agency?" Cameron asked from twenty feet away to get her attention.

"Yes! Are you Mr. Harrington?" the bubbly girl asked.

"None other."

As she approached, she stuck out her arm fully while still several steps away, an exaggerated welcome gesture, as were all her movements. She had an enormous smile displaying large teeth.

"I am called Judy, for my western name. I am an independent

operator, and have been hired by the agency to be your guide. I have a van outside with a driver. I have several suggestions for today, and then tomorrow I am to take you to the river. I understand you are going over to Lao."

"Yes, I am. What do you suggest for today?"

"Most people like to go out to some mountain villages here, which is a very beautiful drive. We can head for Myanmar, or Burma, as it may be known to you, and then to the Golden Triangle, where the three countries of Burma, Lao and Thailand meet. Then return, which will put us back at the hotel around dusk, or a little after. Will that be of interest?"

"Sounds wonderful. I have my camera and am ready."

Cameron said, as they approached the van, "I will sit in the back here," referring to the middle bench seat in the van. Judy got in the front with the driver, and off they went. She had made cassette tapes with copied recordings of western music, and put one on the tape player the van was equipped with.

"You came in this morning from Bangkok, right?" the girl asked.

"Yes. I was there two days," Cameron said.

"Is this your first trip?"

"Yes, this is the first trip, and the first time I have been in Asia."

"How did you find Bangkok?" she asked.

"The floating market was very interesting. The women selling their vegetables and fruits on sampans was an experience."

"How do you find the Thai food so far?" she asked.

"Delicious! The guide in Bangkok took me to a place like a supermarket-cum-restaurant where you pick your own seafood from a long row of fish on ice, and then tell the chef how to make it. You also pick your own vegetables, wine and everything else that way. I left it up to the chef to pick the method of cooking, and he delighted me. It was spectacular!"

"I am glad you are enjoying your trip so far," she said. "What else did you do in Bangkok?"

"The guide took me to a Thai massage place. It was really neat. Do you know of them?"

"Thai massage is a specialty. You can get that here as well. I think the hotel will have that," Judy told him.

The little white van took them to the nearby mountains, and they went up and into windy roads curving about the hills. After an hour and a half of driving, they came to a rounded hilltop, with what appeared to be a plantation off to the right. There was a structure on it and equipment inside. But the eye-catching sight was a very large human, dressed in white. A fence obscured much of the view, and they might not have noticed anything beyond it but for the large man in the bright white suit reflecting so much sunlight towering well above the fence. He stood on the flat part of the hilltop. The majority of the plantation could not be seen from the road as it angled down a sloping hill beyond the flat area on top.

Judy instinctively thought this new feature of the Thai mountains that she had not previously noticed may be an interesting thing to check out. She quickly said to the driver to turn in. He overshot the entrance, but backed up and then turned in the open gate.

"I have driven by here, but have not noticed this place," she told Cameron. "It looks like a tea plantation."

As the van turned in, she said, "Yes! It is! It is a tea plantation. Let's see if we can get permission to look around." She was forward as a tour guide should be, and she was so small, like a pixie, that her action of entering someone's land would not seem like an intrusion.

Cameron could see the tea growing down the vast slope of the plantation, which was not visible from the road. No wonder Judy had missed it before, as it was only the large man in white that caught her eye.

Back from the gate a hundred yards, stood an equipment garage. The big man was out front, looking about. He appeared to be in his late fifties, standing well over six feet tall and very heavy. He wore a wide-brimmed, white panama hat with a black band, an ivory-white silk and thin wool-blended suit with matching vest, and adorning the vest was a gold pocket watch with chain. He did not have his suit jacket on, apparently due to the heat. He sported two-tone tan canvas and light-brown alligator shoes. His belt was matching alligator. The material of his suit was obviously very expensive, as it had a shine in the light, and a character of its own. There was much of it in order to cover the huge man inside it. Under the vest was a white silk shirt with a pale blue silk tie. The French cuffs were fastened with Laotian blue sapphire cufflinks, and a matching sapphire tie tack adorned his tie. In one hand was a rosewood walking stick with an ornate silver handle. He was clearly, by anyone's definition, the perfect dandy.

They exited the van, and bubbly little Judy walked up to the big man. Next to him she looked like an elf.

After a few moments, she turned and walked back to the van with a huge smile, her oversized white teeth shining in the bright sun. She had charmed the man.

"That is the owner. This is a tea plantation, and he welcomes us and will show us around. Come on."

Cameron got out and followed her to the man, who had walked over to some shade of a tree near the structure that held the farming tools and stainless drums to dry the tea leaves.

"How do you do, sir? I am Cameron Harrington. I am from America, and my guide says you have graciously consented to let us admire your tea plantation."

"Certainly, sir," the huge man said with an accent that was hard to place – it was definitely not American. And the "sir" showed old-world respect, not the revolting first name habit that American people had begun using. He continued the introductions, "Allow me to introduce myself. I am the Baron Von Limbach." The way he put it made it seem so old-world formal, and so proper, that it was very impressive.

The Baron continued, "We just completed a harvest of several of the teas. This is a special plantation where I grow only the finest of oolong teas. I grow one here that is completely unique," he boasted. "They bring an incredibly high price in Taiwan and nearly the same price in a few other places. Please note the fields below here," he said, pointing.

The estate was quite large, and was not visible from the road. The tea plants were in neat rows covering many acres of the hillside which they overlooked.

"Is this all a special type of oolong tea?" Cameron asked.

"Yes, it is. I am actually growing several varieties, but all are extremely special. They do well here in these highlands and climate. This is my fourth year at it, and we showed a profit last year and this."

"I regret that I know nothing of tea," Cameron said. "But it is all very interesting. But please, do not let me disturb you."

"Not at all. I enjoy a little company. I have an estate manager, who is off buying supplies at the moment, and there is no harvest at the moment, as we just completed one. Come, let me show you." He took the lead with Spencer and Judy following to the open building. Just inside were stainless drums, five feet high, two feet in diameter, with motors to turn them.

"These are dryers that I had specially made. The tea is dried here. There really isn't much to it. The main thing that is special is the kind we grow, the care in growing and the climate. Would you allow me to show off my tea by sampling it?"

"That would be a treat indeed!" Cameron said. They followed the huge man into an enclosed part of the structure. There was an air conditioner on the back wall cooling the place. The large room was undivided, and was obviously used as the office for the ranch manager. There were three desks towards the rear, and file cabinets. A young Thai girl was present, organizing some papers at a desk. Towards the front was a bar against the wall, with pitchers, teapots and small, sampling-sized cups, although taller than demitasse coffee cups.

"It is cooler here than at the lower altitudes, but as the afternoon approaches it does get warm," the Baron said, putting his panama hat on a hook on the wall, over an ivory-white jacket that was obviously his suit coat. "Please, have a seat," he said, motioning to a table at the front, abutting a big picture window that gave a nice view of the plantation. They sat, situated where they could look over the large plantation.

To Cameron's surprise, the man spoke to the young girl in Thai.

The Thai girl got up, and began tea preparations. She turned on an electric water-heating grill, and prepared cups and pots to steep the teas.

"You speak Thai!" Judy said in surprise. She then spoke some words to him in Thai which Cameron did not understand. He responded, confirming to Judy that he actually spoke her language. She was obviously impressed with his correct Thai from the expression on her face.

"You have quite an impressive command of languages," Cameron said. "How many can you speak?"

"Let's see… In the European languages, German, Italian, French, Spanish and Russian. I can speak Arabic, and can understand a little of some Middle Eastern languages. Of the eastern, Thai, Mandarin, Malay and Lao. I can understand several others."

"No English?" Cameron said jokingly.

"Oh yes, of course!" And they all laughed.

"My God! We have met the world's linguist!" Cameron said.

"Oh, please! You are too complimentary!" the Baron said.

The Thai girl brought over a tray. It had the little sampler-sized tea cups in little saucers. There was a thermos of hot water, and several small containers of different teas. The Baron took over and went right to work making tea himself, enjoying it.

"Here, I want you to try this," he said, pouring. The tea was golden brown.

Cameron and Judy sampled it.

"This is spectacular!" Cameron said.

"Delicious!" Judy agreed and gave a big smile.

"Do you come here often?" Cameron asked. The Baron looked and dressed like someone from a movie from 1920. His outfit, although outrageously dressy, was actually very well done.

"I have an apartment in Chiang Rai. I stop off now and then. But I am about to build a small place here, on this property, so as to have a place to stop off now and then here."

"Where else do you normally live?"

"In addition to Chiang Rai, I have a place in Berlin, Taiwan, Vientiane and on the coast of Spain. I have regular rooms that I stay in but do not own in a few other places. I am in international business. The tea is just a small thing, but last year it was actually quite profitable. That tea you just sampled sells for around one thousand dollars a half kilo in Taiwan. But you see, I love fine tea."

"Wow!" Cameron said. "That must be very exciting."

"May I ask, what do you do, sir?" the Baron asked with his old-world manners.

"I am an architect in the United States," Cameron said.

"What an interesting profession. I love architecture," the Baron said. "Do you specialize?"

"I do mostly small commercial properties, and an occasional home," Cameron said.

"I have some plans here that I would like to show you if you don't mind," said the Baron as he lifted his large frame, and went towards the back of the room and picked up some rolls of plans. "I would be glad to hire you to add to these ideas that I have paid some locals to give me. The local architects, I fear, are not very creative. It seems they just want to add those funny up-turned wooden tips on the roofs to ward off evil spirits. Tell, me," he said, opening the plans, "what do you think?"

Wow, Cameron thought. Here I am, on the other side of the earth, and am being asked to do some architecture. "Let me have a look," he said.

"Cameron asked, "May I draw on these plans?"

"Please!" the Baron said. "I would be honored!"

"I would change the entrance like this," Cameron said, drawing on one of the plans. "Then, I would raise the interior ceiling here, right on up to the second story, and delete the rooms above this area. Then, I would add a section here, in the rear, and reach them with a staircase, like this. I would also move the garage entrance this way around to this side completely. As you can see, it keeps the garage out of sight, and provides for a place that you can store extra cars and things that are not attractive." Cameron paused and looked at the plans.

"But now, if you are willing to make some more dynamic and more interesting changes, why don't we make the corners round, instead of square, like this," Cameron said, drawing curves at the major corners. "Then we could have more interesting rooms, like this entry, which would wind around a curved staircase like this." He drew in a curved staircase to the upper floor as he talked. "We could then have a balcony at the upper level that the staircase leads into, and you have the staircase and the balcony encased in interesting wrought iron. Then we could do arched doorways, instead of the square ones," he said, switching to a different sheet of the plans, and putting in much more interesting doorways than were on the boring plans that had been made by the local architect. Then, in the dining room and main hall, we could do double-recessed ceilings for interesting effect and recessed lighting. I think the entry to the dining room should have a column on either side. We could also have two short columns on either side of the front, right here, under the overhang of the roof. Repeating the round theme, we could do a round observation tower on top of the house, with a staircase to it from the top floor, with a round tile roof, from which you could have a panoramic view of your entire plantation, which you would not otherwise have. Why don't we put the smaller eating area and kitchen up a step, overlooking the family room, and again curve the walls into it?" Cameron was really in his own element now, and his talented hands were drawing rapid and infinitely more appealing designs than the very ordinary rooms that the locals had designed.

"This is amazing!" the Baron said. "If you will stay here to finish these for me, I will pay whatever you ask."

Cameron was tempted, but realized the purpose of his trip, and came back to reality. "I wish I could make you finished plans, but that would take some doing and several days at least. I am unable to stay on for that. But I tell you what. Give me another hour or so, and I will continue with the changes, making the rooms and hallway curved and more interesting, and I am sure that your local people can fill in the details."

With that, the Baron and Judy walked outside to walk about the plantation to let Cameron work.

An hour later, the Baron came back in with Judy. Cameron had completed what he could without starting fresh, and showed the plans to the Baron.

"I am most impressed!" the Baron said. "Please allow me to give you some money."

Cameron said, "It is reward enough that you showed us your plantation, allowed us to sample your tea, and have allowed me to know that I have contributed to a design as far away as Thailand."

The Baron said, "Then you must at least let me give you some of my most valuable tea." He went to the shelf, and took down a metal can. He signaled for the girl who came to provide fresh cups. He took out some of the tea to put it in a pot, saying, "Note the purple leaves. This is most unusual, and sells for two thousand dollars the quarter kilo in Taiwan."

"Wow!" Cameron said. "That has got to be the most expensive tea ever!"

"I believe it is!" the Baron answered with a big smile.

"What a strange color," Judy said, looking at the purple tea leaves.

"Yes, it is. It is what I believe is the finest oolong tea in the world. But of course, I am, how do you say… prejudiced!" and he chuckled.

"Note the unusual aroma," he said while pouring the tea into the demitasse cups.

Cameron put the cup to his nose. He inhaled deeply.

"This is wonderfully fragrant," Cameron said. He took a sip. "I have never had anything like it. I can see why your teas sell for so much."

"I am so glad you enjoy it," the Baron said.

"I have never seen purple tea leaves. This must be very rare," Cameron said.

"Yes, it is. I am the only one who has it," the Baron said. "Here, you must allow me to give you some. I am afraid that there isn't much at the moment, as it was just harvested and shipped off. There won't be another crop for a while. But take this, please," referring to the container.

"If you only have a little left, you should keep it," Cameron said.

"Not at all! Soon there will be another harvest, and I will have a lot of it. Please. Take it. I insist."

The Baron poured out the container, which gave Cameron nearly a pound. He put it in a plastic bag and handed it to Cameron.

"I cannot thank you enough. This is a wonderful gift," Cameron said.

"If you are ever near one of my offices, do not hesitate to call on me. Did you say you were going to Lao?"

"Yes, next stop," Cameron said.

"I will also be there in three weeks, in my office in Vientiane. I export teak from Lao, and also do a little business with the government. Should you be there, call me at the number on the card. We might have dinner." He passed Cameron an oversized business card with multiple languages on both sides.

As he spoke, a new, shiny, pewter-colored Mercedes pulled up in front, with a uniformed chauffeur driving.

"Ah, here is my car. Well, you must excuse me, as I have to go back to town now. Be sure and call on me, to return the favor for your expertise. I have also enjoyed your company," the Baron said.

"It has been a pleasure," Cameron said, shaking his hand.

The Baron took his matching ivory-white suit jacket from a hook on the wall, and put it on as well as his panama hat. They all walked outside, the Baron with his walking stick to his Mercedes, and Cameron and Judy to their little white van, which was now severely outclassed by the big, new, expensive Mercedes. It was one of their biggest models, and very new. The chauffeur opened the back door for him. Cameron could see a navy blue leather interior that looked very nice against the pewter metal-flake exterior paint. Off he went in his white suite and panama hat.

Cameron and Judy got into their little van, and went in the opposite direction.

"What a character!" Cameron said to Judy. He looked with admiring eyes at the treasure in the bag of tea leaves in his hand. "Who ever had such tea? And, purple leaves? This is definitely something new. I doubt that I will ever taste such tea again when this is gone!"

Chapter Thirty-One

Two hours later, they arrived at the Burmese border. "This is now called Myanmar," Judy said. "You used to call it Burma, correct?"

"What was wrong with 'Burma'? Why did they change the name?" Cameron asked Judy.

"I don't know," she told him. "The reason is called 'political', I think?" She was uncertain as the answer involved things she was not involved in: politics.

"Yes, 'political', as in 'politics'," Cameron confirmed for her.

At the end of the 'main drag' of the street before the country line of Myanmar, there was a bunch of shops that got closer and closer together in the last two blocks as the street ended at the border. They sold goods from Myanmar, and apparently the proximity was a selling point to the tourists. Westerners could not just go into Myanmar, he remembered.

Judy said, "Myanmar is still an oppressive government, and does not allow the sort of free enterprise and travel across the border like most of the world. But we can go up to the border."

They got out, and walked about the shops. Judy pointed out things to Cameron. There were woven wall decorations with little pearlescent buttons sewn on. Most were elaborate elephant scenes.

Judy said, "One of the things that Myanmar has is rubies. They sell them here."

"Let's go have a look," Cameron said, and they went up several steps from the street to what appeared to be the fanciest jewelry store. It was located only one hundred feet from the border of Myanmar, which consisted of a white-and-black-striped gate across the road, with a guard gate on either side. A soldier stood on either side, with a cheaply made machine gun.

As they looked towards the border from the landing just outside the jewelry store, several steps up from the street, Cameron said, "What a difference! All these commercial shops, jammed against the border. And, just across the boarder, nothing!" There was only a road that led off into large trees, and no sign of life or activity.

Inside the jewelry store, Cameron looked at the sparkling jewelry in the glass cases. There were many beautiful rubies, set in twenty-two or twenty-four karat gold. He asked one of the salesgirls, "May I see one of these, please?"

The salesgirl, overdone in make-up, came over to him to find out which he wanted to see. He pointed at a ring, marked twenty-two karat gold, which was three-quarters of an inch in length, completely surrounded by rubies that were set in a diagonal pattern. The rubies were huge, two or more karats each. There were eleven of them.

"Are these genuine rubies from Burma?" Cameron asked.

"Absolutely, sir." She turned around, and picked up a booklet of official-looking papers that was four by six inches in size. It had various red chops in it. "We guarantee all are genuine Burmese rubies," she said, showing him the certificates which said that in English and apparently in Thai.

"How much is a ring like this?" he asked. He held it under the spotlights over the glass cases. It was spectacular.

She held out her hand, and looked at the price tag on it. It was in Thai Baht. Cameron could see the price at that point, and could tell that it translated into nearly five thousand dollars. After looking, she turned and spoke to a man who was at a counter behind her. They said something softly to one another, and she then turned and said, "For you, a special price. In US dollars, that would be one thousand five hundred and fifty."

Cameron turned to Judy, and said, showing her the ring, "That is very cheap! I might get this for a present or just to hold on to. Do you think the rubies are genuine?"

Judy said, "If the store guarantees them, they must be."

Cameron turned to the salesgirl, and said, "I thought that it was illegal in Burma to export rubies. Are you certain they are genuine Burmese rubies?"

"Absolutely, sir," she said, repeating her earlier statement. She held up the guarantee form again.

"I will look about a bit, and I may come back later to buy it," Cameron said.

The girl turned to the man behind her, and they said something he could not hear, but it was not in English anyway. "The last price we can offer is one thousand three hundred and fifty dollars."

"Thank you, and I will consider it." He led Judy out the door. They looked about the street, and the afternoon sun was heating the day very well.

Cameron said to Judy, "Let's go snoop about." He led her up the street away from the border, up a block and a half. At that point there was a small street crossing the main one. Cameron decided to go in that direction. They came to an alleyway which led back to the back side of the shops on the main drag. They walked down the alley, and came to the back of the jewelry store they had just been in. There was a large workshop there and it was open. There was no air conditioning, and it was very hot inside. Sitting at little workstations were slender Thai men making jewelry.

"Let's go have a look," Cameron said. Each workstation showed each person's specialty.

At the first workstation they stopped at, there were a dozen little clumps of irregular red objects, looking something like small sweets, a quarter of an inch in diameter. There was a can, with a bunch of what looked like cigars in it. They were rolled-up brown papers, on closer look. They were rolled to a point at the end. The man glued one of the red objects on to the tip of the rolled-up paper, and put it into a flame from a small burner on the small workstation where he sat. It got soft, and the man shaped it into an oval shape. It was opaque, but as it heated it became clear. The man had a stone wheel that turned in water, and he shaped it into a very good-looking, artificial ruby!

"Look," Cameron said to Judy, "these are fake!"

After he shaped it, the man passed it on to the next bench, where another craftsman used finer wet stone grinding wheels to grind the stones into either round or oval shapes. Another dozen other workers sat at tables in the area busily working away. Each was working on some aspect of making the stones into finished jewelry.

"Let's go. These rubies are all fake! I heard of 'cooked' rubies in Thailand. These are literally cooked."

"Did you know they sold fake Burmese rubies in the stores?" he asked Judy as they drove on.

"No, I thought they were real," she said.

Cameron wondered as they drove off. Could Judy actually not have known? Judy seemed so bubbly, honest, and not part of some scam. How could a tour guide from the area not know? He went back and forth in deciding if she knew or not as they went on. Maybe she got a commission on a sale to a customer she brought in. But she seemed so honest. He could not decide what to believe. Many people must get cheated here, he thought. He realized he knew very little about Asians.

An hour and a half later, the van came to the mountain cliffs overlooking the Golden Triangle, where Myanmar, Thailand and Lao all meet at the Mekong River.

"This was the place of major drug traffic in years past, and," Judy said, "there still is some. Life in the mountains is difficult, and dealing in contraband is still done. Drugs were traded for gold, and so the name. Do you see the sandy area out in the middle of the river?" she said, pointing to it. "That does not belong to any of the three countries. I think you call it a 'no-man's-land'."

"This is the stuff movies are made of," Cameron said, walking to the cliffs. The sun was going down soon and the late horizontal rays illuminated the far bank of Lao, casting shadows on Thailand and Myanmar. "I am going over there next," he told her.

On the three-hour drive back to Chiang Rai, the bubbly girl had a package of some sweets which she offered to Cameron, but he declined. She then opened up the glovebox, and took out a cassette tape with recorded American music from different artists. She began singing along with the artist, as they traveled back. The first was John Denver, in "Take Me Home, Country Roads". Cameron could hear her over the music, *Country road, take me home, to a place, where I belong. West Ginger, mountain mama, take me home…*

"Hah," he laughed aloud. "*Ginger!*" Well, she spoke a lot more English than he did Thai, which was zero. At least she tries, which is more than me, he thought. Fun girl.

Chapter Thirty-Two

The following day, bubbly Judy came back with the travel company minivan and driver. Cameron was waiting in the lobby, admiring the architecture of the hotel.

"Good morning," she said. "Are you ready to go to Lao?"

"Good morning. I am ready," Cameron said.

Off they went on the three-hour trip to Chiang Khong, on the Mekong River, with Judy pointing out things of interest along the way.

Arriving at the border on the Mekong River, Cameron found himself in a very small city that seemed to have nothing else to shout about but a port to Lao. The port consisted of only a steep, narrow, long concrete ramp about two tiny cars wide. The van took them halfway down, to a wooden barrier, by which stood a building for an official the size of a telephone booth. The barrier was like a railroad barrier, a piece of wood across the narrow street – except that it was not electric.

"Over there is Lao," Judy said, pointing to the bank on the other side of the river. The Mekong River was a half mile wide at that point.

The driver got out and handed Cameron his bag. Cameron gave him a tip, and then was escorted to the little hut, where a fee was paid for a boat ride across the river. Judy followed him and spoke to the man in the hut about the fee, and got the money from Cameron and handed it to him. She then followed him down to the water, and saw him on to a strange little boat.

Cameron felt that she had more than accomplished her job, and appreciated her exuberance. He thanked her by a substantial tip for which she seemed most grateful. She stood and waved him off politely for several minutes as the boat left the shore.

The boat was comical, Cameron thought. It was a long canoe-like boat, but curved up at the front, but with a small, squared-off front end a foot wide at the bow. The widest part was less than three feet. The length was eighteen or so feet, and it was powered by one of the Thai-styled small, four-cylinder engines on a swivel, with the propshaft coming straight out the back to a propeller, such that the prop was eight to ten feet behind the boat. The motor swiveled from side to side, up and down to raise and lower the prop in and out of the water, like the Thai boats he saw at the floating gardens. He could not understand why or how anyone would build boats with such long propshafts like that. He wondered if it would actually work better, as he watched a trickle of water come in from the bow, and slightly wet the outside of his bag. It was becoming a very hot day, and the wetness seemed not to matter.

At the Lao side, there was another paved ramp even steeper than the one on the Thai side. The boat pulled up, and the fellow got out with no shoes on, and roped it to a small tree trunk. Cameron got out, and the fellow got his bag for him. He put his bag, a canvass type, on the ramp up a few yards from the river, and looked about. There was a small building to the right, up thirty more feet, which appeared to be the official building. On the left was what appeared to be a restaurant, and there was a girl of eighteen or twenty sitting outside looking up the river. She appeared to be connected to the restaurant, but the restaurant had no customers.

What he did not notice was that just as he got off the boat and went ashore, two men just embarked in a similar boat on the Thai side of the river, and were starting to come across the river at the same spot. They were Japanese.

Cameron went up to the official-looking building. It was up some ten concrete steps that were as steep as a ladder. He touched the upper steps with his fingertips as he climbed, to ensure balance; if he was not in good shape, he would have had to use his hands like on a ladder, the steps were so steep.

"No blue handicap parking spots here," he mused.

The building was fifteen feet square at most. Inside were two women, one brushing the long hair of the other. There was a small fellow, in a uniform, who was obviously the official. The two women had on Laotian sinns. One had on a white cotton pullover, and the other a yellow shirt with a collar. The uniformed man could speak no English, but pointed to some signs, and Cameron figured out to give him his passport. The official took the passport, and then opened an old-fashioned ledger that looked like an accounting ledger from many years past. He meticulously wrote down information in hand from his passport. He then pointed to a sign which had numbers on it. Cameron finally realized that there was an entry fee to come to Lao. He worried for a moment, and then took out his remaining Thai bahts. Cameron asked him how much, and the fellow wrote it down, and accepted the bahts. Cameron just held out his hand with the bahts in it and let the fellow take what he wanted, as there was not much in bahts left in his pockets. After roughly figuring the fee, he calculated it to be less than only one dollar, and Cameron felt relieved. The man returned the passport, which he had chopped and signed inside the chop.

Cameron then saw a sign that said money exchange, and the rate of exchange. He did not want to change too much, as he wondered if the change place might also be a communications device to alert some bandits. So, Cameron took out two one hundred dollar US bills, and gave them to the man. He had to open a locked metal box below, and took out brand new Laotian kip bills of five thousand kip each, which Cameron then saw from the sign was a little over one US dollar each. By the time the man counted out the bills, even though new, there was a huge wad of bills to fold and put in his pocket.

There were no taxis waiting or anyone else waiting there at the point of entry into Lao. It was hot, and Cameron did not want to carry his bag, but realized he had no choice. Cameron picked up his bag, and began walking up the steep concrete road to the town, two hundred yards up at a very steep grade. It was hot and tropical, and he was sweating by the time he reached the top.

At the top of the steep road was the town of Ban Houei Sai. "Ban" meant village, he had learned. The steep road ended there, and a level cross-street greeted him. It was the main drag of the tiny little town of Ban Houei Sai.

Parked at the curb was a *tuk-tuk*. There was very little traffic of any kind, but what little there was consisted of little motorbikes, mostly 100 cc size. No one wore a helmet. Cameron thought the helmet laws were ridiculous, and just made one's head bigger, heavier and more likely to cause a spinal cord break in the event of an accident. He momentarily wished he had his Harley there. Cameron noticed a rather nice-looking café sort of place to the right of the top of the hill, on the corner, and it had some outside tables. One of the tables had a group of five young people who were obviously college types – Cameron guessed from England or Germany. They were having beer. A "Laobeer" sign was on the building.

Cameron went over to the parked *tuk-tuk*. The operator got up from sitting on store steps nearby, and walked over to him. Cameron showed him the name of the hotel he was to meet Faint Chance at, but it was in English. The driver recognized it: Arimid Guest House. Cameron started to get in the back, but remembered there were no meters in the cabs. Cameron thought about the taxi cab tricks to overcharge you, and so he turned around and asked the man how much. The driver said "two" holding up two fingers. Cameron said "two thousand kip?" The driver nodded. Cameron got in and then realized that the drive was only going to cost about fifty cents. He had no idea how far it was, or where he was going exactly.

The driver took off in the funny little vehicle, its exhaust popping, down a road which was a combination of pavement and dirt. Cameron hung on to the little bars around the back truck-styled bed, as the little taxi hit some holes and rough spots in the road that was paved, but not in the best of shape. There was absolutely no traffic, and in fact, no other vehicles were seen on the road except for one girl coming the other way on a small motorbike.

Although Faint Chance had been told the day he would arrive in advance, it could not be absolutely certain that he would in fact arrive on the day scheduled, and there was no way at all to set the time. Therefore, Spencer and Candice had told Faint Chance to fly to Ban Houei Sai to meet him at the hotel that they had stayed at, the Arimid Guest House. She was to have flown in the day before on a flight from Vientiane, a fairly short flight on a turbo prop plane of Lao Air. She was to go to the hotel and take a room, and to set up and wait for him.

After several minutes traveling in the back of the *tuk-tuk*, the driver pulled up in front of a beautiful little compound. The compound was protected by a wrought iron gate, with flowers and plants all over the front, vines with flowers on them on the wrought iron gates, and trees and flowers behind the gates, all very picturesque. There was a winding path going down in-between little cottages. The cottages were built out of some sort of natural trees, like wicker, but heavier. The material was interlaced, and made hard from varnish. The color of the material was a natural reddish brown. Notwithstanding the use of natural materials for construction, they were well built, Cameron, always the architect, noted.

The cottages were not attached to each other, but stood alone. The roofs appeared to be some sort of natural material over wood frame. The floors extended out into a porch in front, were made of teak wood planks, and were raised off the ground an average of three feet in the air. Individual cottages lined both sides of the little path that went on down a gentle slope that made up the compound, which had a beer sign in front, saying "Laobeer" and "Arimin Guest House"(not "Arimid"). Cameron thought he might be at the wrong place, but the name was similar. The beer supplier probably got the name wrong in supplying the sign, he thought. He decided to get off and look in, as that might be the place. He gave the driver one of his five thousand kip notes, which was over a dollar, and said, "Keep the change." The driver understood enough to realize that the whole thing was his. The driver's eyes opened a bit, and he put his hands together in the prayer mode, just below his chin, and bowed and said, "*Kop chai lai.*"

Cameron went inside the gate, and stood in a beautiful garden at the front of the cottage compound. The whole width of the compound was nearly one hundred feet, and he could see a curved concrete path wandering down slightly to a back gate three hundred feet away. Along the sides were the individual cottages, each with a porch, with a little teak table and two chairs. There were slender teak trees protruding upwards past the cottages in several spots, and colorful flowers in a garden in front of each cottage. It was absolutely beautiful. A slender man, the owner, was painting the front cottage with a brush, dipping it into a very strong-smelling, clear-colored but with a rich brown tone, old-fashioned natural varnish. Where he painted, the woven natural material of the cottage side took on a very rich natural color, contrasting with the unpainted parts that looked more dried out. He spoke to Cameron, "Yes?" Cameron was pleasantly surprised to learn that he spoke at least some English.

"I am Cameron Harrington, and I am looking for Sangmouane Sayasithsena," Cameron attempted to read from a piece of paper that Spencer had given him. His effort to pronounce the name was so bad that the proprietor had no idea what he was saying.

The proprietor said nothing, apparently unable to understand. After a time, he seemed to realize something, and said in fair English, "I think you are looking for number nine." He pointed towards a cottage. Cameron thanked him and started down the path, admiring the unusual flowers.

He noted the numbers on the cottages, and came upon what was number nine.

On the teak cottage porch, four feet off the ground, was a hand-carved teak table with two chairs. The table was near the edge of the porch, against a handmade teak railing. The porch to the cottage was covered by the roof of the cottage which extended over it. Surrounding the steps to the porch were flowers on either side, well groomed. A girl was sitting at the teak table on the porch.

There she was! Even more beautiful than her pictures that Candice showed him, he was stunned and speechless!

She saw him coming down the flowered path, and quickly got up to come down the few steps off the porch to greet him. She was wearing a bright blue sinn and matching western-styled top. She wore blue eyeshadow and dark red lipstick. As he approached, she put her hands in the prayer position of the *nop* with elegance and feeling. She bowed formally and did not come up, bestowing great respect until Cameron acknowledged her. Her coal-black hair shone richly in the Laotian sun, and her olive skin glowed with the richness of oils, like a model on an ocean beach.

Chapter Thirty-Three

"Faint Chance?" he called out, feeling discomfort at such royal treatment. She rose and he could see her beautiful features more clearly. Spencer and Candice, although they had tried, had not adequately described her beauty. It was an indelible moment he would not forget.

"Yes, I am Faint Chance. You are Cameron Harrington," she stated, not as a question, but more of a statement.

"Yes, and I have heard such wonderful things about you."

"I am honored to meet the brother of Spencer, brother-in-law of Candice, who both have honored me so," she announced like an ambassador of a foreign country making a formal introduction. Cameron thought that she must have practiced it beforehand. The poor thing, he thought, so concerned about having to impress his family so as to not become a burden on them to come over to the US.

She continued, "I am here to take care of you, and to help you in any way that I may be able. I have also heard wonderful things about you."

My God, Cameron thought. He could see why Spencer and Candice were so infatuated with this girl. A person could grow addicted to her in a big hurry.

She said, "Following your brother's instructions, I came ahead yesterday, and took a room here. I was able to fly up yesterday from Vientiane. Your brother and sister-in-law sent me a fortune in money, one thousand dollars, just for this trip and to help you. But as it is so much more than I need I will be able to save enough to pay for my journey to your country when the papers are issued to me allowing me to come."

She continued, "I have taken a room here at this hotel, and have prepared it for you."

She took him to the inside of the cottage. She had cut flowers from the outside with which she decorated the room. "I hope this will be satisfactory for you," she said. The room had what appeared to be a king-sized bed, although the dimensions were not quite the same as in the US. The bed was not high – it was only coffee table height. The floor was made of teak planks, each five inches in width, and they were not quite flush together, such that there was a little slit between them the width of a piece of paper so the ground below could be seen.

The bathroom was to the rear of the bedroom, done in white tile, with an angled ceiling. The back wall was concrete rather than wicker with several angled slits built in the concrete for ventilation for which there was no cover. The weather must always be warm, he thought. The shower was a wand that would spray you and the rest of the bathroom, as there was no shower curtain or enclosure. There was a western toilet, which was a comforting sight, and there was a short hose beside it on the wall, with a sort of trigger that you would expect to see on a watering hose. It was a form of bidet, he figured.

"How much is this room?" he asked her.

"Twenty thousand kip," she responded. That sounded like a lot. He did a quick mental calculation. It was only four dollars.

"So cheap!"

"I can stay on the floor, as the bed is for you. I stayed in the bed last night, and it is very nice," she said. "But I made sure they put clean linen on for you, and I hope everything will be to your liking."

"My God!" he said. "At these rates I could take the whole place! Why don't I get you another cottage for yourself? Or one for me?" he added, thinking that it might be more polite to let her keep her things in this room, but then wondering about the flowers she had obtained somewhere.

"Whatever you would like," she said.

Cameron began to get a few thoughts from that remark, but then realized that it was probably just her way of being polite, open and giving. "I will not have you sleeping on any floor. Let's go take a second cottage," he said, and went to the door, to go get the proprietor. Faint Chance followed behind, to interpret or help as might be necessary.

The proprietor was up at the front cottage, brushing the

varnish on it from a gallon-sized can. When asked if he had a nearby room, he said, "The nearest one is just across." Asked the price, he said, "Twenty thousand kip."

"Is there any room tax or service charge?" Cameron asked.

"No, that is the full price," the man said. "There are no other charges, unless you eat in the restaurant, which is extra."

"I will take the room," Cameron said. The proprietor went for a key inside, and led them to the room. It was then that Cameron began to truly realize what Spencer and Candice were referring to when they said that Lao was more nearly a frontier than any other place, with such hotel rates!

Cameron took the new room, since he had not opened his bag yet and Faint Chance was already set up in the first one. He told her, "I will shower and rest. Can we meet in an hour?"

"I will be waiting for you," she promised.

After refreshing, Cameron walked out onto his front porch. Faint Chance saw him and came to join him for a walk about the compound to admire the flowers.

"How are Spencer and Candice?" she asked.

"They are wonderful, and send you their regards. They are very anxious to have you come over just as soon as you can come."

"And how is Devan?"

Cameron said, "He is a very gifted child. He is only four months old, and he already walks and talks. He is getting lessons from a tutor, and has the intelligence of someone several years of age or more. He is absolutely amazing! They believe you are responsible for it. Are you aware of that?"

"I knew he would be special," she said, "when I summoned the spirits."

Cameron realized that her view of the powers of the plant were quite different than those of his scientist sister-in-law.

"I got two letters from Spencer and Candice, and they told me he was special. And when they called me about this trip, I heard some things about Devan. But I would like you to tell me more."

Cameron said, "Devan is more than special. He is extraordinary. When he was only a month old, he could say his name. At two months, he was speaking. He is learning things all the time at an accelerated rate. He is more coordinated and mentally able than some kids are at several years of age. He is quite in control of himself, and has no fits of crying as other children do. I do not have experience with children, but I am very impressed. Frankly he is the only child I have ever liked."

"I am so happy everything turned out well."

"Candice is studying Devan's DNA at her lab at this time."

"What is DNA?"

"Deoxyribonucleic acid. It is a generic term for any of the nucleic acids which yield deoxyribose on hydrolysis, and which store genetic information." After speaking, he realized that he sounded a bit pedantic. He then added, "She studies things like what differences Devan has from his own parents and other humans."

"Can she study the special abilities that the spirits gave Devan?"

"Well, yes. She can study how he is different from others."

"Did you study science as well as architecture?" she asked, leaving the subject, which was a welcome relief to Cameron.

"No. All you have to do is just go over to Spencer and Candice's house for dinner now and then, and you can't help but learn a few terms!" He then chuckled.

"I am to go and live with them when my papers come through, and I am hopeful to be able to learn a little of such things as well. They are both very smart doctors."

"Yes, they are both published researchers."

"Please tell me about you," she said, as they walked among the sunlit flowers of the compound. "I understand you are a very successful architect. What sort of things do you design?"

"I design homes and small commercial buildings."

"I am hopeful to see your work when I come to America," she said, which made him feel quite proud.

She formed a serious expression and said, "You are here to get more of the *ton mai piiset*. Spencer and Candice told me to take you to my village and ask for more."

"Yes, that is why I am here. Are you worried about that?" Cameron asked.

"Yes."

"What worries you?"

"I am not sure that the spirits in the plant will be taken out of Lao to America."

"What do you think may happen?"

"I really don't know, but I have a feeling of fear."

"Candice wants a sample of the plant, and believes that she can synthesize it in the lab to make it available to everyone. In other words, she wants to make more of it in a laboratory."

"I do not believe it will work without the prayers. Do you?"

Shit! Cameron thought. Now she is putting me to the test. If I tell her I don't believe the mumbo-jumbo about spirits, I may not have her faith and trust. On the other hand, I will also lose it if she knows or finds out I am lying when I say that I do believe in the spirits. What do I say?

"I am only an architect, not a scientist. I really don't know. Perhaps there is a way to add the prayers to whatever she can make in the lab."

"I love architecture," she said backing out of the subject, much to the relief of Cameron.

"After we go to the village, on your return, I will show you some of the Laotian architecture if you would like. We can look in Vientiane and possibly in Luang Prabang."

That came as a big relief! He worried for a moment that she was going to put him through the inquisition over a battle of her beliefs versus the scientific ones of the doctors. One cannot win in any religious battle. On the other hand, maybe she was just testing him subtly. What was she thinking?

They came to the back end of the courtyard, to the hotel's small restaurant. The sides were open without windows or doors. There were metal roll-down curtains for the night, that were now down during all hours of operation. The afternoon was hot, and Cameron was thirsty. A woman who was obviously the owner's wife was behind a small counter on a high stool where the bills were prepared, engaged in bookkeeping. She appeared in her forties. Instead of letting her legs dangle down from the high stool, she put them on a shelf on the counter in front of her, so that she was almost in the same seating position that she would be if she was squatting on her ankles as so many of the Asians do.

The restaurant was "L" shaped, and the counter was in the corner of the "L", in-between the two openings in the walls. They sat at a table and were close enough to tell her their order without her getting up. Cameron was a little afraid to take just anything, worried about getting sick. He had very little travel experience.

"A Lao beer," he said to the lady.

"Coffee," Faint Chance said, and then said something in Lao.

The lady nodded without saying anything and went to the kitchen hidden behind an oriental screen blocking the doorway to the rear.

"What was it you added to your order?" Cameron asked.

"I wanted to be sure that it was the good coffee. Lao has some of the best coffees, but the good kind is sent for export. It is grown up here in the mountains, and so it is available here. They have it."

The lady arrived with the beer and coffee. "Would you like to try the coffee?" Faint Chance asked.

Cameron took a sip as he had never heard of Lao coffee, and curiosity had overcome him. "This is delicious!"

"Have you never had Lao coffee?" she asked.

"I confess that I have never had anything from Lao. I have never seen Lao coffee in any store."

"Was it much of an inconvenience for you to take time off work from the shop where you work?" he asked her.

She answered, "I asked if I could take time off from the shop for a while. I asked my father, and he said it would be all right. He thought it would be a good idea for me to go back to the village one day, as I have not been back since I left years ago. This is my chance. I might not have had the chance if this opportunity had not come along. I am so fortunate."

Cameron shifted the conversation to the plant, "How are we to go about getting this plant?"

Faint Chance said, "The Chief, if he is still alive, must allow us to have some of the plant. Without his approval and help, we would not be able to find the place where it grows. We must go to him, and ask him if he will give us some of it, or, take us to where it grows so that we can get some ourselves."

"Do you think he might not let us have it?" Cameron asked,

worried his long trip might all be in vain.

"I cannot say. But I am sure that the Chief would not want the news of the existence of the plant out because many strangers would begin to come and ruin the peaceful life the villagers have."

"When are we going off to the village?" he asked.

"I have planned for us to leave the day after tomorrow. We have to make some preparations first. We can do that tomorrow, and leave the following morning," she told him. "We will need to find a *tuk-tuk* with the ability to go up a rough mountain road, and we will need supplies. The *tuk-tuk* will not be able to go the entire way. We will have to go in on foot after the *tuk-tuk* can go no further. We will need camping gear.

"Why don't we take a walk down towards the river, as it is too late now to go into town for supplies," Faint Chance said.

"I will grab Candice's camera, and then let's go."

She led him on a stroll towards the river, the other direction from town. Along the way, Cameron, always the architect, observed the way the houses were built. The structures varied considerably in how they were made. There were some primitive structures made of natural materials, and some modern ones of concrete. He took several pictures of the ones that interested him.

After a time, they came to the Mekong River. Leading to the river was a long, concrete ramp used for loading and unloading boats. At the bottom in the water were a dozen or more long, green painted boats of different sizes. The larger ones looked like a family might live on the boat themselves. Cameron took a few pictures.

"Now some with you," he said to her. He realized that Faint Chance should be in his pictures, and put her in the forefront. "Smile!" he told her as he snapped off some shots of her in front of the boats.

Chapter Thirty-Four

Later, they met at the hotel restaurant. In the hard-working tradition of Laotians, the owner's wife kept it open from six to nine. She did not seem to speak English, or at least she did not verbalize it. It was still quite light at seven thirty when they sat down to dinner. There were others now in the restaurant, and also moving about the courtyard. Three girls worked at the restaurant, but they had other duties as well, and the restaurant was hardly full. Cameron noticed the restaurant had an opening to the street in the back, but did not appear to have much business from outside the compound. In the compound, he counted sixteen cottages. The few guests he saw were European students who were on a tight budget.

Cameron remembered once seeing an old book *Europe on Five Dollars a Day*, and, although he had not read it and it was undoubtedly quite dated now, he figured that a person could actually travel in Lao on five dollars per day. The students quickly find out with their ingenuity how to get about and have an adventure on a modest income – and Lao was certainly a perfect spot for that. There was one European family, a balding man of thirty-five, his wife and two very young girls, one in a pram, and the other toted in backpack apparatus. Earlier, he looked around the area, saw that around the back of the small restaurant was a wood-fired stove. Apparently the electricity was used only for the refrigeration and lights. These people do work hard, Cameron thought to himself when he saw the wood-fired stove.

Cameron noticed several bottles of liquor and wine on display on a table against a wall, for sale by the bottle. The owner had apparently bought them in town and kept them there for the convenience of his guests. No liquor control like back home, Cameron mused as he thought about it.

A western girl sat at the next table, reading a book. She wore ankle-high hiking shoes with canvas tops and rubber-cleated soles, the antithesis of feminine. But, they certainly looked practical. She wore jeans and a rustic jacket that went to her knees. It was not a very flattering outfit, for what seemed to be an otherwise attractive girl. Cameron spoke to her when she looked at him. "Hi, I am from the US."

"Canada," she said. "A friend and I are backpacking, and only today splurging on a hotel."

"Have you been traveling long?" Cameron asked.

"Six months, so far. We are traveling as long as our money holds out. We have been in China, and are going back to some parts we have not been to. Because we don't have much money, we are traveling only in areas where it is very cheap. Lao and China are the cheapest."

Cameron had forgotten about such things as traveling on minimal expense, as he had been out of school too long. Imagine splurging on a four-dollar hotel, he thought! "You are very adventurous, camping in such places," he said to her. "Have you run into any trouble?"

"Not really. We have been sick a few times, but so far, so good," she said, and went back to her book.

Looking at the scotch for sale by the bottle, he wondered how much it cost in Lao. Although he had a bottle of scotch in his bag, he was interested to see how much the scotch was as he was sitting right across from it.

"How much is the scotch?" he asked the owner's wife.

"Eighty-five thousand kip," she said. She apparently could handle enough English to handle the cost of things.

"God, that sounds like a lot," he said. Then he calculated and said, "But actually, that is only twenty dollars for my favorite scotch! This is a very civilized country indeed!" he proudly announced to Faint Chance, who looked as if she had no idea what he was talking about.

He pondered that this country was not yet government-saddled enough to have oppressive taxes, and how Europe and America had diminished freedom with their appetite for spending on social causes with ever-increasing taxes. Taxes themselves were Satan, he thought, cloaked in disguise. Imposing large taxes on liquor, cars, and the like was just a way of preventing people from having a better life, he postulated, while picking up the scotch bottle from those on display for sale, and taking it as a spare. Nothing like being prepared!

Cameron asked Faint Chance, "Would you like some scotch before dinner? Or something else?" he added, realizing that he had not given much option in the question, as he was so pleased to see the scotch that he enjoyed so much.

"I will have just a little," she said to him. Cameron opened the bottle, and poured out some for them, neat. After a sip, he dropped in an ice cube in his from a bowl of several cubes that had been brought to the table, due to the heat. They sipped the scotch as the meal was being prepared by the owner's wife in the back.

There were four other tables occupied. He could, for the most part, talk without being heard by anyone else if he kept his voice down. He did not want to broadcast his journey or its purpose, as he did not want some other tourists joining in the conversation to inquire about it. Faint Chance seemed to understand perfectly that the conversation should be done in a manner that did not disclose to any others nearby what it was fully about.

They ordered from the menu, with Faint Chance taking care of interpreting. The main courses were vegetables fried with meat.

Waiting for the food, she asked, "Have you married? When your brother was here, he said you were not married at that time."

"No, I am still single," he told her. And he was glad, now that he was in the presence of such a beautiful girl. "I will show you about when you come to America." He thought that he could hardly get a more attractive date than her, and how proud he would be to show her off to his friends. He would be the object of their envy. He was unsure if she would go for that sort of thing, as he thought, as he knew so little of her ways.

"I still do not have my visa yet. I cannot yet go to America."

"Has anyone given you a date as to when it will come?"

"No."

"Spencer and Candice wanted to come, but could not, as I am sure they told you. They have used up their holidays at work with that year-long sabbatical. And, of course, there is now Devan to take care of," Cameron said. "So here I am," he added, opening his hands and smiling as though to present himself on stage.

The food arrived, and, to Cameron's relief, it was not so strange that he could not enjoy it. He shifted the conversation to her, to try to take himself out of the limelight. This girl had a way of making you feel important. "Is there any special reason as to why you did not go back to the village that you lived in?" Cameron asked.

"Travel is expensive, and it is a long journey. But I have always wanted to, and so this trip will be very wonderful for me, too," she said.

Cameron said, "If we get the plant, we must tell Spencer and Candice not to reveal much about where the plant comes from. Perhaps they could state, when it comes out, that it comes from some completely different place in Lao, or even a different country. Or even better, that they simply invented it. But then, that would be difficult to do in the science journals. In any case, we must not ruin the village with a deluge of interested people, who would no doubt come by the thousands. The village would become a fishbowl for onlookers."

A sense of evil came over her as she thought of exposing the secret of the village to the outside world.

"Where do we go to find the special *tuk-tuk* for the journey?" he asked, turning the topic to the immediate problem of transportation.

She said, "I spoke to the owner of the hotel earlier. I asked him about where to find a *tuk-tuk* that could take us into the jungle. It seems that there are more than one kind. Some have a smaller motor than others, according to him, and when I told him we wanted to go on a jungle expedition, he said we needed to find one with a bigger motor. He said he knows of a fellow who has one, and who offers his services with it for expeditions into some of the remote villages. He said he would be going into town later on in the morning, and would find him for us and tell him we are interested in his service. I did not tell him where we are going, other than to tell him that you wanted to see some of the villages as a tourist."

Cameron asked, "Can we take a *tuk-tuk* close into the village?"

She replied, "No. The *tuk-tuk* can take us to the end of the road. The road in that direction will not be paved after a short time, and is a sandy, rough road, and the *tuk-tuk* will not be able to go very fast. The *tuk-tuk* can only take us in part of the way. We will still have a fairly long journey. The trip in the *tuk-tuk* should take a day, and then we will have to walk in the rest of the way."

"How far do we have to walk into the jungle?"

"I think I misspoke. I mean 'hike', not 'walk'. Yes, that is the better word," she corrected.

"How far do we have to hike?" he asked.

"It depends on the conditions, the path and the weather, and on how fast we hike. It is in the mountains, and the path may be narrow, and difficult at places," she said. "My guess is that we can make it in three days if all goes well. We could run into some very heavy rain, and that will slow us down."

"Jesus! No one told me I would be on a three-day hike!"

"Spencer did not ask that in the call," she replied.

"I get it! No one asked, so you did not mention it!" he smiled, making it into a joke. The worried look he had put on her face by his concern left when he smiled, and she smiled slightly in return.

"I imagined the call from America must have been expensive, so I did not want to waste his money," she said.

"Did you bring any suitable clothes and shoes?" she asked. "Those shoes you have on," she said, looking at his slip-on loafers, "will not do."

"I did bring sort of hiking-styled shoes, as my extra pair, by coincidence," he said. "They are not hiking boots, but ankle-high tie shoes with those cleated rubber soles that are popular now. They are kind of like hiking shoes. They will do." He wondered if he could ever buy something like a hiking boot in Ban Houei Sai, and doubted it, remembering how small the town was.

"Although it will not be very cold, the highlands at night will be cooler than here in Ban Houei Sai. I bought some things for us in Vientiane with a little of the money your brother and sister-in-law sent. I bought backpacks, sleeping bags and a fold-up tent."

"Well, Spencer and Candice did not tell me that I needed any such things. Do you think it may rain?" he asked.

"Quite likely at this time of year," she said. "This is the rainy season. The rain can be very hard in the wet monsoon. Let us go into the central part of town tomorrow to find things we will need on the trip."

Having finished their meal, they walked up to the area of their cottages, taking the bottle with them that he bought at the restaurant. "Let's sit out here at the tables," leading her to the teak table and two chairs on his cottage porch. She followed, and joined him at the table.

"Would you like another drink?"

"I will have another if you are," she told him. He went for the glasses inside and poured two glasses, setting them at the table in front of each of the two chairs on the ends of the porch table. They sat at the ends of the small table, and looked at one another, in a romantic way.

He lifted the scotch and took a sip. As he soaked up the tropical evening, he looked across the teak table at the beautiful creature and said, "You must tell me your story about your life and the village life first-hand."

He prepared to relax the evening away before retiring, drink in hand. And so did she, and he became mesmerized. Cameron realized that was very enticing and that there was a very distinct possibility of him falling for such a girl of Asian blood, something that he had not previously considered.

After an hour, having come a long way that day, starting from Chiang Rai, Thailand, checking out of the hotel, then traveling by car, then boat, and into Lao, Cameron realized that he was exhausted. He told her, "I am very tired now, but I have enjoyed hearing your story. I heard it from Spencer and Candice, but it is much better first-hand. If you will excuse me, I really must go to bed. Whoever is up first, wake the other."

She bowed her head to him in the style of the *nop*, and said, "Goodnight, Cameron. I have been honored to meet you."

Chapter Thirty-Five

Cameron was up early, just before daybreak. He went outside, and walked about the compound as the morning light introduced itself to the day. The light of the morning was over to the east, not yet overhead at six, when the owner's wife opened the metal door to the restaurant. It was a door of ten feet in width that rolled up. The restaurant was thus open to the atmosphere all the time while open for business. The temperature must be stable enough not to close off the doorways, he thought. There was no heat or air conditioning. Cameron saw the owner's wife moving about inside getting it ready for the day.

"Coffee?" he asked her – she did not do too well with lengthy sentences in English. One word seemed to work well.

She nodded and went to the kitchen. While waiting, he walked about to look at the flowers and plants in the courtyard.

One of the young girls who worked there brought out the coffee after ten minutes. She did not speak any English. Cameron sipped the coffee, as the sun crept into the courtyard.

The owner's wife came back out, and Cameron told her, "It is wonderful coffee."

She responded, but Cameron did not understand what she said. He wondered why he had not so much as heard of Lao coffee. He had sampled Jamaican and Hawaiian coffees, both good but expensive. Indian and Brazilian coffees were equally good and much cheaper. He had never seen it for sale in America. Then again, he realized, he had hardly even heard of Lao. The only people, excluding his brother and sister-in-law, whom he had ever met who had been to Lao, were still under the impression that they were still under orders to not reveal that they had been there – those were pilots that had rained bombs on Lao during the Vietnam folly of the American government. Waiting for the sun to fully illuminate the day, sipping the delicious coffee, he thought about the military action in Lao years earlier, and the bombing of Lao on the Ho Chi Minh trail. He thought of the lack of ability of some that governed America, especially those who conducted a war in a way destined to lose.

But then, he thought, who was he to criticize? It was nice being an architect and not in politics. He stopped thinking of such things and brought his focus on the surroundings, realizing that he should not be wasting the beauty of the trip by wasting time on politics like an Irishman in a pub, and should concentrate on taking in as much as he could on this trip. The sun was now bringing bright rays of light to the picturesque flowers and teak trees of the compound.

Appearing from her cottage was Faint Chance, who illuminated the day more so than the sunlight. She approached the restaurant with a big smile.

"Did you sleep properly?" she asked him as she approached.

What a strange way to put it, he thought to himself. Then again, this is a strange place. He almost said that he slept like a log, but he stopped himself, as he realized how funny that would sound if she had not heard the expression. Odd, as he thought of it, comparing oneself to a fallen tree.

"Yes, I did. I slept 'properly'." He utilized her choice of words. "And you?"

"Yes, thank you," she said.

"What shall we order for breakfast?" he asked her. "I am hungry. But I fear I cannot communicate what to order."

To help him get along, she gave some instruction, "To say 'I am hungry' in Lao, you say '*koy heo kao*'. It literally means 'hunger rice'. Or, you can say '*kay yahk kin kao*', which literally means 'I want eat rice'. To say 'I am thirsty', you say '*koy heo nahm*'. That means 'hunger water'. Or you can say '*koy yahk kin nahm*'. That means literally 'I want consume water'."

Cameron laughed lightly. "How strange to define 'hunger' as 'a want for rice'." Then he tried several times to get the sayings right, and she helped him as he repeated them clumsily.

She looked at the menu in Lao, and asked him, "Do you like rice noodle soup? The soup is '*mee nam*'."

Trying his best to get the accent right, he said, "*Koy yahk kin mee nam.*"

"That's right!" she complimented. "You are doing well!"

Rays of the sun changed their angle as they sat, and the brightness of the day intensified. The noodles came in steaming bowls and were placed on the table by one of the young female assistants to the owner's wife.

Cameron tried his as Faint Chance was busy adding some additional spice from a small plate provided. "This is delicious!" he said.

"To say that in Lao, say '*Ahn-nee sehb lie-lie*'," she told him.

"*Ahn-nee sehb lie-lie*," he repeated after her.

As they ate, they watched the sun intensify its rays on the flowers and the trees through the large opening in the wall they sat next to. When the owner came by, Faint Chance spoke to him in Lao. "The owner has told us where we can go in town for provisions for the trip, and where we can find a good *tuk-tuk* to go into the mountains."

At nine in the morning they reconvened and hailed a *tuk-tuk* to take them downtown in a short trip in the small town. Faint Chance spoke to the driver in Lao, and then to Cameron. "He will take us to the shop the hotel owner spoke of."

At the provisions store, they walked about looking at things they might need. The store was only sixteen feet square, not exactly the sort of sporting goods store Cameron was accustomed to at home.

"Let's get some of these canned foods," Faint Chance said, "but not too much." Cameron picked out four cans of food and took them to the counter.

"How about this papaya?" Cameron said.

"If we eat it in a few days it will be good," Faint Chance said, and so they added that. Spencer picked up some fresh bananas. Dried, processed meat in a plastic bag looked light and edible. Those were added to their supplies.

Cameron said, "What about water?"

Faint Chance said, "Let's take the plastic bottled water. We can refill the bottles from mountain streams, and also at the village for the return."

They purchased the provisions, and looked about the store to see if there was something else they might need. On the shelf were a machete two-and-a-half feet long with a wooden handle, and a leather sheath with belt loop.

Picking up the small machete, she said, "This may be a good thing to carry, even though we should travel as lightly as we can."

"Good idea," he agreed. He took it, and held it as though to be cutting brush.

They walked down the street to the place that the proprietor had told them to look for a special *tuk-tuk* suitable for an expedition. They came to a spot with a more substantial-looking *tuk-tuk* in front, its owner sitting nearby. It had slightly larger wheels, more tread on the tires and a larger engine than the 100 cc kind they had previously seen. It was otherwise the same configuration. Presumably this could go up the mountain roads.

Faint Chance talked to the fellow at some length about where she wanted to go. Cameron just listened, but had no idea what they were saying, other than what he could suspect. The conversation went on for some time. Finally, it looked as though they had reached an agreement, and she turned around and spoke to Cameron.

"I am asking him if he will take us as far as he can go, and then come back again for us later. I think that if we allow a day in the *tuk-tuk*, three days to hike, maybe three days there, and three back, another day in the *tuk-tuk*, and then add another two or three for emergencies so he doesn't leave us, that would be about right. What do you think?"

"You are the boss," he said to her. "How much does he want?"

She spoke to the driver at some length. After a time, she then spoke to Cameron.

"He will give his *tuk-tuk* a service today, to make sure it is in good order, and then tomorrow we will go. He will take us into the mountain jungles for the day, as far as he can go, and then come back for us in ten days. He will wait for us for three more days in case we are late. The price will be three hundred thousand kip. But he will charge an additional five thousand kip for each day that we do not return and he has to stay overnight in the *tuk-tuk*. But he only has to wait three days, and then he can return without us."

162

Cameron translated that into dollars. "That is roughly seventy dollars. Tell him we agree."

She told that to the driver, and they discussed the matter and repeated it a few times to make sure they both had it correctly. They reached an agreement, and the deal was done. The driver told them that he will finish the service, get some extra gas in cans, and be done in two or three hours. He told them that, if they wished, he could take them somewhere that afternoon in his vehicle, saying he would be accepting no jobs until after he had dropped them off in the mountains the following day.

They looked at each other approvingly. They had obtained a bonus of a chauffeured vehicle to take them about that afternoon. After all, they had already collected their provisions, and all they had left to do was make arrangements at the hotel to store their bags for them while they were gone. Faint Chance spoke again to the driver in Lao.

"I have asked him where we might go this afternoon. He says there is a spot he thinks you would enjoy seeing not far away. It is a very small village, of only forty or fifty people, where there is a lady who makes Laotian whisky. Apparently, the majority of the village is supported by her, and they collect the supplies she needs for the whisky."

She continued, "We will return before dark tonight, and then make our final preparations. We will leave the hotel early in the morning, at daybreak, so as to utilize the daylight to its best advantage. Is that agreeable? There will be no further charge for the driver for today's service."

"Sounds perfect to me!" he said.

She told the driver in Lao that they could use a ride back to the hotel to drop off their provisions, and that he should come for them after he had serviced his *tuk-tuk*, at noon. He agreed, and off they went to the hotel.

At the hotel, they took in the provisions and packed them in the backpacks that Faint Chance had bought.

On the patio waiting for the *tuk-tuk* driver to come back for them, Faint Chance said, "The ramp we went to at the river is for the slow boats down the river. The fast boats are on the other end of town. On our return trip, I plan to take you down the river to

Luang Prabang. There we can fly to Vientiane. You have a choice of either the slow boat or the fast boat."

She continued, "The slow boat takes two days to get to Luang Prabang, the fast boat only one. On the slow boat, it is necessary to spend the night halfway at a place called Pak Bang. The fast boat makes the trip in one day, and only stops at Pak Bang as a checkpoint."

The *tuk-tuk* driver arrived at the back side of the hotel, right by the restaurant. "There he is," Faint Chance said to Cameron when she saw him pull up. They went to the blue *tuk-tuk* and stepped up in the back. It was open on the sides, with a metal top that curved down slightly. There were three very thin horizontal bars to hold the structure together with an occasional vertical post, all three-eighths of an inch in diameter. Each side in the back had a shelf seat that extended from the front to the back, and they each took a side, sitting on the metal seats – there were no cushions. Off they went to see Laotian whisky being made.

The place where the local whisky was made was a little over an hour away. When they arrived in the small village, there was a woman working under a canvas tarp supported with bamboo. The woman looked to be twenty-five. She was hard at work, and had dust and some smears of something on her pretty face. There were two black metal barrels there, two feet apart. They looked to be the size of the fifty-five-gallon metal barrels that were common in America. Each had a small dugout underneath, and logs were burning underneath. The top had a pipe coming in, pouring in cold water from a mountain stream source. There was a pan inside the top that the cold water went into, and it drained the cold water out and towards the road.

These were stills, Cameron realized. The cold mountain water was to condense the steam inside. Nearby were thirty ceramic pots, fifteen-gallon size, covered with some sort of natural material on top that was tied around with string. A pipe stuck out of each still below the water condenser pan, from which a clear fluid dripped. The nearest one was dripping into an old, light-green, plastic, one gallon, British Petroleum container, which had the top cut off. The sight of the motor oil container to catch the whisky amused Cameron. It was a very makeshift container to catch the finished product.

Faint Chance spoke to the lady off and on, and the lady explained the process. Faint Chance interpreted for Cameron. "The name of it is 'Lao Lao'," Faint Chance explained.

"The ceramic bowls have sticky rice in them, and water. Also added is a special local mushroom," Faint Chance said, after interchanges with the lady. Her house, which was also the supply warehouse, was only ten feet away. She went inside to get one of the special mushrooms. She held it up, and passed it to Cameron to examine. It was nearly black in color, and hard. It must have been dried out for some time.

"She says that mushroom is used in the making of Lao Lao in the north here, but some other things that are used to make it work in the south," Faint Chance went on, interpreting. "This mushroom only grows here in the north. It is what makes northern Lao Lao different from southern Lao Lao."

Faint Chance continued to interpret, "Sticky rice is put in the bowls with water, and some of the mushrooms are added. The bowls are then covered, and left to stand for fifteen days. Then they are ready to be put over in those," she interpreted, pointing to the stills. Cameron heard names given the things she was pointing at, but the names apparently did not translate well into English, or more likely, Faint Chance did not know the English equivalents.

Cameron assumed the sticky rice fermented, and then it was distilled in the barrels. As they spoke, the British Petroleum plastic container filled, and the lady had to go to the still and change it. She put another in its place, and brought over the full one to them. She had glasses nearby, and poured out two. Cameron wondered if she sampled it often, as the glasses were handy. The lady passed a glass to them. It was still very warm from just coming out of the still.

"Not bad!" Cameron said aloud, expecting burnt diesel oil. Faint Chance interpreted to Laotian for the lady, but it was obvious, and the lady gave a big smile.

"How much of this do you make in a day?" Cameron asked.

"Two hundred and seventy bottles a day," Faint Chance interpreted.

They looked about at the supplies, and Cameron marveled at the differences in making an alcoholic beverage in Lao versus in the West with the west's industrialization and health standards. They sipped the drink, and had another, as the lady tended the stills.

Faint Chance spoke to the lady and then said, "She supports most of this village, and they collect the supplies for her, in barter."

"Sort of a one-purpose town," Cameron joked. Actually, it wasn't too bad, he thought, and asked for more. But then, she was the only bar in town.

Chapter Thirty-Six

The next morning, Faint Chance came out of her cottage to the restaurant where Cameron was waiting at daybreak, sipping his newly-discovered Lao coffee. She was wearing faded, button-front blue jeans, and ankle-high tan walking shoes with rubber soles like hiking shoes, only more stylish. She had on a pale-blue knit top, and she looked very sexy. Cameron tried to keep his mind off her body, but it was not easy. She had a natural sway in her walk, which made ignoring her impossible.

"Good morning!" Cameron greeted her. "Did you sleep properly?" He thought that he would try it on her.

"Yes, thank you, I did. Did you also sleep properly?"

"Yes, very good. I see our driver is all ready to go," he told her.

The driver was already faithfully waiting just outside the gate. They checked their gear again to make sure they had everything, and she took a coffee. He had already ordered the noodle soup for two, and it was just arriving.

The owner came by, and Faint Chance told him in Lao, pointing to their bags that were stacked up against the wall, "Hold our bags for us. We should be back in ten days, or a few more." The owner acknowledged this and took them to the back side of the restaurant room where there were other bags and guests' laundry.

They went through the town in the same direction that they had gone in to see the Lao Lao whisky being made. However, the driver took a different fork in the road sometime after they left the town before they came upon the Lao Lao place. The road was largely paved in town, but after that it turned to dirt and sand. It was the local highway, and there was an occasional other vehicle. Cameron estimated their cruising speed to be nearly thirty-five miles per hour, but once in a while the driver would slow to five miles per hour or even less to avoid being tossed in the air by large ruts.

They passed some beautiful valleys, and luscious green land-scapes. Cameron took out Candice's camera and took a few photos, a gamble of questionable quality due to the bouncing vehicle.

After another three hours of bouncing about, they came to a small roadside place that was near a very small village that they could see from the road. There was nothing for sale, and no store to buy anything from. The driver pulled up and looked back to see if Faint Chance wanted to stop. She said something to the driver and he stopped.

Cameron stretched and walked about to recover from the bouncy ride. "Should we take some papaya?" he asked Faint Chance.

"That would be good," she said, and Cameron got one of the pieces and cut off a little. He gave a piece to Faint Chance, and also to the driver.

"Is this the last village before the mountain village we are going to?" Cameron asked.

"I do not know, as I have not been anywhere near here for years, and then I was little." She consulted with the driver, and turned back to Cameron. "The driver says that we will pass close to another village later on, but it is not directly on the road."

After they pulled out of the village, and were almost out of sight, another *tuk-tuk* pulled in the village and two men got out to take a break. They were Japanese.

A half hour later, a small dirt and sand road came up on the left. Faint Chance told the driver to go in that direction. It was the direction of the higher mountains. Their speed slowed as the road was not as good. Water that had passed over the road had created dips, and slowed them to a walking speed at many spots. In places water was streaming over the road on its way down the mountain, but not deep enough to stall the *tuk-tuk*. There was no other traffic or people anywhere for over an hour, until they finally came upon a young man riding an elephant going in the same direction.

"A working elephant," Cameron said.

"Yes," Faint Chance said. "The man uses him for work. He is very lucky to have an elephant, but the elephant eats a lot."

"Hah! 'Eats a lot'." Cameron said. "That is funny. That should be his name."

The *tuk-tuk* driver went around the elephant at the first opportunity. Cameron and Faint Chance held on in the back tightly as they bounced along, up and down on the sandy road. The jungle growth smacked the sides of the *tuk-tuk* much of the time. The sides and the back of the *tuk-tuk* were open except for the three little horizontal strips of round metal that did their best to keep out the slapping green foliage trying to whip in and smack them.

The road seemed to endlessly wind up a gradual trail up the mountains. The road did not wind back and forth like a road climbing a big cliff. Rather, it just curved from side to side, with an occasional sharp turn to go around some huge rock or miss a cliff. The driver did a good job, all in all. Once in a while an obstacle would come up with little notice, and the driver would come down hard on the brakes, and the two of them in the rear would be propelled to the front part of the back of the *tuk-tuk*, even though hanging on with both hands. The hard bouncing about was seasoned with occasional light rain lasting usually only several minutes.

Three hours outside the last stop at the small village, Cameron felt he was about to scream for a break when they came to a scenic spot where there was a widening of the road and a good place to stop. It was a level spot fifty feet wide, on a cliff, next to which the mountain dropped away steeply.

It was not more than five hundred feet or so to the bottom, but they had been in such thick jungle growth that they could hardly see much at all most of the time.

On the cliff, the view surrounding the area was spectacular. The sky was a strange combination of heavy broken clouds surrounding parts of the mountain tops, but there was an equal amount of bright rays of sunlight coming in-between them. It was an eerie sight, one that Cameron had never seen. It gave a sense of entering a strange land.

As he took a picture with the camera that Candice had lent him, he said to Faint Chance, "I feel like I am going into a strange land looking for King Kong."

"What is King Kong?" Faint Chance asked.

"Oh, never mind. It is from an old movie," Cameron said.

"Are you ready to get going?" she asked.

"Yes," he told her. They mounted the *tuk-tuk* and drove on.

After three hours, they came to a clearing with a small stream in its middle. There were huge rocks in the stream, and, even though it was only a foot or two deep, there was no way for a vehicle to cross it. And, just ahead of it, was another small mountain, giving no place for a vehicle to go if it went on.

"I guess this is the end of the trip for the *tuk-tuk*," Cameron said.

The *tuk-tuk* stopped, and Faint Chance began talking in Lao to the driver. This was clearly the end of the road. There was a pathway to the left and to the right as well, and it was obvious to Cameron that each was a path to some village. One would take them to their destination, he figured.

Faint Chance spoke at some length to the driver as they took their gear out of the back of the *tuk-tuk*, and made ready for the trip. Cameron did not understand a word. Cameron noticed that even questions do not give themselves away to the westerner, as in Laotian a question does not end by a raising of the tone.

Faint Chance then turned to Cameron and said, "I have told the driver to return there in ten days. I have told him I do not know what day we will return, but that he should try to be at this spot at midday if possible so that they could get back to the main road before dark for the return trip. I have told him that if we are not here on the tenth day, that he should sleep in his vehicle for three more days, in case we are delayed. I told him that if we are not back after three full days' waiting, that he go and report us to the military to come and look for us. I have told him what direction we are going."

Cameron asked, "And just what might happen to us?"

"Well, there are a number of things that might delay our return. Difficulty in finding the plant, heavy rain, getting lost, injury and several other things," she said. "And, if the Chief is still alive, I will want to visit for some time. It would also be very rude to rush off."

"Getting lost!" he said excitedly. "In the jungle! And what are the 'other things'?"

"It is best not to think of the dangers. Let us go on," Faint Chance said. "I have looked at a map, and spoken to people, and believe we will not get lost. There is a pathway there, and there may be occasional hunters, and other villagers working fields that we can talk to if we take a wrong turn. So don't worry," she said with a big smile.

The driver stood by politely. Faint Chance repeated her instructions to him several times, asking him to repeat them back to her. There was daylight left, and they set off on foot towards the village.

The driver waited for them to walk off and out of sight before he left to drive back to Ban Houei Sai. As they walked along, she said, "I did not tell him where we are going exactly, to protect our purpose at your instructions. I told him that you were exploring remote villages and the local ways of life, and just told him the general direction we are going in case he has to report us," she said.

Cameron said, "We should make whatever distance we can, and then look for a good place to set up for the night."

After an hour more of hiking, they saw some women carrying on their heads and in their hands wicker baskets of harvest they had just picked. The women were not on the road, and were moving alongside the road, apparently living nearby. Cameron looked over to Faint Chance.

"They live in a village nearby, and are taking back some crops they have harvested," Faint Chance said to him in response to his puzzled look to her.

Soon dusk was upon them, and Cameron noticed that in the mountains the shadows would make it dark sooner. Evaluating spots for a place to camp for the night, they looked about into the very dense forest of tropical vegetation on all sides. Finally, they came upon a place where there was a clearing off to the right of the trail.

"Does this look okay?" Cameron asked her, assuming she

might know better where to stay the night.

"I think so," Faint Chance said. A fallen tree lay ahead, covered with growth at the end of a flat spot in front of it that looked perfect as a place to set up their new tent.

"Let's set up the tent here," Cameron said. They took off their gear, and began to set up the tent just in front of the fallen tree to act as a headboard to their tent.

The tent had bows to set it up with. Faint Chance had just bought it, and had not opened it yet. Cameron struggled with it for a while until he figured it out, and set it up. It was a rounded shape, and was just right for two people. After finishing setting it up, they opened their sleeping bags and placed them inside beside each other in preparation for the night.

Dusk set in, and the partially-cloudy sky cut off the light rapidly. "Here, let's have some of this food," Faint Chance told him, pulling things out of her bag.

Cameron sat down on a rock nearby the tent, looking up at the quickly-darkening sky and asked her, "Do you think it will rain?" He could feel a different wind, coming from the southwest.

Just as he said it, the sky opened up, and a Laotian monsoon rain that Cameron had never seen the likes of came down.

Rapidly, the two scurried inside to hide from the rain that began to fall very hard. The spot they picked for their camp was a little higher than the surrounding ground, and to one side there was a run-off. It looked to them like they had succeeded in setting up where they would remain mostly dry in the event of running water over the terrain.

"Are you hungry?" Faint Chance asked, rummaging through the provisions.

"Starving," he replied. "What is the *spécialité de la mason*?" he mused with her.

"Let's eat the meat we brought. It may not be good tomorrow in this heat," she said.

The storm pounded on the tent as they ate. It came down so hard that it drowned out all other noise. Cameron normally loved the rain, but this was of some concern as it was coming so hard. He worried that the tent might get taken away in some wall of water.

"There is no satellite dish and big screen with this tent," Cameron said as he ate.

"Excuse me?" Faint Chance responded.

"It is just a little joke," Cameron said. "Never mind," realizing they lived, literally, a world apart, and his jokes were not understandable to her. Luxuries he was used to made the primitive camping quite the inconvenience.

"We might as well go to bed, and get up at first light. I hope the rain stops by morning," she told him, as she organized the food back into the bag and put things aside to make room in the small tent for them to sleep.

With the sun setting fast, and the clouds broken, but heavy, darkness came quickly. Cameron had a small flashlight which took two AA batteries. He had propped it up in a corner of the tent and pointed the light up, such that it reflected about the tent almost uniformly, and with a soothing luminescence. The rain cooled down the hot day very quickly – a welcome relief.

Cameron said, "It is a good thing you brought these sleeping bags. It is getting a bit chilly in this rain. I think I will get in, if you don't mind." There was no room to stand up in the tent. He unzipped the bag. He took off his shoes and socks, and wondered how much else to take off in the presence of this girl with God-only-knows-what customs.

She said, "These bags zip to each other so that we can make more warmth with our bodies. Why don't we do that if you are a little chilly?" He did not object, and she then zipped the bottom zipper of the two bags together and then the top. Once done, she then straightened them out, and unzipped the top halfway as though to make a bed turned down and ready for the night.

"Will this do?" she asked him.

"It looks very inviting and warm," he complimented her.

Trying to suppress any thoughts of sexual contact, still overwhelmed by all of the newness of the surroundings, he did not know what to do. Spencer and Candice had told him that she wanted very much to come to America, and had so little, that he thought he might inadvertently take advantage of her, which he did not want to do. And, besides, she was acting the perfect hostess in her own country, which he had entered only a few days ago, and he wanted to act the ambassador. Under no circumstances would he impose himself on her.

But any idea of diplomatic behavior was not to be. Faint Chance also took off her shoes and socks, and then began taking off her jeans! As she took them off, Cameron was elevated by the sight that she wore nothing underneath. He tried to turn his head to be polite, but she continued, and took off her top and bra, which let loose her breasts, which were quite large compared to other Asians. But then, he remembered, she was of mixed blood and seemed to have the best of both the East and the West.

He did his best to pretend to continue to find something to preoccupy himself with so he could look away, all the while looking with peripheral vision. In moments, she was stark naked.

She turned to face him with her breasts exposed and her legs folded. Her pubic hair was visible, but he tried not to look. It was dense, and formed a triangle in-between her legs, as though a pointer as to where he should look.

She said, "I prefer to sleep without any clothes, if you don't mind."

Mind! He tried not to think about the comment so he would not have to pole-vault into the sleeping bag.

Her nakedness was visible in the reflective light of the torch – absolutely beautiful! The long and beautifully-shaped legs, and breasts with very large nipples were engulfing his attention. These were going to be hard to ignore, he realized.

She seems so different from any other woman I've known, he thought. Resisting any idea that she was inviting him to approach her, still trying to assume this is how people in Lao normally behaved, however that might be, he tried to think of other things. Architecture maybe?

It was apparent that she was facing him to see if there was anything he wished to address. When nothing else was said by him, she did not hesitate longer and slipped into the waiting bag. "I will warm it up for you," she said, "since you are feeling chilly."

He thought, when in Rome… and so he said, "Yes, I prefer to sleep that way, too." Actually it was almost true, except that he normally wore a T-shirt at home in the cooler season. He too took off his jeans, and shirt, and was naked. He slipped into the double bag with Faint Chance in it.

"Actually," he said, "I am enjoying myself immensely on this trip, thanks to you, rain and all." He was trying to take his mind off the senses that engulfed him in the nest that she had made up for him. The rain continued its pounding without letting up.

"I am glad. I told your brother and sister-in-law that I would do my best to see you are properly taken care of."

Surely she could not mean that the way it sounded. Naaaaaaaaww, he said to himself. Couldn't be. Anyway, she used that word "properly" when she referred to whether or not he had a good night's sleep yesterday morning. It had to be taken in a different way than his first instinct. Suitably? Fittingly? Thoroughly? Admirably? In accordance with social ethics and good manners? With propriety? As best he could remember the definition of "properly" might have included those different meanings, and surely she meant something like the latter ones.

Cameron lay face up, more to his side of the double bag. He occupied more of it of course than she, as he was larger. He turned off the flashlight to conserve the batteries. Faint Chance then inched her way towards him until her naked body pushed up against his. She put her arm around him and pulled herself up close to his side.

The rain intensified even more, and was very loud on the tent and whatever it pounded down on nearby. It insulated them from any other outside noise or disturbance, it intensified their senses. Cameron began to lose his thoughts and concerns that he should stand off from what was burning inside, as they lay and listened to the rain. Faint Chance made several movements that rubbed her alluring, warm, soft cocktail against his thigh. She pulled herself closer in with the arm that was over him, and pulled lightly on his far shoulder. Accommodating the light pull on his shoulder, he rolled over on his side so as to face her. In the process, she positioned, and then repositioned herself such that when they came to rest, his tumescent member was moving on its own into the warm area between her thighs, as though having an engine and global navigation system of its own. The shape of her thighs was such that they opened with ample access to her large sex. His member, without being touched, was practically entering her. In a movement he would never forget she, without using any hands, made a few movements, relaxing, positioning, such that he felt himself slide right in her without so much as his moving. This girl had unnatural talents.

Well, he thought to himself. There may be a clue in here somewhere...

"SHOW TIME!" he said aloud.

Chapter Thirty-Seven

"My name is Mrs. Priscilla Hargrove. How do you do," she said as she stood outside the door of the Harrington home. She was dressed in a blue suit, skirt below the knees, a white shirt and a dark tie. Her hair was pinned up, and she looked the essence of "proper". She had a slender briefcase in which she carried a copy of her references and diplomas.

"Do come in. I am Candice Harrington, and my husband, Spencer, is here also. Come over, Spencer, and meet Mrs. Hargrove."

"How do you do," Spencer said. "We spoke on the phone."

"Please have a seat. Would you like some tea?" Candice asked.

"That would be very nice. We English drink a good deal of tea," Priscilla said. Candice went to the kitchen for tea, and returned with it shortly while Mrs. Hargrove settled at the table.

"Here are my credentials and references," Priscilla said, handing a package to Spencer. He looked through them as they continued the interview. "You may keep them as your copy. I also have a copy of my social security card, and green card."

"Tell us a little about yourself," Spencer said. "Apparently you decided to maintain British citizenship?"

"Yes, I have not yet applied for American citizenship. I have a degree from Oxford in English Literature. I have worked as an Associate Professor in England in English Literature. I later married, and migrated to America with my husband. We have two children, and this year the youngest is off to college along with the first. So now I have free time, and I saw your advertisement. I rather miss teaching."

"Our son, Devan, is what we call a gifted child. We are seeking a special educator for him. Candice and I believe that communication is the key to success, and we both feel that Devan should learn proper English, rather than just adequate English. So

Candice and I both believe that someone such as yourself from England is best-suited."

"How old is Devan?" Priscilla asked.

"He is much younger than you might imagine. He is only four months old," Spencer said.

"Four months?" Priscilla said politely, but in shock. "I think there is a mistake! I rather doubt that he needs someone versed in English literature. I was expecting to tutor someone in his late teens. I think you must have thought I was looking for employment as a nanny?"

"Before you make any rash prejudgments, please meet Devan," Spencer said.

With that, Spencer went for Devan. He came back into the room leading little Devan by the hand. Devan was in pants and shirt, not nappies as Priscilla anticipated for a four month old. He walked by himself.

"Devan, this is Mrs. Priscilla Hargrove. She teaches English."

"How do you do, Mrs. Hargrove?" Devan said to Priscilla, offering her his little hand. "I am Devan Harrington."

"My goodness!" Priscilla said. She covered her mouth in shock. She regained composure after a few moments and finally answered, "Very well, thank you."

"I am pleased to meet you," Devan said. "I hope that I can learn from you."

"Do you see now that he needs special tutoring?" Spencer asked.

"Indeed! This is most interesting," Priscilla said.

"We think mornings would be sufficient, Mondays through Fridays. We are both research doctors, and work regular hours. We have a wonderful Yugoslavian woman who is also here the entire day, Monday through Friday, who takes care of the house and prepares his meals. She will look after him in the afternoons, and you would keep him busy in the morning. We have set up a study with blackboard and suitable furniture. We will show you now if you like," Spencer said.

"Yes, this is a most unusual assignment," Priscilla said. "But I must warn you that I have no such particular experience in teaching such a young person. I have only taught older subjects."

"We are confident that you will find Devan very much like an older pupil, and also well-behaved," Spencer said. "However, we must ask you not to speak about his unique talents to others, as we do not want to draw attention to him."

"I understand," she said. "Yes, this will be a most interesting assignment indeed!"

Chapter Thirty-Eight

"BOOM! The sound of a mellow drum awoke the two of them – it was the sound of a large drop of water falling from a tree leaf many feet above the tent.

"AWK AWK!" The chirp of a very loud jungle bird followed the drum noise.

Faint Chance and Cameron were awake. Rays of sun made the tent material glow inside.

"Good morning," she told him, snuggling up next to him in the cool air of the mountain.

Cameron held her tight, savoring the moment, realizing that he would remember that point in time, his awakening in the jungle after making love to Faint Chance for the first time.

They lay and looked up at the sunlit top of the tent, moistened and cooled by the heavy rain.

"The rain is over," Cameron concluded.

"This is the rainy monsoon. It may rain again any time."

Cameron opened the little round tent to look outside. A strong ray of sunshine struck his face, but dark, broken clouds surrounded the bright rays streaming through them. He took a deep breath of the cool, refreshing air. Everything seemed so peaceful. He leaned back into Faint Chance, and kissed her cheek.

After packing the tent and their things in the backpacks, Cameron decided to sit on the fallen tree that they had set their tent up against the night before, to have a slice of papaya.

"This is really beautiful, this jungle, after the rain like this," he said, eating the sweet papaya. He leaned back to look up at the tall trees and the sky. As he did, his movement set the fallen tree in motion backwards, and it rolled backwards almost enough to let them fall backwards over it.

"Whoa!" Cameron exclaimed, leaping forwards off the tree, and helping Faint Chance who also nearly fell over backwards. The tree stopped after it rolled a quarter turn. The sun struck and reflected off a shiny spot on the tree that became exposed when the tree rotated.

What is this?" Cameron said, and stooped to look at the shiny spot. He rubbed it with his hand to remove the moss that covered most of it. Western letters started to show up. Rubbing it more, they became clear: "US Ordinance. 2,000 lbs.".

Rubbing the object, which was now loosened by the first movement, caused it to roll over a little further, and one end of it struck a tree trunk nearby. A loud clicking noise was made by the touching of the two together.

"Whirrrrrrr," the noise came from the object. The movement had triggered the time-delay fuse inside.

"Jesus! It is an unexploded bomb! Run!" he shouted.

They grabbed their packs and ran as fast as they could to the path and to distance themselves from the monster bomb. After running a stretch, there appeared a small cliff dropping down fifteen feet. An enormous tree grew on the cliff's edge with a trunk fifteen feet in diameter. It had an enormous set of roots growing exposed below the cliff, providing good cover. They jumped down, and Cameron pulled Faint Chance under the protection of the huge tree.

KA-BOOM!

The explosion shook the earth they were standing on. The blast blew entire trees and rocks right past them, in a deafening blast. A huge rock, nearly eight feet in diameter, came straight down and crashed into the ground not twenty feet away. Debris from the explosion rained down around them for the longest time. They stayed there, huddled up, somewhat deafened from the blast.

They stood up and looked back to the area that the bomb blew away. It had made a crater and a clearing nearly the size of a football field in the spot where it exploded.

They could not hear a thing. They moved in closer to see the magnitude of the crater created by the bomb and took a seat near its edge to gape at the aftermath. It would be several hours before their hearing would return.

Chapter Thirty-Nine

Resuming their hike along the sandy road, they went around a curve in the path, and just ahead was a man pointing a long rifle into the trees off the side of the road!

Cameron put his hand on the machete handle on his belt, but dared not draw it against the man with the firearm. Cameron took Faint Chance by the hand, and they prepared to run, duck or otherwise take cover. They backed up very slowly, hoping he had not seen them, so as to hide behind the foliage of the side of the road. They could see him through the branches of the dense foliage on the side of the road, as they watched and stayed still, thinking movement might give them away if they had not been spotted already.

"What is he doing?" Cameron asked of Faint Chance softly.

"He is a hunter from some village," she concluded.

As they spoke, the hunter put down his rifle, and gave up whatever he was hunting. He looked disgusted.

They assumed that he was not hunting people, and stood up as the hunter approached. They both thought that would be better than surprising a man with a gun from up too close.

Cameron observed that the hunter did not appear to have fear just because he and Faint Chance were present. The hunter, with his obvious keener senses for critters in the area than Cameron would ever have, realized that they were foreign to the area. The hunter was in search of some prey to feed his family. The hunter could tell instinctively that the couple were no threat, which was good for them. He looked like a fierce, effective hunter, although he had a very small frame.

The hunter appeared to be twenty-five years of age. Even though Cameron thought he was in hiding, the hunter knew very well that there were two of them, and exactly where they were. He walked towards them slowly, with his long rifle in both hands in front of him, but not pointed towards them.

He slowed his pace as he came closer, but he did not appear to want a fight. It was as though he was upset at the presence of the couple which had scared off the game he was pursuing.

Faint Chance stood and spoke to him in Lao.

She interpreted, "We scared off a turkey he was chasing."

"I hope he is not too mad about it," Cameron said.

Cameron could not help but look at the rifle of the hunter. He had an interest in guns when he was younger. The rifle that this young hunter was carrying was a very long, thin, muzzle-loader. The gun looked like it came out of some museum, from a collection of civil war relics. However, it was thinner. "Tell him that is a very fine rifle," Cameron said.

Faint Chance told the hunter in Lao that her friend admired his weapon. He seemed very proud of his rifle, and displayed it to Cameron. He then lowered the hammer slowly, and passed it to Cameron, but kept his hand on it. He was obviously not only proud of it, but concerned that it might hurt someone.

The gun was truly amazing. The barrel had a bore of three-eighths of an inch, with a thin wall, obviously made for light-weight carrying. The stock appeared to be teak. It had brass metal bracing much like the early American muzzle-loaders from the civil war period. The hunter took out a pouch, and displayed some things for the muzzle-loader.

The hunter showed some natural fibers bundled up, and told Faint Chance, who interpreted, "This material is to put behind the lead."

The hunter showed some lead balls. "He says he makes the lead balls himself." He had taken out of his pocket a stick of lead three inches long to show where the lead shot came from.

Faint Chance interpreted, "He says the government says everyone has to turn in their guns. He used to grow opium, but it has been illegal to grow it since 1996. He refuses to give up his gun, as he needs it to feed his family. He says they don't have much to eat. He says most of the deer are gone, but there are still birds."

Cameron said, "Tell the hunter that we apologize for making his family go without food today. Give him this," as he took out four, five thousand kip notes, which was a small sum in dollars, less than five. "Tell him it is a present, that we want to buy him some food for his family since we ruined his hunt today."

She spoke the words, and the hunter's eyes lit up at the size of the money. He took it slowly, and then stared at it for a time.

The hunter bowed humbly with a *nop*, and thanked Cameron, and then Faint Chance, in Lao several times. He looked genuinely moved.

Four hours of hiking later, they came to a stream crossing their path. Rounded rocks protruded out of the stream. There was no way around.

"We can walk on top of the rocks," Cameron said.

Stepping across the tops of the wet rocks was precarious. At the far side, a short rest and some bottled water seemed overdue, so they sat on a big rock near the water. The loud noise of the rapid stream winding around the rocks provided a soothing, but loud, sound as they rested.

"We had better press on, so as not to waste the daylight," Cameron told her, and, tired as they were, they put on the gear and headed out again, greeted by a small shower. The shower was not so strong that they needed cover, and they walked on in the rain.

After a time, a good spot appeared for the night. "That looks like a good spot ahead," Cameron said. "We should set up camp here if it looks okay. It will be dark soon, and I am exhausted. How about you?"

"Yes, me, too."

The tent opened up easily and looked like a good shelter in case it began to rain again. Sitting outside, they opened up some of the canned goods they had bought in Ban Houei Sai. The remaining minutes of the sunset between the mountains provided a nice golden glow in the sky, and within an hour and a half stars could be seen, as the sky had cleared of the heavy rain clouds. A full moon illuminated the sky for them, as Faint Chance sat next to Cameron. Cameron had no idea that he might become so enchanted with this girl that his brother and sister-in-law had both spoken of with so much regard. They retired for the night, and went inside the tent, closing the insect flap which doubled over itself at the edge so a person could go out by going in-between the nets.

Here I am, in the middle of the jungle, Cameron thought, as he lay motionless. The inside of the tent was illuminated somewhat by the moon and stars.

Faint Chance, who had been quiet, curiously said after several minutes, "Is your blade nearby?"

"Yes, I have it here."

Cameron trusted her instincts, and, although he did not hear or sense anything, he rolled over, and took the machete out of its sheath, and put it out above their heads on the ground for easy access in case of danger. But nothing was apparently threatening them at the moment.

Exhausted from the long day of difficult hiking in the mountains and the excitement of the bomb, the two were soon off to sleep.

Chapter Forty

As the night unfolded, the noises outside changed slightly. Faint Chance opened her eyes. Something was wrong. Her body was tucked into Cameron's, and her arms were inside the sleeping bag.

Cameron was beside her, sound asleep, but one of his arms was outside the bag, wrapped around her on top of the bag.

The insect flaps of the tent were pushed apart by a long, white object that entered the tent two feet above the ground. It was a foot in diameter, and came in right over the couple, a foot-long, thin, black, slimy, straight object sticking out in front of it, moving in and out.

Seemingly endlessly long, it glowed white from the light of the stars and moon illuminating it as it came into the tent – a thirty-foot-long Burmese Albino Python Constrictor! Its white color glowed in the light of the moon that penetrated the tent, in an eerie fashion.

The monster snake stuck its long, dark tongue out over the couple, and it sensed the warm bodies of the humans below it with the heat-sensitive pits on its head and lips. Its head came in several feet, and then it drooped its incoming body under the blissfully dreaming twosome in their double bag so as to wrap itself around them in its death squeeze, to later swallow them when dead.

As the body of the beast began to go under the bag, it caused the bag to rise. Faint Chance quickly jumped, but she could not move out of the bag as her arms were trapped inside.

"CAMERON!" she yelled.

Cameron opened his eyes abruptly. The huge white snake had already gone about the sleeping bag once and was now tightening its grip, with more of the body coming in, trying to make a second wrap about the sleeping bag – if it did, there could be no escape by anyone. The snake was quickly tightening its grip about the bag, and would in no time squeeze the life out of him to later swallow him for its next meal.

Cameron was able to slither out of the bag, as his arms were free and out of the bag to begin with, whereas Faint Chance was trapped. He jumped quickly, and grabbed the machete and squatted next to the opening of the tent. More of the snake was coming in quickly, and more of it slithered around Faint Chance in the bag. It now had a full loop around Faint Chance in the sleeping bad and began to tighten the loop, only seconds from crushing her.

He raised the machete and with both of his arms and all of his strength brought down the blade as hard as he could over the one-foot-diameter body near the tent opening.

WHACK!

The blow cut the huge python neatly in two, with nearly half of it inside the tent, squirming about, and relaxing its hold on Faint Chance. Out she came from the sleeping bag, very scared.

When it finally came to rest, he stabbed it with the machete, and dragged the heavy piece of it outside. Once outside, he could see the length of the beast.

He thought he should drag the body parts away, wondering what else might be attracted to a freshly-killed snake. The thing was so big it was difficult. After ten minutes of dragging the snake body only a short distance away, he came back inside the tent. Faint Chance was waiting for him, still very afraid.

He crawled into the double sleeping bag with her and she held him with her arms, her naked body squeezed tightly up to his. His heart was still running fast, and so was hers – he could feel it. She held him tightly, but said nothing. It took some time before their heartbeats slowed enough to let them sleep.

Chapter Forty-One

On the third day, the path became tighter with overgrown plants and trees, and was only one person wide in many spots. They traveled one ahead of the other, Cameron first, machete in hand. They came to a steep hill, and had to go down with the occasional help of their hands clutching plants and branches as they went down to keep from slipping. A large white-and-black bird had a nest on the mountainside, and flew above watching them. There was a small but fast-moving stream at the bottom, and the path led them back up the other side, winding up the mountain until they crossed the top. The back side was very green, and there were wild flowers growing.

Faint Chance said, "I think the village is not much further. These mountains look familiar."

Exhausted, hours later, the path widened and the signs of people and activity appeared ahead of them. Faint Chance recognized the terrain, and became excited. Trees surrounded the entrance over the path in. The clouds above were thick, but allowed strong rays of sunlight to come in-between them into the village entrance.

"This is it!" she exclaimed excitedly.

The village was at the top of a mountain, but not on a peak. It was obviously remote, and entirely inaccessible except by the narrow path that they had come in on. It spread out over gently-rolling hills. The houses were made of wood, and were built up on stilts, apparently to protect them from the monsoon rains, Cameron thought. The height of the stilts varied from two feet to five feet to make them level on the uneven terrain. The thatched roofs were made of a natural tree material that had dried out and was grayish-brown in color.

Four youngsters came to look at them as they came into the village. They did not get too close, but did follow along with them as they came into the village, off to one side. They were very curious, and a little afraid, of the strange-looking newcomers.

Off to the left, and inside the village a short walk, was a very old, small-framed woman, standing over a stone apparatus. She was very slight, perhaps eighty pounds. As they walked in, they veered over to her to see what she was doing. With both hands, she was turning a round stone a foot and a half in diameter around and around, by way of a stick that stuck up at the edge of the stone. The stone was on top of a larger stone. There was a hole in the middle of the upper stone, and in the hole, she gradually trickled in a few corn kernels every minute or two. The corn kernels came out ground from below on one side where there was a groove in the stone below. The ground kernels went into a container. Although she did turn when they walked out to face them, she did not greet them, nor did she pause her work. It looked very difficult for her, and she had to put her whole body into it, given her slight frame. She continued at a steady pace, not letting up just because visitors had come. Faint Chance spoke to her. The woman replied, but she did not break her rhythm of turning the stone.

"Corn for animals. She is crushing the corn to feed animals," Faint Chance said to Cameron.

"Was that the Lao language?" Cameron asked.

"No. That was the local dialect. I still remember it, but it has been a long time."

They stood there, a few feet away from the lady who was crushing the corn, and looked all around them, turning around several times. Cameron noticed that the eyes of Faint Chance had become a little watery, apparently as she remembered that she had lived there some years ago.

Cameron asked, "Do you think anyone here will remember you?"

"Some may, and surely the Chief will. If he is still alive. I will ask her who the Chief is." She did, and it was apparent from the conversation and the expression on Faint Chance's face that he was still alive. They went on into the sprawling mountain village. Cameron could see perhaps a hundred houses, and wondered what the population was.

They arrived at the Chief's house. A guard for the Chief, who was sitting at the door stood up. Faint Chance said to him in the dialect, "I am Sangmouane Sayasithsena, and used to live here. I wish to see the Chief."

The man went inside, and then came out, holding the drape open to invite them in.

Inside, Faint Chance looked around. There were six people inside. She stopped at an elder man, who Cameron guessed must be the Chief. Faint Chance put her hands together in the *nop* prayer position, and bowed her head to him.

Faint Chance then, in the local dialect, said, "I am Sangmouane Sayasithsena." The Chief then recognized her. "And this is Cameron Harrington from America. He is designer of houses."

Cameron looked about the Chief's home. It was roughly twenty-five by twenty feet, larger than the others in the village. The walls were a single layer of boards, just under three-quarters of an inch thick, and in varying widths of eight to ten inches. The length of the boards averaged between ten to fifteen feet. The boards had been cut by some sort of hand saw, with irregular edges. The roof was thatched, made out of the tree foliage, and was dried out and brownish-gray in color. Light shone through the edges of many of the boards making up the walls. Two of the walls had a window opening. It was obvious that these houses were built in the same way for many hundreds of years, and the people had no building materials such as glass for windows brought in from the outside.

It was not immediately clear how many of the six people they saw in the single, open, dark room lived there. There was a sort of split-level effect at one side, a third of the floor space, which was elevated eighteen inches. The elevated spot was the sleeping area, and there were a number of mats to sleep on, resembling Japanese futons, rolled up and put back up against the wall so as to make the floor space available for the day. There were some woven blankets there as well.

The Chief appeared to be very healthy, and only in his late forties. He stood and Faint Chance went to him and gave him an enormous embrace. Faint Chance interpreted a few things back and forth, but it was her moment, and Cameron stayed back to let them reminisce. They took seats, short stools of wood, while the others who lived there just squatted on their ankles – something Cameron could not even try.

The Chief spoke to her in Lao, and they spoke of those people that she remembered. Cameron could not understand a word, but it seemed sort of obvious what they were saying, with Faint Chance telling him all what had happened to her since she left.

Others in the room listened intently. Cameron observed a very old lady squatting on her ankles, listening intently, who may have been a relative. She had no teeth left, as far as Cameron could see. All seemed very interested to hear what had happened to Sangmouane Sayasithsena.

Faint Chance said, "The Chief says this is a special occasion, and wants to offer us some Lao Lao."

The Chief went to a wicker storage container against the wall, and produced a bottle of clear Lao Lao. Faint Chance said, "Lao Lao is not made here, and only the Chief has some. It is from barter with some Lao Lao-maker at some other village." He produced some small wooden cups, and gave Cameron, Faint Chance, the elders and himself a glass. They sipped it and there was much conversation, but only in Lao and the local dialect. The Chief asked her about the city where she lived, the Indian who adopted her and the type of work that she did. The reunion was wonderful to watch for Cameron.

After the reunion in the Chief's home for an hour, of which Cameron was largely excluded due to language, Faint Chance said to Cameron, "Let's take a walk around the village."

"Sure," Cameron said.

Faint Chance led Cameron on a walk around the village. A red sky above was saying goodbye to the day. Picturesque little thatched huts covered the hilly village, and the residents seemed to hurry slightly to get what they had to do before there was no more light, as there was no artificial light to be had in the village. Word was getting around the village already that one of their own had come back, and as they walked about they could tell that some of the people knew already who they were. They came to a nearly flat spot below the area of houses, which ended with a drop off on a cliff that gave a nice view to the rolling hills below. They stopped near the cliff's edge, and Cameron put his arm around her waist.

Faint Chance said, pointing off to one side, "That is one of the areas for crops. To the other side are banana trees, mangoes and papayas. I remember it very well. Let's go walk there."

At the fruit trees, Faint Chance stopped and turned to Cameron and said, "This is all very wonderful. I am so happy you and your brother and sister-in-law made this possible."

She put her arms around him, and kissed him on the mouth. She then said, "I think there is something in my karma with you."

Cameron put his arms around her, and kissed her passionately. Faint Chance responded, connecting feelings that the two had not yet experienced.

When they got back to the Chief's hut, the elder lady had organized some sleeping mats for them to spend the night. Later, they found themselves sleeping with six other people in the Chief's home. At least they would not get lonely, Cameron thought.

Chapter Forty-Two

The following day, the Chief was occupied settling the problems of the villagers. He was definitely the seat of power in the village, and many came to him that day with problems for him to resolve. Finally, by mid-afternoon, the Chief was free to have a discussion with them. The Chief told a guard outside his house not to send anyone in, which gave Cameron the feeling he was getting a special audience with the Chief.

Faint Chance said to the Chief (in dialect), "I first met Cameron's brother, Spencer Harrington and his wife, Candice. They are research doctors. They were in Vientiane last year. They have invited me to come live with them in America, and I have accepted. I will go when the government lets me."

"Will you then live there?" the Chief asked.

"They will become my new family in America. I have heard much about the West, and about America. I am very excited about going." She continued, "But I must tell you why I came here. I apologize that it is not just to see you. My new American friends paid for my trip here, as they want me to ask you for the special plant, the *ton mai piiset*. I gave my new American family, Spencer and Candice, my wedding present from you. I wanted them to have the special child that might have been mine had I married and undertaken the ceremony. It was my present to them for bringing me to America. They took the *ton mai piiset* when in Vientiane last year, and I performed the ceremony for them. I wanted to repay them for offering to make me part of their family and move me to America."

The Chief said, "Did they have a child from the *ton mai piiset*?"

"Yes."

"And is the child special?" the Chief asked.

"Yes, he is special, like you. The spirits were good to him. He may become a leader of his people like you."

The Chief said, "And now I believe you are here to ask me for more of the plant to give to the research doctors, isn't that so?"

"Yes, it is so. You are so wise – you already know. They want to study the plant leaves in their laboratory. I have told them that it will make no difference what they study, as without the special prayers that you taught me, it will make no difference what they do. I have told them they cannot make chemicals to beget special children without the prayers to get the help of the spirits, but they wish to try."

The Chief said, "The discovery of the *ton mai piiset* by the West may have a greater impact on the world than you think, my daughter."

"I do not understand how, Father, but I am sure you know," she said. "Have I done wrong?"

The Chief said, "I hope that it does not bring the outside to our village too quickly, as there is much greed and evil in the world outside the village. But I knew when I gave you the *ton mai piiset* and sent you off to the outside world that I was risking an invitation to the outside."

He continued, "But the *ton mai piiset* is now almost extinct. It only grows in soil that has minerals from ages past, and in only one place, on a mountainside, right where I found you. I was there not long ago, and I could only see one plant left."

He looked at Cameron, and then at her and asked, "What do the doctors intend to do with the plant leaves if I let you have some?"

Cameron answered, and felt that he should provide an honest answer. "My sister-in-law intends to study what the plant leaves are made of to see if she can duplicate the substance. Her plan is to make it available to the world if she can synthesize it. She believes it can be done."

"So, they intend to make it available to the world? That would be quite a change in mankind," the Chief said.

Cameron wondered if he had come all this way to be turned down. He asked, "I would very much like to hear the history of the plant, if you would be kind enough to tell me."

Cameron politely waited for interpretations between Faint Chance and the Chief. Cameron noticed that the Chief did not always have to wait for completed translations before he understood – he was very astute.

"I will tell you now the history of the *ton mai piiset*. My father, the *Maw Pii* before me, discovered it. It only grows, so far as I know, in one spot. No one has seen it elsewhere.

"My father saw its strange colors, and was beckoned by the spirits to sample it. He found that it put him in touch with very powerful spirits."

Cameron remembered Spencer and Candice speaking of visions and hallucinations when they took the plant – obviously the plant has some strong substance in it, he thought.

The Chief continued, "My father is the first person to take the plant. The spirits told him to take the plant on his wedding day and they would make a special child for him. He took the plant upon his wedding, and I was born with special abilities given to me by the spirits."

"Are you his only child?" Cameron asked.

"Yes. My mother died when I was young, and my father was killed in the jungle when I was thirty-five. I was made *Maw Pii*, and have been since that time."

"How long ago was that?" Cameron asked, wanting to know the Chief's age.

"That was eighty years ago."

Cameron asked Faint Chance to correct the question and answer, as there was obviously a mistake. She repeated his question and the answer, "That was eighty years ago."

Cameron was silent. Is something missing here in the translation, he wondered?

Cameron looked to Faint Chance and said, "Ask the Chief his age."

She spoke to him and turned to Cameron and said, "One hundred and fifteen."

Outside the village, on a high spot, were two Japanese men camped out, looking at what was going on in high-powered binoculars, waiting for the appropriate time to make their move.

"What do you think, Kumi-cho?"

Morio Uto answered, "There is no sign that they have the plant leaves yet. When it appears that they have them, we will make our move."

"Ask the Chief if he has achieved the age of one hundred and fifteen because of the plant," Cameron said to Faint Chance.

Interpreting his answer Faint Chance said, "Yes. I was intended by the spirits to be the *Great Maw Pii*, the leader of those who speak to the spirits, and also the wisest leader. Only a person of years has the experience to be very wise. The spirits of the plant also give longevity so that the person born of it can accumulate great amounts of experience and wisdom to pass on to others. The spirits also gave me the ability to ward off things which afflict the aged. This is why I am so healthy at one hundred and fifteen."

"My God!" Cameron said. "This plant is truly the next step for man. Ask him if anyone else has taken the plant leaves besides him."

"He says he is the only one, except his widow, who was killed in an accident."

"Ask him why?"

"There is not enough for the villagers, and thus it has been saved for the Chief's son to become *Maw Pii* to follow him. There is less and less of the plant each time each year."

The Chief spoke to Faint Chance, asking his own question. "The Chief would like to know if he can ask you some questions?"

"Of course," Cameron answered. Faint Chance interpreted.

Faint Chance said, "He says it has been some time since the village had a visitor. Sometimes military scouts come by. Two were here a year ago."

She continued to interpret, "Four years ago, Christian missionaries from Australia came trying to teach their ways, but I would not let them. The Lao Government does not allow them to come in and try to convert villagers. They were posing as educators, but in reality were trying to spread their religion. The military came in afterwards and asked me what they were doing when here. That is when I found out that they had been arrested for trying to spread Christianity. I don't want Christianity in the village either."

Faint Chance continued to interpret, "Have there been any new wars in the last four years since the missionaries were here?"

Cameron replied, "There has been fighting in the Middle East, with people of different religious faiths killing each other. And there is also violence caused by the Muslims in Indonesia. They are jealous of the Chinese in Indonesia and have been looting their shops and property, and running them out of the country."

Faint Chance interpreted after clarifying with Cameron what he meant by the term "Middle East". As Cameron thought about it, he realized that he was not too sure what exactly it was himself.

Interpreting in Lao from the Chief, she went on, "The problems caused by the Muslims will go on for many more years. Maybe a hundred."

That remark shocked Cameron. How this remote villager would even ask about the outside, let alone predict events was very surprising.

The plant! Cameron realized. The Chief is living proof that it works! No wonder he is so intelligent!

The Chief took the opportunity to ask Cameron about Cameron's government, how things were going in unified Germany, and how the collapse of the communist state was developing in Russia. Cameron realized he was talking to a person who knew about a great deal of the world, and he did not have a TV or a newspaper! The Chief had just learned what he could when some missionaries or government troops came through, which was rare. This was like Shangri-La.

Finally, the Chief changed the subject. "Tell me what advancements have been made in curing cancer."

"None," Cameron answered.

"Medicine is the one thing the Chief says he would like to bring here."

"Can the tribesmen read and write?" Cameron asked.

"Only myself and my son. But that may change, too. The government is hiring educators to come to remote villages, and one day an educator will probably come to this village. These villages of *Lao Sung*, or the highlands, are more difficult to get to, as you may have witnessed coming here."

"That is the understatement of the year," Cameron said. "But don't translate that," he added, realizing that such remarks might come across as quite unusual in a strange language.

"Are your people religious?" Cameron asked.

Faint Chance continued her interpreting. "They are animists. They believe that living souls live in natural objects. They believe in a spiritual world."

Cameron thought about that. This was truly a remote village. The people are living as they had for many centuries, with hardly any change at all.

"Do you think it will be appropriate for me to ask the Chief if he is religious?"

Faint Chance said, "I think it is not bad to ask." And so she did.

"No," was his answer.

This was most interesting. Here was man in one of the most remote jungles in the world, born, raised and living with animists who believe spirits live in objects, with no formal education, and he is not religious. Then again, he had been isolated from organized religion – probably an excellent idea! I wonder if he has heard of Karl Marx and the saying that religion is the opiate of the people? Cameron then mused to himself that if Karl Marx had been born this day he would have probably said, "The Internet is the opiate of the people!"

"I would love to hear your views on religion," Cameron asked.

"The best way for me to simply define religion for you as a westerner is to say that 'man invented religion so he could have a day off'."

Cameron was taken aback as he thought about the answer given him. *Man invented religion so he could have a day off!*

Cameron was spellbound. He vaguely recalled the philosophy courses he took in the university, and remembered having to study the elaborate theories and lengthy reading of philosophers such as René Descartes and St. Thomas Aquinas as to the existence of God.

But the Chief's was the most profound theory of religion he

ever heard, and it made more sense than any other. He strained his mind to think if he could ever remember studying about some religious people that did not have a Sabbath. Originally a Saturday, the Sabbath was the seventh day of the week. A day of religious rest. Since the Reformation, the word became applied to the Lord's Day, the first day of the week, observed in commemoration of the resurrection of Christ. But this man lived in the world of followers of Buddha, the enlightened one from India, of the fifth century BC but whose teachings had reached far into Asia.

He strained to think of any religion that did not have a day of the week off from work. None! He thought of his youth, at a time when the Sunday holiday was largely consumed by having to go to a Christian church – everyone dressed up, met the other members, acted polite, followed by a big ceremonial afternoon meal or early dinner. A day off. It was perfect! Religious people claim it would offend Jehovah, Jesus, Muhammad or God by any other name to work on their Sabbath. Jews have a day off – Muslims, Christians, Hindus and Buddhists as well. And, they all *claim* it would offend God if they worked that day. Hah! What a beautifully simple way to define religion! Any idiot can define something in a whole book by talking in circles around it until you are put to sleep, but it took a genius to say it in a sentence. What did *all* religions have in common? Christ for the Christians, but not for the Jews. Muhammad for the Muslims. Some of these people had to be wrong, as they are mutually inconsistent. Eat pork, don't eat pork. Eat beef, don't eat beef. Eat only vegetables. Fast on some days. The Koran versus the Bible. Face Mecca and be cleansed. Get born again or go to Hell. Speak in tongues. Meditate.

But what did they *all* have in common? *They all had a day off, and they took it under the guise of religion*! The day off was the common denominator, and hence the primary purpose. Religion was used as the excuse for the day off. The details of the how and the why, all differing, were to fill in the blanks, and to give man's small brain comfort that he had been put here for some purpose.

The Chief was a genius. How ironic that Cameron would come to a village in the middle of nowhere, where there is no electricity, no TV, no newspapers, no mail service, no Internet, and take his most profound lesson in life! It was like having an audience with the High Lama in the story of Shangri-La!

What are the chances of coming to the other side of the earth, meeting up with someone who had never been to school and learning things of life not available in the best western universities, he wondered. A *faint chance*, he mused.

Cameron thought he would push his inquiries a step further, given the intellect of this master. He asked Faint Chance to interpret. "Have you intentionally kept the outside world away from your village?"

The Chief said, "Your government was dropping bombs like rain very near here just a generation ago. There was madness and killing. I can take you on a fairly short journey to see several large, unexploded bombs dropped from airplanes. I am still waiting for the government to clear those dangerous bombs that did not go off when dropped. Many of my people were killed by bombs during the war, and even recently there have been deaths to hunters who came upon an unexploded bomb unknowingly."

"We slept next to one without knowing it on the way in a few days ago," Cameron said. "I will always remember that! We were nearly blown to pieces!"

He continued, "Undoubtedly, your civilization will one day be here, but I do not believe that keeping it out so far has been a mistake."

"I am sure you are right!" Cameron answered. The Chief could see that the younger man appreciated his wisdom, or at least respected it, and he did not mind parting with some of it.

"How about inventions and the luxuries of the West? Are you aware of much of these?" Cameron asked.

"I am not aware of many of these things, but along with these comes the bad as well as the good. Our people were able to stay out of the Vietnam war by being in this remote village. One day the village will be in contact with the rest of the world, but that should come later. I leave such changes for my son when he becomes Chief, as he wishes. Or his son, if he does not wish it. Such major changes are best left to the youth."

Cameron realized that not only was this man incredibly

intelligent, but smart enough to realize his limitations. That took even *more* intelligence, and even more wisdom.

The Chief said, "I knew that my giving the wedding gift to my adopted daughter might bring an outsider here some day. And so here you are. Others will probably follow. I hope it will not bring trouble."

This remark set Cameron back again. Cameron realized that the Chief could see the likelihood of the outcome of his acts years in advance. Cameron wanted to ponder what he had learned, and told Faint Chance, "Please ask the Chief if I can walk about the village to consider what he has taught me."

"The Chief would like to show you about," Faint Chance interpreted.

The Chief led Cameron and Faint Chance for a walk about the village, and to some vantage points. Faint Chance interpreted for Cameron. "Over there you can see the mountain stream. Over there, the corn growing. Fruit trees over there," she said, pointing. The Chief spoke at times to Faint Chance about the past and the village, about things that he did not need to have interpreted. Cameron could see she was ecstatic as she remembered things from her past.

Although picturesque in their hillside settings, the thatched roofs on all the houses made Cameron, always the architect, ask the Chief, "Aren't those natural roofs impractical?"

The Chief said, "Sometimes parts of the roofs have to be replaced each year, but they last many years and provide very good insulation from the heat and cold."

"Isn't that quite a bit of work, replacing parts of the roofs each year? Wouldn't it be better to use something else?"

The Chief said, "The thatched roof material is readily available just paces away. It is light in weight and requires no outside cement or other materials to make it work. It is easy to find and gather, easy to take up on the roofs and requires no maintenance, other than occasional partial replacement. And, just because it dies off and needs to be replaced now and then, does not mean it is not worthy as a building material. Everything you take out of the earth eventually goes back there."

Everything you take from the earth eventually goes back there! Another sample of this man's incredible wisdom! How wonderfully put. As an architect, he dealt in building materials all the time, and the useful life of materials was in some cases a numeric figure, and something that had to be certified by an engineer. The Chief's statement was not just profound, but *inspiring*. Where on earth did this man, who had not been to some fancy college, or *any* school, learn such incredible things, put so concisely, so correctly, so insightfully and with so few wasted words!

They sat in the Chief's house that evening, and finally he announced to them, "I have made my decision. I will take you to the place of the plant so that you can get some leaves. I will allow the leaves to be taken to your America. But in order for the spirits to go across the ocean with you in the plant leaves, it will be necessary for you to pull the plant leaves out of the ground yourself, and for me to conduct a special prayer to ask the spirits to follow the plant leaves across the ocean with you to their new home. I will ask them to follow you."

He then said, "I have a few conditions."

"What are they?" Cameron asked, entering the subject cautiously rather than simply saying "of course" or otherwise promising before he heard the terms. Who knew what his terms might be.

"If the doctors are successful at making more of the *ton mai piiset*, I want you to bring enough to our village so that everyone in the village getting married can have it. Then their offspring will be special, and also long lived like me. I want our village people to succeed and not fall backwards while the world passes them.

"And the second is not to tell anyone where the plant comes from or that it came from this village or anywhere near so as to keep the world out, as it will surely flock here if the information gets out.

"Do I have your word on these matters?" He looked first to Cameron.

"You do. I promise to do as you say, Chief," Cameron assured him.

"And you, Sangmouane. I am going to give you more for yourself, which you are to use for your wedding one day. Do you promise not to give away your wedding present and to use it if I do this for you and Cameron?"

"Yes, my father."

"Good! Then we will start out in the morning for the plant leaves. My son is still on a hunt, so we will go without him. Do you know how to use this?" he asked of Cameron, picking up one of the antique-looking muzzle-loader rifles.

"Yes, if you will show me how you load it," Cameron answered.

"I will show you. I prefer my bow and arrow," the Chief responded.

Chapter Forty-Three

"Please wake up," Faint Chance said as she shook Cameron lightly.

Still dark, Cameron was not yet awake. Faint Chance had awakened early and was up and had things ready to go.

The Chief had arranged food for them to eat along the way, which Faint Chance put in their backpacks, the Chief carrying his own in a bag attached to his belt. The Chief put his bow and quiver of arrows over his shoulder, and machete on his belt. He handed Cameron a muzzle-loader, which Cameron held up to his shoulder, and then familiarized himself with the primitive flint lock mechanism.

Off they went, the Chief in the lead. The village was only making a few noises from getting up as they left it behind. The sun was hinting it might come up soon in the eastern sky.

The jungle that they were led into was obviously uninhabited. The noises of various animals were very loud, alerting of the intruders. Cameron realized he must be more silent, and adjusted his footsteps to make less noise.

AWK AWK! The sound of a strange bird filled the air and startled Cameron, but the bird could not be seen. The jungle was simply too dense to see very far anywhere. Daylight was just rearing its head as they started.

The pace the Chief was keeping was exhausting. He was in much better shape than either Cameron or Faint Chance – very impressive at one hundred and fifteen. There was little breeze in the dense trail, and Cameron was soaking wet after a few hours. Faint Chance was also hot, but not as much, as she was used to the hot climate. The Chief did not seem to notice the heat, or tire.

The trail widened, and a clearing was ahead in bright sunlight. Just inside the clearing, the Chief stopped suddenly. Faint Chance saw it, and lowered herself to one side. Cameron then saw it.

Eating the carcass of some unlucky animal was an enormous

tiger! Its head was a foot and a half in diameter, and the beast was eight feet long – eleven if the tail was added. It had not noticed them yet, its sense of smell apparently satiated in the flesh and blood of the unfortunate creature that had not outrun it.

All three instinctively became motionless. The Chief kept his bow and arrow in hand and ready, and backed up a few paces with extreme slowness so as not to make noise by crumpling the fallen foliage on the ground.

It didn't work.

The tiger stopped eating and turned its head. It looked right at them. Everyone, including the cat, went absolutely motionless. Cameron realized he might not be breathing. Blood was dripping out of the beast's mouth from its prey. A piece of the prey's skin hung from one of the cat's giant teeth.

The Chief continued to back up, ever so slowly, a few slow-motion steps at a time – his bow and arrow were ready. Cameron wondered if the Chief could sink an arrow into a charging cat of that size so that it would stop before it got to them. Cameron held his muzzle-loader ready at his waist, pointing it directly at the brute in case it charged.

The Chief increased the tempo of the backwards motion, moving away to make the cat think that they were not going to try to take away its catch.

As they walked backwards, less of their presence imposed upon the beast. As luck would have it, the huge tiger decided it had enough in its recent kill to eat, and these humans were not going to try to take it away. It turned its huge head, and tore off another bite of flesh.

The Chief turned, led them quickly back to the path, and said, "We have to go around."

"Understatement of the year!" Cameron said.

They came to a cliff going straight up forty feet, with vines on it. The Chief said, "We have to go up here to go around."

"Jesus! This is the jungle walk Spencer and Candice talked me into?" Cameron said.

The Chief went up the cliff by pulling himself up the vines on it like Tarzan in a movie. At the top, he called down for them to come.

Faint Chance grabbed a vine, and did her best to scale the cliff. The Chief made it possible by pulling up the vine at the same time from the top.

"Okay, it is my turn," Cameron said.

Cameron went up, but he could not have done it without the Chief pulling the vine.

Cameron and Faint Chance followed their guide some distance around the opening where the monster was, and began an uphill hike for several hours. Cameron and Faint Chance were becoming exhausted.

"Let's take a break," Cameron told Faint Chance. They stopped at a small clearing that had some tree roots suitable to sit on. There were some rocks about. Cameron took the water out and drank. Faint Chance took a little. The Chief declined any.

While sitting and resting, Cameron noticed an interesting line of identical insects – two inches long each, with long, skinny legs that were marching towards him in a neat column. Cameron watched intently. There were seven of them, and each stood just over an inch tall, and had a bright-blue colored bump on the head. They were getting closer and closer to Cameron. He put his finger down in front of the column to see if they would stop or go around. They did neither, and the one in front was a matter of inches from his finger, when suddenly something startled him.

WHAM! The sound of a rock smashed on the ground right in front of Cameron, and startled him so much that he leaped off the tree trunk, unaware of what was going on. Faint Chance had picked up a rock and smashed the first two insects in the column.

The Chief joined Faint Chance and the two of them scurried about to try to smash the remaining insects with a rock in hand. After killing two more, three were missed, and instead of running off, they continued to pursue Cameron at a faster pace! Cameron backed up, still startled, while Faint Chance and the Chief pounded at them with a rock in each of their hands, smashing the insects that had been initially missed.

The Chief smashed the last one, inches away from Cameron, who was now backed into a hill of dirt and could retreat no further. His heart pounded. He puzzled at such actions over some tiny insects.

"What is all this about?" Cameron looked to Faint Chance for an explanation.

Faint Chance said, "That insect is extremely poisonous. If it bites you, you will either die or become totally paralyzed for life. One or the other, for sure."

"God, that tiny little insect? It can do all that? One bite?" Cameron asked.

"Yes. I had a friend that lived in Vientiane who went on a jungle expedition and became paralyzed from the bite of one of those," Faint Chance said.

The Chief spoke. "I have witnessed the results of its bite. It has paralyzed and killed members of my tribe. At the very best you would be paralyzed for life if one bites you. There is no question about it."

"Good Lord!" Cameron said. He started looking around as though maybe there were more. "Thank you and the Chief for the quick moves."

She spoke to the Chief, who then smiled and looked at Cameron, enjoying the compliment.

"Tell him I am rested, and ready," Cameron said. And, he thought, there is no way in Hell that I am going to sit down here again!

It became a little cooler as they hiked uphill and the hot sun was dropping. The trees were large, and between the small mountains and the trees, it appeared that it would get dark soon. They continued on until the Chief selected a place to sleep for the night.

The Chief said, "It will be dark soon. We will sleep here. The place we are going to is three more hours away, and we will go at dawn. Rest now. I will watch for danger."

Watch for danger, Cameron thought. How do you sleep so lightly as to be able to watch for danger in a place like this? Oh well, he has made it to this age, so he must know some ways of doing it. Then he thought about the massive tiger and the tiny insects that nearly ended his stay on earth that very day.

Cameron and Faint Chance set up their little tent, but the Chief was apparently going to sleep on the ground. He had taken no extra baggage, so as to make him more agile in the jungle. A smart move, Cameron thought. Still, the tent seemed like a nice luxury. The Chief had no blanket or pillow, utilizing only leaves and plants to create a place to sleep. Cameron wondered what sort of things, like snakes, tigers and insects might be in the area. He was tired, and fell asleep quite quickly.

Chapter Forty-Four

Cameron's eyes opened, and it took him a while to remember where he was, he had slept so hard. He opened the tent, and stuck his head out to see if the Chief was all ready to go.

"Faint Chance, are you up?" he asked her. Her eyes opened, and she looked at him. She gave him a hug and then sat up and yawned.

Outside the tent, the Chief spoke to Faint Chance.

"Ask him if there was any problem last night," Cameron said.

She spoke to the Chief, and then interpreted, "Yes."

"So, what was it?"

She spoke to him again. "He says to look at where he is pointing."

Cameron walked over to where the Chief was pointing. Something five feet long and limp was lying near the small clearing where they had slept. The Chief went to it and picked it up by the tail, which added to its length. It was a black cat, resembling a jaguar, with an arrow in its chest, looking very dead. It had been a perfect shot to the heart with the bow and arrow.

"Oh my God!" Cameron said. "What happened?"

The Chief said, "I sensed the cat coming and waited for him. I positioned him in the moonlight so that it lit the cat's eyes so I could see him when he was close. Then I got him with my arrow."

"Was he going to attack?" Cameron asked, through Faint Chance.

"Yes."

"Why did we not hear anything?" Cameron asked.

"The cat made no noise, not even when he took the arrow."

"It is a good thing we didn't come here alone," Cameron said. "What is the word for that huge animal in the local dialect?"

Faint Chance asked and then said, "Cat."

"Hah!" Cameron chuckled. "Cat."

After three hours of continuous hiking, they came to the enormous cliff with the gorge below where the plant grew and where the Chief had found Faint Chance. The drop-off was sudden, and the cliff actually went straight down eight hundred feet to what looked like a tiny river from so high up. A dizzying sight – it was no place for someone with vertigo.

"Jesus!" Cameron said. "This looks like the end of the earth!

Faint Chance spoke to the Chief, and said, "This is the place. The plant grows here. The place of the *ton mai piiset*."

"Where is it?" Cameron asked.

The Chief led them along the cliff's edge to a place some distance away. "Here."

"Where?" Cameron asked.

The Chief walked over to the cliff and pointed down, and said something.

Faint Chance said, "That is the place of the *ton mai piiset* – the special plant."

"On the side of the cliff?" Cameron asked frantically.

"What is it about this place that grows the *ton mai piiset*?" Cameron asked.

The Chief answered, "There is something in the earth there on the mountainside that comes from ages past, that makes the *ton mai piiset* grow. The *ton mai piiset* is not known to grow elsewhere."

Cameron went over to the cliff, and was struck with dizziness, looking at the tiny little river a zillion miles below. He regained his composure, and looked again to the spot where the Chief was pointing. He could see some unusual strata of strange colors of soil. And there it was, the *ton mai piiset*!

There, twenty-five feet below, on the vertical cliff, in the soils of the strange colors, was one of the colorful plants – only one. The Chief had said that it grew only in soils from ages past, and the cliff side had a strata of strange-colored soils; the plant was growing from a point positioned beneath many years of accumulated earth.

"Follow me," the Chief said. He led them to a cut-out in the cliff fifty feet away, and below the cut-out was only a suspicion of a path, less than a foot wide, sloping downhill, traversing across the otherwise vertical cliff.

Cameron said, "Oh God! We have to get it from down there? This looks like a place where mountain goats come when they commit suicide. I am glad that he is here to do it. I would probably fall off the cliff. He is in good shape for this sort of thing."

The Chief and Faint Chance spoke for some time in what seemed to be an involved conversation.

Finally, Faint Chance turned to Cameron and said, "There is a problem. First, the Chief says you should be the one to remove some leaves from the plant in the soil so as to put yourself closer in touch with the spirits, if you want them to cross the ocean with you."

"Won't they just understand and come along?" Cameron asked.

"No. And, there is one more problem," Faint Chance explained. "There is a group of very large, dangerous birds that live in nests on these cliffs. They attack anyone they see on the cliff. The Chief says that if you go down for the plant leaves, he will sit on the edge with his bow and arrow and shoot any bird that attacks you."

"You mean *I have to go there to get it*?" Cameron asked frantically.

"He says you should go. Be careful."

Cameron said, "Jesus! I better not think about it – just do it!"

Cameron went to the little path, and took deep breaths as though that might help cure the fright. He could not take the muzzle-loader, as he would surely fall if he did not have both hands to cling on to the cliff with the occasional rocks and brush sticking out.

Oh well, there is only one way to do this, he thought, and that is to just do it and not think about it. He began side-stepping very slowly along the trail moving down the cliff towards the plant. He had his arms outstretched along the side of the cliff as he inched along, grabbing on to what little plant life or rocks that were available on the cliff's edge. The Chief sat on the edge of the cliff, just over where the plant was situated, bow and arrow ready for anything.

When Cameron had nearly approached the area of the plant,

by inching his way, Faint Chance yelled out, "Brace yourself, a bird is coming!"

A bird? Cameron thought. No wonder the Chief is sitting on the cliff's edge. He saw something coming in.

"Oh, shit!" Cameron said. He braced himself, mainly by hugging on to the cliff as tightly as he could. The Chief readied with his bow and arrow, but the bird was coming in from the side, along the cliff, but below the edge so he could not get a shot. Only the outside wing was in his view.

A huge bird, black in color, with red wing tips, ten feet in wingspan, came in parallel to the cliff at a high speed and struck Cameron with its talons on his shoulder. The impact nearly knocked him off the ledge. The talons made deep scratches on his shoulder, drawing blood. He felt a sharp pain after the initial shock of the impact.

What sort of strange bird is this? Cameron wondered. This is probably one of the few places on earth where it lives. It attacks people. Will it come back? I think it will. Maybe it thinks I am going for its nest, wherever that might be.

The huge bird had bounced off Cameron on the first strike, and went out, away from the cliff, flying very fast. In just moments, it was a quarter of a mile out, nearly to the other side of the gorge. But it was not content with that, and it turned and came straight on for a full-on frontal attack. Cameron saw it coming in straight at him, at an alarming speed. As it approached, it rotated into a stall flight mode with its wings open to slow and to hold its talons out in front to tear into its human prey.

There was nothing Cameron could do. He could not back off the cliff quickly enough to escape.

The bird was unaware of the danger posed by the Chief's archery skills. He did not have to calculate lead since the beast was coming straight in, and all he had to do was hold steady. He pulled back his bow very hard, and let go when it was only eighty feet out. There would be no time for a second shot.

With the bird rotating its lower part forward to stick its talons out to dig them into Cameron, it exposed its chest and stomach section to the Chief. As it was coming frightfully close into Cameron, the Chief released his arrow. The arrow went *thiiiiiiiiip*. It hit the huge bird squarely in the chest.

The bird lost control, and smacked into the cliff only a foot below Cameron, and then tumbled down the cliff.

"Nice shot!" Cameron yelled out, his heart beating what seemed like a thousand times a minute.

Cameron moved on quickly, wondering if Godzilla had a relative. In another ten feet of traversing the cliff, the Chief said, "It is just below you now. Reach down to it. Don't take the entire plant, as there are no more. Just take some of the leaves."

Just reach down to it, they say, Cameron thought. Here I am on a little ledge, eight hundred feet over a river, with nothing to grab on to, with a goddamned monster species of bird that hunts humans, and they say, "Just reach down."

He went to his knees, and then carefully to his stomach. He could see the colorful plant within reach from the ledge. There was only one to be seen. Could it really be that this is the last plant of its kind on the planet?

He got hold of the leaves, and pulled some of them off and put them in his pocket. He took another handful, and put them in his pocket as well. He did not want to strip the plant, worried about killing it and making the last of its kind extinct. Having removed what seemed like enough, he stood up, and moved slowly back, inching his way.

When he arrived back at the cliff's edge, the Chief came and took Cameron's arm and helped him over the cliff top. Cameron moved away from the cliff and lay down on the ground to rest for a few moments. His shirt was torn from the talons of the monster attack bird, and his shoulder was bleeding. He arose and took out the plant leaves and showed them proudly to his two companions with a big grin. The leaves were purple and orange, two distinct colors.

"What beautiful colors," Faint Chance said. "You were very brave to get it."

Cameron grinned even more. He felt like a hero.

"Okay, we got what we came for. Let's get back," Cameron said. And he put the plant in his satchel.

The Chief spoke. "It is going to rain. That is good because it will keep our scent down from cats."

Faint Chance, interpreting, added, which apparently was not something that the Chief had said, "I think he is talking about our scents, as we are perspiring more than he is."

"Well, I am not used to jungle trekking," Cameron said. "I am not insulted."

They started out, and within an hour it began to rain. Soon it was raining very hard. They marched back on the same trail, soaking wet. Water ran across the trail at many points, and very rapidly in some, as the water found its way down the mountain.

Cameron's scratched shoulder hurt when the leaves of the overgrown foliage smacked it on the trail at its narrow points, on the trail which was so seldom used. They would have got lost without the Chief, he realized, as the trail was not so well-defined in spots, and appeared to have several junctions at spots.

At dark, Cameron and Faint Chance set up their little tent again, and made ready to retire. After the cat incident, Cameron wanted to stay on alert with the Chief, but realized that he was far too tired not to sleep, and went in, with the comforting sight of the Chief sitting and watching out for dangers.

Chapter Forty-Five

Late the next morning, they arrived at the village, the protection of the villagers a welcome sight to Cameron and Faint Chance after the dangers of the jungle.

After settling in the Chief's house, the Chief and Faint Chance told the others in the house about the cat they saw and the bird attack, as it was a custom of the villagers to tell of what happened on a hunt or a journey. Some of the stories were legends in themselves.

After dinner, when the village people had mostly retired, the Chief had Cameron and Faint Chance gather around inside his house, and he laid the plant leaves they had obtained on a piece of cloth.

After obtaining quiet in the room, the Chief said, "I will communicate with the spirits of the plant and ask them to follow you to America." He began a chanting prayer, aloud. At some points, the others in the room joined in with a noise, apparently adding emphasis to something. Cameron did his best to follow along with the chant and the sounds the others in the room would make while getting wound up in the prayer. The prayer lasted fifteen minutes.

"There," he said. "I have asked the spirits residing in the *ton mai piiset* not to stay in Lao, and to follow you across the sea to America to work their powers there."

He crushed the leaves in his hands, and divided out a small amount of it and put it into a little cloth bag. "Now, Sangmouane, this is for you for your wedding, and you are not free to give it away again." He was obviously displeased that she had given away the first batch he had given her years earlier. Faint Chance took the little bag from him and tucked it away, not mixing with the rest, as it was special to her, it coming from her first adoptive father, the Chief.

"And these," he said, putting the majority of it into a larger bag, "you may take to America and to your relatives." He then placed the bag on a little wooden block.

"Now I wish to speak to Sangmouane for a short time," he said to Cameron. Faint Chance interpreted that as, "He wants to speak to me alone, if you don't mind. Could you please take a short walk outside?"

Cameron got up and went outside to let them be alone, most likely to discuss something between father and daughter. He took a stroll about the village. When he returned, Faint Chance had the bedding ready and all were turning in for the night. He lay next to her and went right to sleep.

Chapter Forty-Six

The next morning, after all were up, a young man of the village asked permission to enter the Chief's house. The Chief told him to come in.

The young man said, "There are two more outsiders coming."

The Chief asked Faint Chance, "Are there any more people in your party that might be coming late?"

"No."

"Get some help," the Chief told the young man.

There was a sense of danger in the air, and the Chief went to a storage place under the raised portion of bedding area and pulled out a large machete and stood it up against the wall near the door. Unknown to him was the fact that the two men had been observing the area of the village where he lived with binoculars, unseen to anyone in the village, and they knew right where the Chief lived.

Before any help arrived, two Japanese men stormed into the house. They were in their late twenties, and their clothing was soiled from lying outside the village on the ground observing. It was Morio Uto and an accomplice. Uto took his pistol out of his jacket, which he had not taken out on the way in, allowing whoever saw him to think that they might be part of the same group of new visitors as Faint Chance, who were welcome.

Uto went right past the Chief into the middle of the house, with his accomplice standing behind near the door. Sensing danger, the Chief moved quickly towards the wall where he had set the machete.

The other bandit called out a warning, "Kumi-cho! Abunai!" (Watch out!)

The Chief had picked up the machete off to one side to attack Uto but the warning alerted him. Uto turned to see the Chief attacking with machete in hand, and shot him in the chest with his pistol.

The freshly-picked plant had been placed in a little bag and was sitting like a prize on top of a small, square piece of wood where the Chief had placed it the night before. Uto grabbed the bag with the plant and began to back towards the door, all the while holding his semi-automatic pistol in front of him in case anyone else challenged him. He spoke to his accomplice in Japanese.

His accomplice said to Uto, "Back out behind me."

The accomplice was backing out ahead of the Kumi-cho, when his head suddenly split open from the top down.

The village hunters had gone on alert at the command of the Chief, and several had just arrived at the Chief's house. One caught on, and had come up behind the accomplice, raised an axe and brought it down with all his might. He opened the head of the accomplice as if slicing a coconut or melon. The blade went right down into the bandit's neck. It was a sight that Cameron would not forget.

The hunter was now with his blade in the man's head down to his shoulders, and the Kumi-cho turned and shot him, killing him instantly. By now, several of the other hunters were there and swarmed onto the Kumi-cho. He struggled and fought with them, and in the fight dropped the bag with the plant leaves, and began running for the jungle with several hunters in hot pursuit, with more following shortly behind as it became known that these were bandits. He stopped to turn and shoot once, downing another hunter. His pistol made them stop in place and distance themselves from him, and he was then able to make his way into the dense forest. The hunters did not give up, and chased after him.

Sangmouane Sayasithsena knelt over the slain body of her wonderful Chief, her first adoptive father, the person who saved her from dying from exposure when she was four, and wept. It was the saddest day of her life. She realized that she had brought this evil upon her village and to her father. At age one hundred and fifteen, he was now dead, and it had been brought about by evil following her into the village.

Chapter Forty-Seven

Every hunter and able-bodied man came in to protect the village. Several joined in the chase of the escaped murderer. The entire tribe was alerted from outlying areas that were farming crops or hunting. The women came in from the fields. They were also on alert for the return of the Kumi-cho, who had not been found and killed, and who had dropped the bag with the plant leaves, which was the thing he came for.

The slain Chief's son came back that day from his hunt to learn that his father had been murdered by evil from the outside. He met Faint Chance and Cameron, but there were no greetings. Guards were everywhere, all the hunters taking over guarding the village. The Kumi-cho was still not caught.

Faint Chance and Cameron were told to stay inside the house, as preparations were made for funerals the next morning. Coffins were made for the slain Chief and the two hunters. The bodies were put in boxes at the end of the day, and set in a special place in the center of the village. More than half of the hunters stood guard overnight, prepared against a night-time attack. Cameron noticed that there were two guards not far from him and Faint Chance at all times, and he was not sure if they were there for protection or to prevent them from leaving.

The following day, Cameron saw a ceremony he would never see the likes of again, as long as he was to live. Almost everyone, except for a few hunters at the perimeter standing guard, gathered completely around the caskets, in a circular pattern, and there were many more people in the village than Cameron originally thought. Many had been out harvesting crops, gathering fruit or hunting so that they were not readily visible to Cameron when they arrived, all of whom now came in for the sad event, the burial of their leader, the one who could talk to the spirits, and the two other slain men.

They were all sitting on the ground, surrounding the caskets.

Chanting prayers in complete unison, each would touch the person in front of him or the person next to him with the tips of the fingers on one hand only, the hand extended, usually touching the side or the back of the other person while chanting some part of the prayer. They were talking to spirits, and to the spirits of the slain men. Faint Chance was one of them. Cameron participated as best he could by humming the extended syllables, not having any idea what they meant, but wanting to participate in the mourning.

After two hours, the caskets were taken by pall-bearers, held over their heads, to a special burial place just outside the village, with everyone following, chanting and praying along the way.

There was not enough room for everyone at the burial site, but the villagers all followed and got as close as they could, continuing their chanting and praying, as the caskets were put into the ground. Their beloved Chief was gone to the spiritual world. The Chief was legendary to those who knew him, and that included Cameron and Faint Chance.

Chapter Forty-Eight

Back in the village, the son of the Chief, already designated by his father, took over as the new Chief. He had not married, and lived in the same house with his father. In the house, he spoke with Faint Chance. "Knowledge of the *ton mai piiset* has already brought death to my father and two more village men. If we capture the Japanese bandit, and neither of you leave, it will put our village back to safety from future attacks."

Cameron was struck with fear, and asked of Faint Chance, "Does he mean to kill us?"

"He will decide what is to become of us."

Cameron realized that the Chief had the power of life or death over them – there was no other form of tribunal as to their fate. They might not be allowed to live, so as to keep the location of the plant a secret forever. He and Faint Chance might simply not be heard of again.

The new Chief gave some commands to his men, and an armed group commanded Cameron and Faint Chance to get up and follow them to a small house that was empty, ten feet square inside. It had no windows, and four of the men stood guard by the doorway, covered with a drape. It was dark inside, except for little rays of bright sunlight that shown through the cracks in the wooden sides and a few knot holes.

"I guess all we can do is wait!" Cameron said. "We have brought evil to the village, and caused the deaths with avarice from the outside world. He may put us to death!"

Faint Chance did not respond. She seemed calm, as though taking whatever was to come in her stride. He lay down on the dirt floor and wondered if this day would be his last. He began to think of home, his brother Spencer and his sister-in-law Candice. He wondered how he had got involved in this ordeal, an architect now in the middle of thatched roof huts in the middle of nowhere. True fear overcame him, realizing he might be at the end of his life.

Chapter Forty-Nine

Four hours after first light, the drape opened on the small house, and two guards came in. One spoke to Faint Chance.

"We are to go to the new Chief's house now," she said to Cameron.

"Did they say anything else?" Cameron asked, very worried.

"No."

At the new Chief's house, they were led in and pointed to where they were to sit, in front of and below the new Chief. The new Chief was sitting down on the raised portion of the built-up floor, a foot and a half higher than the dirt floor, the place where the mats were rolled out for sleeping at night. The elevated position, with his legs folded under him, made him appear situated like a courtroom judge presiding over their lives. And presiding over their lives was exactly what he was doing. In the village, there were no police to call on, Cameron realized. No courtrooms, no twelve jurors of your peers, no public viewing, no media attention, no appeals of lost cases, only the final word of the Chief. No doubt the sentence would be carried out that same day.

Several elders were behind him, and it was apparent that he had been discussing with them what to do. The old lady who lived there was squatted on her heels against the wall, observing. There were several others in the house, and standing in the back were two armed guards, looking like court bailiffs to Cameron.

Cameron felt like a defendant accused of murder, and was brought into the courtroom to hear the verdict – and that was just what was happening. Sweat formed on his brow as everyone readied for what the edict would be.

The new Chief spoke. "The *ton mai piiset* has brought the evil of the outside to our village. We have not known such evil since the skies nearby rained with bombs in the war with the Vietnamese.

"My father, our *Maw Pii* is with us now in spirit. He will always be. Our *Maw Pii* granted Sangmouane Sayasithsena, his adopted daughter, the right to summon the spirits to make her a special child on her wedding day. She gave away the *ton mai piiset* to those who would take her to the West, where the world travels at a pace unknown to us. That world has wars, evil and crimes that we do not. She then led the outside here to get the *ton mai piiset* to make it available to the rest of the world.

"Knowledge of the powers of the *ton mai piiset* is now out in the West. If I kill all who have the knowledge of how to find our village, I may be able to keep others from coming to look for the *ton mai piiset*. There is very little *ton mai piiset* left. It only grows in the soil of ages past, and it may not flourish much longer. Sangmouane and her western friend wish to take some of it to the outside world to see if more of it can be made. It is now my decision whether to let the plant go to the world, or to bury it, and the directions as to how to come here, forever."

He paused, and looked at Faint Chance and said to her, "Tell the white man what I have said, and then I wish to hear what you and he have to say."

Faint Chance dutifully interpreted his words to Cameron. Thoughts of survival raced through his mind. This plant was only taken by the Chief's family, and now it was being decided if everyone would become his equal one day. Would he allow that? Or would he, out of jealousy, want to hang on to his superiority over others? Did the additional intelligence brought about by the plant reduce the primitive instinct of jealousy? What about the outside world coming here? Surely that was equally threatening. Cameron could feel his heart pounding away, realizing that what he would say would determine if his head would be chopped off or if he would go back home. The language was so different, and so too the customs. Surely he would not say the right thing.

Faint Chance asked Cameron, "Do you wish to say any words to the new Chief?"

Cameron said, "I better say something!"

Faint Chance said, "Cameron Harrington, designer of houses, requests the right to speak."

The new Chief acknowledged Cameron's last right to speak and looked to him.

Cameron gathered his thoughts for a moment, and then spoke. "You are now the *Maw Pii*, the wise one who talks to the spirits now that Father is gone. As the wisest one, you must decide if you are to hide the biggest secret of the world, and let it perish, or to let it be known to benefit mankind. If you believe that the next generation of man should have the special powers from the *ton mai piiset*, then you will release it. If you do, you will truly be the greatest *Maw Pii* ever, the one who brought the spirits to the rest of mankind."

The new Chief did not look impressed with his plea. No doubt if he let these people go, and when the news of the spiritual powers got out, the village would be swarmed with people from everywhere, and more of the same events would surely happen. It was obvious that he had decided to put them to death and retain the secrets of the plant and the spirits. Cameron realized he was going to die!

Just as the edict of the new Chief was to be passed, ending their lives, Faint Chance spoke. "I demand my right to hear from the spirits in the *ton mai piiset*!"

The new Chief raised his eyebrow and acted quite surprised. "That is your right," the new Chief said, much to the astonishment of Cameron and Faint Chance. The Chief got up and went to the *ton mai piiset*.

"What luck!" Cameron said softly to Faint Chance. "Apparently there is at least some form of criminal justice system here! You get to call on spirits for your witness!"

The new Chief brought out the bag of the plant leaves and also a bottle of the northern Lao Lao whisky. He opened the bag and poured out on a wooden plate some of its contents. He then took a healthy pinch of the leaves in his fingers, put it in his mouth and chased it down with a drink of the northern Lao Lao. He then chanted a prayer to summon the spirits.

He sat quietly for a time, his feet folded under him, waiting.

Cameron remembered the story from Spencer and Candice as they told it to him when they had taken the plant. Spencer had said he had had an epiphany, a vision. Candice had had hallucinations. Clearly there was something powerful about the substance in the plant leaves.

Quiet consumed the room. After several minutes, the new Chief began to gaze out into the room, not focusing on anything. It was apparent that he was being influenced by the plant leaves and having his own vision, or something similar. He then put his hands in the prayer position and mumbled softly. Given the solemnity of the occasion, all were quiet as the new Chief had his experience. After what seemed like an eternity, but which only took ten or fifteen minutes, the new Chief bowed his head in a position of respect and went motionless. Was he communicating with spirits? Cameron wondered. Having a hallucination?

No one dared to speak. Finally, the new Chief stopped, raised his head and chanted a prayer softly. He then opened his eyes and looked at Cameron and Faint Chance. He said something in the local dialect.

"I have been told to allow you to leave with the *ton mai piiset*, and to let the world have it."

Cameron thought he might pass out. He took Faint Chance in his arms to share the moment with her. She too was moved, knowing how close to death they were. With tears in her eyes, she embraced Cameron, with whom she just nearly went to the spiritual world.

"Did you hear what he said at the conclusion of his prayer, when he spoke something aloud?" Cameron asked.

"Yes," Faint Chance answered.

"What was it?"

"He said, 'Yes, father'."

Chapter Fifty

"You are to do as my father asked," the new Chief told them.

"Yes," Faint Chance answered for them, without consulting Cameron.

The new Chief spoke. "You are free to leave, and you may take the plant leaves with you. The bandit may be in pursuit, so you must be careful. I will send some of my best men with you to take you to the end of the path." He continued, "You are not to disclose where the village is to the outside world, and not to tell of where the *ton mai piiset* grows."

Faint Chance and Cameron spoke of the bandit to one another, and then she said, "We will not disclose the location of the village or where the *ton mai piiset* comes from. But the Japanese bandit knows, and he may return."

The new Chief spoke. "He knows of the village, but not where the *ton mai piiset* grows. He wants it for himself, so I do not think he will bring the world back. The location where the plant grows will remain a secret. And," he looked to Faint Chance, "you know that he cannot make it work."

What was he referring to? Cameron wondered. Oh yes, he thought. The prayers that Faint Chance knows. That must be it.

Cameron and Faint Chance got up and went outside into the bright sunlight of day. They walked to the cliff side overlooking the valley of the crops and sat down. Cameron realized his heart rate had been so high for so long that he was sweating and exhausted. He turned around, lay his head in Faint Chance's lap, and passed out.

Chapter Fifty-One

It was the next day, and time to go. The new Chief arranged an armed escort for them. Four were with muzzle-loaders, and four were with archers. Several had long blades slung at their waists. They looked very fierce, and some had scars, no doubt, Cameron thought, from fights with jungle animals that they hunted.

Surrounded in the front and back by the escort of guards, Cameron and Faint Chance left the village. Because the hunters knew the way, and were setting a faster pace, they made much better time than on the way in.

"It is quite impressive to be in the center of an armed escort that will shoot on sight, with no Miranda warnings," Cameron said to Faint Chance as they were walking.

"What are Miranda warnings?" she asked.

"Hmmmm. How to describe it," Cameron pondered, and then he came up with what he thought would work as an answer. "Sort of like verbal warning shots."

When they came to a resting place for the night, Cameron, exhausted, lay down to ease his aching muscles. The guards explained that they would not be making a fire, which could be seen, in case the bandit was following. Dinner was to be fruits and unheated things brought along with the guards. The guards spent the night surrounding their charges to protect them, with four awake and on alert at all times.

On the second day, they traveled even more distance. It rained for a few hours, but they continued on, as the hunters were not bothered by it. They saw some wild birds, but did not shoot any of the game they saw en route, as they wanted to be prepared for human targets. They would be able to look for something to take home on the way back to their village.

At mid-morning on the third day, they reached the end of the path. And there was the *tuk-tuk* driver, waiting for them loyally. It was such a welcome sight!

They said goodbye to the hunters, and wished them well. Once again in the blue *tuk-tuk*, they were off on the bouncy trip back to the hotel in Ban Houei Sai. Faint Chance said to Cameron, "On the way back, I am going to have the driver take us back to the lady who makes the northern Lao Lao. I want to get some."

"Sure," Cameron said. "You must miss it, eh?"

Chapter Fifty-Two

Cameron awoke at daybreak. He found himself in the nice little hotel cottage in Ban Houei Sai.

Cameron said to Faint Chance, who was sleeping next to him, "Wake up! We should go early, to stay well ahead of the bandit if he is still following us."

Outside, Faint Chance spoke to the owner, and got directions to where the "fast boats" were docked and said to Cameron, "The fast boats are on the other side of town, to the south."

Ten minutes south of the little town the driver of the *tuk-tuk* pulled off to the right to a small concrete-block building, painted green. There were window openings, but without glass, and a doorframe with no door. It hardly looked weatherproof, which no doubt accounted for the fact that the only things in the building were two tables, each with a chair, somewhat back from the open windows. The rooms were otherwise nearly bare. On one side was a place where the fast boat tickets were for sale, and on the other, an official-looking person who took passports and wrote down the information at a checkpoint. He used an old-fashioned ledger, which he must have taken home at night with him. There was no electricity in the building. Several young men, who were obviously the pilots of the fast boats, stood about outside. It was unclear if the fast boats were government owned or belonged to some agency.

Cameron and Faint Chance did not enter straightaway to get tickets. They instead walked over to the cliff at the edge of the Mekong River, twenty feet high. Going down to the boats were a series of steps, but not made of concrete or even wood – the steps were simply cut into the hillside with a shovel. They were irregular, somewhat soft from rain, and treacherous at some points. Cameron looked at the fast boats. What a difference from the slow boats!

Cameron was amazed at the shape and style of the fast boats.

They looked like racing boats for some modern race in the US, a most unusual sight in this poor country. Cameron estimated that they were eighteen feet in length, three feet wide and only a foot deep. The bow had a sharp point and tilted up in the air. They were very bright yellow and trimmed with painted geometric shapes, mostly of red, blue, white and black. On the back, sticking up from each boat, was a four-cylinder, twenty-four valve (it was marked in English on the valve covers), Japanese car engine, with a four-into-one exhaust collector that ended in a completely unmuffled megaphone that pointed back and slightly up – pure racing style. This was going to be very loud. The engine swiveled from left to right, as well as up and down. Sticking out of the back of the engine was a ten-foot long shaft with a completely exposed propeller on it. The method of steering was a handle on the front of the engine, with a throttle on it. The pilot would take this handle, which looked something like the collective on a helicopter, and move it from side to side, or up and down. There was no seat for the pilot, who sat to one side of the engine on the rear deck of the boat with his feet in the engine well. The pilot would keep from falling out by holding on to the steering rod. Helmets were provided for the travelers, as an option. It seemed so unlikely to see such things in Lao. Nothing like this would be allowed for public transportation back home, Cameron thought. What great excitement!

The fast boats could hold as many as eight people, two abreast. This was done with removable wooden seat backs that slid down into wooden guides on the insides of the thin hull to hold them in place. With the wooden seat backs in place in front of another seat, there was only thirty inches between the seats. The seats were simple cushions on the bottom of the boat. If the vertical board which formed the backrest for the people in front of you was in place, you had to fold your legs in tight in order to seat yourself in the boat.

Cameron went back up to the building and talked to Faint Chance. He told her, "Tell the man that we want to rent an entire boat for ourselves."

They gave their passports to the official to write down the information about them in his ledger. The small building had a divider, equally dividing it into two rooms, but the divider only came out halfway. It was to separate the official with the ledger from the other man who collected for the boat trip. They walked around the divider to the man who took money for the fast boat ride to the river. Posted on the wall over him were the rates. The rates were for one person, and were either to Pak Bang, which was halfway, or to Luang Prabang, which was at the end of the journey.

"Faint Chance, I think it would be a good idea to ask which of the pilots is the fastest. The bandit may be following us. Ask the group of pilots over there which of them is the best."

She walked over to the group of pilots who were waiting for a trip and talking to one another, and said, "Which one of you is the best and fastest boat pilot?"

All of them formed together and pointed out one young man who was just a few feet away. He seemed to blush somewhat with the compliment. The others laughed somewhat, but it was clear that this was not a joke; this young man who they pointed out was clearly the best pilot amongst them.

Cameron said to Faint Chance, "Go tell the man inside we want that pilot."

She got his name, and did that. The man inside agreed, and they went to the perilous dirt steps cut in the hillside, which were all different sizes and shapes, to get to the fast boat.

The pilot had hustled on down ahead of them to the fast boat, and was making some quick preparations to the boat before they got to it. He took out the extra boards for the seat backs, leaving only one in place for his two exclusive passengers. They had to get into the boat carefully, as it was light, and stepping on the edge might capsize it, especially with Cameron. The pilot took off his shoes, rolled up his pants and stood in the water a foot deep to give them his hand and assistance with getting into the racy yellow boat. He put two vinyl-covered cushions side by side where they were to sit, which the pilot had determined so as to get the best planing and performance out of the fast boat, given the overall load. He placed them back of center, not far ahead of the end of the motor compartment. He had already taken their bags and put them in the bow, and then tied them across with some thin rope.

He offered them two life jackets, orange in color. They were rather small.

Cameron asked, "Can you swim well?"

"Yes, I can."

"Take one if you want, but I will pass," he told her. She also declined one.

Cameron waved the life jackets away. Cameron disliked such things. He did not want to spend the day with a big orange "Mae West" around his neck. The pilot next offered them helmets. The helmets were full cover, with no face shields. Cameron declined those also.

The pilot made his final preparations, secured two cans of extra petrol and put their bags in the front, tying them down with ropes.

The pilot then stood in the water near the shore, and turned the boat towards the center of the river, and gave it a big push. He then took a few steps and jumped over the back and into his position.

He then went through the procedures of starting the boat. He turned on the gas, primed the engine and put on the choke. The engine ran, and the pilot warmed it up by going around in two circles not far from the shore, to make it easier to come back in case something went wrong, like engine failure. The river was fairly narrow at that spot, perhaps one thousand feet wide. On the other side was Thailand. But there was a visible current in the river, most easily seen where there was a branch or rock sticking out, as the water made a wake around any such obstacle.

Everything seemed to be in proper order, and so the pilot yelled something back to another standing by on shore, who was waiting to make sure all was well. If the boat failed, they might need a rescue if the current was too strong, Cameron thought. The current might take them downstream a few hundred yards before they could get over to the shore to moor.

"Well, off we go!" Cameron said to Faint Chance. "Have you ever been on one of these?"

"No, I haven't," she replied.

"Neither have I."

The pilot tried the engine a few times by revving it up with the long shaft out of the water. It seemed to be clear and running well. He put the shaft down in the water and turned on the throttle. Cameron and Faint Chance were pushed back in their seats, and the speed they attained in no time was quite scary at first. Cameron tried to estimate it, and put it at fifty to sixty miles per hour.

But in just a minute, they slowed down to a slow pace. There was a dock ahead to the left, and it was sticking out into the river fifty feet from the shore. It was obviously a petrol dock.

The pilot brought the fast boat up to the dock. The level of the dock was two feet above the boat. A young man was lying on the dock, resting. He got up when the boat came. It all looked like something out of the past from an old *National Geographic*. There was a plastic tube sticking up in the air, six inches in diameter, with little black lines and numbers painted on it. There was a good-sized hand crank, and that was attached to a hose that went down into the water and towards the shore, which Cameron figured was where the petrol stores were kept. The pilot and the young man on the boat spoke, and a rubber hose from the apparatus was put into the primary petrol tank. The young man then turned the crank, and petrol, red in color, filled the plastic tube to the top. Then the young man stopped and turned a valve, and the contents of the tube ran down the hose into the boat tank. Cameron figured the marks must be in liters. Gravity was the method used, after the young man turned the pump to fill the tube.

The filling process took quite a few fills of the plastic tube, and each time the tube was filled, the young man made a mark right on the wooden boat's deck top with some sort of chalk or other marking instrument. The pilot filled the main tank, and then checked the extras, adding to one. The pilot gave the young man money from a small purse that also had some papers in it – probably some documents that allowed him to go down the river and be cleared at the government stops. They were now ready.

Off they went, down the Mekong River. There were clouds,

and occasional mist, but it was not enough to wet them. The sun broke out from time to time, and when it shone, it was hot. The pilot was very good. Cameron could tell from the way he expertly handled the boat. Cameron was glad they had asked for the best pilot.

The river was not cleared of rocks, like the navigable rivers in the United States. There were rocks as big as ten or more feet high, sticking up now and then. There were sand bars underneath the water, making it very shallow at spots. The rocks that jutted out of the water varied from a few inches to ten or fifteen feet in height. There were currents around the rocks, and it was obvious that the pilot knew the river very well. He could tell when to slow down slightly, when to slow a lot and when he could run the boat wide-open. He was also a very fast pilot. No other boats had passed them.

As they traveled awhile, Cameron noticed that the rocks seemed to come in groups, rather than just a single rock sticking out of the water. Cameron tried to estimate the depth of the river, but it was not clear, and he could only guess from the rocks sticking out that it was not very deep. The fast boat had a flat bottom, obviously designed to be able to navigate the shallows of the river. On occasion, the pilot went rather close to some of the big rocks. Cameron wondered at first if that was daring or careless, but as the trip continued, he realized by continued observation that the pilot knew exactly where to take the boat, and Cameron began to get much more comfortable with the pilot's ability. As fast as they were going, they could easily demolish the boat and get killed if they smashed into one of the rocks.

Cameron was surprised to see that the shoreline of the river looked in many places like wonderfully clean, white sandy beaches on the ocean somewhere. Cameron had never seen nor heard of a river that had so much sand on it. The water was not clear like ocean water, but the beaches looked very clean.

As they traveled further, Cameron noticed that many of these white, sandy shores had green things growing on them in some places, all in neat rows, obviously planted. Cameron occasionally saw some sort of water buffalo wandering about. As he studied them as they went down the river, it became more clear. The locals had come down to the sandy areas as far as they could, depending on the height of the river and what season, and placed bamboo stakes to stake a temporary claim. Some sort of natural fiber was wound around the bamboo stakes to form a fence, to keep out the water buffalo and God knows what else. They had planted crops inside the fence in the sand. Apparently they knew how long the river would be low enough to utilize the sandy area for a crop, probably a few months at most. He was very amazed at the fact that anything would grow in the sand, but grow it did. He saw different kinds of crops growing at different stages.

He asked Faint Chance over the roar of the engine, "Do you know what those crops are?"

"Yes, I recognize them. They are sweet potatoes and peanuts."

And so they went down the Mekong River, weaving in and out of the rocks at times, traveling at sixty miles per hour. They looked at the growers of the sweet potatoes and peanuts when they saw them, and Cameron marveled at how industrious these people were. It was wonderful, and the two of them enjoyed every minute.

There were occasional mists of water from the broken clouds that looked like rain clouds, but there were also distinct sunny portions between them. In the sunny spots it was hot. It was an unusual sky.

Faint Chance occasionally hugged him, wanting and needing him, still very upset about the evil that had followed them to the village.

After a half day, the pilot began to slow a little, even though there were no rocks. He spoke to Faint Chance. She turned to Cameron and said, "This is Pak Bang. It is halfway. Here we will stop to rest, and you can get something to eat."

Cameron looked up, and he saw a boat dock on the left, thirty feet long, a few feet from the shore. There were fifteen or more boats docked there. A hundred feet up, on a ridge overlooking the river and the dock below, was a cottage hotel where the slow boat people stayed overnight. The steps up were the irregular "cut in dirt" type, and the midday sun shone brightly on them. The only thing at the top was the cottage hotel for the overnight passengers that had taken the slow boat. They did not feel the need at the time to check out the hotel. The steps looked too gruesome just to go have a look.

There was a most unusual bathroom, consisting of a wooden outhouse built on top of the dock at the corner towards the river. Inside, there was a simple hole in the floor that was four feet down to the river. There was no seat.

Inside the open-sided dock were a dozen or more tables of varying sizes. The food preparation was done in the center towards the rear by a heavy woman and a pretty young assistant. The dock was floating and tied only a few feet from the shore, anchored by ropes. It had a walking ramp to the shore, ten feet long. Several of the tables had customers. Some were local river people, and there was one table of four European students.

"Order me a Laobeer," Cameron told Faint Chance. "Get us something to eat. You pick."

Faint Chance ordered beer for the two of them, and also rice noodle soup from the short, wide woman.

The short woman brought two bottles of beer and opened them for them. They were a welcome treat in the hot day and after a long ride sitting in a single position. She returned with two large soup bowls, with a clear broth, noodles and various small bits of green vegetables.

"This is really good beer," Cameron said, taking quite a bit of it to quench his thirst. It was sunny at the boat dock, but dark clouds surrounded the mountain tops. As they drank the soup, they could see the boat pilot checking the boat, adjusting the ropes on the baggage and transferring petrol to the main tank. A good man, Cameron thought, as he watched him off and on. He polished off the beer quickly in the heat of the day, and then ordered another by holding up the empty bottle to signal the woman in charge.

Faint Chance had her hair forced back by the wind, and looked a little like a sports athlete. He imagined he did too, but there was no mirror in the bathroom, just a hole, so he did not know how on earth he looked.

After forty-five minutes on the dock, the woman who ran the place told them something in Lao. Faint Chance interpreted, "The boat is ready."

They boarded the little boat for the rest of the trip to Luang Prabang, another three hours away. There were several other fast boats coming and going, as it was midday, and the stop at Pak Bang was halfway. The fast boat was pushed out by another pilot assisting, and their pilot fired up the noisy engine. Off they went.

The rest did them good, especially Cameron, as he was not used to sitting in the same position as they had in the boat all morning. They were both refreshed.

They did not notice across the lake, near the other side, another of the fast boats that had its motor off. It was just sitting in the water, waiting for something. It had a single passenger in it, in addition to the pilot.

Chapter Fifty-Three

"Thank you very much for taking me down the river in this manner," Faint Chance told him over the roar of the megaphone exhaust before it reached full volume as they pulled out of the dock at Pak Bang. "It is beautiful!" she told him, looking around her at the shoreline and the jungle surrounding the Mekong River on all sides. They hugged each other as the speedboat roared off.

The sky was mixed with heavy, dark clouds and rays of sun coming in-between them off and on. It continued to look like rain, yet none came, except for occasional light mists of moisture, which felt cooling and good on the hot river.

Twice they saw a "slow boat", the larger green ones for passengers like the ones they saw at the ramp on the north side of Ban Houei Sai, coming up the river, en route in the other direction, heading from Luang Prabang to Pak Bang. There was an occasional fast boat coming up the river as well. However, no one overtook their boat going down the river. Their locally-notorious pilot had passed several other pilots in fast boats going the same direction, two in the morning and another two in the afternoon by that time. He was, it turned out, the local "hot shoe", that is, qualified to be a contest racing driver with one of the fast boats.

After an hour, the pilot turned his head to the rear, off and on. Cameron did not think anything of it at first. As the pilot continued that off and on for a while, Cameron turned as well. Cameron did not have the vantage point that his pilot did, as Cameron was down in the bottom of the boat, whereas the pilot was sitting up on the deck near the engine. Even though it was only a foot higher, it gave the pilot a considerably longer view up the river, and he could face the rear easily, while Cameron could only strain and try to see around the engine, which was screaming away. The bumping up and down, the very fast speed and the turns in-between the occasional rocks made it impossible to stand, or even get up on his knees without risking falling out. Something was bothering the pilot.

Finally, after another half hour, when they were in a turn so Cameron could see around the engine behind him, he saw what the pilot had been turning to see. There was another fast boat up the river, behind them several hundred yards. The boat was visible once in a while, as they made turns and straightened out going down the Mekong River for the next half hour. The boat behind them was catching up little by little. Perhaps the following boat had no passengers – then the pilot did not have to worry about a very rough ride.

They approached some rock formations coming directly out of the middle of the river. There were quite a few of them, and the pilot slowed and maneuvered around them. This gave the boat behind, which had not yet slowed for the rocks, a chance to get close enough for Cameron to see that it did have a passenger, only one, and a pilot.

After they cleared the rocks, the pilot of Cameron and Faint Chance's went back up to speed. The boat behind them had gone through the rocks faster than they had, and was now closer. Their pilot looked about once in a while, but did not seem to change his pace. It was as though he was going as fast as he could without tossing about his human cargo unnecessarily. There were turns, and slower sections of the river to navigate through, and within nearly fifteen more minutes, the boat behind was catching up.

The boat behind came up on the right side slightly behind their boat. It had one of the local pilots, and a Japanese passenger, in his late twenties! It was the same bandit!

Cameron said excitedly, "That is him! It is the Japanese man who killed the Chief. Tell the pilot whatever you have to. Tell him there is danger if he does not distance himself from this other boat, and a big bonus if he gets us to Luang Prabang well ahead of it."

She spoke to the pilot over the roar of the engine, and he appeared to be getting most of it when the other boat came up much closer, just behind, and forty feet to the side. The boats were bouncing in the river, motors roaring.

The Kumi-cho took out a semi-automatic pistol and began

shooting at them! One of the bullets hit the boat just a few feet ahead of Cameron and Faint Chance, making a hole above the waterline. The bouncing boat made it hard to aim.

There was little they could do except go faster. Cameron told Faint Chance, "Tell him to go as fast as he can!"

She yelled that to him, but off to the side something was happening. They all looked. The pilot and the Kumi-cho were fighting! Apparently the pilot of the other boat was not going to allow shooting from his boat, and the Japanese man was fighting him to get rid of him! Their boat slowed, as no one was at the throttle. Cameron and Faint Chance sped on.

As they watched and gained a little distance, they could see the Kumi-cho successfully knock the pilot overboard into the river. Then the Kumi-cho took over the throttle himself, replacing the position of his former pilot. The chase was on again.

Their pilot got the message, and started to go wide-open. He was going now as fast as he could, and barely slowing to go around the big rocks sticking out of the water.

Their pilot expertly maneuvered through the rocks and the sand formations sticking above, or nearly above, the water as they raced down the river. There was no way for the Kumi-cho to equal his skills, but he had the advantage of following. On a racetrack, a driver with less talent can follow a more talented driver behind and just imitate, and go faster than he normally would. In this case, even though the Kumi-cho was not familiar with the boat, going wide-open on the straight parts took no talent, and winding through the rocks at speed was done by knowing where to go without hitting an obstacle just below the waterline. Their pilot was showing him how, by simply being ahead. And, the following boat had only one person, whereas the boat in front had three. The Kumi-cho was closing in little by little, in spite of his lack of experience in piloting one of the boats.

The race was on. All of a sudden, Cameron and Faint Chance heard two loud whistling noises beside their heads, and they turned around to see that the man following them was shooting his pistol with one hand while holding the control stick with the other. He was eighty yards back at that point, and there was a straight stretch that allowed him to take some time to aim.

Cameron said to Faint Chance, "Tell the pilot to weave back and forth without losing speed, and to try to lose him in the rocks ahead with some tight turns."

She yelled at him, as the roar of the engine, only two feet behind them, now going wide-open, made hearing difficult. He understood, and turned expertly a little from side to side, weaving, as the bullets continued. One bounced off the engine of their boat.

The race continued, and the three of them all knew that they either had to lose the man following them, or somehow get him to make a mistake. Otherwise, they would be killed. The pilot was traveling without much slowing at all, and Cameron and Faint Chance had to hold on tightly. As the rock formations came up, it seemed that the boat was pulling several Gs in the tight turns it was making.

Cameron yelled to Faint Chance over the engine noise, "Tell the pilot that the man does not know how to pilot one of these. Tell him to try to lose him in the rocks if he can."

Faint Chance could not be heard well by the pilot from where she was, so she turned to the rear on her knees to keep from being thrown overboard, and yelled the command to the pilot in Lao. On the second time, he got it. He understood, and acknowledged with an expression and a nod. Faint Chance turned and sat back so as not to be thrown out. The boat was slapping up and down. The pilot leaned forwards into the wind and closer to his control stick, as though to pick up even more speed and to brace for some tight turns. Cameron and Faint Chance held on tightly to the sides of the boat and to each other.

Another rock formation was ahead. The river was only two hundred feet wide at that point, and the rocks stuck up sharply towards the sky. Passage space was narrow between the larger rocks near the center of the river. Normally, a pilot would slow to ten miles per hour to go through this dangerous part. Their pilot knew it well, as he had been going up and down the river for several years, almost daily, and had a plan. The Kumi-cho was shooting with his right hand, steering with his left by holding the steering stick that stuck out straight in front of the engine. He was sitting, as the pilot did, on the right rear of the boat to the side of the engine.

There were two large rocks jutting up ahead. They were tall, twenty feet high. On the sides of them were many smaller rocks also sticking out of the water. The big rocks were staggered, the one on the left further downstream by twenty or thirty feet than the ones on the right, which the pilot knew very well from his regular trips.

As they approached the rocks, the pilot went slightly to the left, as though he needed some room to turn right. The Kumi-cho did the same, his pistol in his right hand, waiting for a good shot. The staggered rocks obscured another big rock in-between them, which became dead ahead once you went through the two forming the opening. Once through the first two rocks, it would be necessary to make a very sharp turn to the left to avoid the third rock, which was fifteen feet wide and a little shorter in height. Going through slowly was the only way to safely pass. The experienced pilot turned sharply to the right to go between the two rocks. The turn was very harsh, and the boat pulled several Gs. Cameron and Faint Chance had to hang on tightly as the boat rolled up on its side, nearly flipping over.

The pursuer behind did not slow, and the distance between them became less. He was now one hundred and fifty feet behind them, steering carefully, aiming for the opening in-between the two tall, staggered rocks.

The pilot knew that just after the opening, it was necessary to make a hard turn to the left to avoid the other rock that was ahead but obscured before going in-between the rocks forming the opening. Normally, the speed he would enter would not be over ten miles per hour. Instead, he did not slow. By doing this he went out of sight of the boat behind, as the rock on the right obscured them from their pursuer.

Just after going through the opening, and when they were momentarily out of sight of the boat behind, the pilot cut the throttle somewhat and leaned back and out to the right hard to turn left. In this manner he was out of the way of the steering stick which he yanked hard towards him. He pulled it right over his chest with both hands on it. The boat nearly flipped over as it went up on its other side, in as tight a turn as it would make to the left, narrowly missing the rock dead ahead. Cameron and Faint Chance were nearly thrown out in the amazing maneuver. The pilot then resumed to the speed he had lost in the turn. All that the man behind could see was that the boat in front had gone in-between the rocks.

Had their pursuer seen what they had done, he would have cut his throttle. But he did not, and he went between the tall rocks at full speed not knowing he was being led into a trap. He did not know what they had done, and could not see the rock directly ahead. He could not hear that their engine speed had been cut, as his own was so loud. He was steering with his left hand, his gun in his right. He turned to the right after entering the opening.

There it was, directly ahead – a massive rock! The only path to avoid it was to turn hard left, which he realized he had to try to follow. He could not automatically drop his weapon because of his instinct not to part with it. When he saw the huge rock ahead, he tried to move quickly, but he had a problem that the pilot for the boat in front had arranged. The control stick stopped short of coming all the way to the right in order to make the hard left turn needed to avoid the big rock, as it stopped right into his mid-section. He did not have the experience to lean backward quickly enough pulling the steering stick over him to get more turn out of the boat. He tried to lean to his right to allow the control stick more movement, but to do so quickly enough to turn the boat that fast he would have had to instantly pull the stick past the point where he was sitting by leaning back to draw the stick over him as the experienced pilot had done, flinging the boat to its limits. The boat did turn, but not enough.

The Kumi-cho crashed, not quite head-on, into the massive rock. His boat exploded into splinters, and parts went flying. Cameron and Faint Chance saw, and felt sure that he was dead. However, they had no weapons, and dared not go back to see.

Cameron told Faint Chance, "Tell him not to stop, and to make good time the rest of the way to Luang Prabang." She told him that, and he complied.

They reached the little dock of Luang Prabang in thirty

minutes. There were no other boats at the primitive dock. The driver moored the boat, and they got out.

Faint Chance told him in Lao, "If you report the incident, we will all be detained until it is sorted out. It is better you say nothing."

The pilot did not seem at all interested in being detained, or involved with police. He told Faint Chance in Lao, "I will say nothing."

Cameron said to the pilot in English, "You have done very well," and he put something in his hand. With the compliment, the pilot gave a big smile. When he looked down at the two one hundred dollar notes in his hand, his eyes opened wide. He probably made a dollar or two per trip, and that was the most money that he had ever held at one time. He gave the *nop* bow to them as they walked away.

The docking area was forty feet or more below the banks, and it was necessary to climb another steep dirt path with some occasional steps cut with only a shovel. At the top, off to the right and back away from the cliff, was another checkpoint and another man in uniform with a ledger. It consisted of a wooden roof, five by eight feet in dimension, just under seven feet in height, and with four posts holding it up with no walls whatsoever. Sitting behind a simple desk underneath was a man in uniform, with a big book resembling an old ledger.

They gave him his passport and her identity papers, and he took down the information in his ledger. It was apparent that the government had these checkpoints along the Mekong River and logged who embarked and disembarked. However, there were no communication devices, and whatever information the government might get elsewhere would take some time – perhaps if they were looking for someone they might set up a communications radio, as otherwise the information was for records only.

Not far away from the official was a single *tuk-tuk* and driver waiting, hoping to get a fare from someone off a boat, like theirs, that might arrive that afternoon. Cameron looked at his watch. It was four thirty in the afternoon.

Cameron said to Faint Chance, "Tell the *tuk-tuk* driver to take us to the airport. We do not know for sure that the man is dead.

There will be an inquiry when the pilot who was pushed into the river shows up and tells how he was pushed out of his boat by a man shooting with a gun. We should go to the airport and see if there is a flight that we can still take today to miss any such inquiry."

They got in the back of the *tuk-tuk*, and the driver drove them to the Luang Prabang airport, a thirty-minute ride away. The road for the first part was a narrow, sandy, bumpy road ten feet wide.

All of a sudden the *tuk-tuk* driver stopped, the deceleration jerking Cameron and Faint Chance forwards in the back of the *tuk-tuk*. Jumping out in front of the *tuk-tuk* were three men, holding weapons. One came up and held a gun on the driver. The other two moved in.

"Get out!" he yelled at the driver, and then he looked at Cameron and Faint Chance in the back. He was holding a Colt M-16. One of the others was holding an AK-47. The third had a gun that Cameron could not identify, but was also an automatic weapon. They were not in any uniform, but were dressed like bandits.

The driver did not hesitate, and jumped out quickly. He stood with his hands up and looked very scared. The two men in the front moved in closer and kept their guns pointed at them all. The one that had approached the driver with the M-16 stuck it at Cameron and Faint Chance through the semi-open sides of the back of the *tuk-tuk* and barked out the same command to them. Once outside the vehicle, the nearest armed man motioned for them to raise their hands, barking out the command at the same time. The two of them raised their hands in the air. They were then motioned to stand off to one side with the driver, with one of the bandits standing guard while the other rifled through their backpacks that were taken from the back of the *tuk-tuk*.

Standing back with their arms in the air, Cameron asked of Faint Chance, "Who are they?"

"They are Hmong."

Cameron and Faint Chance talking came to the attention of the Hmong, and one came over to them, machine gun raised, and shouted something that Cameron did not understand.

Hearing nothing from Faint Chance, he asked her, "What is he saying?"

Not obeying his command, the Hmong went around to the back of Cameron, raised his machine gun butt and hit Cameron over the head. Cameron went unconscious.

Chapter Fifty-Four

A throbbing head was the first sensation that came to Cameron.

As he looked about, the world was upside down. Was it a dream?

As his senses slowly came back, he remembered what happened – he was hit on the head. Had he become dyslexic? Then he realized he could not move his arms.

As he looked about, he realized that he was hanging from a tree by a rope tied to his ankles, and his arms were tied with another behind his back. The ground was several feet below his head. He saw his backpack and that of Faint Chance, and all the contents laid out in a pile – someone had rifled through everything. One man with a machine gun sat on a rock standing guard.

As he turned his aching head, he saw Faint Chance strung up similarly, only eight feet away from him. She appeared to be unhurt.

She saw him move and said, "Are you all right, darling?"

Cameron said aloud in his dizziness, "She called me 'Darling'!"

He then answered, "Yes, I think so. Now I know why hotel rooms are only four bucks in Lao. Where are we?"

"They have brought us to a campsite not far from where they met us."

"Do you know what they intend to do with us?" Cameron asked.

"Not yet. A group of them have gone off somewhere and will be returning soon."

"What happened to the driver and his *tuk-tuk*?"

"I don't know."

"Who did you say these people are?" he asked.

"Hmong."

"What is Hmong?"

"You don't know?" she asked. "They worked for the CIA in

the Vietnam war. Better be quiet, I hear some people coming!"

There was rustling in the jungle nearby, and someone called out some signal to the guard, who responded. Soon five men appeared in the clearing where they had been taken to, weapons in hand.

One of them barked out something at Cameron. Not understanding, he said nothing.

"I will answer for us," Faint Chance said. She then said to the man (in Lao), "He is from America. He does not speak Lao. I now live in Vientiane. We are not involved with the government in any way."

One of the men, presumably the leader, said to her, "We can see that the man is from America from his papers in his satchel, and his clothes and camera. Where have you been, and where are you going?"

She answered, "We have been to the village in the far north mountains where I came from. We are going to Vientiane and later to America."

The same man asked of her, "What business did you have in the village? Are you looking for the Hmong to report our whereabouts?"

"We are not seeking the Hmong. We went to visit my father, the *Great Maw Pii* of the north, the greatest shaman ever. He was killed by a bad man when we were visiting him, but his spirit travels in the plant leaves that we bring. He is traveling with us, and will put a curse on you if you harm us or don't let us go."

That comment sparked a completely different tone out of the men. They began talking among themselves. It seemed there was some debate as to what to do.

They then untied them from the tree and lowered them to the ground, but left their hands tied behind their backs.

Cameron had to lie out on his back, as the world spun in dizziness as he went from being inverted to right side up after so long. Eventually he sat up, and could see Faint Chance sitting next to him.

The same man came over near Faint Chance and began to talk to her. "Exactly where is your village in the north?" He was testing her to see if she was lying.

Faint Chance then told him where her village was, and who her father, the Chief was. His expression changed completely.

The man then said to her, "Tell me of the *Great Maw Pii*. We have heard of him. His powers as the greatest shaman of all are well known."

"I have just come from the village, where I visited him until he died. He is now in the spirit world. Before he died, he gave me *ton mai piiset* where spirits reside. He told me to take the *ton mai piiset* across the ocean, and he told the spirits to follow the plant and me there. He also attached his spirit to the *ton mai piiset* when he died."

The man became very frightened and then untied her hurriedly. "Show me the *ton mai piiset*."

Faint Chance went to the things that had been dumped out of their backpacks and found the bag with the plant leaves. She held up the bag to him, and opened it only a little, saying, "This is it. You must not touch it now that you have done this to us, and you must help us leave. If you do not, you and your ancestors will be cursed forever by the great spirit of the *Great Maw Pii*. If you help us, I will speak to the *Great Maw Pii* and tell him to forgive you and your ancestors."

The man spoke to the others, and they immediately put their guns down, untied Cameron and brought them water.

The man who did the talking said to Faint Chance, "We did not know that you were the daughter of the *Great Maw Pii*. Please do not curse us or our ancestors. We return your things."

"Will you escort us back to the road to Luang Prabang?"

"Yes," the man said.

"Very well, I will speak favorably to my father in the spirit world about you."

They were allowed to go and collect their things. Cameron's money and camera had been taken by them, which was returned to the pile apologetically.

Cameron decided things were going well and he better just shut up. They put their things back together and got ready to hike back to the main road to Luang Prabang, again traveling with an armed escort.

Chapter Fifty-Five

As they walked another jungle trail, this time to the former capital city of Luang Prabang, Cameron could finally speak in safety. And, they had no less than an armed escort of two tough-looking Hmong, each with a machine gun in hand.

"So what is a 'Hmong'?" he asked her, now that they could talk.

"I am surprised that you do not know of the Hmong," she answered. "We know all about them here in Lao. Hmong are a northern Lao race of people of eighteen clans. They worked for the CIA during the Vietnam war, fighting the Viet Cong and doing dangerous things for the CIA like rescuing downed American pilots. They were considered to be the bravest and most efficient warriors in Lao – some say the bravest in the world. Many years ago they were a wandering group in Central Asia, and eventually ended up in Lao fleeing persecution in China. When not fighting, they settle and burn forest patches to grow rice, corn and of course their cash crop, opium. But especially now, having become such fierce fighters, it is hard to take that away from them, and a small number of them are a challenge to the government. Lao has actually hired Vietnamese troops to come into Lao to help find the militia groups."

"This is all completely new to me. How many of them are there, and how many were involved in the Vietnam war, if you know?" Cameron asked, wondering how he could never have heard of these people.

"Three hundred thousand now live in Lao. Twenty thousand died in the Vietnam war. Many died afterwards in Lao. After Vietnam, many Hmong were gassed with toxic gas in some places by the communists, and had to flee to avoid death. One hundred and twenty-five thousand, which was nearly half of them at the time, went across the Mekong River into Thailand hoping to go to America, and waited in refugee camps for years before being allowed to come to America. Some did not leave and remained here or in Thailand. The Lao Government discriminated against the Hmong and they have very hard lives. Under the communist government that took over in 1975, of those who remained, over forty-six thousand were arrested and put in re-education camps where three-quarters of them died. Others have died of hunger and disease as life is very hard for them."

"Since Lao became a republic, what is it like for them in Lao?" Cameron asked.

"Even after our government became a republic, they did not believe that they were receiving the same benefits as other Laotians, and they have organized militia groups that receive money from their own kind in America, which they buy weapons in Thailand with that they smuggle into Lao. Those in America send money to those here for support as well. These militia groups now cause terror to the Lao Government."

"This is the first I have ever heard of them!" Cameron repeated.

"What do they think of Americans?"

"By and large they are still loyal to America as many now live there and are supported by the US Government. But that is not universally the case. Several years ago, there was an attempted assassination of the then US Ambassador to Lao, Wendy Chamberlin."

"I suppose that working here as an ambassador does have its risks," Cameron said.

"Yes, but the attempt was in America when she was giving a lecture!"

"My God!" Cameron realized how little he knew of world affairs. No one he knew ever spoke of anything like that. The Middle East was the main topic of foreign affairs news, and so little was heard of places like this. No wonder he hated the US news and refused to listen to it. They had their own agenda and tried to make ridiculous things into a mini series, completely omitting major parts of the world.

"Now, you must tell me what it is that you said that got us out of there. Whatever it was, it was very clever."

"The Hmong are said to be the strongest of shamanists."

Cameron interrupted, "What is a shamanist?"

"Shamanism is the ancient Laotian practice of contacting spirits of the dead. It is also practiced outside of Lao. A shaman is one who can do that. The Hmong go to a shaman to talk to ancestors, to obtain spiritual and psychological healing, and to heal illness."

"Does the Lao shaman have his own special ceremony?" Cameron asked.

"Oh yes, certainly. They chant, and jump about using a ring of metal discs in front of an altar for several hours to summon the dead."

"So what did you tell those Hmong that was so moving? They cut us down at once, then acted apologetic, let us live, gave us back everything and are now providing us with an armed escort to the road?"

"I told them who my father was, the *Great Maw Pii*, who the Hmong considered to be a shaman. They are from the north, and they had heard of his great powers to talk to the spirits, and his wisdom. I told them that he died during our visit, and that his spirit lives and is being carried in the *ton mai piiset* with us on our journey."

"I remember the part where you showed him the plant," Cameron said.

"I told them that they had wronged us and that if he touched the plant, and did not let us go, that the *Great Maw Pii* would curse them and their ancestors forever."

"Wow!" Cameron exclaimed. "That is fantastic! And they believed it!"

She looked at him seriously and said, "It is true."

Cameron became quiet, realizing that the plant, or whatever was in it, was certainly very powerful. And so was the *Great Maw Pii*.

Chapter Fifty-Six

Arriving late at a hotel in Luang Prabang, Cameron realized it had been the most eventful day in his life, and he jumped right into bed with Faint Chance after showering. The high-speed chase down the Mekong River with the Japanese bandit shooting at them, being captured by the Hmong... what a day to remember! They went right to sleep.

The next morning, Faint Chance came into the room and woke Cameron. He slept so soundly that it took him a while to remember just where he was.

"I have checked with the airline, and there is a plane to Vientiane at five o'clock. That means we have the day to show you about here at the old capital, where you will find some interesting architecture. How does that sound?"

"Wonderful," he said.

In her hand were brochures from the lobby. "Here is what I have in store. We will see the former Royal Palace, the Wat Mai architecture from the eighteenth century, the Wat Xieng Thong and the Buddhist architecture from the sixteenth century. Then we will go to the airport and fly to Vientiane. How does that sound?"

"Maybe I can get some ideas," he said, realizing this really was an opportunity. And he jumped out of bed. Surely he would be influenced and get some ideas. He fired up Candice's camera.

Later at the airport, they stood at the counter of the only airline, Lao Aviation. "How much is the fare to Vientiane?" Cameron said in English.

The girl pointed just behind her to a white-colored board hung on the wall just a foot behind her, where fares to several locations were handwritten with a broad green marker pen: VIENTIANE $US100 CASH ONLY.

"One hundred dollars for each passenger," Cameron read

aloud as he read from the crude form of rate announcement.

The girl did not respond, but it seemed that he read the message correctly. He pulled out his wallet and handed over a credit card. Nothing like plastic, he thought, with a feeling of satisfaction.

The girl declined the credit card, and again pointed to the board behind her.

"Yes, I see that," Cameron said. "Here. We will take two seats. Charge it to this card."

She refused to take the card and continued to point to the board.

Faint Chance broke the stand-off. "Cameron, I think she only accepts cash, not credit cards."

"What about Laotian kip?" Cameron asked, hoping to get rid of some of the kip in his pocket, somewhat resentful that he could not use his standard form of currency – plastic – that he used when traveling in America.

Faint Chance spoke to her in Lao, and said to Cameron, "No, only dollars. No kip."

"This is amazing," Cameron said to Faint Chance. "An airline that will not accept its own country's currency. What about other tourists? Who would know that Lao Aviation will not accept its own country's currency, and no credit cards? It is a good thing we are not carrying yen or deutschmarks. We would have to hire an elephant to take us there."

Faint Chance said, "I am sorry, but I do not travel and do not know of such things."

"What would we have done if the Hmong had taken our cash and let us go? What if we had lost it? It's a good thing I have some American currency left," Cameron said. "We might never leave!"

Chapter Fifty-Seven

After arriving at the Vientiane airport, Cameron said to Faint Chance, "If the bandit is alive, or has accomplices, they will try to find us here as they would know we are coming back here. You pick a hotel, but don't tell the driver which one, in case he might be asked where we are staying. Have him take us a block or so from the hotel, without mentioning its name. We cannot be sure the bandit is dead, or that he does not have accomplices."

At the hotel room, she asked, "I would like to stay with you, if you do not mind?"

"Of course."

In the room, Cameron opened the bag with the plant. It was now somewhat dried out, and only occupied half as much space. It retained its purple color, although less intense from having dried out. The orange leaves of which there were fewer, had lost most of their color and had become a sort of purplish brown.

"Look at this," Cameron said to Faint Chance. "These leaves have the same color as the Baron's exotic oolong tea!" He took out the Baron's tea leaves to compare. "Check this out!"

Faint Chance came over and looked at the comparison of the Baron's exotic oolong tea leaves to the *ton mai piiset* leaves. "Yes, they are nearly the same."

"I am worried that if the bandit is still alive, or if he has accomplices, and they find out where we are staying, they will come for the plant. So, I have an idea for a hiding place for the plant," he said. Cameron grabbed Candice's camera, and dismounted the bayonet mount lens off the 35 mm camera body. He then locked up the reflex mirror. This made a neat little storage space directly in front of the focal plane shutter and behind the lens mount. He put the plastic bag containing the plant leaves inside that space, which barely fit in with some tucking. He put the bayonet lens back on.

"See?" he announced. "Who is to know?"

Cameron put the precious tea gift from the Baron into two bags and said, "I will put one bag of the tea into the camera bag, as a decoy, and the other in our bag in the room here. If someone goes into the camera bag looking for the plant, he will think the tea leaves are the plant and hopefully leave the camera with the real stuff alone. The other is if he gets into the luggage in the room – if he gets these he will think he has the plant and take off. I will take the camera bag down to the hotel clerk and tell him to put it in the hotel safe."

That done, they were exhausted. They showered and sat in the room, quietly thinking of the day's events. Cameron poured himself a scotch whisky, and put it beside the bed, which he lay down on. Faint Chance came out of the shower. "Would you like a drink?" he asked her.

"Yes, I would." He poured it for her.

"There is some massage cream here in the bath. Would you like a massage for your sore muscles?" she asked Cameron.

"That would be wonderful!"

She wore a hotel terry robe from the shower. She came to the bed with the cream, and told Cameron to turn over on his stomach and relax. She took off her robe. Cameron took a gulp of the whisky, and relaxed his muscles as Faint Chance began her massage technique.

As she massaged him, he asked, "I have been wondering, when we were before the new Chief – how did you know that he would be told by the spirit world to let us live?"

"I didn't."

"Then why did you ask him to communicate with the spirits?"

"The new Chief was going to put us to death. I relied on my father to save us. He did."

"All this 'spirit business' is new to me, dear."

"But you can see that it is real, can't you?"

"I really don't know what to believe at this point," he said, so as not to offend her, but still tied to his skeptical analysis of the spiritual world.

He rolled over on his back as she continued the massage. She could tell he would not hold up for much longer, but she could also tell that he had some other energy left.

"I can give you a special massage now."

He wondered what on earth that might be. Faint Chance put her legs on either side of him and squatted over him without sitting on anything, in the sitting manner of the Laotians. She then lowered herself slowly over his body, and began squeezing him with only her sex! She started at his feet, and went up and down his front, passing over him.

Cameron, exhausted from the day, became consumed by his senses. He was alert enough to realize that he had never experienced anything like it in his life! After a time, she closed in, and Cameron concluded that this Faint Chance could definitely summon spirits of ecstasy not found on planet Earth.

Chapter Fifty-Eight

The rainy monsoon continued its deluge on Lao. The hotel window was open a few inches for ventilation, and the noise of the heavy rain pounded away and awakened Cameron. He slept so hard, it took him a while to realize all that had happened the day before. He turned over, and Faint Chance was not there. He heard her moving about the room, then saw her. She was drying her hair with a towel.

"Good morning," he said to her.

"Good morning. Did you sleep properly?" she asked.

"Yes, I did," he answered that unusual question of hers.

"I have already ordered up some Lao coffee," she said.

"Sounds wonderful."

"I should go to the shop," she told him. "My father will be worried about me, and he can use me there so he can run some errands."

"Is it going to be difficult for you to leave your adoptive parents and move to America?" Cameron asked.

"Yes. But if I stay here, the most likely thing that I would do would be to find a husband one day, and marry and have a family. In Lao, the wife takes care of the husband and the home, and that takes all of her time.

"It is not fair on my parents to have them supporting me forever. I hope to get good work in America. I have heard that the jobs pay a lot of money there, and one day I may be able to send some money home to my parents when they are too old to work any longer. So, it will be like my leaving to marry, except that I will be far away. I will write often, and after a few years I hope to have saved up enough from working hard to be able to come back and see them again. I love them very much."

Cameron could not help himself and said, "Would you consider living with me instead of Spencer and Candice?"

Faint Chance stopped what she was doing. Cameron was

putting her in a predicament. Spencer and Candice were her sponsors, and wanted her to live with them.

"I have promised Spencer and Candice that I would live with them. If I was to live with you, they would have to consent. They are to be my new American family, and I must do as they say."

Cameron realized that they wouldn't mind, but there was no way to relate that to Faint Chance at this time. Should he offer to marry her? But then she might want kids, as she was most likely very traditional. Well, he could find out. Maybe she would not even want him as a husband, with or without a child?

"I want to look into expediting your visa. I would like you to come and live with me in America, assuming that Spencer and Candice consent, of course," he added, to respect her loyalty to her sponsors to America. "I will go over to the embassy and see if you can come under some expedited visa, like a tourist visa. I would like you to come back with me, ahead of your immigration, if that is possible. Would you like to come over earlier?"

"Yes. I did not think it would take so long for me to get approval to come."

"Good. I will go to the American Embassy tomorrow and see if a tourist visa can be arranged for you ahead of your main visa. Today I think I will rest."

Her face glowed. He wondered after he said it if he could arrange what he had suggested.

He hoped he had not suggested something he could not deliver.

Across town at a hotel, Morio Uto, the Kumi-cho, quite badly beaten up from the crash, with fresh cuts on his face and arms, was talking long distance to Japan.

Uto told the Oyabun enough of the story and its status and asked if the Oyabun had instructions.

The Oyabun spoke. "I will arrange to put pressure on the brother and the sister-in-law in America to tell their brother in Laos to give you the plant. I have people there now who can do that. Call me back in two days."

Uto hung up, and felt good that he was working on this

project for the Oyabun, who had impressive and far-reaching influence.

Chapter Fifty-Nine

There was a knock on the front door of the Harrington household. That was unusual for ten in the morning. Priscilla Hargrove was giving English lessons to Devan. Rina, the housekeeper, heard the knock and opened the door.

Three men, wearing sweatshirts, gloves and black nylon screens over their faces held in place by their sweatshirt hoods, stormed inside. They drew out their guns when they were inside the door so that the neighbors could not see – they had also put on their face gear near the door so as not to attract attention.

"Don't move!" one of them yelled. Each had a pistol out and Priscilla and Rina found themselves looking at gun barrels.

"Where is the baby?" another said. Then he found Devan before anyone answered. He was sitting in his chair, where he had been receiving his lesson.

Their actions were swift and decisive. One stuck a gun in Rina's neck, and another put one in Priscilla's face. They went for the baby, and quickly wrapped the baby up in a blanket and carried him outside towards their waiting car. They walked backwards out the door, and one left a folded letter on the table near the door. In just a few minutes, they had successfully kidnapped Devan.

The note had typing on it. It was addressed to Spencer and Candice Harrington. The note said:

> *Take no action. Call no police or the FBI. If everything is done by you and Cameron as we demand, you will get your son back, unharmed. If not, the baby will be killed and left in a field somewhere.*

Priscilla Hargrove called her employers at once. "Mr. Harrington! Three men just came in here and kidnapped Devan! They left a note." She read it to him. "What shall I do?"

Spencer told her, "Just sit tight! I will get Candice and we will be there immediately."

Candice had ridden with Spencer that day, and he got her in her lab and they hurried towards home. He told her en route, "Candice, it is the plant! It has already started! Word has leaked out, and the criminal element has already learned of it! That plant is evil!"

Candice said, "I wonder just where Cameron is? Would he have the plant by now? We really have to wait for him to contact us to know what is going on over there. He must have the plant since they refer to him doing what they demand. Oh God, I am so worried about Devan!"

Chapter Sixty

Faint Chance was working at the jewelry store, allowing her father a chance to run errands.

A messenger came in. (In Lao), "Is this where I can leave a message for a Mr. Harrington?"

"Yes, I will give it to him," Faint Chance said. Faint Chance accepted it from him and asked, "What is this about?"

The messenger said, "I do not know. I was instructed to leave the envelope at this shop, nothing more."

An hour later, Cameron came to the shop. The father had returned and they both were there.

"Hi!" he said to her father, and gave Faint Chance a big smile.

"Here, this was delivered here for you." She held out the envelope for him. He opened it and read it.

> *Cameron Harrington: Call your brother and sister-in-law at once. Be at the Euro Café at 2.30 P.M. tomorrow with the plant from the village. Contact no one else.*

He showed it to Faint Chance, and said, "It must be the same man, or an accomplice. But why call Spencer and Candice? I had better call at once!"

The only phone in the shop was in the center of the store, at a desk that was surrounded by a square of jewelry cases. It was not private. He hurried back to the hotel for the call.

One could not dial out directly from the hotel room overseas, as the phone system was primitive by western standards, and so Cameron placed the call through the hotel operator. Ten minutes later, the phone rang and his call was put through.

"Cameron!" Spencer exclaimed with excitement. "Devan has been kidnapped! Have you been contacted by anyone? Your name is mentioned in a note that was left."

"I have been given a note to call you, and to bring the plant to someone at a café tomorrow," Cameron told his brother.

"So you got it!"

"Yes, and we were followed. There was violence. I will tell you later." Cameron did not know who might be listening, and he was still worried about being arrested and detained indefinitely by the Laotian police.

Spencer said, "Some men came into our home when Candice and I were working, when the tutor and the maid were there, and took Devan at gunpoint. We have been told not to contact the authorities, and we have not done so yet. We believe that these people would not stop at murder to get the plant leaves."

Spencer said, "Whoever wants the plant has kidnapped Devan, knows about us and has international connections. What do you think we should do? Can we really risk Devan's life? Candice and I would never be able to live with ourselves if we allowed our Devan to be killed just to get the plant specimen."

"There is a problem with contacting the police," Cameron said. "You will have to reveal the 'ransom' of the plant, and the news of it will get out. Then the village where it came from will be invaded by the outside world, and we have already caused violence to come there."

"Candice is worried sick," Spencer added. "I think you should relinquish the plant."

"I have been sent a message to go to a meeting tomorrow. I think the only thing to do right now is for me to go and then I will call you. Here is the name and number of the hotel that I am staying at."

Cameron went back to the jewelry store for Faint Chance. They went out to a café to be able to talk. "Devan has been kidnapped! These people are big time! They have the ability to send gunmen to Lao and nearly simultaneously have someone kidnapped in America. Having seen how ruthlessly they killed the Chief and the others, considering the violence and daring involved in a kidnapping, and with their international connections, I believe they are fully capable of killing again without hesitation! I do not want to be responsible for the death of my brother and sister-in-law, not to mention the loss of that extraordinary child himself.

They would then do violence to Spencer or Candice as a next step until they get the plant. I am sure of it."

"Is the plant all that valuable?" she asked.

"Whoever synthesizes it first can patent the formula and process, and can make billions."

"But if they stole it from you, how could they sell it legally?" Faint Chance asked.

"Stole what? A naturally growing plant? The first one to make the synthesized formula is the one who has something to steal. If someone gets it analyzed first at some lab, then synthesized and made into a digestible potion or pill that can be taken when creating a child, that person, or entity, will own it. It would be impossible to go to court to claim it is yours since it would be a formula that he came up with, not you. All we could do is try to convincingly prove he stole or misappropriated the natural plant from us. The plant is free for the taking in the jungle, if it can be found. And, with the kind of money and muscle that we have seen already, these people could fabricate undoubtedly convincing evidence that they had found the plant first. And we must not forget, with the kind of muscle behind these people, that we might run into some accident and never finish a court challenge. I would bet on that happening for sure.

"So," he continued, "I think we had better show up with those strange purple plant leaves tomorrow at the Euro Café, or we can expect them to kill Devan, and then come after Spencer and Candice. They have already come after us!"

Silence prevailed for a time as they looked at each other, trying to grasp the scope of the events. Finally, Faint Chance broke the silence. "The Baron's special oolong tea leaves are purple."

Cameron's eyes opened wide as he thought about what she said. "Do you think we could substitute the purple oolong tea leaves?"

"How would he know the difference?" Faint Chance added. "They look the same."

"It might take some time, days or longer, for them to get the leaves to a lab, analyze them, and finally determine that the leaves were not the genuine article, and were nothing more than exotic oolong tea! Devan would probably be returned unharmed soon after they got the leaves. Do you think we dare?"

"I don't know about these things," she admitted, not wanting to take part in a major decision for something that she knew so little about.

"I must think it through carefully," he said. "I could never face Spencer and Candice if I let Devan get killed over this."

Chapter Sixty-One

Cameron called Spencer in the US from the hotel room. "I am going to turn over the plant leaves tomorrow as I have been told to. If they contact you, go ahead and tell them what I said."

He dared not mention that he was thinking of the oolong tea substitution. There was no way to debate such a subject halfway around the world.

Spencer said, "We have not called the police. We doubt if there is anything they could do in such a short time. They would probably want to monitor the phone line to trace the calls coming in. I am sure these bastards are aware of that and would take precautions from where they call."

Spencer said, "Here is Candice. Please reassure her. She has been sort of a basket case since Devan was kidnapped."

The newspaper article read:

DEVAN HARRINGTON, INFANT SON OF SPENCER AND CANDICE
HARRINGTON, KIDNAPPED AND FOUND DEAD.

A picture in the newspaper showed a field where the small body of young Devan was found, and another was a picture of Devan himself when still alive.

Cameron's eyes opened and he sat up abruptly. How could this happen! Then he saw the hotel room, and the paper was no longer there. It was only a dream!

He would be responsible for Devan's death if he did not give up the plant! How could he ever look Spencer and Candice in the face again if he caused Devan's death? On the other hand, coming to Lao and finding the biggest discovery for mankind and simply letting it go would make it impossible for him to live with himself. This was the biggest decision he would ever make. This was his moment.

He looked over to Faint Chance sleeping next to him in the hotel bed. He lay back down, and tried to lower his respiratory rate as he found himself soaking in sweat.

Hours later, Cameron's eyes opened. He remembered his dream. The dream was so real, he thought. He wondered if the dream was a view into the future, or just an ordinary dream. What should he do?

Chapter Sixty-Two

Cameron sat in the chair sipping coffee sent up by room service. Faint Chance stirred and moved about in bed. She saw Cameron and asked, "Have you made up your mind as to what you are going to do? Are you going to give him the tea, or the plant leaves?"

"I am going to take a chance," he said, announcing his decision. "I figure that if the gangster sees the strange purple tea leaves, he will think he has the plant. He saw the plant with its purple color at the village, and no one has seen purple tea leaves like the Baron's. So when he gets the tea, he will think he has the plant leaves, and then report that he has the plant leaves and head back to wherever, probably Japan. They will release Devan, so as not to cause Spencer and Candice to call the FBI. I realize it is a gamble, but so much is riding on this discovery, that I am going to go for it. If I were to just go back home having relinquished the plant, after all I went through to get it, I would always regret that I did it. So, the gangster gets oolong tea. That is my decision."

"I want to come along," she said. "And I want to be part of it."

"These people are dangerous," he warned her.

"I know the Euro Café," she said. "I will get you there, and I want to be there. This is my future, however it turns out."

At midday, Cameron put the Baron's exotic purple tea leaves in a silk purse she brought from the jewelry store. The special plant leaves remained in the camera body where they had been put. Soon thereafter they called for a *tuk-tuk* to go to the Euro Café.

The *tuk-tuk* pulled up to the Euro Café, a neat wooden cottage, stopping in the dirt drive by the steps. It was all very newly decorated in beautiful teak inside and out with a large western-styled bar inside. The several tables in the small but neat place were covered in tablecloths of blue-and-white checks. The motif of the newly-decorated establishment was designed to give it a European flare. At an off hour in the new place, no other customers were there – the gangster picked a perfect meeting place.

As they sat at one of the empty tables, the waiter approached with menus.

"Just two coffees," Cameron told him, so as to order something to be permitted to remain. The waiter seemed to understand as he nodded and went away to get the coffees.

At 2.35 P.M., Morio Uto walked in the door. It was the same man whom they had seen in the Chief's house. He was alone. His face was scratched up, no doubt from the river accident. He had a bandage on his left hand.

Cameron had immediate ideas of jumping him as the earlier scene at the village went through his mind. The Euro Café had western utensils, as it catered to westerners. There were knives, forks and spoons on the table at each setting, and Cameron thought of taking one of the knives and plummeting it into him. Faint Chance also had an intense reaction of hatred and desire for revenge.

She could sense the coldness of the gangster.

"What is your name?" Cameron asked the gangster.

Uto looked Cameron straight in the eyes and said coolly, "You do not need to know my name. What you do need to know is that I hold the power of life or death over your brother and sister-in-law's baby. If you do not give me the plant, he will be found in a field somewhere very dead. Then harm will come to your brother or sister-in-law next. You can be sure of it."

The threats had a very convincing tone. After a few moments of silence, he asked, "Did you bring the plant?"

"If I give you the plant, how soon will the baby be returned?" Cameron wanted to make it look like he might or might not have the plant, and wanted further assurance that the baby would be released if he turned it over.

"Within a few hours after I call, and I will call as soon as you give me the plant. We have no reason to hurt the baby if you give me the plant."

Cameron had no reason to suspect otherwise. If they killed the child, there would be a very great motive for the FBI, police and international authorities to track him and his accomplices. But if the matter was over and done with in just a few days, with the baby returned safely, the matter would be treated completely differently even if reported. So they had a motive not to harm the kid if Cameron gave them the plant. But they sure as hell would have to take some protective measures once they found out they had oolong tea!

The very edge of a multicolored paper was sticking out of Uto's shirt pocket. Only a quarter of an inch stuck out. Faint Chance recognized the colors, but said nothing. The colors were pastels. It looked like the bound edge of an airline ticket.

Cameron took the silk bag of the Baron's exotic purple tea leaves out of his pocket and put it on the table. Uto picked it up and opened it. He smelled it as though he might recognize it, but realized he could not. The distinct purple color was present, but dulled, just as he had anticipated it would be.

"If this is some sort of trick, or if you notify any authorities, you can be sure of swift and certain retaliation!"

In order to divert the gangster's attention from studying the plant, Cameron introduced his own form of drama and said, "It is no trick. We have not contacted any authorities anywhere. However, if Devan is not returned in a few hours, the FBI and other authorities will be notified, and worse for you, I will fixate on you for the rest of my life and utilize all of my resources to locate you and put you in the ground."

Uto was used to living in a world of threats and did not feel particularly threatened by Cameron, but he did read into his statement a very firm resolve – it took his attention off the plant. He closed up the bag with the plant and said, "I will make the call." Uto got up and left the café.

The waiter came with the coffees. "I hope I have not made a big mistake," Cameron told Faint Chance, worried. "Let's hope that he doesn't find out about the fact that he has oolong tea before they release Devan!"

"I wish I could find out who he is," he said, frustrated. "As it is now, we have no idea who he is, what country he lives in or anything else about him. There is little we can do, other than try to get the plant leaves out of Lao and get back and take precautions against retaliation."

"Did you notice the paper in his pocket?" Faint Chance asked.

"I saw a paper with some colors on it," he said.

Faint Chance said, "Those are the colors of the new airline that just started up last month here. It is called Silkair, and is based in Singapore. The only flight from here on Silkair is to Singapore. To get a ticket on it, you must go to the office, which is only two blocks from my father's shop. It is new, and has only one full-time girl and an assistant girl helping. The girl in charge is my very good friend whom I have known for a long time. Let's go there."

"Can we get her to help us?" Cameron asked, wondering if her friend would jeopardize her position for Faint Chance.

"I know her very well."

The *tuk-tuk* driver took them near the ticket office, but not right in front in case Uto might have gone there himself. There was no sign of Uto. The same pastel colors of the ticket in Uto's pocket decorated the place, as the airline colors. They went inside where two Laotian girls in their twenties, the Silkair staff, sat behind the counter in the narrow office. A young Asian couple walked out and no one else was present. There were large books of schedules around them, below the counter, and a single computer screen. Scheduling for international flights in Lao had to be physically done at the ticket office, old-fashioned style.

One of the girls recognized Faint Chance and got up with a big smile on her face. They spoke in Lao. They were obviously good friends. After they spoke a bit, Faint Chance switched to English and said, "This is Cameron Harrington. He is from America."

The Silkair girl also spoke English, and looked approvingly at him. "I am pleased to meet you."

"Likewise," Cameron said. "This is a new airline?" he asked.

The Silkair girl replied, "Yes. It is Singapore-based, and at this time, the only flights out of Lao are on Mondays and Thursdays, and those are to Singapore."

It was Tuesday, Cameron thought. Just maybe the Japanese

man had already booked a flight out, knowing he would get the plant. Or had just planned ahead in case he got it so as not to delay in the country where he had already killed three people. Booking in Lao was not something you did from your hotel room, and so maybe, just maybe, the man would be in the reservations information.

Faint Chance took over and switched the conversation into Lao. She told her friend that they wanted to find a Japanese man whose name they did not know, and would she please look and see if any of the passengers were Japanese on this week's Thursday flight out of Vientiane to Singapore.

Without so much as even hesitating, the girl sat at her computer screen to check the flight. Since the airline was new and Singaporean, it had a computer for reservations, even if only one. The plane was obviously not a big one like a 747, as the number of people going to Lao had to be small. Cameron thought it would not be too hard to locate a Japanese person.

She said. "The next flight is Thursday, at 9.30 A.M. It is Silkair Flight No. 2. It is a direct flight to Singapore. There are no other flights until next week." As she looked at the screen, she said, "There are only two groups of parties with Japanese names. One group is four people, and the other just one person."

"Do you remember them buying tickets?" Faint Chance asked.

"Yes. The four people are two couples, the Yasumis and the Omoris. They are traveling together. They did not buy a ticket, as they already had one. They came in this morning together to confirm their flight."

"Can you describe them?" Cameron asked.

She started speaking in Lao, and Cameron was not sure if she realized it or not. Faint Chance interpreted, "They are elderly, probably retired."

"Who is the other person?" Faint Chance asked her in English.

"That is Morio Uto. He is a young man. He came in this morning also, and bought a ticket."

"Uto!" Cameron said aloud. Both girls looked at him. Cameron thought he had better not say too much in front of the Silkair girl. He recognized the name, that of Candice's assistant,

Tadashi Uto, who had been to two parties at Spencer and Candice's home. The connection came together. It must be a brother or close family relative of Tadashi Uto. Tadashi knew of the plant, as the only one that Candice had confided in. He talked! Was he involved? He had to be!

"That is the person you want?" the Silkair girl asked.

"Yes," Cameron said. "When is he leaving?"

"He is taking the Thursday flight to Singapore. He is traveling on a Japanese passport."

"Do you know where he is staying?" Cameron asked.

"Yes. We require a number to be reached as part of the reservation. He is staying at the Manoluk Hotel, in room twelve. Here is the phone number." She wrote it down for Cameron. "Do you want me to look up the address?"

"I know where it is," Faint Chance said.

"Do you have his passport number as well?" asked Spencer.

"Yes, we get that on international flights," and she added that to the paper, which she then passed to them.

Faint Chance thanked her girlfriend, who did not think it was any big favor at all. Quaint place, this Lao is, Cameron thought to himself. They left and went back to the little café next to the shop only two blocks away. They sat there, and ordered cold drinks. It was another hot day.

Cameron said, "So, we know he is going to Singapore for sure, on Thursday, unless he changes his plans. The only flights out are on Thai Air and Silkair. It takes some doing to make or change a booking, and he will probably keep the one he has made. So, we have only until then to report him to the police for the murder of the Chief, or he will be out of the country. I am afraid that if we report him to the police, and he is arrested, two things will happen that we do not want. The first will be that he might let his contacts know, and if he finds out we are his accusers, he may leave word to have Spencer and Candice's child killed. The second is that if the police are told, they will detain us as well until they make their inquiries. By the time they go to the village, obtain witness information and conduct an inquiry, many days will have passed. In the meantime, if they find out about the plant, which will undoubtedly happen, they will seize our supply as well as Uto's for evidence, and possibly because they may think it has value."

"There is corruption at high levels," Faint Chance added. "If the value of it was found out, they would take it and not let you out of the country with it."

"So," Cameron said, "reporting to the police is out." He thought for a while, and then said, "I think I have a plan that may work. I visited the Golden Triangle coming in from Thailand, and heard of the drug trafficking. Is there still drug trafficking in Lao?"

Faint Chance said, "Yes. It was not illegal to grow the opium poppy in Lao until 1996. It has been a major crop, and there are still a lot of people who make their living off of it."

Cameron asked, "Do you have any contacts that know where to get some opium, or heroin?"

"Yes, I do. There is still trading of that here in Vientiane, as it is only recently illegal."

"How do we get a considerable amount, such as a pound or so?" he asked her.

"I know some people who will know where to get it. Do you really want to go buy some?" she asked, wondering why he was suddenly interested in drugs.

He told her, "I have a plan that I believe will solve everything, but it will take some quantity of a strong drug such as heroin. Do you know how much heroin costs here? I have never bought anything like that, but back home it is very expensive, according to the papers and arrests that I read about occasionally."

She replied, "I do not know exactly, but I know of people who deal in it. I doubt that it is very expensive as long as you buy it here, inside the country. I think it gets expensive once it is smuggled out and arrives in its destination country."

"If I come along, will those people sell it to us, or do you have to go alone?" he asked her.

"I think they will, as I will be introducing you as a buyer from America," she said.

"What is the penalty for possession of heroin here in Lao?" Cameron asked.

"I imagine jail for a few months, as it has not been long since it was completely legal to grow and deal in it," Faint Chance said.

Cameron said, "First, let's go back to Silkair. I want to get a phone number in Singapore."

Back inside the Silkair office, Cameron asked the girl, "Do you have a phone number for the Singapore International Airport where the Silkair plane lands?"

The girl looked in a book, and replied, "Here it is. It is called the Changi International Airport. There are several numbers. What department do you want?"

Cameron replied, "Customs."

The girl wrote down the number and gave it to Cameron.

Outside they hailed a *tuk-tuk*, and off they went to her contact. After a fifteen-minute ride, Faint Chance told the driver to pull over in front of a home. She said, "Please stay here," and she went inside.

In a few minutes, she came out and told the *tuk-tuk* driver the next destination. She told Cameron as they drove off, "That was a fellow who knows where to go. We are going there now."

The *tuk-tuk* driver was instructed to go to another residence. As it was a bit out of the way, at Cameron's suggestion, Faint Chance told the driver to wait for them to take them back after they conducted their business inside.

Inside, there was a man and a woman. They all spoke in Lao, and the couple spoke no English. Faint Chance spoke to them for some time, and Cameron could hear some numbers and guessed they were discussing prices. There she was bargaining down the price of heroin. Finally, the man went to the back and came out with a plastic bag of white powder that looked to be a pound or even more. Faint Chance told Cameron, "For this he wants two hundred dollars. He says it is pure heroin, and of the best quality."

Cameron looked at it, and really had no way to determine if it was real or not. He asked Faint Chance if she knew if it was real. She told him, "I have heard of this man before. He has a reputation for selling heroin, and I am sure he is selling the real thing. It is easy to get here, and there is no reason to think it is not."

Cameron took her aside a bit so the dealer could not hear and said, "From what I know of it, the price is too low for it to be real, or concentrated. I would expect something like this to be many times that, even in the country of origin. But don't tell him I think it is cheap – just tell him I am concerned it is not pure."

Faint Chance looked surprised at that, as though she had some idea of the local price for the heroin, and the two hundred dollars was not cheap for it. She spoke to the man again. After a time, she said in English to Cameron, "He says he has heard of people reducing heroin by adding things to it. He says there is no need to do that in Lao as there are many poppy fields, more than there are people to harvest them. And, he would like your repeat business." At that she smiled at Cameron, as it did seem like a joke at that moment. Cameron chuckled. Nothing like relying on "reputation" for repeat business.

"Everything is cheap here in Lao," he said to Faint Chance. She did not respond as she did not have any experience outside of Lao and could not compare. Also, she thought things cost a lot there in Lao.

Cameron gave the man two one hundred dollar bills, and he split the heroin into two bags instead of one after obtaining another from the dealer, as one would not fit well into one of his single pockets without sticking out. Cameron put a bag into one of each of his front jeans pockets and they returned to the hotel under a late afternoon sky of pink and red.

Inside, Cameron said, "It may be a little early to call Spencer and Candice. Maybe we should wait a few hours, given the time change. This will also give the gangsters time to return Devan. I want to somehow get into Morio Uto's bag or bags at his hotel before he leaves the country to put the heroin in. I don't yet know how to do that. Do you have any friends at the Manoluk Hotel, like the girl at the Silkair office?"

"No, I don't. I have only been by it, never inside."

Cameron said, "We must give Uto time to call and for his accomplices to return Devan before we do anything to get him caught. So, tonight is out. I think the best time would be to wait until tomorrow. Perhaps he will leave the room to eat or do something, and then we can find a way in. Tomorrow is Wednesday, and he leaves on Thursday."

After dinner in the hotel, Cameron said, "It is still too early to call the United States. It would be best to wait a few hours before calling. Do you have any recommendations on how to pass the time?"

"Why don't we have a drink?" she asked him.

"That would be nice." She poured them each a drink from his bottle. As Cameron sipped his drink, she took a little of hers, and set it down. She then went to a bag she had brought along with her from home to the hotel room, and opened it. Inside were clothes, which she took out. She went to the bathroom to change her clothes, out of sight of Cameron. What was she up to? Cameron wondered.

She then came back into the main room in her change of clothes. She wore a traditional type of costume, made of silk, in a one-piece outfit. It had long, flowing lengths of silk, all with intricate flower patterns.

She then took out of her bag a small metal incense cup. Inside was a block of incense, which she lit and got going well. She then set the burning incense on the floor in the middle of the hotel room.

A small quantity of smoke began to come out of the spout of the cup, which after coming just a few inches out, turned invisible. It made a wonderful fragrance, which he could still only slightly detect as it was apparently going to take some time to reach him from across the room. He would soon learn that the fragrance's method of transportation to his senses was not quite what he had anticipated.

There was a radio in the room on the side of the bed, built into the night stand. She went to it and turned it on, and there was a station playing some sort of combination of modern music and Lao which was apparently in Lao. Cameron had no clue – it might have been from neighboring Thailand.

Faint Chance went to the middle of the room, and began a traditional dance of Lao. Her hands moved about in circles with the fingers wide apart as she rolled the hands around at the wrists. Her head moved from side to side as though she had a double-jointed neck, in the traditional style of Lao, which reminded him of a movie he had seen of a girl doing such exotic dancing in

Thailand. As she danced, he could see how light she was on her feet, as she occasionally turned full circles, and sometimes multiple circles. As she did, the loose silk dress that he could see the outlines of her legs through spun out and exposed her legs, and at one point he could see that she was wearing nothing underneath.

As she went around and danced the traditional dance, she would occasionally cross over the burning incense, and on occasion paused over it while moving her hands and arms about in the traditional, exotic dance moves.

As she paused over the incense, to move her arms and head from side to side, he realized that the purpose was not only to show the dance but also to provide stimulation. The purpose was for her to take on the fragrance of the incense up her legs for his later delight.

She danced over the incense, with her legs apart, just enough to remain delicate, but yet enough to allow the fragrance of the incense to rise up into her as she undulated over it. It was something Cameron had never experienced.

"Can this actually be happening to me?" he asked aloud, but to no one in particular. As he watched from the bed, her movements became even more suggestive, and she began to move her steps in more closely to the bed where her spellbound audience awaited.

Chapter Sixty-Three

Before retiring with an enormously satisfied feeling, Cameron called Spencer and Candice in the United States through the hotel operator. It was early morning there.

Candice answered, "Hello?"

Cameron said, "It is me. I have turned over the plant leaves."

There seemed to be little reason to alarm her, although threats of retaliation if Uto found out did make him wonder if he was doing the right thing. It would take some time for the gangster to find out he had oolong tea. How long? Should he warn them now?

"Have you got Devan back yet?"

"Yes, just minutes ago! A woman came up to the door. We went to the door, and saw her entering a car and leaving. Devan was at the front door. We are so relieved! I have been worried sick! Devan is fine and unhurt. We did not call the police. Do you think we should do so now?"

"Not yet. I am working on something here, and will call you soon." He then spoke to Spencer, and they talked and repeated how relieved they were that Devan was safe and sound.

"Was the event traumatic for Devan?" Cameron asked.

"Actually no. In fact, something they may not have known, but Devan is so smart that he can recognize who did it if the police can show him suspects!"

Cameron said, "By the way, a man named Uto is involved. He must be related to Tadashi Uto. Do not confide any further in Tadashi."

So it was done, Cameron thought. The kidnapping was over. Devan was safe.

But, now it was payback time, for taking the Chief's life, and for what he and his accomplices had done.

The next morning Cameron put the heroin that was in two plastic bags into a shopping bag, under a shirt. They hailed a *tuk-tuk*, and had it take them to a spot down the street from the Manoluk Hotel. The hotel was a two-story building of white stucco. It sat back from the street, separated by a flowered garden with palm trees. It had balconies trimmed in teak. There were gates in the front to open to a small circular drive. They were opened in the morning.

There was a row of little shops across the street. One shop was a little stall, with a rack of sundry items in it. Behind was a lady with an infant in her arms. The store had a modest amount of things like toothpaste, tissue, combs, chewing gum, sweets and things like that. The lady behind the counter was moving about, bouncing the infant up and down to keep it from crying. Next to that was another shop, further away from the hotel, that appeared to be a new business. Some fellow was bringing in boxes off the back of a motorbike. Another man was inside organizing things. There were boxes in the shop not yet opened, and Cameron could not tell what was in them.

Cameron and Faint Chance discussed hiding in the new shop, behind the boxes to wait and see if Uto would leave the hotel, as from there they could clearly see the front of the hotel.

Faint Chance asked the man unloading the boxes if the two of them might wait inside there for a while. He agreed, and allowed the two of them to stand behind the boxes in the front that formed piles four and five feet high, providing a form of cover as they watched the hotel entrance.

They waited for an hour, with the young man returning once in a while with more boxes tied to the back of a motorbike. The boxes contained small appliances, as one was opened inside and had a new electric fan in it. It was apparently a new small appliance shop, and the owner or someone else was bringing in the appliances to set up to sell.

"There he is!" Faint Chance said, the first to see him. Uto was out in front of the hotel, looking around, smoking a cigarette. He did not seem to be in any hurry to go anywhere. Cameron and Faint Chance ducked in tightly behind the new appliance boxes, as the man inside the shop watched curiously. After Uto had smoked half the cigarette, he raised his arm to a passing *tuk-tuk*.

The *tuk-tuk* pulled over and stopped. Uto spoke to the driver, and it took a while for him to explain where he was going. Cameron and Faint Chance were out of hearing range. After a minute or so, Uto climbed in the back of the *tuk-tuk* and off they went.

"So far, so good," Cameron said.

When Uto was out of sight, they came out from behind the boxes, with the man quite puzzled as to what they were hiding from. They walked to the hotel.

As they approached, Cameron said, "We know his room, number twelve. Let's just walk in deliberately like we are staying there. The morning desk operator will assume we came in last night, or are perhaps meeting someone. Just look like we know where we are going."

The entry was handsome teak. Just inside, to the left, was a wide spiral staircase leading to the second floor. How beautiful, Cameron thought, as he recalled how the uniform building code in America did not allow spiral staircases in commercial properties. Just because some fat people might not be able to negotiate spiral stairs well, something as nice as this becomes illegal, he thought. Too many laws! He realized he could not help but let his architectural background influence his observations.

Just beyond the staircase on the first floor was the reception desk. It too was in teak. As they walked in, it did not appear that the first floor, at least in front, had sleeping rooms. Cameron took Faint Chance's hand and made an abrupt turn to the stairs and led her up. They walked up the stairs as though they were going to their room. Up the spiral stairs, there was a huge sitting area, with teak floors. There were no windows on the arched stucco openings on the two outside walls. Against one inside wall was a big teak bar, but no one was there. Behind the bar were cabinets with locked sliding glass doors in front of various liquors the hotel was proudly displaying. There was only one of each bottle, unlike a western hotel. Just past the bar to the right was a wide hallway, also in teak, where there was a single elevator. They walked that way, and right across from the lift was number twelve.

The sitting area was obviously a meeting place for the hotel, to conduct parties. It looked like it might take between fifty to seventy-five people. They went over to a couch on one of the outside walls, from where they could see the door to number twelve. They sat on the couch, and tried to look like tourists waiting for their guide, or other traveling companions. Occasionally a maid or other staff person walked by, but paid them no attention. They hoped they were not too late for the cleaning maid.

As time passed, Cameron got anxious that Uto might return. What would he do when he saw that his identity was known? Where was the cleaning lady?

Finally, the cleaning lady came along pushing a cart. On the top of the cart were towels, soap and the things that were used to supply the rooms. In the bottom was a laundry basket and cleaning things. A mop was on the front of it, and there appeared to be some brushes in a bucket. She opened the door to number twelve and went inside, leaving the cart partly in the doorway.

Cameron said, "Get her out of the area somehow for a minute or longer if you can."

Faint Chance went to the room, stood at the door and said in Lao to the cleaning lady that she was waiting for some hotel guests, and needed to use a bathroom. The maid told her about a bathroom on the first floor, but Faint Chance acted like she could not understand where it was and asked if the maid would show her. The maid said yes, and led Faint Chance down the steps.

Cameron had only a very short time to act. He jumped to his feet, and quickly entered the room. Inside on a luggage stand was a soft bag, already packed. There were a few articles of clothing not in the bag on a chair. The bed was yet unmade.

Cameron quickly looked in the bag, towards the bottom. In the bottom were some jeans, that were soiled and rolled up. Apparently Uto had not given these to the laundry, not knowing when and how quickly he might have to move. Since Uto was leaving tomorrow, he would not be giving these for laundry, or he would have done so by now. Since they were soiled, Uto would most likely not bother them in the bag. It looked like a good place to stash the heroin. Cameron took out the jeans, and removed the heroin from his bag and put one each of the two plastic bags in the front pockets of the dirty jeans. He rolled the jeans back up, and put them as they were in the bottom of the bag.

He hurried quickly out of the room. The maid was returning. He walked right by her, trying to look natural about what he was doing, over to the wall adjacent to where he had been sitting, which faced the front of the hotel, and overlooked the courtyard and the street. The upper portion of the wall of the sitting room had arched openings with no glass.

Uto was getting out of a *tuk-tuk*!

Cameron quickly ran to the steps, and went down them two and three at a time. He slowed as he came in sight of the front desk so as not to attract attention.

He looked about, and then asked, "Where are the bathrooms?" A girl at the desk pointed to a hallway just past the elevator. He went there, assuming Faint Chance was in there, and might come out face to face with Uto. At the hallway, there was a men's and a women's. He could stay out of sight by standing just inside the wall, standing right in front of the women's.

Uto came to the front desk, and Cameron could hear him ask, "Any messages for number twelve?"

The clerk said, "No."

Uto came towards the lift. Just as he was approaching, Faint Chance opened the door from the bathroom! Cameron was standing in front of the bathroom door, just around the corner from the lift. He stood up against the wall. From where Uto was walking, he could see her if she came out from the hallway, as the door was only a few feet away. As soon as she appeared, Cameron put his hand on her mouth and grabbed her arm, pulling her to his right side, away from the corner.

They were lucky, as Uto had not seen her or heard the commotion. He pushed for the lift, and entered it when the door opened. Cameron and Faint Chance walked at a fast pace outside, went to the left entrance to the courtyard, turned left and began walking down the street, trying to look normal.

There was nothing more to do about the retaliation for the moment, according to Cameron's plan. Cameron asked her, "Lunch?"

Chapter Sixty-Four

The next morning at ten, Cameron and Faint Chance returned to his hotel room after breakfast to use the hotel phone. Faint Chance called her girlfriend at Silkair, to make sure the Silkair plane to Singapore was on schedule. She put down the receiver.

"Everything is on schedule," Faint Chance said, repeating what she had been told.

Cameron went to the phone and picked it up. He dialed the hotel desk, took the piece of paper he got from the Silkair office the day before and said, "I want you to call this number in the country of Singapore." The clerk said to Cameron that he would do so, and it would be a few minutes. Calling in Lao was like in old Europe, Cameron remembered, where one had to wait for the operator to find a "trunk line" when one called overseas like in the old movies.

After ten minutes, the phone rang. The clerk said to Cameron, "I have Singapore on the line for you, sir."

"Is this the Singapore Government Customs Office at the Changi International Airport?"

On the other end, a person who spoke English said, "Yes. It is. How may I help you, sir?"

Cameron said, "I do not wish to be identified, and so I prefer not to give you my name. This is an anonymous tip, but a good one."

The customs official said, "Yes, sir, we welcome anonymous tips. What is it you have to report?"

"En route at this time to your country is a Japanese man named Morio Uto, traveling to Singapore on Silkair from Vientiane, Lao. He is on Silkair Flight No. 2. It left Vientiane at nine thirty this morning, Lao time, which was thirty minutes ago. He will be arriving in two hours in Singapore, at the Changi Terminal. He is in his late twenties. His passport is Japanese, with the number 87949322. He is smuggling into Singapore over a pound of pure heroin. It is in his jeans pockets, rolled up inside his bag. He is a dangerous gangster and drug trafficker."

"We thank you for this tip. Can you give us a description of the man?"

"He is Japanese, five feet nine inches tall, with dark, medium-length hair. He is traveling alone."

The customs official said, "Very good, sir. I will make the alert." Cameron hung up the receiver.

"Why did you wait to turn him into the authorities in Singapore, instead of here?" Faint Chance asked.

"Don't you know about the Singapore Government and drugs?" Cameron asked.

"No, but I heard that Malaysia puts people to death for possession. Is Singapore the same?" Faint Chance asked.

"Yes."

"But won't he tell them that the heroin was not his, and that someone put it in his bag without his knowledge?" she asked.

"Sure!" Cameron answered. "But then all the smugglers say something like that. No one admits to it. He is obviously a gangster, and he will never be able to convince the Singapore Government that he did not know about it. The Singapore Government is known for not making exceptions in drug smuggling cases. He will be hanged within six months. It is a sure thing."

Chapter Sixty-Five

As international airlines do, there is always a stewardess or steward aboard the plane who speaks the language of the country that the plane embarks from and goes to. In this case, there was an attractive Laotian girl as one of the two stewardesses on the small new Silkair jet heading towards Singapore. At the beginning of her presentation of telling people how to use the seat belts, and in accordance with her customs, she bowed deeply to the passengers. She had a very sweet, high voice, and when she used the intercom she was very pleasant to hear. However, she drawled her vowels, but in a very delicate way. She also spoke Thai. Her accent in English was more Thai than Lao. She told them how to use the seat belts, and in the Asian tradition, she did not have the amplifier turned up too high to add importance to her little speech. When she finished, she went about serving the passengers with the help of another. Uto paid no attention.

The Silkair jet flew over Thailand, and then over Malaysia, on its way to Singapore. As the small jet passed Kuala Lumpur, Malaysia, the same stewardess, in her unusually nice, high voice came on the intercom and said, "Ladieeeeees and gennnntlemennnn. We have just passed Kuala Lumpuuuuurrrrrr, Malaaaaysi-ahh. Wee weeeel bee landeeeng in twenty meceenutes. Dee Capitaaannn has asked me to tell you to return to your seeeeeeets, to put de seeeeet backs up and to prepare for dee landeeeeeeng."

After a short pause, she added, "Pleeeese be advised that dee laws of Singapore prohibit druuuugs. Dee peennalteeee is deeeeeaaaaatthh."

Uto heard the stewardess, which almost sounded like a cat purring. He said to himself sitting in the airplane seat, "Only the stupidest guy in the world would try to smuggle drugs into Singapore."

Morio Uto strutted off the plane into the modern Singapore

airport terminal with a sense of accomplishment. He had got what he came for, he thought, and felt good about it. The Oyabun would reward him handsomely with a small percentage of the proceeds from the synthesized plant formula, and he would never have to work again. He thought of buying a red Ferrari.

The automated conveyor belt moved the passengers down the long hallways of the Singapore Changi Airport to the customs area. His baggage consisted of two carry-ons which he carried, with nothing checked in. The precious cargo was in one of them, he thought. At a mirror on the wall next to the conveyor belt he checked himself out to see if he looked as "cool" as usual. He satisfied himself that he did, wearing his sunglasses.

At the first check, for the passport, there were several of the numerous stations staffed with personnel. Several anxious Singaporeans got ahead of him, and he stood in line patiently to have his Japanese passport chopped into the country.

When it was his turn, the attractive Indian female official in a blue uniform-styled shirt with epaulettes took his passport. She ran it through the computer scanner, and waited. On her screen appeared a small warning visual signal, designed not to alert the person entering the country. She saw it, and nonchalantly pushed a hidden button with her knee that no one could see.

"Please go to the customs area with your bags for inspection, sir," the pretty Indian girl said. Instead of the usual white card, she put a pink card into his Japanese passport – its length made it stick out of the passport such that it could be seen ahead of him as he held it in a hand that was carrying one of his bags.

Six police were already waiting ahead, scattered about so as not to alert anyone standing in the general path of the incoming passengers. They had been pre-warned.

Nearby in a room were more airport police, waiting, drinking sugared coffees and teas. Due to the near absence of crime in Singapore, whenever a known criminal event was to occur, an abundance of police were always available. A buzzer rang in the room.

One of the two standing officers held out his arm with his neatly white-gloved hand pointing over to the section for inspections, as opposed to the section that permits people to go through, on their honor that they have nothing to declare.

All the remaining officers came out and went to the area of customs inspection. They covered the exits so as to block any attempt to escape. Several slowly moved more closely towards Uto, but not so much as to let him know he was their target for an arrest yet.

"Place your bags up here, sir," the customs inspector told Uto.

Uto hoisted his bags up on the examining bench. "Please open the bags, sir," the polite customs officer said in English.

"Sure," Uto said.

"Have you anything to declare, sir?"

"No."

The customs officer took out several articles of clothing, some soiled, and began leafing through them. He came upon the plastic bag of the Baron's exotic purple tea leaves, and held it up. "What is this, sir?"

Uto, experienced at crime, without any change in expression said nonchalantly in English, "That is a herbal remedy for certain pain. You mix it in hot water and drink it." The Chinese, which is the predominate race in Singapore, took all sorts of such remedies, Uto recalled, and it would not seem unusual to the customs official that someone would travel with such a potion. The customs officer set it aside, as though to determine later if it was as had been represented by the traveler while he continued to look further.

The customs officer looked further. He came to mud-soiled jeans, rolled up. He looked in the front pockets, as that was where he had been told to look. Out of each front pocket came a large bag of white powder. He held them up, for the armed officers to see.

Uto's eyes opened wide as he stared in amazement. He had been set up! Who was behind it? Why were the plant leaves not taken? But now he was caught with heroin, and in Singapore!

He did not realize at that time that he was only carrying tea instead of the plant. All of the armed officers, except two guarding the exit, moved in and surrounded Uto, guns drawn. Uto looked about to see if escape was possible, but realized it was useless.

Chapter Sixty-Six

Cameron had the plant, and Devan was returned to his worried parents. With the Singapore police holding Uto, there were now a few days available for a short holiday before returning to America with his precious cargo. And Faint Chance. Which was more precious?

Cameron walked to the American Embassy. Inside, he walked up to the counter, and said, "I must have a temporary visa for a Lao citizen to come to America. What is involved in obtaining one? The person has already applied for a permanent visa some months ago, so it should be no problem."

"Oh, sir, I am afraid you have been operating under some misconception. Once a person has applied for immigration and is waiting for papers, immigration will not grant a tourist visa. They find that people who enter America in that manner tend to stay, even when the immigration visa is not granted."

"What? Just because she has applied to come in permanently, now she can't come early as a tourist when she might have otherwise?"

"I am afraid that is the case, sir," the lady told him.

"What else can be done? I must have this person in America right away. How long should it take? Months? Years? I cannot wait for that! I want the person to come over right away."

"You and many millions of others, all over the world, sir. I am sorry. But as much as I would like to help you, it is not the embassy that makes these judgments, but the Department of Immigration and Naturalization in America. I believe that you may have had an unrealistic idea of a Lao citizen coming to the US. There are quotas, and frankly, I would not depend on her coming for quite some time. It could be several years, and there is no guarantee at all. I want to be candid with you. And, there has been a change in immigration policy just recently, and it is much more difficult to get a visa. It could take a very long time, even years."

Cameron remained silent and motionless for a time and then said, "Thank you, but I may be back. I appreciate your help." Down and out, he walked slowly back to the hotel. What had happened? Spencer and Candice must have been misinformed about her chances of coming over soon. Years? That will not do! What was he supposed to do? Just go back to architecture and forget Faint Chance?

Later, after her work, Faint Chance came to the hotel room. She came in with a smile, but could at once see that something was wrong. Cameron had a very sober expression that telegraphed something was wrong.

"What is it?" she asked.

"I am afraid I have some very bad news. I will not be able to take you back with me," he said sadly. "And worse, they told me at the embassy that your visa is not certain. There are new policies and efforts to curb migration to America. It will take a long time at best. However, I will go to work on it when I get home, and see what I can do from there. There must be something I can do."

Her eyes watered. "It was all really too good to be true. I may not get to come to America after all. Maybe it is my karma to live and die in Lao."

"I cannot lie to you or mislead you. At this time you cannot come. Maybe when I get back I can find a way, but I don't know what to do from here."

Faint Chance sat down quietly, wondering about her future, and cried.

Chapter Sixty-Seven

Two days later Uto was allowed to make a limited number of supervised calls in order to assist his defense from the Changi prison where he was being detained pending his court date in Singapore. He called the Oyabun on a special number the Oyabun had given him for such calls. It went to a bar in Tokyo, and then was routed through a device that routed it as an untraceable call to Oyabun's mobile phone.

Uto knew he was being monitored in Singapore, but he felt that he could communicate his message. "Someone planted heroin in my luggage. I am in big trouble. Can you get me out?"

"Not out of Singapore," the Oyabun answered. "I will send money to a solicitor for you – that is all I can do. What happened to the thing you were supposed to bring?" He did not mention anything by name or description, so as not to alert anyone listening.

"All I know is what I have been told by the police in interrogation sessions. I am told that I brought over a pound of pure heroin and also some oolong tea!"

That was what he had been told was in his bag. He figured the authorities must have thought it was tea.

"Oolong tea? What are you talking about? Tea?"

"That is what the police have told me. Pure heroin and oolong tea."

The Oyabun said, "Do you think that the American and the girl still have the plant leaves?"

"Well, I can't do anything to find out here in the Changi prison!"

He told Uto, "Leave an instruction to give your things to this person." He gave the name of a courier. He wondered if he could get the tea turned over to him as part of the personal belongings of a condemned man.

"Isn't there anything you can do for me?" Uto pleaded.

"Singapore does not allow bail in such cases," the Oyabun answered, "where there is a death penalty. And, the Singapore Government is not open to influence." He was obviously referring to the pay-offs that sprang his men from jails in places like Indonesia and Latin America.

"But I am innocent!" Uto pleaded.

"Maybe you can convince them of that. I will send money for your solicitor," the Oyabun said. "And, if there is anyone you want money to go to, let me know." That was the tradition with the gangsters and the Oyabun, to provide some assistance to any family. But Uto had no wife or children.

Chapter Sixty-Eight

Cameron awoke at daybreak. He got up, and called for coffee. No one answered, as it was still early for the restaurant to be open. As much as he wanted to stay on, he would have to go back soon. His job required it.

He thought of the system of America depriving immigrants such as Faint Chance entry. Then again, there were undoubtedly so many people trying to move to America, the country had to have some system of making it difficult to get in. But why did that have to include Faint Chance? Wasn't there something that he could do? Did he have to wait to get her to America? He did not know any politician. He would probably go back and return to work, writing letters to various places and getting nowhere with her immigration status as months and months passed. Maybe years...

He moped about the room, trying not to wake up Faint Chance. She looked so innocent, sleeping in the bed. She had so little, apart from her hope chest. At least now she had her hope chest restored. Some dowry! He fantasized of how the richest men in the world might want her for making a special offspring. Perhaps if he became rich, he might gain the influence to get the government to allow her to come? But how long would that take? Would she wait?

He sat at the table, and began organizing his passport, tickets and papers, tossing things he did not need into the wicker bin nearby. He organized the nearly useless kip, the local money, in its huge numbers, by the bill size. He reckoned that stationery in America cost more than kip – it wasn't worth the paper it was written on back home.

In the papers, airline tickets and schedules, receipts and things he had accumulated on the trip, he came to the oversized card of the Baron Von Limbach. He looked at it intently, remembering the dandy fellow from nearby Chiang Rai, Thailand. It had writings on both sides in many languages.

Then he remembered. The Baron was going to be at his Vientiane office at this time for his teak exporting!

As he showered, he wondered if the Baron might help. He would go to his office after nine in the morning. He went to the bed where Faint Chance slept and said, "Faint Chance! Wake up please. There is someone I want you to meet."

Cameron and Faint Chance entered the Baron Von Limbach's office. It was in a single-story commercial trade building, that was trimmed inside in teak. It was very handsome, and old-fashioned. Although air-conditioned, it appeared to be an older building converted to modern offices. The reception area was not overly large, and staffed by only a secretary-receptionist. The furniture was elegantly carved wood.

The secretary-receptionist looked to them to see what they wanted. No doubt she could handle simple communications in several languages, and was waiting for a clue.

"I am Cameron Harrington, and this is Faint Chan... I mean Sangmouane Sayasithsena. We would like to see the Baron Von Limbach."

"Will he know what this is about?" she asked in perfect English.

"No, but he knows me. Tell him I am the architect he met in Chiang Rai, Thailand."

She picked up a phone, and announced Mr. Cameron Harrington and a female guest. She put the phone right back down. The Baron did not have time to say anything. In just moments, he came through the door, through which he barely fit, with his big, inviting smile. He was in a beige linen three-piece suit, with a green silk shirt and green silk tie. What a sight, Cameron thought.

"Well, what a pleasure! I am so glad you came to see me! Please, come in, Mr. Harrington, and now you must tell me, just who is this beautiful girl?" He was so properly polite and yet so to the point. He must know that the visit is regarding her, Cameron thought.

"This is Sangmouane Sayasithsena, from here in Vientiane, but I call her 'Faint Chance'."

"HO HO HO," the Baron laughed with his oversized lungs, in a voice that filled the room. "Faint Chance! I like that! 'Faint Chance'." And then he greeted her in Lao. What a master of languages, Cameron thought.

His office was considerably larger than it appeared to be from the reception room. Inside, Cameron saw hand-carved desk furniture with inlays of different woods.

"This is just a modest office I keep here for what little business I do in Lao."

Cameron imagined that, to the Baron, a little business might mean several million. What did this man really deal in? Better not ask.

"You might be pleased to know that I have incorporated your ideas into the new house, and set the locals to making the changes. You are a genius. If I ever build anything else, I will call on you to see if you are available."

"You are too kind," Cameron said. "But I am taking the liberty of calling on you for a favor."

"Certainly! You need only ask. I am so glad to try to repay you for your design in Chiang Rai for me."

"Faint Chance has applied to immigrate to the United States. She met my brother and his wife, both research doctors, last year, and they wanted her to come to the United States to live with them. They have applied to be her sponsors. It was thought that it would only take a few months to get things through. But that turns out not to be the case. Now I am here, and I want to bring her back to come and live with me, before her papers come through from immigration."

It was the first time that he had announced to Faint Chance that she would be living with him. He had asked her about it at the hotel, but she had said she would have to ask Spencer and Candice.

"I went to the American Embassy, and I was told that now that she has applied for immigration, she will not be given a tourist or other visa, and will have to wait until her papers come through. Further, I was told that the papers might not come through.

Apparently the US is tightening up on its immigration policies for foreigners."

"My oh my! This is a very popular girl," the Baron chuckled. "It seems everyone wants her! What is your secret, my dear?" he asked, looking at her. She did not answer.

What a coincidence that he should ask such a question, Cameron thought. If he only knew. She holds the secret to the next step in human evolution. And now, she has the most valuable dowry in the world. What super-rich man would not take her, if not for her charm, but to have the smartest child in the world? Yet, the Baron must bargain with people from all over the world, and must be able to see that there is something very special about Faint Chance. Could he really detect that she had a secret? Maybe so…

Cameron said, "You travel so much, I thought you might be able to help. Do you know of anything that can be done?"

"Well now, I just might. Let's see," and the Baron leaned over to a leather personal phone directory on his desk. "Ah yes, here." He picked up the phone, and called a number.

"Hi. Baron Von Limbach here. How have you been?

"I have been wonderful, too. Say, I have a request. A very good friend of mine from America is trying to get a visa for a Lao girl. They are here in my office. It seems that she has been turned down since she already applied for immigration last year. Can you fix that?" The Baron looked at Faint Chance as the person on the other side of the line was talking to him. It was obvious that he was also taken by her looks and that he was wondering just what other secrets or charms she possessed to make such an influence on Cameron and his brother and sister-in-law.

Cameron looked at Faint Chance. He had no idea who the Baron was calling. It was obviously a private line to someone, as he did not go through a receptionist.

"Her name? Sangmouane Sayasithsena." Then he spelled it aloud, looking to her to make sure he got it right."

The Baron then said, "Wonderful! I am much obliged. Yes, I will tell her to go to the American Embassy tomorrow after lunch. Everything will be there, right? I can't thank you enough. Bye."

He hung up. Cameron was speechless. He had never seen

such influence so close up before. Cameron had just met a person at the embassy the day before who said that she wanted to help, but could not do so as the Department of Immigration had to handle the matter, and the Department of Immigration was in the United States, with no office in Lao. But one call from the Baron to someone, and it was fixed! What influence!

The Baron said, "So, all you have to do is to go to the American Embassy tomorrow after lunch, and you will have an unrestricted, multiple entry visa without duration waiting for you. Will that be satisfactory?"

"We are very impressed!" Cameron said. "We are in your eternal debt."

"Now, now, what are friends for?" the Baron said. "It was nothing. Well now, you must excuse me. I am preparing for a meeting with some Lao Government officials, and I have to see them in just minutes. And, I am afraid I am leaving the day after tomorrow, early, so I will not have time to entertain you. Perhaps next trip?"

"Baron, we shall always be in your debt. Whenever you want some architectural work, it will be my pleasure to do it for you wherever you are. Please allow me to repay my debt to you!"

"That is very good to know."

And with that, he stood up. Cameron and Faint Chance stood, and Faint Chance provided the Baron with her *nop* of great respect. She told him, "You have changed the course of my life, and I will always carry you in my prayers." Her eyes watered, and she could not resist going to him and putting her arms around him, giving him a hug and kiss on the cheek.

The Baron spoke to her. "It was nothing. I am so pleased to be able to help my architect and such a beautiful girl."

On the way out, an older Lao man in a suit, followed by a younger man and two armed soldiers, one on either side, passed them in the hallway. Outside was a limousine, and a military car behind it, with several soldiers standing about with machine guns.

As they walked away from the building, Faint Chance said, "That older man in the hallway is the Lao Minister of Defense!"

"He is an arms merchant!" Cameron said to her, now beginning to understand the incredible influence. With just a phone call, the Baron could make things happen with different countries. "Architecture was never like this!"

Chapter Sixty-Nine

The morning sun came in horizontally through the small window next to them in the small jet as it taxied to the small terminal in Luang Prabang.

"I wonder if you will accept my offer to live with me, rather than your living with the doctors?" Cameron said.

With that, Faint Chance glowed, and gave him a kiss on the cheek. She asked, "When are you going to tell Spencer and Candice that you did not give the *ton mai piiset* away, and that you will now be bringing it?"

"Well, I am taking a chance, I know, by not telling them. Uto's things must have been seized by the Singapore authorities and held. But there is the possibility that he might find out that he did not have the plant. I don't really know what those chances are. So, we should leave soon after we go back to Vientiane."

At a shop that sold spices, Cameron said to Faint Chance while holding up a glass jar, "One cannot bring plants or fruits into the United States. So, we must crush up the plant leaves, and put them in something like this. Let's take it to the hotel and prepare it."

Back at the hotel, he dumped the spice in the gutter outside on the way in. Once in the room, he got the plant leaves out and began putting them in the spice jar. "Customs will think it is spice. If they knew it was a plant, they would confiscate it and destroy it. Can you imagine, after all the effort to get it, to have it dumped out by some cretin at customs?"

"Will they let me bring in my northern Lao Lao?" she asked. "It is very important to me."

"Yes, we can bring in two bottles each of anything, but for the life of me I cannot imagine why you want to bring that bilge water to America. One would think you would use up your two-bottle quota for some XO brandy that you can get cheaply without duty."

"It is very special to me," she said.

Cameron wrote off trying to convince her that she should buy some fancy liquors with her two-bottle quota to bring into the US. She probably wants the Lao Lao as a reminder of her homeland, he thought.

Faint Chance then asked, "What is a 'cretin'?"

Cameron answered, "That is another name for a government employee."

Chapter Seventy

In the dark of night, a man came up to the Harrington home, and walked in a stooped position around the house until he found the telephone utility box. From a satchel, he removed a small box. It was painted white to match the color of the house, and unless someone knowledgeable looked closely, it looked like some utility box from the phone company. He fastened it with two-sided tape to the house, and secured it with a set screw for security. He then connected the wires to the phone service. The sophisticated device had a lithium battery charged from the line voltage, and connected the phone service to an internal mobile phone. It was a dual system, as the Harrington home had two lines. When anyone called in or out, the cell was activated to relay the number over a mobile transmitter to a person working for the Oyabun. It made no clicks or drop in line volume.

Some distance across town, two Japanese men sat in a private office with a special desk phone, connected to the Harrington household. A bilingual Japanese man called Japan on another phone, a regular line. The Oyabun himself answered.

"Everything is in place, sir."

"I want to know anything said about a plant or the brother, Cameron Harrington, coming back to America, and as soon as it is said," the Oyabun commanded.

"Yes, sir. Just as soon as we hear anything, we shall call you, day or night."

Chapter Seventy-One

"This is south Indian food," the Tamil Indian, and second adoptive father of Faint Chance, said to Cameron. "It is more spicy than that of the north. How do you find it?"

Cameron sat at the farewell dinner in Faint Chance's mother and father's home. With his mouth burning from the spices, he said, "Very tasty! With all this spice, you don't need to eat as much to be satisfied. It is quite delicious, Mrs. Dorasamy. What are these dishes?"

"I am so glad you like them. Please call me Janu," her mother said, now sitting after serving the various curries. She wore a traditional Indian sari, a colorful outfit that left a portion between the lower part and the top bare, and the end of the cloth flowing over the shoulder. Cameron thought saris were just naturally beautiful. "That is meen curry, which is fish curry," she said, pointing. "This one is idli, which is rice cake to dip in the curry. This one sambar, which is a south Indian vegetable lentil curry. This one is mutton dalcha, which is mutton ribs in coconut curry and lentils. This is chicken biryani, which is rice baked in chicken and spices. This one is murtabak, which is wheat flour bread stuffed with lamb and peas. Sangmouane helped prepare these as well. She will be able to make these in America."

Cameron looked to Faint Chance and they smiled at one another. Faint Chance also wore an Indian sari that evening, as opposed to her usual tubular sinn dress, and Cameron could not help but notice how utterly sexy she looked in the flowing form of the sari. Her sari was dark blue, with magenta, orange, white and light blue flowers, and she wore a dark blue top that left several inches of stomach showing below where the sari wrapped around her. What could be more sexy than a sari, Cameron wondered? Her glowing olive skin radiated and Cameron found himself trying not to stare at the mesmerizing hostess that he would soon have in America.

"And please call me Krishnan," her adoptive father said. "We are so sad to see our Sangmouane leave us. But her happiness will be ours as well, as we want her to be able to migrate to America so much. We migrated here from south India, from Madras. We would have migrated to America, but it was impossible for us to consider. We could not get visas even if we had the money at the time."

"She will be able to return to visit you every year, and next year, I invite you to come to America to visit her. The tickets will be my gift to you," Cameron said. "And I will have a place for you to stay."

"We would be so honored to come, but we will pay for our own tickets. It would be quite an experience," Krishnan told Cameron.

"Will you please take very good care of our daughter?" Janu said. "She is grown-up now, but she will always be our little Sangmouane."

"You have my promise!" Cameron assured them. How not to look after this beautiful creature, he wondered – it would be a crime against nature not to.

After dinner, Janu and Faint Chance cleared the tables. Krishnan said, "Let us all go to the family room now," and he led Cameron there. Janu and Faint Chance followed.

Krishnan went to a drawer, opened it and took out a silk jewelry bag. Opening it, out came a beautiful woman's chain of twenty-four karat gold, and attached to it was a large locket made of intricately-woven strands of tiny gold thread, woven in a pattern of loops and turns in several layers. It was obviously an old piece from India, into which hundreds of hours had gone into its making. The necklace chain was equally interesting, consisting of little swastikas, a quarter-inch square each, laced in-between with elaborate designs of twenty-four karat gold as well. Unlike the German kind, they were not turned slightly but straight, one after the other.

"This was my mother's, before that her mother's, and before that her mother's. Now it is to be yours, my Sangmouane," Krishnan said, standing in the room to present it to her. "It is very old, and very precious to me. You are our only heir. Please think of your Indian family when you wear it."

Cameron commented, "Wow! Wearing something like that with those swastikas can get you into some trouble in America. The Jewish community is very strong."

Krishnan said, "I am aware of Hitler's use of the swastika, but if anyone says anything, you simply tell them they are uninformed, as the Indian 'swastika' goes back four hundred years before the birth of your Christ. It is a very old design. That is where Hitler got it from, as he did not invent it. They should understand."

Cameron said, "Well, as long as you don't flaunt the chain in public, I guess it won't cause trouble. It is beautiful, although not what one might call politically correct," Cameron mused. "Anyway," he looked at her, an olive-skinned woman in a sari, "you really don't look like a Neo-Nazi!"

Cameron realized that his making light humor of these most important matters of generations of saved jewelry was in bad taste and decided to be quiet.

Faint Chance took the locket from her father, and put it on her neck. She realized it was his family heirloom, and the importance of his giving it to her. She began to cry, and went to her father and hugged him with tears in her eyes. "I will not need the locket to think of you." And then she went to her mother, and hugged and kissed her, and said, "Or you." Both the mother and Faint Chance had tears in their eyes. Their daughter was now fully mature, and making her decision to leave the nest – and her choice was to take her to the other side of the earth.

"Now stop that, or you will have us all crying," Krishnan said. Cameron could see Krishnan's eyes watering also. It was such a scene that Cameron thought he was getting teary-eyed as well, when he realized that the girl whom everyone wanted was coming with him – there was no need for him to be sad!

Later, Faint Chance went to the bathroom to dry her tears. In the private way of Asians over personal matters, unlike her American host Cameron, she took out the small bag of the *ton mai piiset* that the Chief had given her. The new locket was just right for holding the quantity of the leaves he gave her, and she put them in the locket. She put the chain and locket around her neck.

Now she had combined her heirlooms from both of her adoptive parents into one, a perfect match. She would be able to remember them both and pray for them at the same time by holding the locket. She held the locket in her hand, squeezing it, and said a small prayer for the slain Chief before going back outside to the others.

Chapter Seventy-Two

Faint Chance brought her things to the hotel as it had been agreed that they would leave from there, and her parents would meet them at the airport for the parting goodbye. She had only two large bags of clothes and things, as that was all she owned.

Cameron took the *ton mai piiset* from the plastic bag. "We have to put this into a spice jar so that it will pose as spices. Candice and Spencer said they would confiscate any plants. One cannot bring into America plants for fear of medflies and similar insects."

"What is a medfly?" she asked.

"It is an insect that can come into a country and breed, and then can ruin a whole fruit crop of a region."

"Oh."

"But I don't think that spices have them. Only plants and fresh fruits, so we should be okay with the plant in a spice jar."

"Let me help," she said, and took over the job, putting the plant leaves into the emptied spice jar.

"Where shall we put the jar of the *ton mai piiset?*" she asked as she helped him pack his things.

"It is too valuable to check in. Let's put it in our carry-on and take it with us on the plane," he told her.

The hotel room's phone rang. Cameron answered it.

"Your call to the United States, sir," the hotel operator said.

"Spencer!"

"Cameron! How is everything?"

"Fine! I was able to get Faint Chance a visa! She will be coming with me tomorrow. We will fly to Bangkok for a short layover, then to Tokyo for another layover and then on home. Let me give you the flight numbers and information."

"Sir, I have just heard the schedule for Cameron Harrington's return," the Japanese man in a private office across town from the Harrington home said over a long distance phone connection to the Oyabun. He gave him the flight information. "He is traveling with the Laotian girl. Nothing was said about any plant or cargo."

"Excellent!" the Oyabun exclaimed. "They will be in Tokyo at the Narita Airport for a two-hour layover! Good work. Continue to monitor for any changes."

"Yes, sir."

Chapter Seventy-Three

Although the sun shone brightly the next morning, it was the saddest and the most exciting day for her at the same time! She had to say goodbye to her parents and friends but also enter her dream – to migrate to America.

Her Indian parents and several of her friends were at the airport, and teary, parting goodbyes were made as they headed for the small jet that would take them to their first stop, Bangkok. Cameron had his carry-on with the spice jar containing the *ton mai piiset*. Faint Chance had an open bag with her two bottles of Lao Lao. Cameron was a little perplexed by her insistence at bringing such potion to America – she might have brought back some good stuff duty-free – instead of that paint remover.

After arriving at Bangkok, Cameron went to the Thai Airlines ticket counter to buy the tickets to take the two of them to America. Given all that had happened, he decided to treat Faint Chance and himself to first-class tickets. The journey would be a memorable event for Faint Chance, and he thought to spruce it up with first-class treatment. They were to fly to Tokyo, with a layover of two hours there, and then on to America on the same plane.

When the big 747 was ready, they heard the announcement in the first-class lounge. To the front of the plane they went, enjoying the first-class treatment of boarding before the masses.

"Champagne?" the pretty Thai stewardess asked, holding a tray of it already poured into tall champagne glasses. Faint Chance and Cameron looked at each other, and he said for them, "Yes."

Soon the big 747 took off, a little late, during which Faint Chance held Cameron's hand tightly, as she had not experienced such a thing before. Cameron went to the first-class magazine section, and looked for a paper written in English. It had been some time since he had any news from the US, which was rather nice, considering the US news.

Cameron picked up the *Straits Times*, the Singapore newspaper, written in English, from the numerous newspapers available to the first-class passengers in the newspaper rack on the plane. Returning to his seat and reading, he soon saw an interesting article on the second page.

"Faint Chance, let me read you something of interest:

Yesterday at Court Twenty-Six of the District Mentions Court of the Subordinate Courts of Havelock Square, a Mr. Morio Uto, of Tokyo, Japan, was charged with trafficking diamorphine. Trafficking of more than fifteen grams of diamorphine is an offence of Section 5 of the Misuse of Drugs Act, Chapter 185, and carries a mandatory death penalty. Mr. Uto was arrested at the Changi Airport, entering Singapore from Vientiane, Laos, on Silkair last week. In his possession were .7 kilograms of pure heroin. Trial is set in forty days at the High Court. The accused is held without bail. The trial is not expected to be a prolonged one. There has not been such a large quantity of heroin seized in Singapore for twenty-three years."

Cameron looked at Faint Chance. They smiled at one another. "Perfect," Cameron said to her.

Chapter Seventy-Four

Narita Airport at Tokyo was as busy as usual. The international travelers in transit used the portion of the terminal that didn't require them to go through customs. As first-class passengers, they got to go up the small lift to the top floor to make use of the first-class lounge that overlooked the airport while they waited in transit.

Inside the first-class lounge, they picked out a seating area of well-stuffed chairs that was unoccupied and set down their carry-ons.

Neither of them noticed a group of four very tough-looking men move over not far away to sit down. One was a monster of over six feet and three hundred pounds, and without a trace of a visible neck.

"You go ahead," Cameron said to her, encouraging her to use the facilities and free drinks in the first-class lounge, "while I watch the bags." She complied, and went to the toilet while Cameron looked at the multitude of jumbo jets coming and going.

She returned, and it was Cameron's turn. The two bags, his carry-on, and her open bag, were bundled together in the seat next to her. She looked around in amazement, having so little travel experience.

Cameron returned, and, instead of sitting down, he stood by her and said, "Well, we have some time to kill. Shall we have a drink?"

"Whatever you are having, fix me one too, lover. I am so excited!"

As Cameron went over to where the liquor was, he thought to himself, *She called me lover!*

Cameron looked over the bottles available for the first-class passengers – it was a help-yourself bar. After looking them over a second time, he decided to go for vodka on the rocks.

He looked over and saw Faint Chance standing, looking towards the planes outside coming and going. He picked up the vodka bottle, and started pouring the drinks.

Cameron noticed a man with no neck at all hesitating near where his bag had been placed. Cameron put the bottle down and looked up again.

The man had picked up the carry-on bag with the plant!

He was heading for the toilet, holding Cameron's bag. Cameron started moving quickly to go after him towards the men's room. Quickly standing up were the other men, three of whom went towards the men's room behind Cameron. One remained, apparently to watch the area for police.

The neckless man went into the toilet at a fast, but walking pace so as not to attract attention. Right behind him was Cameron. The door closed in front of Cameron, and he pushed it open and went in and turned.

A sharp pain was felt on the back of his neck, and the room turned once and went dark.

The neckless man had chopped Cameron on the back of the neck so smartly that he had passed out. The neckless man and his accomplices made their way at a fast walk to a security door to a restricted area on the first floor, where a well-bribed airport worker was waiting to open the door for them. They quickly went down into the cargo loading area, and were escorted to a loading vehicle for small containers. They went in the back of the van, the doors closed, and they were gone.

Cameron awoke, lying on a white tile floor. A concerned-looking Japanese businessman was holding his head up from behind. A few moments passed.

Then he realized! He sat up, and he felt a sharp pain in the head and neck. He slowed his movements, and looked around. Over on the floor was his bag, lying open, with his things strewn about the floor.

Looking as he rose, he could not see the spice jar. He got up, and collected his things. It was nowhere to be found. The man had known what he wanted! He must have been connected to Uto and the kidnappers!

Cameron had to sit back down for a minute, as he was dizzy.

Someone went for a policeman and one came in the room. He had on a white policeman's hat and white gloves. Faint Chance came in as well, and a few people were gathering about looking. Soon a medical team of several people showed up, and began to fuss over him, checking his pulse, looking in his eyes and observing him.

Cameron declined any medical attention, and stood up. The policeman requested that he follow him to a room, and Faint Chance followed. In the room, a person who spoke perfect English appeared, and asked him what happened.

Cameron told him what had happened, making no reference to his special cargo. When asked what might have been stolen, he thought he would simply reply, in case they happened to apprehend them, "Some spices from Laos. That is all."

The police seemed to chuckle somewhat, as though it was no crime at all. But they were concerned that the security of a passenger was threatened. Cameron filled out a report with his name and realized that getting the plant back was not to happen. Cameron looked at his watch. They could still make the flight.

"We might as well go on back to the flight," he said to Faint Chance. "I don't think we are ever going to see the plant leaves again. We could try to go back to Lao for more, but that would be another ordeal, that we would have to set up again. I did not see any other plants growing on the cliff when I was there, only the one. And, who knows if the new Chief would welcome us coming to look for more plants after what happened the first time we came. And, you are en route to your new home; time to look ahead. I think that going back now is not the right thing to do at this time. Let's just go on home – that is, to your new home."

Back at the boarding area, sumo wrestling matches were on the TV. "Well, as far as Spencer and Candice think, the plant is gone anyhow. I really underestimated the powers of whoever is behind Uto and the efforts to get the plant," Cameron told her. Depression set in from the loss of the plant.

At the Oyabun's home, the four men came in the front door. The neckless one held the jar with the *ton mai piiset*. The Oyabun came out to greet them. He had a big smile on his rough face. He had just had Narita Airport held up and no one had been caught.

"Here is what you wanted, sir," the neckless man said to his boss.

"You have all done very well. There will be a bonus for you." The three extra men left, and the neckless one went to his room where he stayed as one of the Oyabun's most trusted men. The Oyabun held up the spice jar with the purple leaves in it, and his eyes opened as he carried it back to his study to call the scientist he had already lined up to get to work on immediately synthesizing the plant contents into a chemical that could be reproduced. With a gleam in his eyes, he looked up, imagining things and said aloud, "I am going to be the richest man in the world." He said to himself, "And, I will also have a son by this plant to carry on my name!"

Chapter Seventy-Five

For the last leg of the trip, the loss of the plant leaves left Cameron very somber. The purpose of his mission had failed. Spencer and Candice had suffered by having their Devan kidnapped, and now would never get their ultimate medical research publication, having lost it to others. The Chief had been murdered. The mission was a failure, except for making Faint Chance's acquaintance. Cameron led Faint Chance into the plane and they started their journey to America.

On the plane to America, Cameron, still very quiet and let down, said to Faint Chance sitting next to him, "Whoever has the plant leaves, probably someone in Japan, will race to make the formula to synthesize it. They will get the patent, and Spencer and Candice will lose their ultimate medical research publication. There is also a huge amount of wealth that will follow the patent, by the way – more than you might imagine."

Faint Chance said, "It is now time to tell you something. I have a secret."

"What is that?"

"To keep the powers of the plant from being taken by another, the Chief left something out when he gave you the plant leaves."

"What did he leave out? What are you talking about?"

"Do you remember when we were in the Chief's home, in the evening, and he wanted to speak to me alone and you took a walk about the village without me?"

"Yes, of course I do."

"He predicted others trying to steal the plant leaves and told me not to tell you about the additional ingredient needed to make it work until I thought it was time to do so. He was so wise, he predicted trouble and trouble came."

"He was the smartest person I have ever met," Cameron freely admitted, in awe of his wisdom.

"But now it is time. My karma is now tied to you, and it is time for you to know."

She revealed her secret. "The plant leaves do not summon the spirits without an additional ingredient."

"WHAT! We have Devan as proof that it does!" Cameron retorted.

"I gave Spencer and Candice the plant leaves during the ceremony with Lao Lao from the north. Do you remember visiting the lady who made the Lao Lao near Ban Houei Sai?"

"Of course."

"Do you remember the special black mushroom that she used in the Lao Lao?"

"Yes, I do! What about it?"

"The northern black mushroom is necessary to make the plant leaves summon the spirits. Unless it is mixed with the leaves, it won't work. Following what I was taught to do by the Chief, when I gave the plant leaves to Spencer and Candice, I gave them Lao Lao from the north. It was made with the special northern mushroom. Since the mushroom will not last outside, but its powers will last in the Lao Lao, the Chief told me to use northern Lao Lao when no mushroom was available. Recall when you told the new Chief to take the leaves, he was asked to take it with Lao Lao as well."

"My God! So all this time I have had only half the facts! That is why you wanted to use up your two-bottle quota of imported liquor into the US by bringing in Lao Lao!"

She smiled. "I hope you will forgive me. But the Chief made me promise not to tell. If someone came to the village, or comes again in the future, they might be able to get the plant. But without the secret it is no good. The Chief said I could tell you at the right time, and to make sure no one else knows. I think he knew much more about what was going to happen than us."

Cameron said, "So whoever stole the plant from us will never figure out why they cannot synthesize it or make it work! Whoever stole the plant will spend millions trying to figure it out and never get it! That is great justice!"

"I have some really good news for you," she said, with a big smile. She took off the gold chain with the locket on it that her Indian parents had given her at the going away dinner. She held it in her hand over her lap carefully, and then opened the locket.

As she opened the gold locket, the contents were revealed to Cameron. It was filled with the purple plant leaves of the *ton mai piiset*!

"My God! You have it! Where did you get this?"

"Did you forget that the Chief gave some to me for my wedding?"

"Of course! I completely forgot!" Cameron was practically shouting, and several people in the first-class cabin turned to look.

"But you specifically promised him that you would save this second batch only for you and for your wedding. He might curse you from the spiritual world if you do not!"

"The Chief said it only takes a little. I think there is enough here for me, and the rest to go to Spencer and Candice to use to make more," she said. "I only need enough to summon the spirits."

Cameron closed the locket, and put it back on her neck. As she came close to him when he put it around her neck, they kissed. A prolonged kiss, it made the other first-class passengers begin to notice.

He sat back in his chair to stop the show that was entertaining other first-class passengers. The mission was saved. And, they would now control the manufacturing of the substance, rather than some sinister corporation. All was well.

"Will you ever have a child when you marry, Cameron?"

Cameron was startled by the question, and looked at her. He started to say no, but then realized that he would not want her to marry someone else, and said, "Well, I have always hated the thought of having to care for an infant. But I confess, with all this discovery, if I were to have a child like Devan, I might change my views."

Faint Chance smiled, and squeezed his hand. She knew he would, and that she would make him very happy.

Cameron thought, how on earth could anyone resist her? He had to have her. Price was no object.

As the jet motors made their usual muted, hissing, background sound, Cameron hoped that his future, or "karma", as she had put it, would include Faint Chance.

The Thai stewardess came by, and asked him in a heavy Thai drawl, "Seeeuuuuuuuurrrrrrrr, is there anytheeeeeeeng I can do for yooouuuuuuuuuuuu?"

Cameron said, "We left Tokyo an hour late. My relatives are picking us up, and I hope they don't have to wait long. What are the chances that we will arrive on time in the United States?"

"I weeeellll go ask dee Capitaaannn." And she went just ahead from the upper deck first-class seating area to the pilots' cockpit. She entered the door and closed it behind her. Cameron could see some of the many switches and gauges in the cockpit while the door was open, and the interesting glowing lights of the navigation instruments.

After a few minutes she came back out the door, and walked back to their seats with the answer to their question. She said, in her country Thai way, "Oh, Seeeuuuuuuuurrrrrrrr, dee Capitaaannn says the jet stream winds are blowing strongly weeth us and weeel speed our arrival. That is good *feng shui*. As to whether or not you will arrive as you weeesh, dee Capitaaannn says that you have *faint chance*."